ARTEMIS FOWL

THE ARCTIC
INCIDENT

THE GRAPHIC NOVEL

Adapted by

EOIN COLFER
&
ANDREW DONKIN

Art by GIOVANNI RIGANO
Color by PAOLO LAMANNA

Lettering by CHRIS DICKEY

DISNEP • HYPERION BOOKS
New York

ARTEMIS FOWL:
A Psychological Assessment

Extract from *The Teenage Years*

By the age of thirteen, our subject, Artemis Fowl,
was showing signs of an intellect greater than
that of any human since Wolfgang Amadeus Mozart.
Artemis had beaten European chess champion Evan
Kashoggi in an online tournament, patented more
than twenty-seven inventions, and won the archi-
tectural competition to design Dublin's new opera
house. He had also written a computer program that
secretly diverted millions of dollars from Swiss
bank accounts to his own, forged over a dozen
Impressionist paintings, and cheated the Fairy
People out of a substantial amount of gold.

The question is, why? What drove Artemis to get
involved in criminal enterprises? The answer lies
with his father.

Artemis Fowl Senior was the head of a criminal
empire that stretched from Dublin's docklands to
the backstreets of Tokyo, but he had ambitions to
establish himself as a legitimate businessman. He
bought a cargo ship, stocked it with 250,000 cans
of cola, and set course for Murmansk, in northern
Russia, where he had set up a business deal that
could have proved profitable for decades to come.

Unfortunately, the Russian Mafiya decided they
did not want an Irish tycoon cutting himself a
slice of their market, and sank the *Fowl Star* in
the Bay of Kola. Artemis Fowl the First was
declared missing, presumed dead.

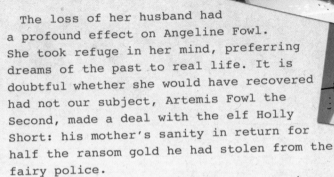

The loss of her husband had
a profound effect on Angeline Fowl.
She took refuge in her mind, preferring
dreams of the past to real life. It is
doubtful whether she would have recovered
had not our subject, Artemis Fowl the
Second, made a deal with the elf Holly
Short: his mother's sanity in return for
half the ransom gold he had stolen from the
fairy police.

With his father missing, Artemis Junior was now
the head of an empire with limited funds. In order
to restore the family fortune, he embarked on a
criminal career that would earn him over fifteen
million pounds in two short years.

This vast fortune was mainly spent financing
rescue expeditions to Russia. Artemis refused to
believe that his father was dead, even though
every passing day made it seem more likely.

Artemis avoided other teenagers and resented
being sent to school at all, preferring to spend
his time plotting his next crime.

So even though his involvement with the goblin
uprising during his fourteenth year was to be
traumatic, terrifying, and dangerous, it was
probably the best thing that could have happened.
At least he spent some time outdoors and got to
meet some new people.

It's a pity most of them were trying to kill him.

*Report compiled by: Dr. J. Argon, B. Psych,
for the LEP Academy files.*

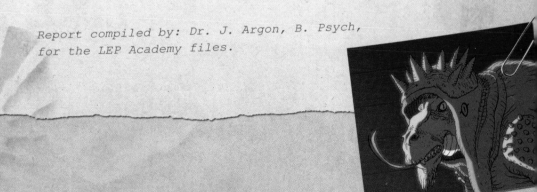

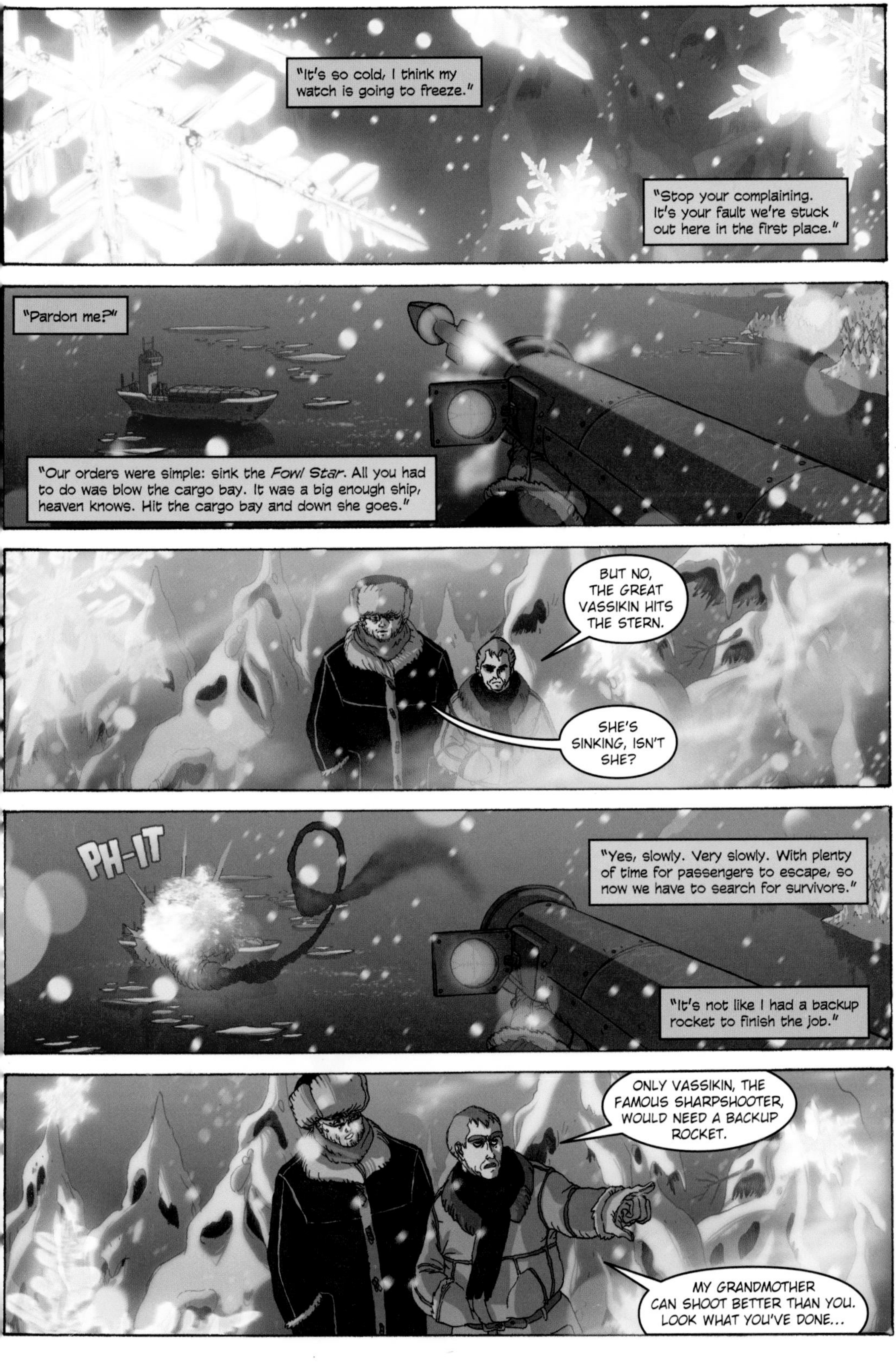
"It's so cold, I think my watch is going to freeze."
"Stop your complaining. It's your fault we're stuck out here in the first place."
"Pardon me?"
"Our orders were simple: sink the *Fowl Star*. All you had to do was blow the cargo bay. It was a big enough ship, heaven knows. Hit the cargo bay and down she goes."
BUT NO, THE GREAT VASSIKIN HITS THE STERN.
SHE'S SINKING, ISN'T SHE?
PH-IT
"Yes, slowly. Very slowly. With plenty of time for passengers to escape, so now we have to search for survivors."
"It's not like I had a backup rocket to finish the job."
ONLY VASSIKIN, THE FAMOUS SHARPSHOOTER, WOULD NEED A BACKUP ROCKET.
MY GRANDMOTHER CAN SHOOT BETTER THAN YOU. LOOK WHAT YOU'VE DONE...

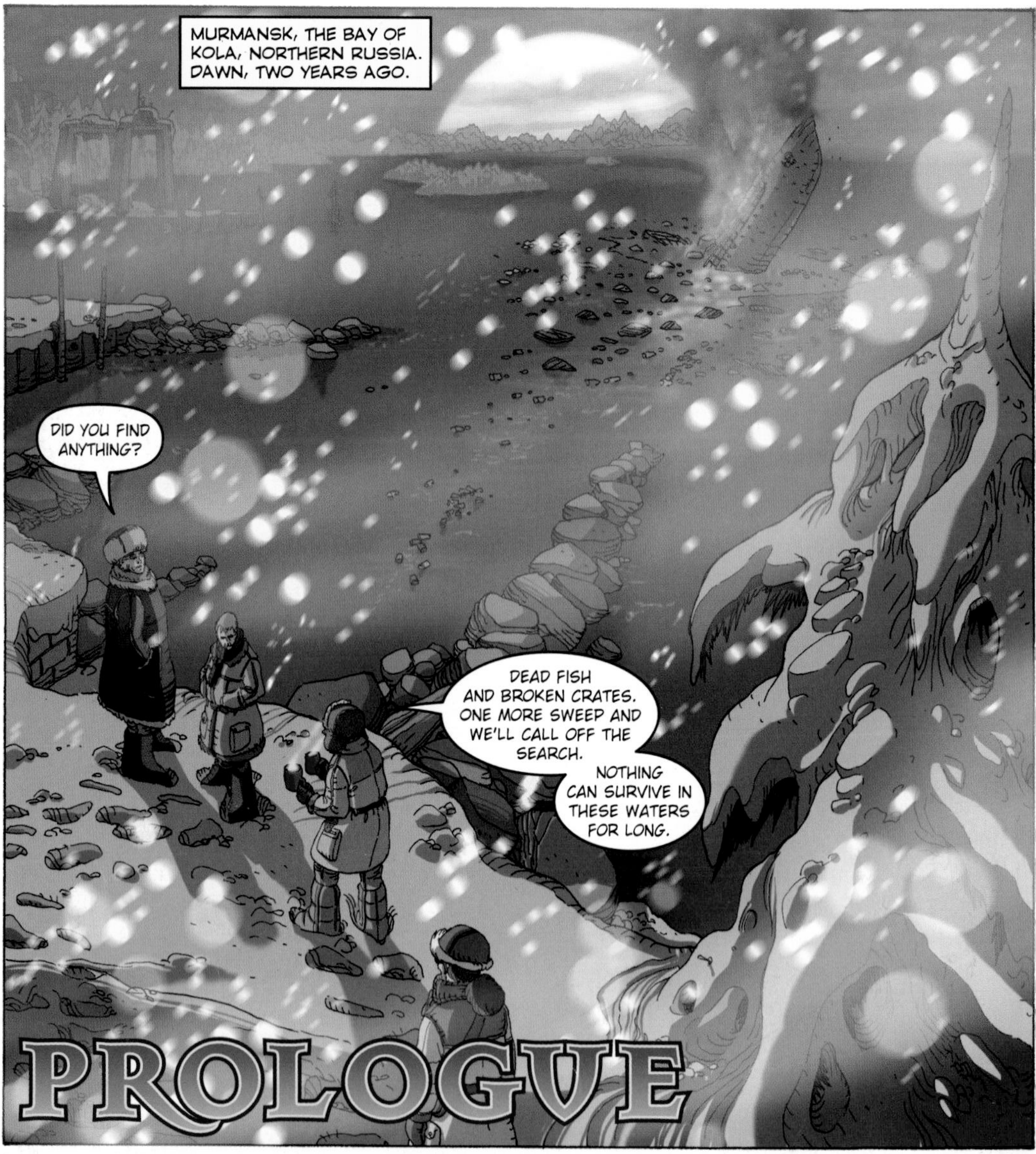
MURMANSK, THE BAY OF KOLA, NORTHERN RUSSIA. DAWN, TWO YEARS AGO.
DID YOU FIND ANYTHING?
DEAD FISH AND BROKEN CRATES. ONE MORE SWEEP AND WE'LL CALL OFF THE SEARCH.
NOTHING CAN SURVIVE IN THESE WATERS FOR LONG.
PROLOGUE

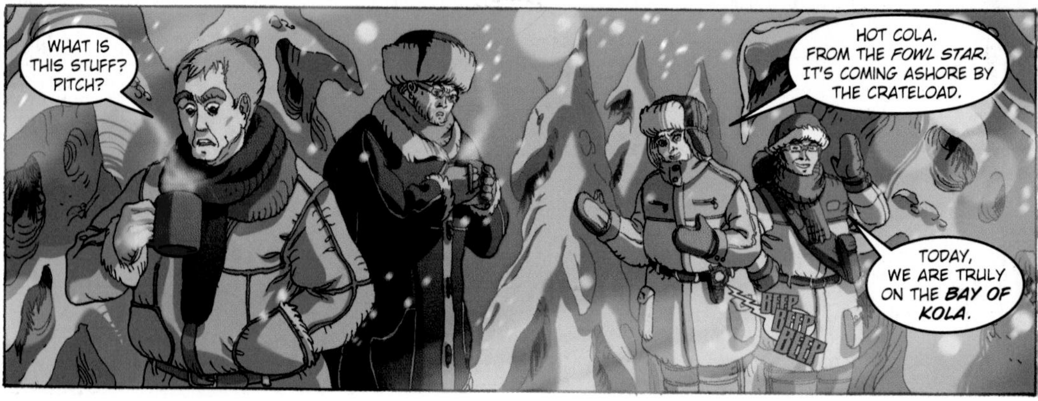
WHAT IS THIS STUFF? PITCH?
HOT COLA. FROM THE *FOWL STAR.* IT'S COMING ASHORE BY THE CRATELOAD.
BEEP BEEP BEEP
TODAY, WE ARE TRULY ON THE ***BAY OF KOLA***.

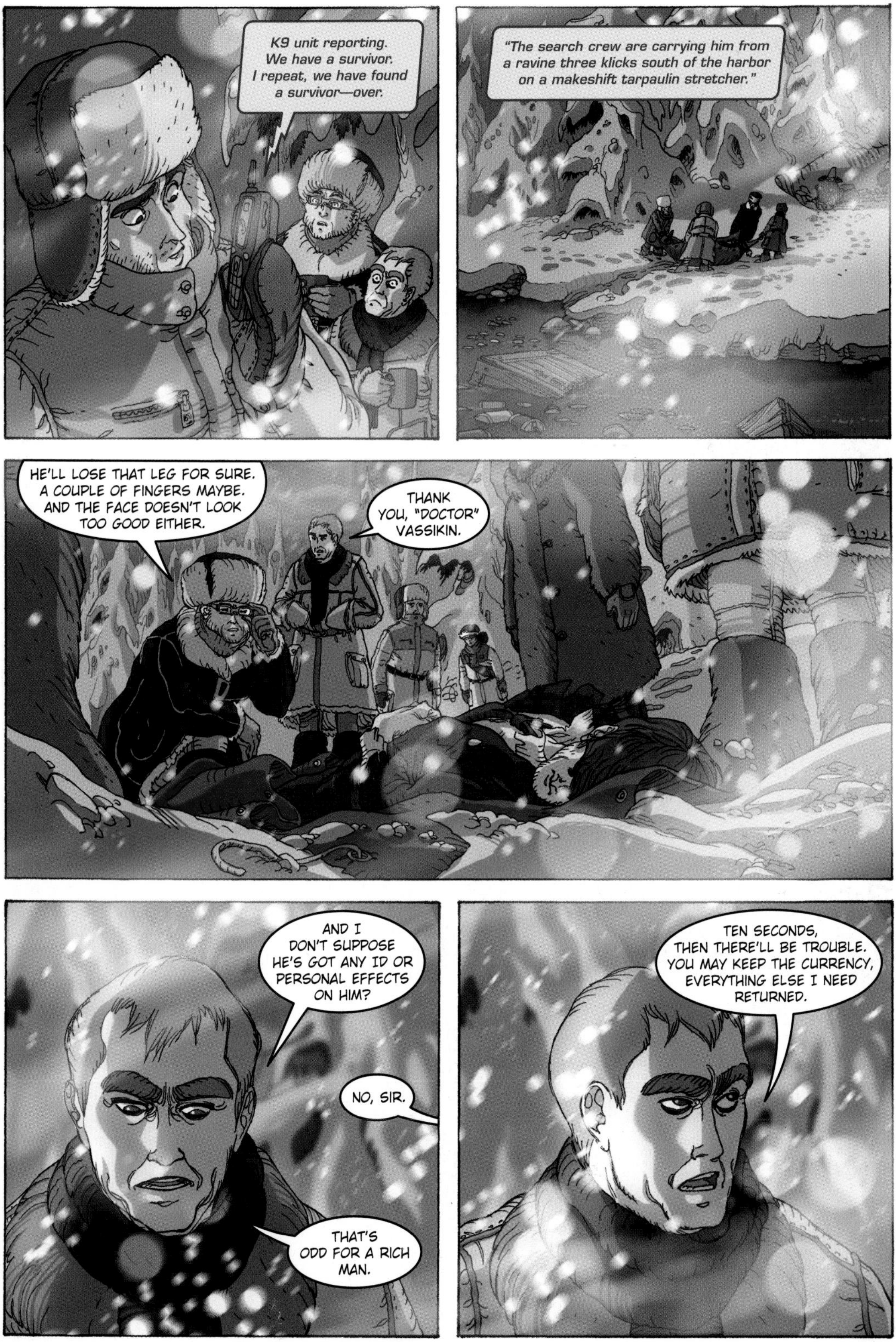
K9 unit reporting. We have a survivor. I repeat, we have found a survivor—over.
"The search crew are carrying him from a ravine three klicks south of the harbor on a makeshift tarpaulin stretcher."
HE'LL LOSE THAT LEG FOR SURE. A COUPLE OF FINGERS MAYBE. AND THE FACE DOESN'T LOOK TOO GOOD EITHER.
THANK YOU, "DOCTOR" VASSIKIN.
AND I DON'T SUPPOSE HE'S GOT ANY ID OR PERSONAL EFFECTS ON HIM?
NO, SIR.
THAT'S ODD FOR A RICH MAN.
TEN SECONDS, THEN THERE'LL BE TROUBLE. YOU MAY KEEP THE CURRENCY, EVERYTHING ELSE I NEED RETURNED.

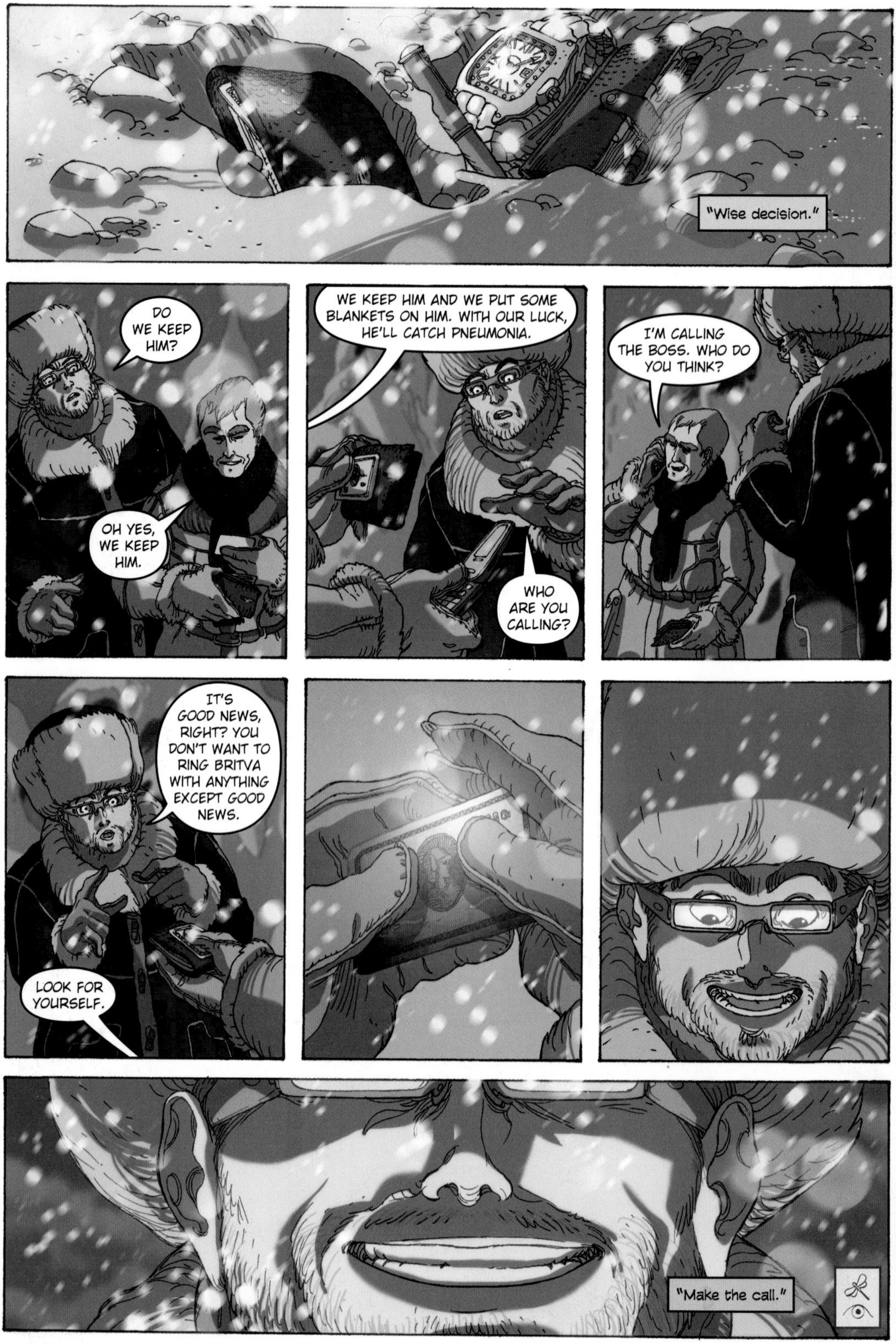
"Wise decision."
DO WE KEEP HIM?
OH YES, WE KEEP HIM.
WE KEEP HIM AND WE PUT SOME BLANKETS ON HIM. WITH OUR LUCK, HE'LL CATCH PNEUMONIA.
WHO ARE YOU CALLING?
I'M CALLING THE BOSS. WHO DO YOU THINK?
IT'S GOOD NEWS, RIGHT? YOU DON'T WANT TO RING BRITVA WITH ANYTHING EXCEPT GOOD NEWS.
LOOK FOR YOURSELF.
"Make the call."

PROLOGUE II

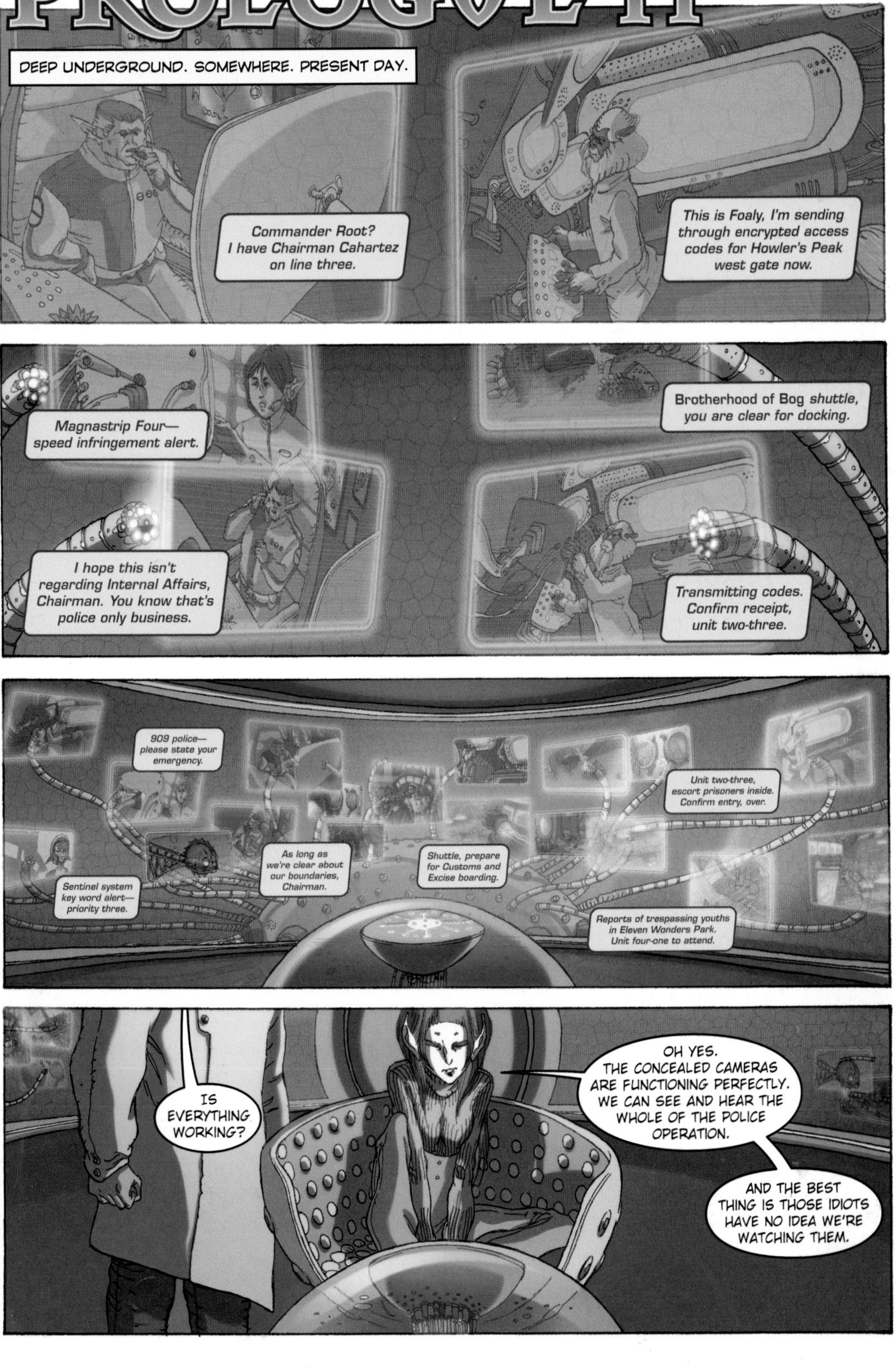
DEEP UNDERGROUND. SOMEWHERE. PRESENT DAY.
Commander Root? I have Chairman Cahartez on line three.
This is Foaly, I'm sending through encrypted access codes for Howler's Peak west gate now.
Magnastrip Four—speed infringement alert.
Brotherhood of Bog shuttle, you are clear for docking.
I hope this isn't regarding Internal Affairs, Chairman. You know that's police only business.
Transmitting codes. Confirm receipt, unit two-three.
909 police—please state your emergency.
Unit two-three, escort prisoners inside. Confirm entry, over.
As long as we're clear about our boundaries, Chairman.
Shuttle, prepare for Customs and Excise boarding.
Sentinel system key word alert—priority three.
Reports of trespassing youths in Eleven Wonders Park. Unit four-one to attend.
IS EVERYTHING WORKING?
OH YES. THE CONCEALED CAMERAS ARE FUNCTIONING PERFECTLY. WE CAN SEE AND HEAR THE WHOLE OF THE POLICE OPERATION.
AND THE BEST THING IS THOSE IDIOTS HAVE NO IDEA WE'RE WATCHING THEM.

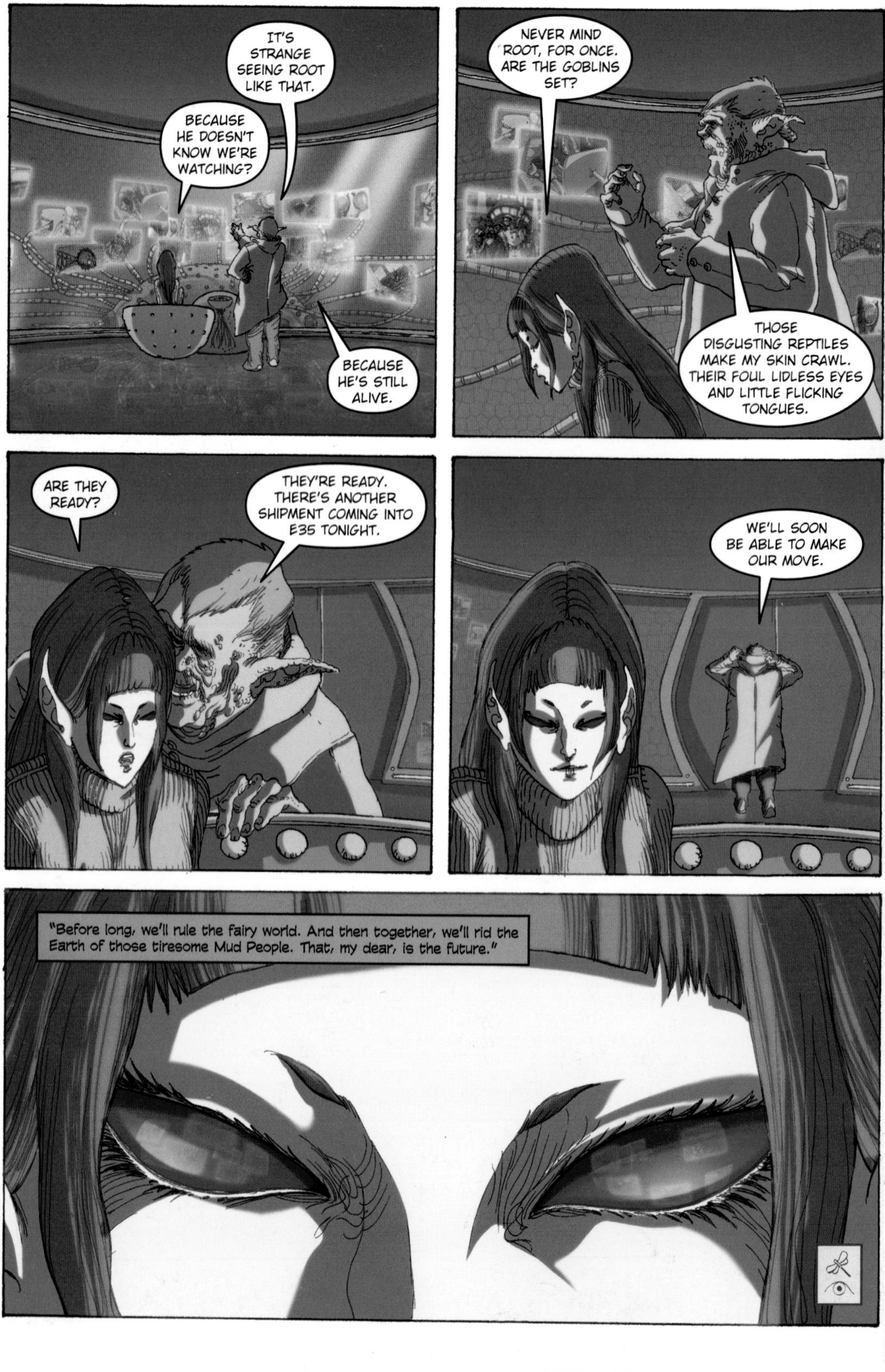
IT'S STRANGE SEEING ROOT LIKE THAT.
BECAUSE HE DOESN'T KNOW WE'RE WATCHING?
BECAUSE HE'S STILL ALIVE.
NEVER MIND ROOT, FOR ONCE. ARE THE GOBLINS SET?
THOSE DISGUSTING REPTILES MAKE MY SKIN CRAWL. THEIR FOUL LIDLESS EYES AND LITTLE FLICKING TONGUES.
ARE THEY READY?
THEY'RE READY. THERE'S ANOTHER SHIPMENT COMING INTO E35 TONIGHT.
WE'LL SOON BE ABLE TO MAKE OUR MOVE.
"Before long, we'll rule the fairy world. And then together, we'll rid the Earth of those tiresome Mud People. That, my dear, is the future."

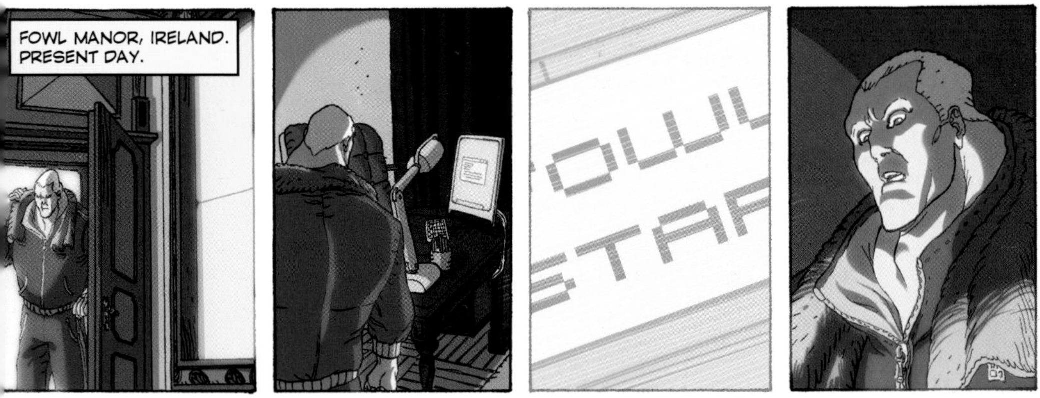
FOWL MANOR, IRELAND.
PRESENT DAY.

CHAPTER 1: FAMILY TIES

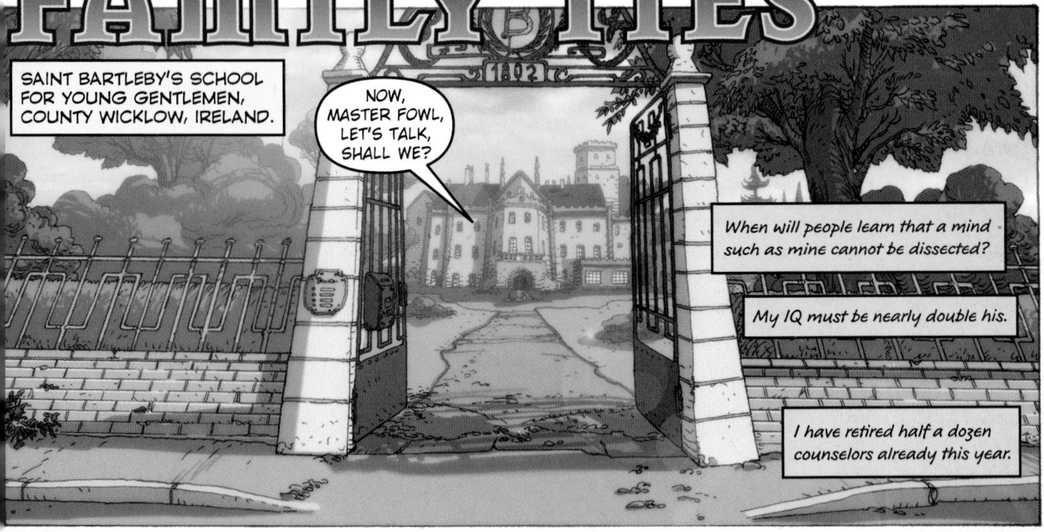
SAINT BARTLEBY'S SCHOOL FOR YOUNG GENTLEMEN, COUNTY WICKLOW, IRELAND.
NOW, MASTER FOWL, LET'S TALK, SHALL WE?
When will people learn that a mind such as mine cannot be dissected?
My IQ must be nearly double his.
I have retired half a dozen counselors already this year.

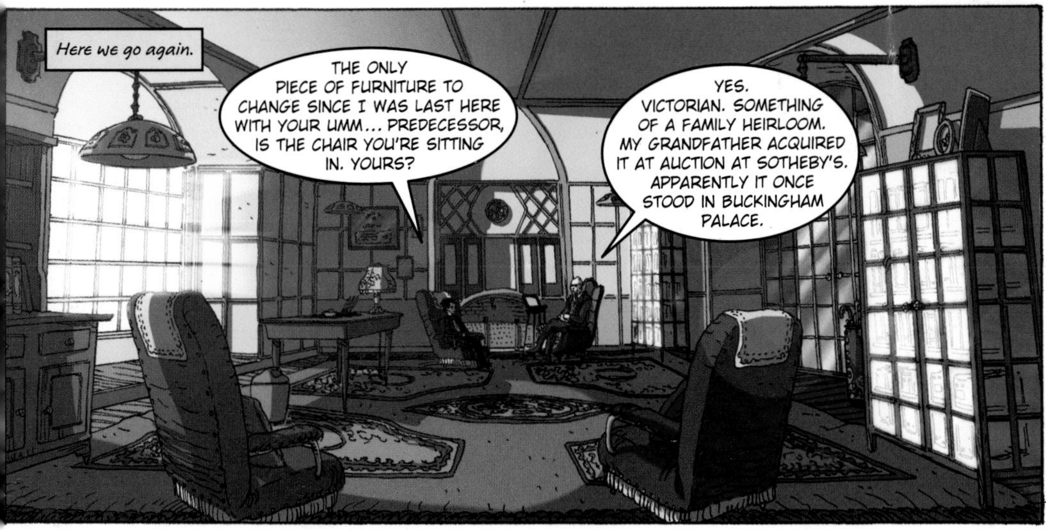
Here we go again.
THE ONLY PIECE OF FURNITURE TO CHANGE SINCE I WAS LAST HERE WITH YOUR UMM... PREDECESSOR, IS THE CHAIR YOU'RE SITTING IN. YOURS?
YES. VICTORIAN. SOMETHING OF A FAMILY HEIRLOOM. MY GRANDFATHER ACQUIRED IT AT AUCTION AT SOTHEBY'S. APPARENTLY IT ONCE STOOD IN BUCKINGHAM PALACE.

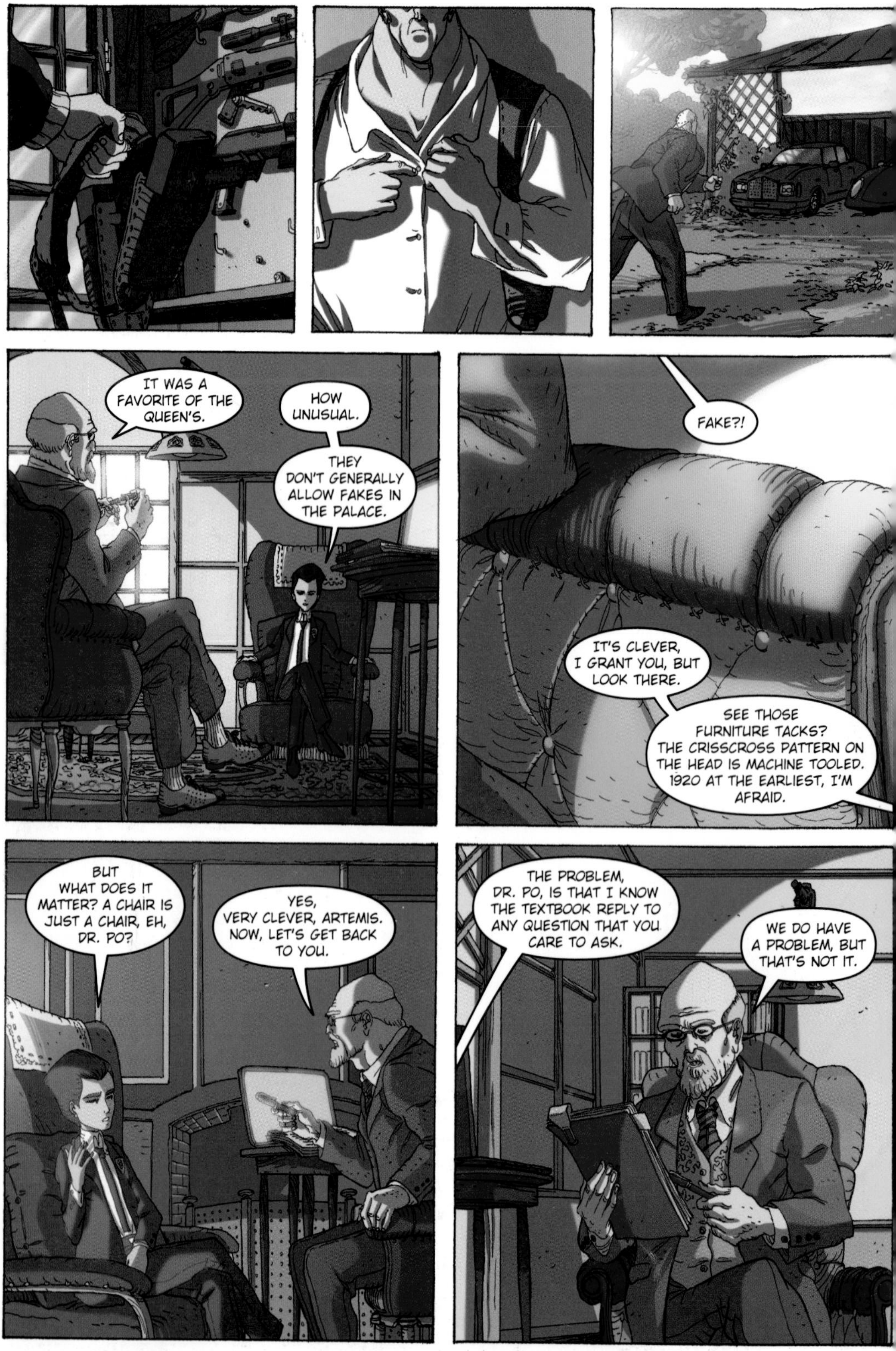
IT WAS A FAVORITE OF THE QUEEN'S.
HOW UNUSUAL.
THEY DON'T GENERALLY ALLOW FAKES IN THE PALACE.
FAKE?!
IT'S CLEVER, I GRANT YOU, BUT LOOK THERE.
SEE THOSE FURNITURE TACKS? THE CRISSCROSS PATTERN ON THE HEAD IS MACHINE TOOLED. 1920 AT THE EARLIEST, I'M AFRAID.
BUT WHAT DOES IT MATTER? A CHAIR IS JUST A CHAIR, EH, DR. PO?
YES, VERY CLEVER, ARTEMIS. NOW, LET'S GET BACK TO YOU.
THE PROBLEM, DR. PO, IS THAT I KNOW THE TEXTBOOK REPLY TO ANY QUESTION THAT YOU CARE TO ASK.
WE DO HAVE A PROBLEM, BUT THAT'S NOT IT.

For a second I allow myself the luxury of wondering what predictable disorder this quack will apply to me.

Multiple personality?

Pathological liar?

THE PROBLEM IS THAT YOU DON'T RESPECT ANYONE ENOUGH TO TREAT THEM AS AN EQUAL.

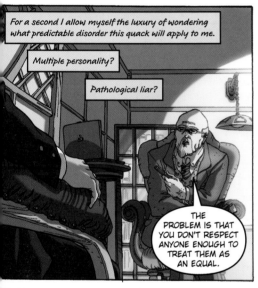

For one second I am thrown.

This doctor is (slightly) smarter than the rest.

THAT'S RIDICULOUS. I HOLD SEVERAL PEOPLE IN THE HIGHEST ESTEEM.

REALLY? WHO?

ALBERT EINSTEIN... ARCHIMEDES.

ANYONE ALIVE? ANYONE YOU ACTUALLY KNOW?

I think hard.

No one comes to mind.

I THINK YOUR FILE EXPLAINS A LOT. ACCORDING TO THIS... YOUR CLOSEST COMPANION IS A MILITARY-TRAINED BODYGUARD.

YOUR MOTHER HAS LITTLE, IF ANY, INFLUENCE OVER YOU. AND YOUR FATHER WASN'T MUCH OF A ROLE MODEL EVEN WHEN HE WAS ALIVE.

MY FATHER IS STILL ALIVE AND I WILL FIND HIM.

His last remark stings.
But I don't let him see how much.

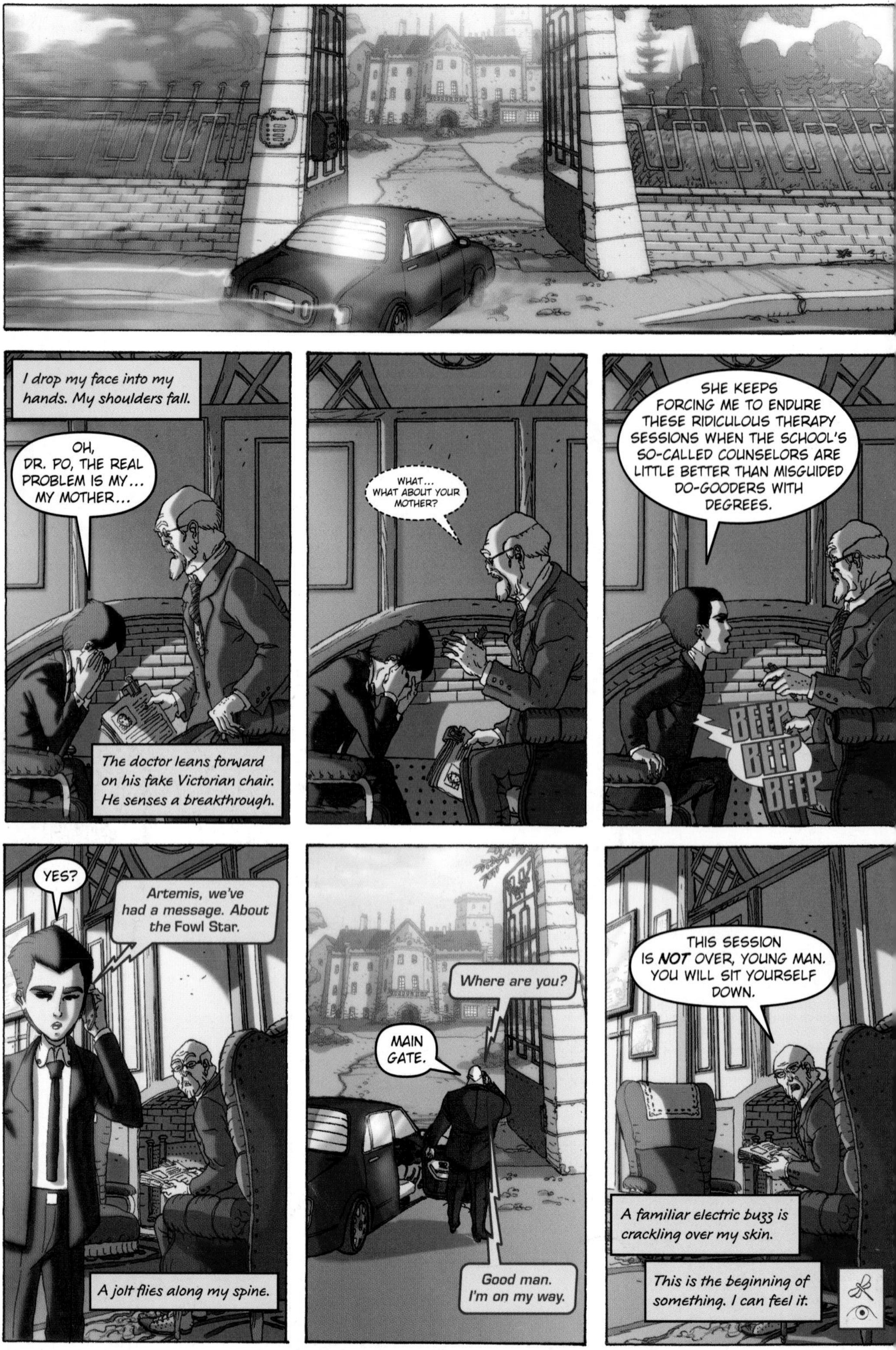
I drop my face into my hands. My shoulders fall.
OH, DR. PO, THE REAL PROBLEM IS MY... MY MOTHER...
The doctor leans forward on his fake Victorian chair. He senses a breakthrough.
WHAT... WHAT ABOUT YOUR MOTHER?
SHE KEEPS FORCING ME TO ENDURE THESE RIDICULOUS THERAPY SESSIONS WHEN THE SCHOOL'S SO-CALLED COUNSELORS ARE LITTLE BETTER THAN MISGUIDED DO-GOODERS WITH DEGREES.
BEEP BEEP BEEP
YES?
Artemis, we've had a message. About the Fowl Star.
A jolt flies along my spine.
Where are you?
MAIN GATE.
Good man. I'm on my way.
THIS SESSION IS NOT OVER, YOUNG MAN. YOU WILL SIT YOURSELF DOWN.
A familiar electric buzz is crackling over my skin.
This is the beginning of something. I can feel it.

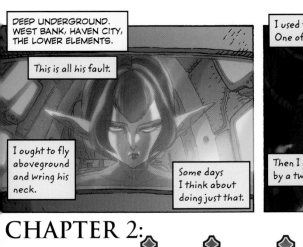

DEEP UNDERGROUND. WEST BANK, HAVEN CITY, THE LOWER ELEMENTS.

This is all his fault.

I ought to fly aboveground and wring his neck.

Some days I think about doing just that.

I used to be Captain Holly Short. One of Recon's most respected officers.

Then I got captured and held for ransom by a twelve-year-old human boy.

It cost a lot of fairy gold to get me back. Ever since then, my career has taken a one-way fall down a deep dark hole.

CHAPTER 2:
CRUISIN' FOR CHIX

This is the hole.

Surveillance duty on a disused pressure chute leading to the surface world.

If it wasn't for Commander Root, I wouldn't even have this.

It's important work. I tell myself that smuggling is a serious concern. I tell myself that the B'wa Kell goblin triad have been getting worse.

I tell myself all it would take is for one thick goblin to forget to shield, and photos of real, live goblins are all over the human news.

I tell myself that then Haven City, the last Mud Man—free zone on the planet, would be discovered and—BANG—it's the end of fairy civilization.

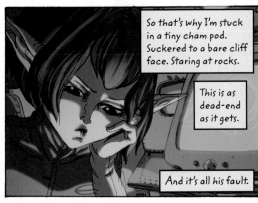

So that's why I'm stuck in a tiny cham pod. Suckered to a bare cliff face. Staring at rocks.

This is as dead-end as it gets.

And it's all his fault.

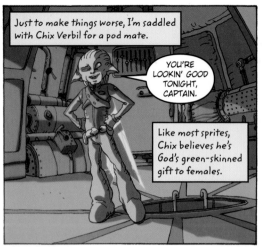

Just to make things worse, I'm saddled with Chix Verbil for a pod mate.

YOU'RE LOOKIN' GOOD TONIGHT, CAPTAIN.

Like most sprites, Chix believes he's God's green-skinned gift to females.

YOU DO SOMETHING NEW WITH YOUR HAIR?

CONCENTRATE, PRIVATE. WE COULD BE UP TO OUR NECKS IN A FIREFIGHT AT ANY SECOND.

I DOUBT IT, CAPTAIN. THIS PLACE IS AS QUIET AS THE GRAVE.

He's right, but we've still got a job to do.

CHIX, I WANT YOU TO DO A FLYBY. WE'LL RUN A FULL THERMAL SCAN.

ROGER, CAPTAIN.

The thermoscan bar on his chest will bathe the whole area below with heat-sensitive rays.

Sprites love to fly. His wings are all natural.

RUNNING THERMAL SCAN.

Any living creature will show up in a thermal scan. Even hiding behind a layer of rock.

HEY, CAPTAIN. SHOULD I DO ONE MORE SWEEP?

Okay, Chix. One more. Be careful.

Even before the words are out of my mouth, I see something move on my screen.

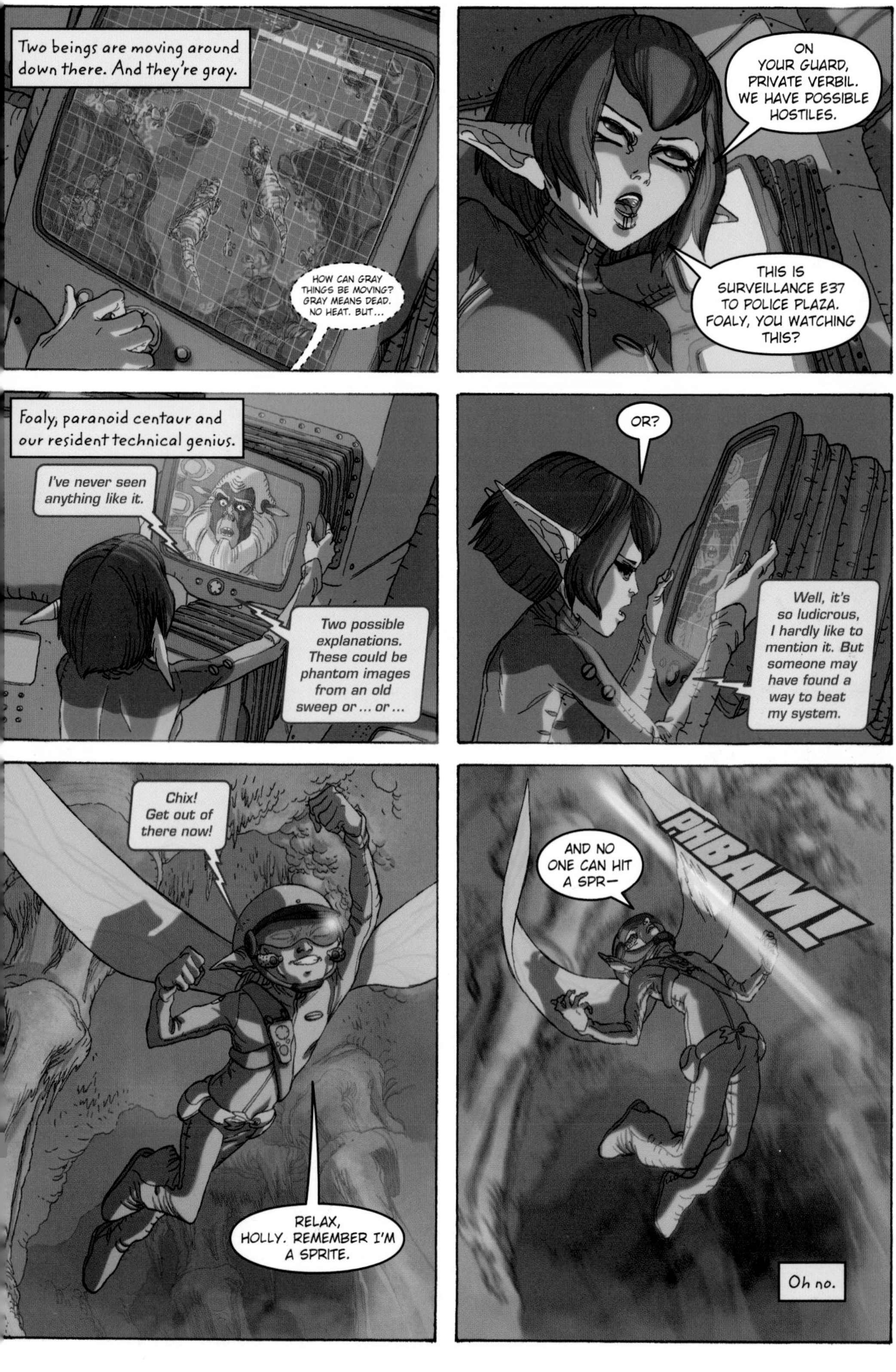
Two beings are moving around down there. And they're gray.
HOW CAN GRAY THINGS BE MOVING? GRAY MEANS DEAD. NO HEAT. BUT...
ON YOUR GUARD, PRIVATE VERBIL. WE HAVE POSSIBLE HOSTILES.
THIS IS SURVEILLANCE E37 TO POLICE PLAZA. FOALY, YOU WATCHING THIS?
Foaly, paranoid centaur and our resident technical genius.
I've never seen anything like it.
Two possible explanations. These could be phantom images from an old sweep or ... or ...
OR?
Well, it's so ludicrous, I hardly like to mention it. But someone may have found a way to beat my system.
Chix! Get out of there now!
RELAX, HOLLY. REMEMBER I'M A SPRITE.
AND NO ONE CAN HIT A SPR—
PHBAM!
Oh no.

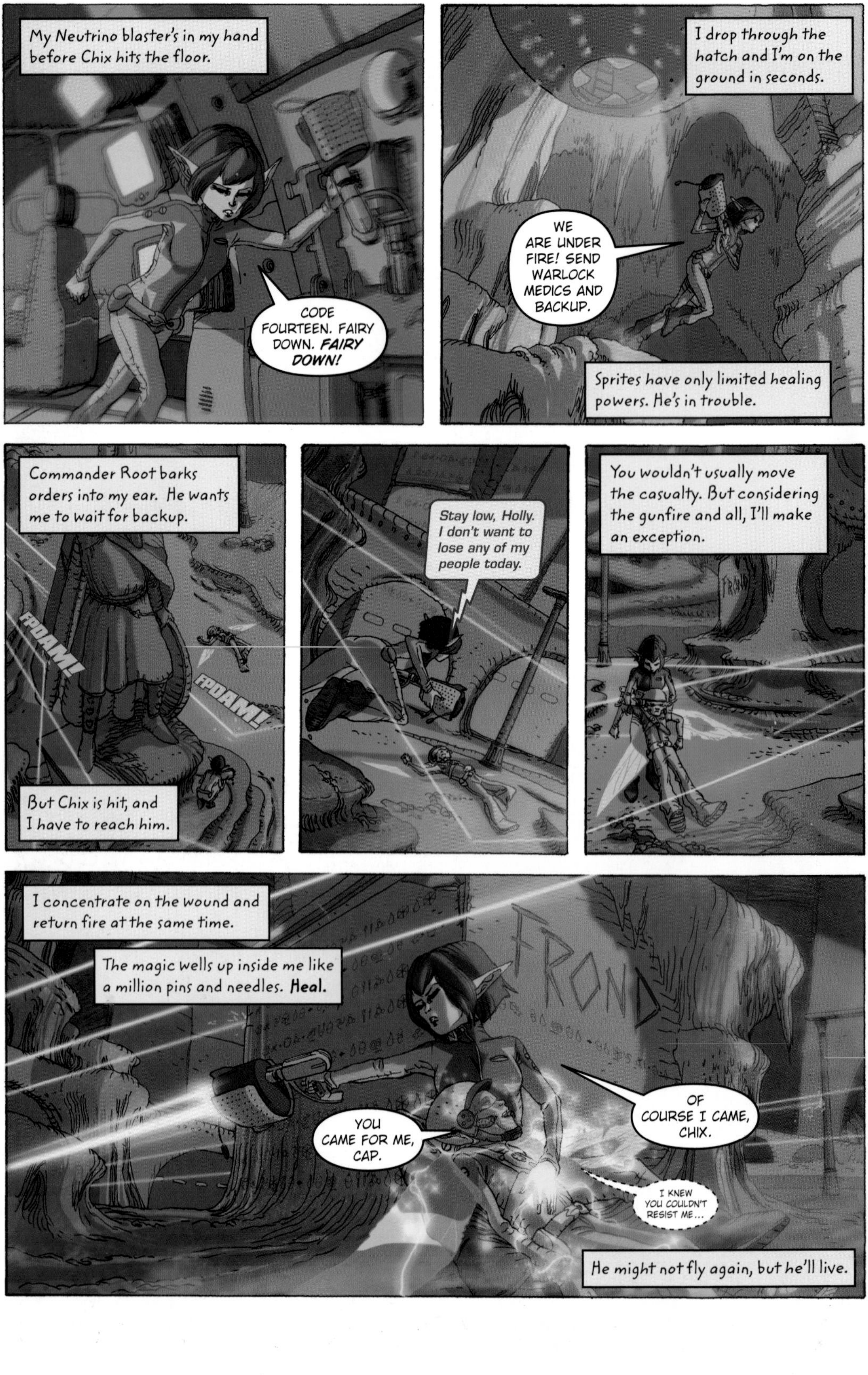
My Neutrino blaster's in my hand before Chix hits the floor.
CODE FOURTEEN. FAIRY DOWN. ***FAIRY DOWN!***
I drop through the hatch and I'm on the ground in seconds.
WE ARE UNDER FIRE! SEND WARLOCK MEDICS AND BACKUP.
Sprites have only limited healing powers. He's in trouble.
Commander Root barks orders into my ear. He wants me to wait for backup.
FPDAM!
FPDAM!
But Chix is hit, and I have to reach him.
Stay low, Holly. I don't want to lose any of my people today.
You wouldn't usually move the casualty. But considering the gunfire and all, I'll make an exception.
FROND
I concentrate on the wound and return fire at the same time.
The magic wells up inside me like a million pins and needles. **Heal.**
FROND
OF COURSE I CAME, CHIX.
YOU CAME FOR ME, CAP.
I KNEW YOU COULDN'T RESIST ME...
He might not fly again, but he'll live.

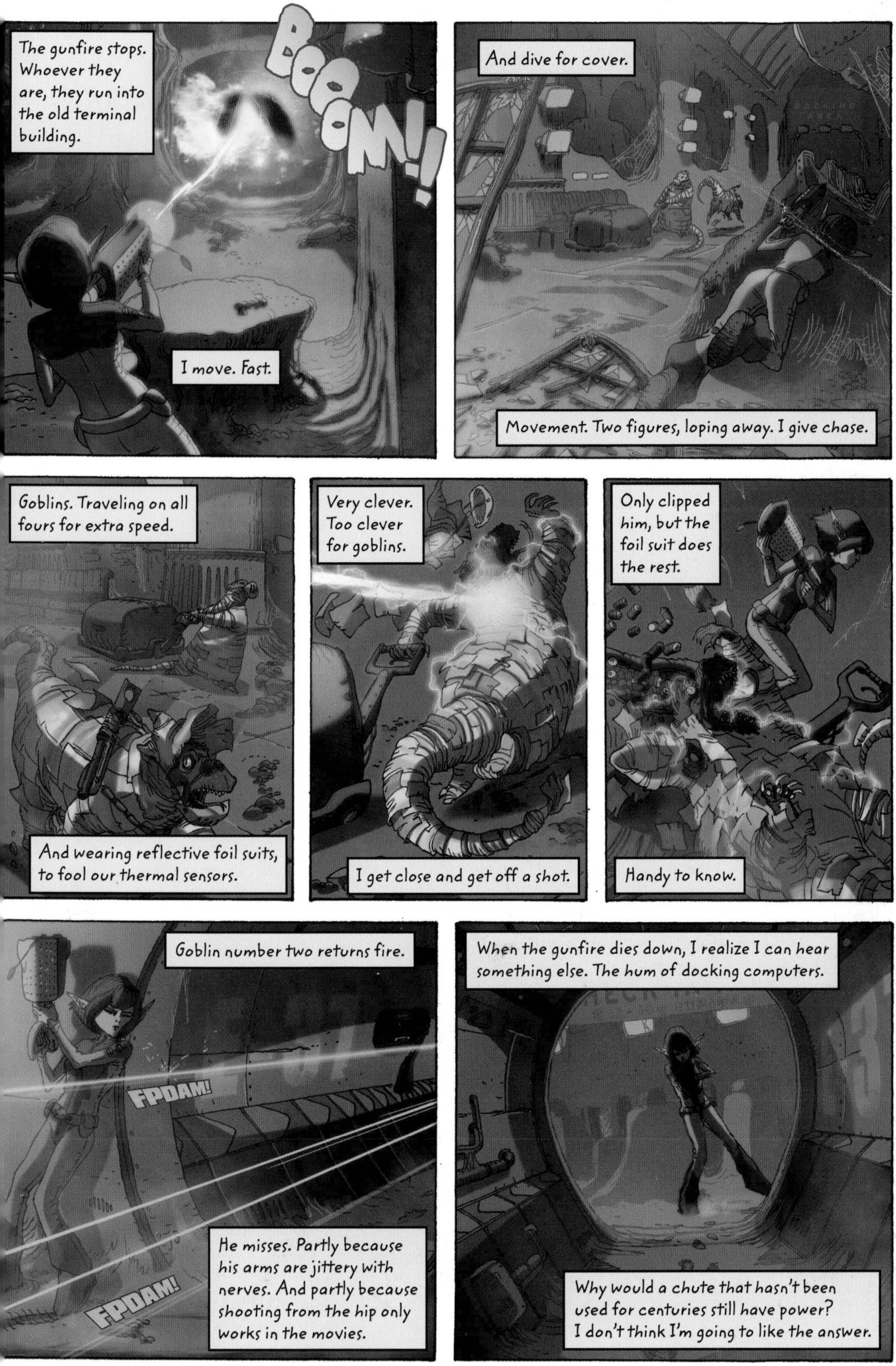
The gunfire stops. Whoever they are, they run into the old terminal building.
BOOOM!!!
I move. Fast.
And dive for cover.
Movement. Two figures, loping away. I give chase.
Goblins. Traveling on all fours for extra speed.
And wearing reflective foil suits, to fool our thermal sensors.
Very clever. Too clever for goblins.
I get close and get off a shot.
Only clipped him, but the foil suit does the rest.
Handy to know.
Goblin number two returns fire.
FPDAM!
FPDAM!
He misses. Partly because his arms are jittery with nerves. And partly because shooting from the hip only works in the movies.
When the gunfire dies down, I realize I can hear something else. The hum of docking computers.
Why would a chute that hasn't been used for centuries still have power? I don't think I'm going to like the answer.

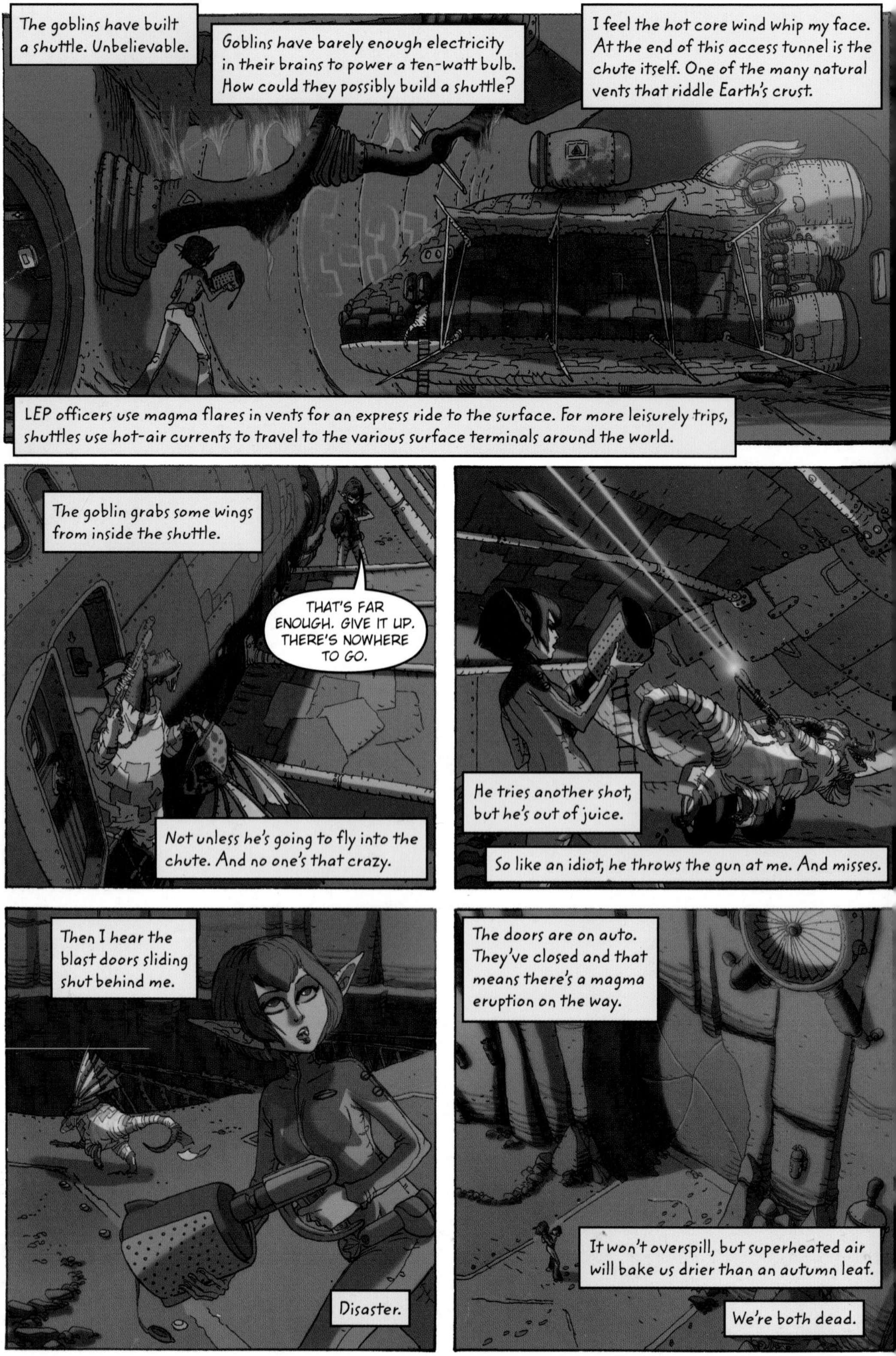

The goblins have built a shuttle. Unbelievable.
Goblins have barely enough electricity in their brains to power a ten-watt bulb. How could they possibly build a shuttle?
I feel the hot core wind whip my face. At the end of this access tunnel is the chute itself. One of the many natural vents that riddle Earth's crust.
LEP officers use magma flares in vents for an express ride to the surface. For more leisurely trips, shuttles use hot-air currents to travel to the various surface terminals around the world.
The goblin grabs some wings from inside the shuttle.
THAT'S FAR ENOUGH. GIVE IT UP. THERE'S NOWHERE TO GO.
Not unless he's going to fly into the chute. And no one's that crazy.
He tries another shot, but he's out of juice.
So like an idiot, he throws the gun at me. And misses.
Then I hear the blast doors sliding shut behind me.
Disaster.
The doors are on auto. They've closed and that means there's a magma eruption on the way.
It won't overspill, but superheated air will bake us drier than an autumn leaf.
We're both dead.

I see the goblin edging out toward the chute. And then I realize.

The goblin's not crazy.

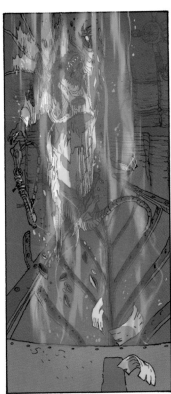

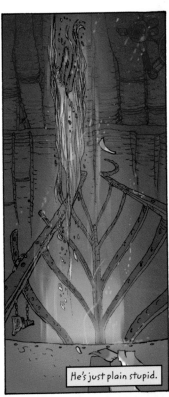

He's just plain stupid.

There's a line of old coolant tanks along the roof. I start blasting.

The tanks split. Empty except for rancid air. Useless.

One tank is black and oblong, out of place among the older LEP models.

I get under it and aim.

Behind me I hear the heat wave come billowing in from the chute. I fire.

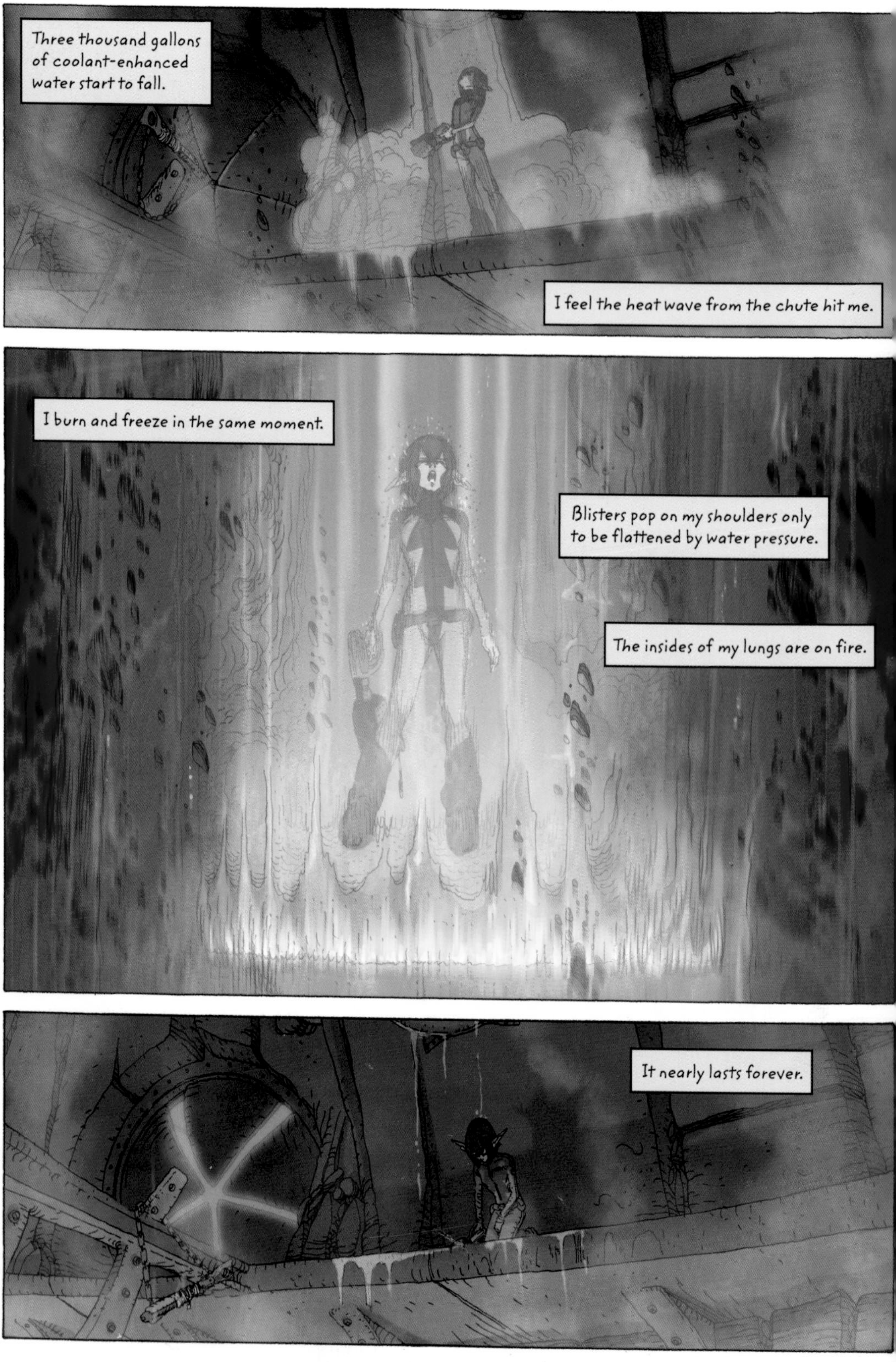
Three thousand gallons of coolant-enhanced water start to fall.
I feel the heat wave from the chute hit me.
I burn and freeze in the same moment.
Blisters pop on my shoulders only to be flattened by water pressure.
The insides of my lungs are on fire.
It nearly lasts forever.

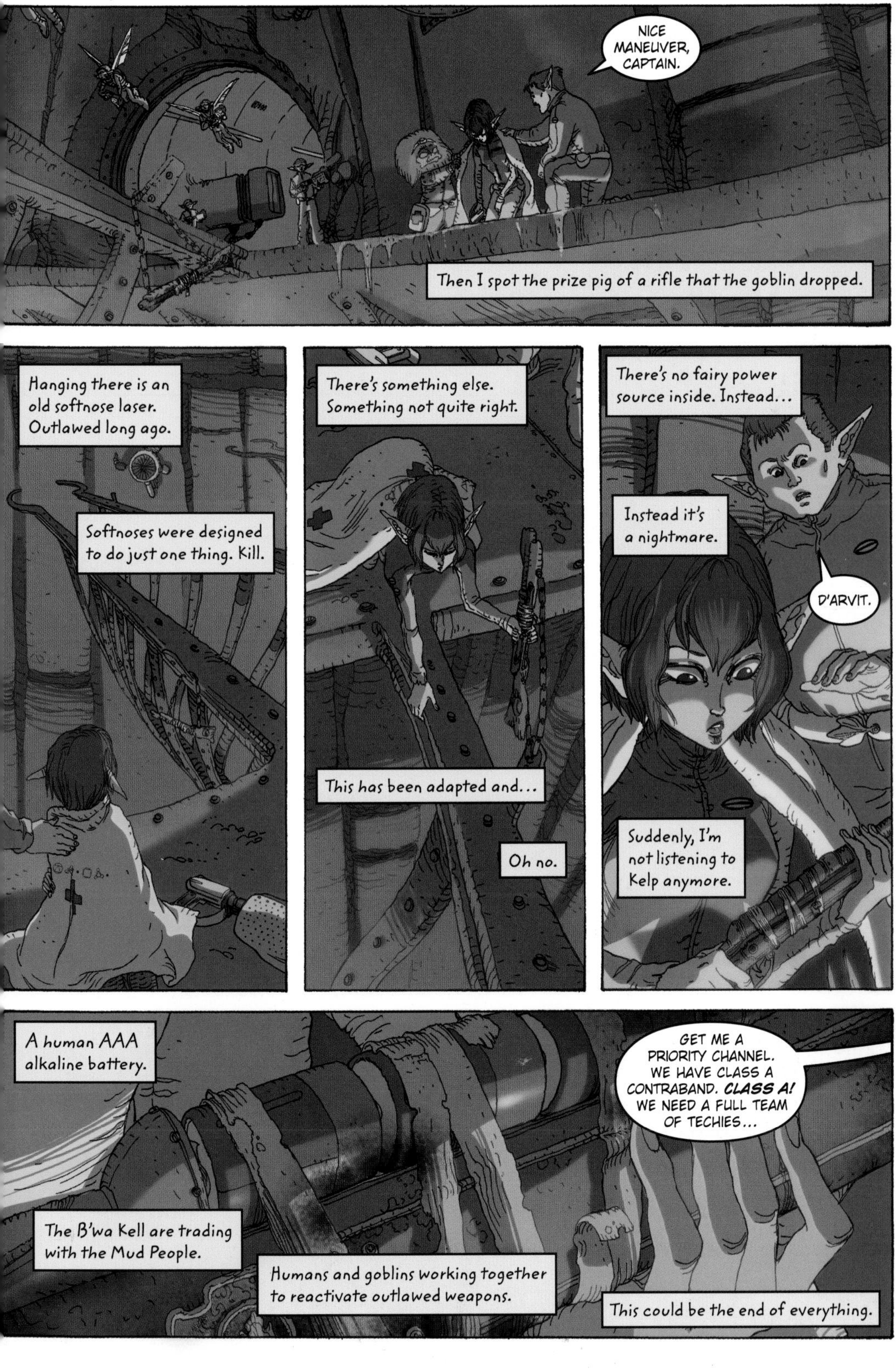
NICE MANEUVER, CAPTAIN.
Then I spot the prize pig of a rifle that the goblin dropped.
Hanging there is an old softnose laser. Outlawed long ago.
Softnoses were designed to do just one thing. Kill.
There's something else. Something not quite right.
This has been adapted and...
Oh no.
There's no fairy power source inside. Instead...
Instead it's a nightmare.
D'ARVIT.
Suddenly, I'm not listening to Kelp anymore.
A human AAA alkaline battery.
GET ME A PRIORITY CHANNEL. WE HAVE CLASS A CONTRABAND. CLASS A! WE NEED A FULL TEAM OF TECHIES...
The B'wa Kell are trading with the Mud People.
Humans and goblins working together to reactivate outlawed weapons.
This could be the end of everything.

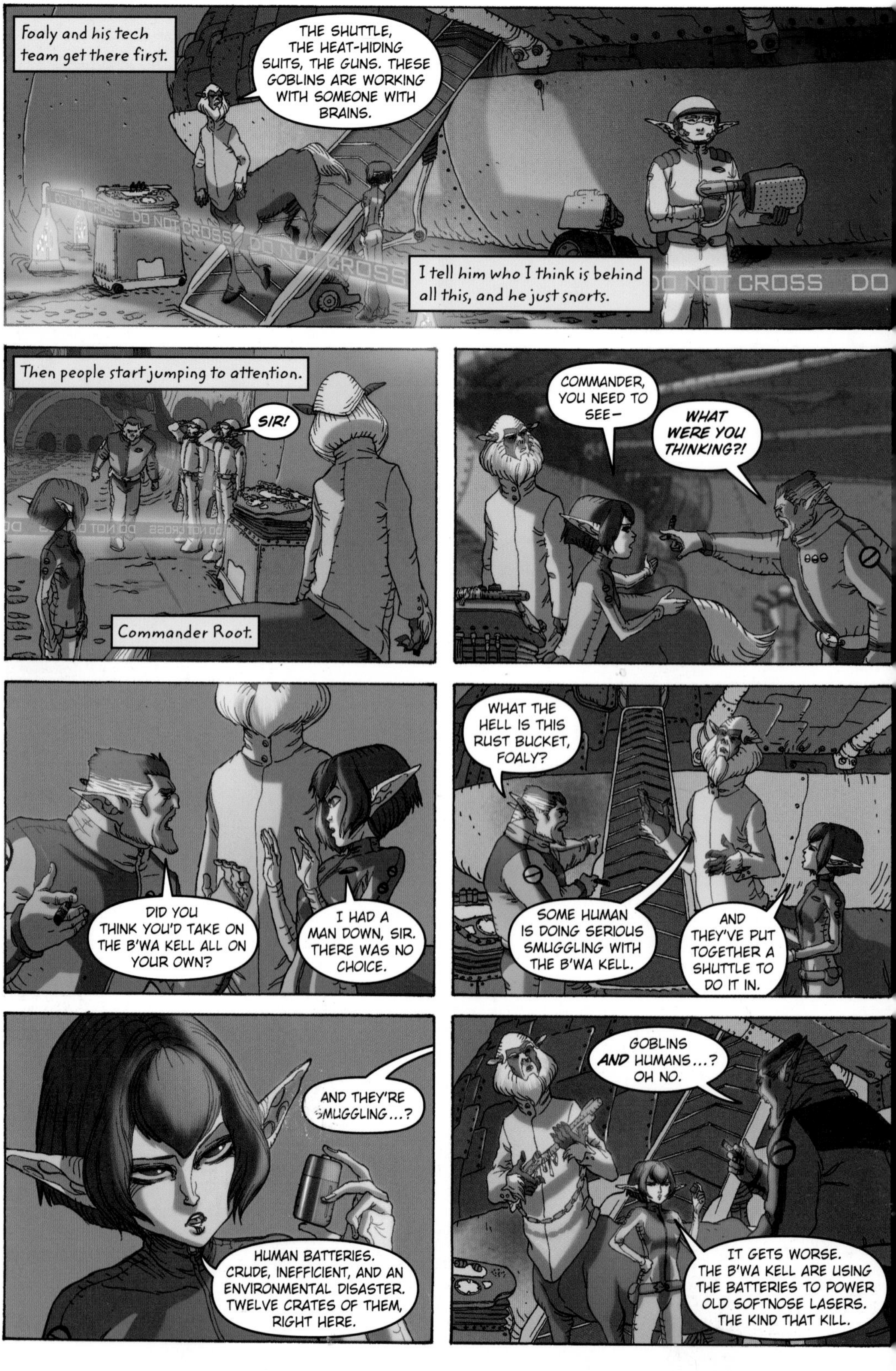
Foaly and his tech team get there first.
THE SHUTTLE, THE HEAT-HIDING SUITS, THE GUNS. THESE GOBLINS ARE WORKING WITH SOMEONE WITH BRAINS.
DO NOT CROSS
I tell him who I think is behind all this, and he just snorts.
Then people start jumping to attention.
SIR!
Commander Root.
COMMANDER, YOU NEED TO SEE—
WHAT WERE YOU THINKING?!
DID YOU THINK YOU'D TAKE ON THE B'WA KELL ALL ON YOUR OWN?
I HAD A MAN DOWN, SIR. THERE WAS NO CHOICE.
WHAT THE HELL IS THIS RUST BUCKET, FOALY?
SOME HUMAN IS DOING SERIOUS SMUGGLING WITH THE B'WA KELL.
AND THEY'VE PUT TOGETHER A SHUTTLE TO DO IT IN.
AND THEY'RE SMUGGLING...?
HUMAN BATTERIES. CRUDE, INEFFICIENT, AND AN ENVIRONMENTAL DISASTER. TWELVE CRATES OF THEM, RIGHT HERE.
GOBLINS AND HUMANS...? OH NO.
IT GETS WORSE. THE B'WA KELL ARE USING THE BATTERIES TO POWER OLD SOFTNOSE LASERS. THE KIND THAT KILL.

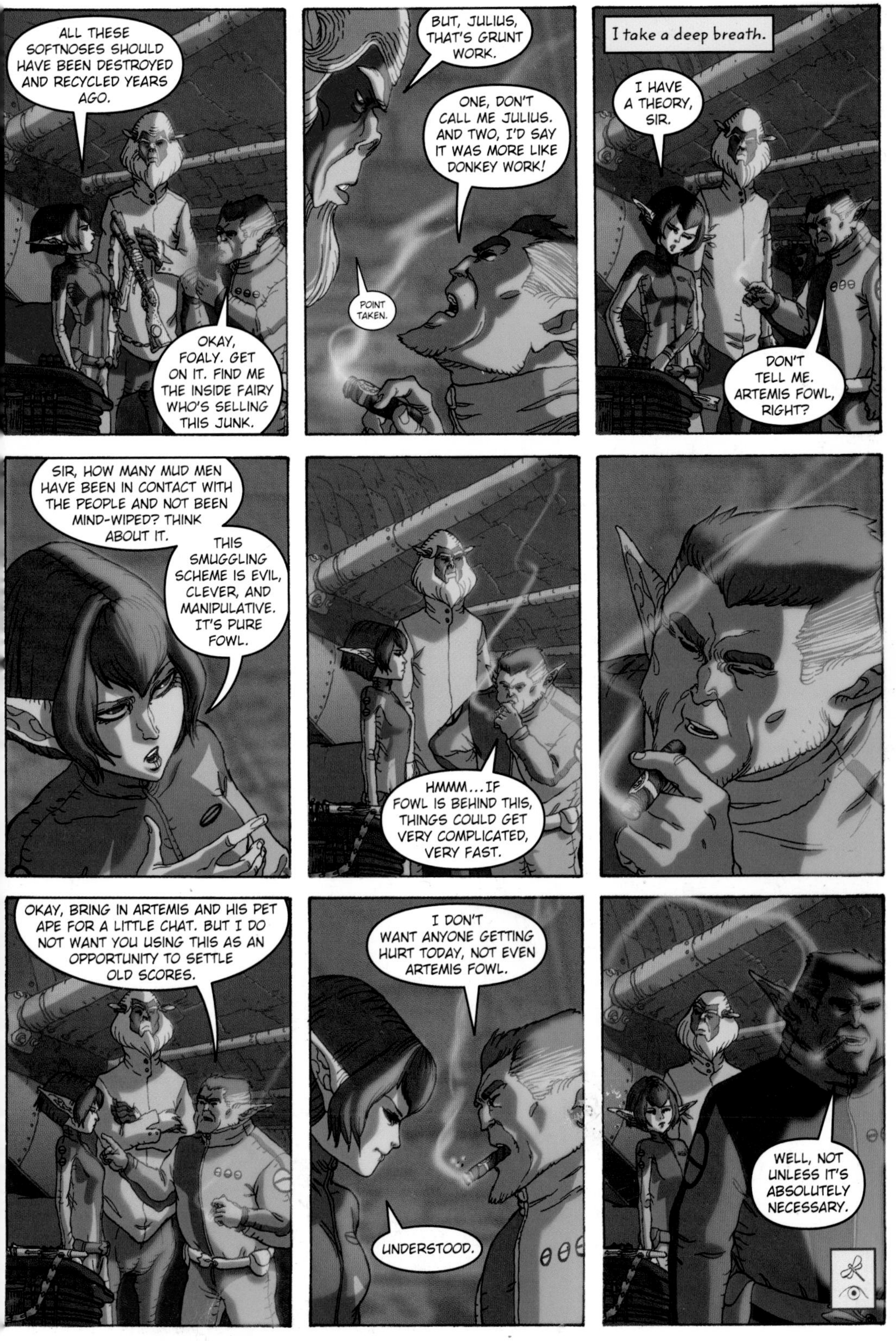
ALL THESE SOFTNOSES SHOULD HAVE BEEN DESTROYED AND RECYCLED YEARS AGO.
OKAY, FOALY. GET ON IT. FIND ME THE INSIDE FAIRY WHO'S SELLING THIS JUNK.
BUT, JULIUS, THAT'S GRUNT WORK.
ONE, DON'T CALL ME JULIUS. AND TWO, I'D SAY IT WAS MORE LIKE DONKEY WORK!
POINT TAKEN.
I take a deep breath.
I HAVE A THEORY, SIR.
DON'T TELL ME. ARTEMIS FOWL, RIGHT?
SIR, HOW MANY MUD MEN HAVE BEEN IN CONTACT WITH THE PEOPLE AND NOT BEEN MIND-WIPED? THINK ABOUT IT.
THIS SMUGGLING SCHEME IS EVIL, CLEVER, AND MANIPULATIVE. IT'S PURE FOWL.
HMMM...IF FOWL IS BEHIND THIS, THINGS COULD GET VERY COMPLICATED, VERY FAST.
OKAY, BRING IN ARTEMIS AND HIS PET APE FOR A LITTLE CHAT. BUT I DO NOT WANT YOU USING THIS AS AN OPPORTUNITY TO SETTLE OLD SCORES.
I DON'T WANT ANYONE GETTING HURT TODAY, NOT EVEN ARTEMIS FOWL.
UNDERSTOOD.
WELL, NOT UNLESS IT'S ABSOLUTELY NECESSARY.

THE SCROLLS OF CAPALLA

Centaurian—possibly the oldest form of writing in the world. It dates back well over ten millennia to when humans first began hunting centaurs. All centaurs are considered to be paranoid, but perhaps with very good reason since there are less than a hundred left alive on or under the entire planet. Humans have killed off their cousins, the unicorns, altogether. There are probably a mere six centaurs who can still read ancient Centaurian, one of the foremost experts being Foaly, the LEP's resident techno-genius. It is believed that Foaly uses the ancient language as a basis for most of his computer encryptions. Only one illuminated Centaurian manuscript from the old times still survives, "The Scrolls of Capalla."

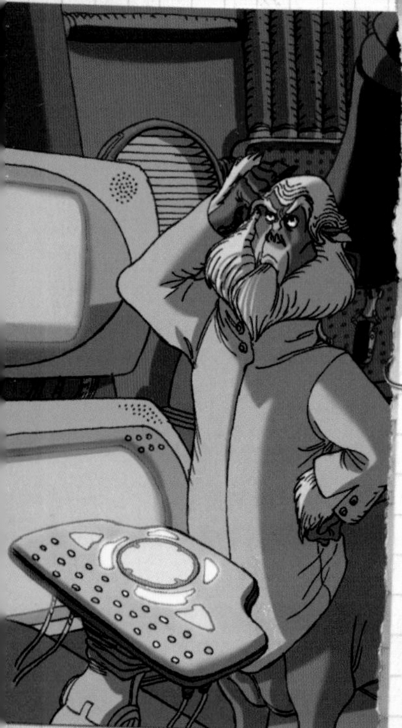

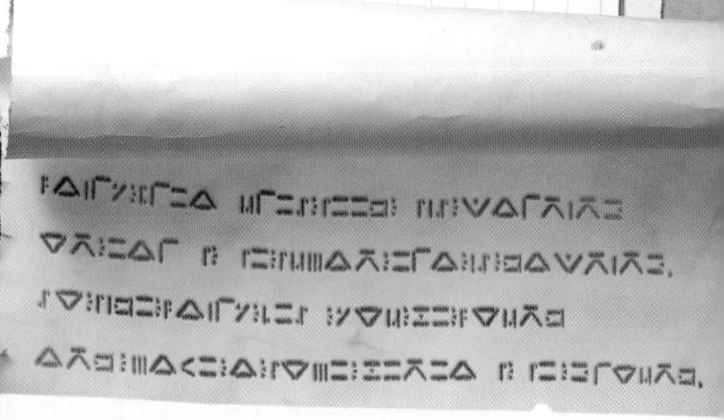

Fairy creatures, heed this warning,
On Earth, the human era is dawning.
So hide, fairy, lest you be found,
And make a home beneath the ground.

Centaurs known for their intellect, not their poetry.

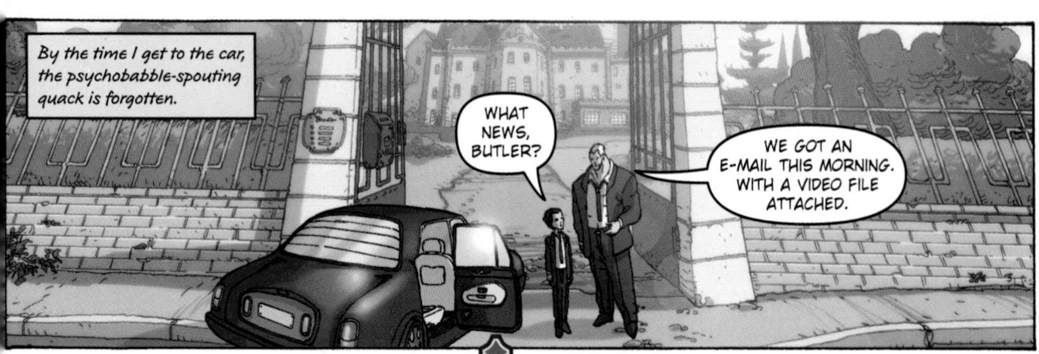
By the time I get to the car, the psychobabble-spouting quack is forgotten.
WHAT NEWS, BUTLER?
WE GOT AN E-MAIL THIS MORNING. WITH A VIDEO FILE ATTACHED.

CHAPTER 3: GOING UNDERGROUND

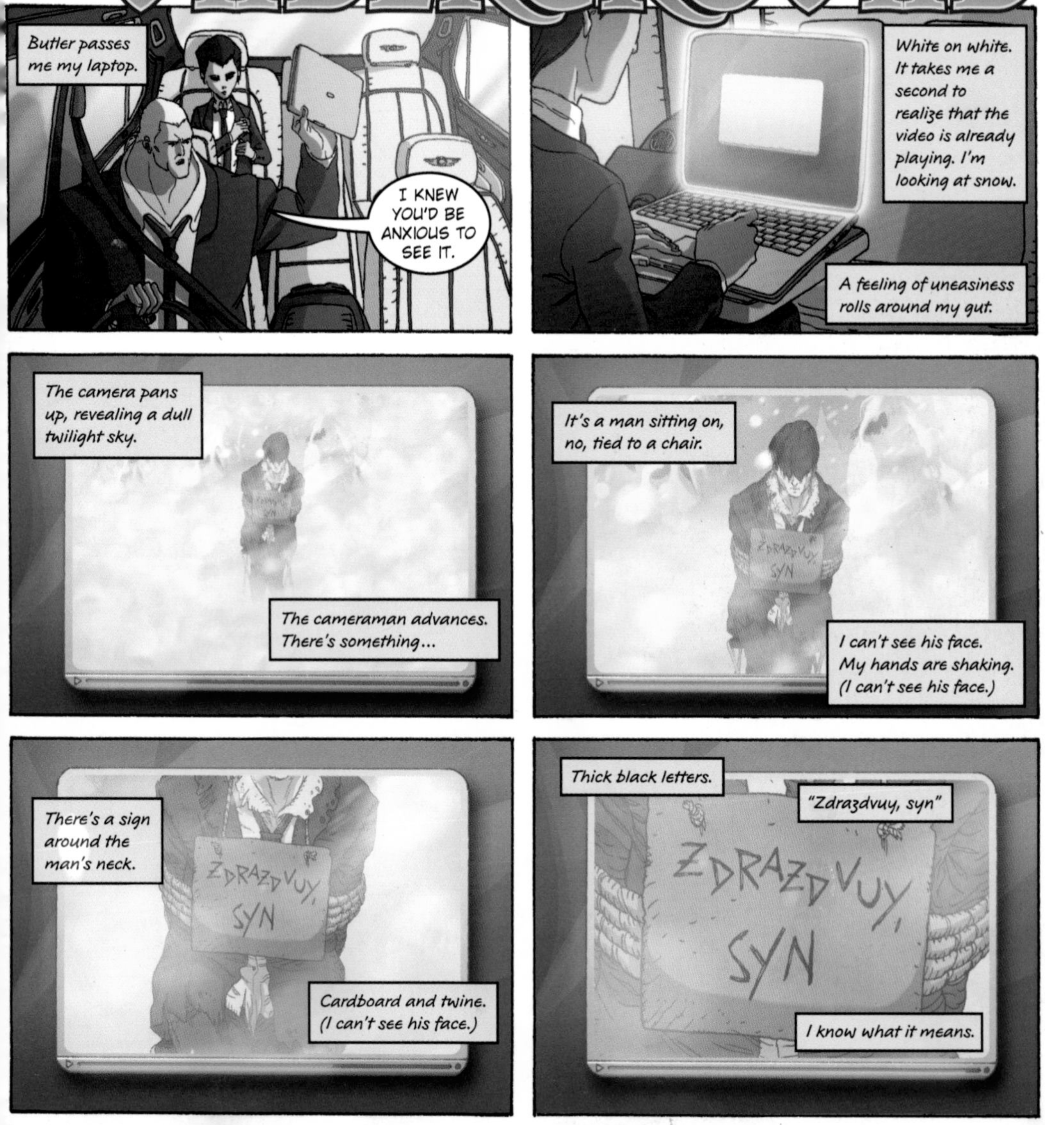
Butler passes me my laptop.
I KNEW YOU'D BE ANXIOUS TO SEE IT.
White on white. It takes me a second to realize that the video is already playing. I'm looking at snow.
A feeling of uneasiness rolls around my gut.
The camera pans up, revealing a dull twilight sky.
The cameraman advances. There's something...
It's a man sitting on, no, tied to a chair.
ZDRAZDVUY, SYN
I can't see his face. My hands are shaking. (I can't see his face.)
There's a sign around the man's neck.
ZDRAZDVUY, SYN
Cardboard and twine. (I can't see his face.)
Thick black letters.
"Zdrazdvuy, syn"
ZDRAZDVUY, SYN
I know what it means.

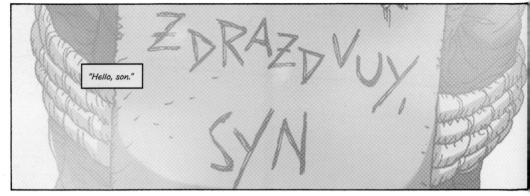

"Hello, son."

DO... DO YOU THINK IT'S HIM, ARTEMIS?

I THINK SO, BUTLER. BUT THE PICTURE QUALITY IS SO POOR I CAN'T BE CERTAIN.

Butler lost someone too when the *Fowl Star* went down. Unfortunately, Butler's uncle, the Major, had soon turned up in the Tchersky morgue.

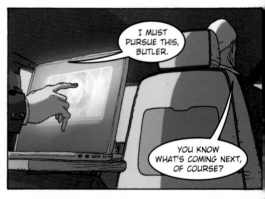

I MUST PURSUE THIS, BUTLER.

YOU KNOW WHAT'S COMING NEXT, OF COURSE?

A RANSOM DEMAND. THIS IS MERELY THE TEASER TO GET OUR ATTENTION. I'LL NEED TO CASH IN SOME OF THE PEOPLE'S GOLD. WE SHOULD CONTACT LARS IN ZURICH IMMEDIATELY.

I'M AFRAID THAT EVEN PAYING THE RANSOM WON'T GUARANTEE YOUR FATHER'S SAFETY.

IT IS QUITE POSSIBLE THAT THE KIDNAPPERS WILL TAKE THE MONEY AND THEN TRY AND KILL ALL OF US.

YOU'RE RIGHT, OF COURSE. I SHALL HAVE TO DEVISE A PLAN.

My last plan almost got Butler killed, not to mention plunging the world into a cross-species war. I see Butler shiver.

The future of the fairy race is at stake and it still takes me half an hour to get my surface visa.

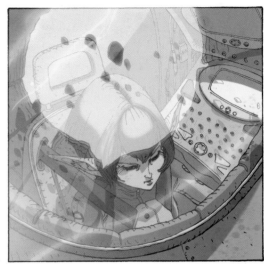

The fairy shuttleport at Tara is concealed beneath an overgrown hillock on the McGraney farm.

For centuries, the McGraneys have respected the fairy fort's boundaries. For centuries, the McGraneys have enjoyed exceptional good luck.

As soon as I hit the surface I turn my shield on. I fly, invisible to human eyes.

The mechanical wings are a set of Koboi DoubleDex from Koboi Labs. New design.

Sunset.

Perfect.

A thermal scan tells me the house is empty. I need to wait.

Now the question. What's the best way to abduct a thirteen-year-old criminal genius?

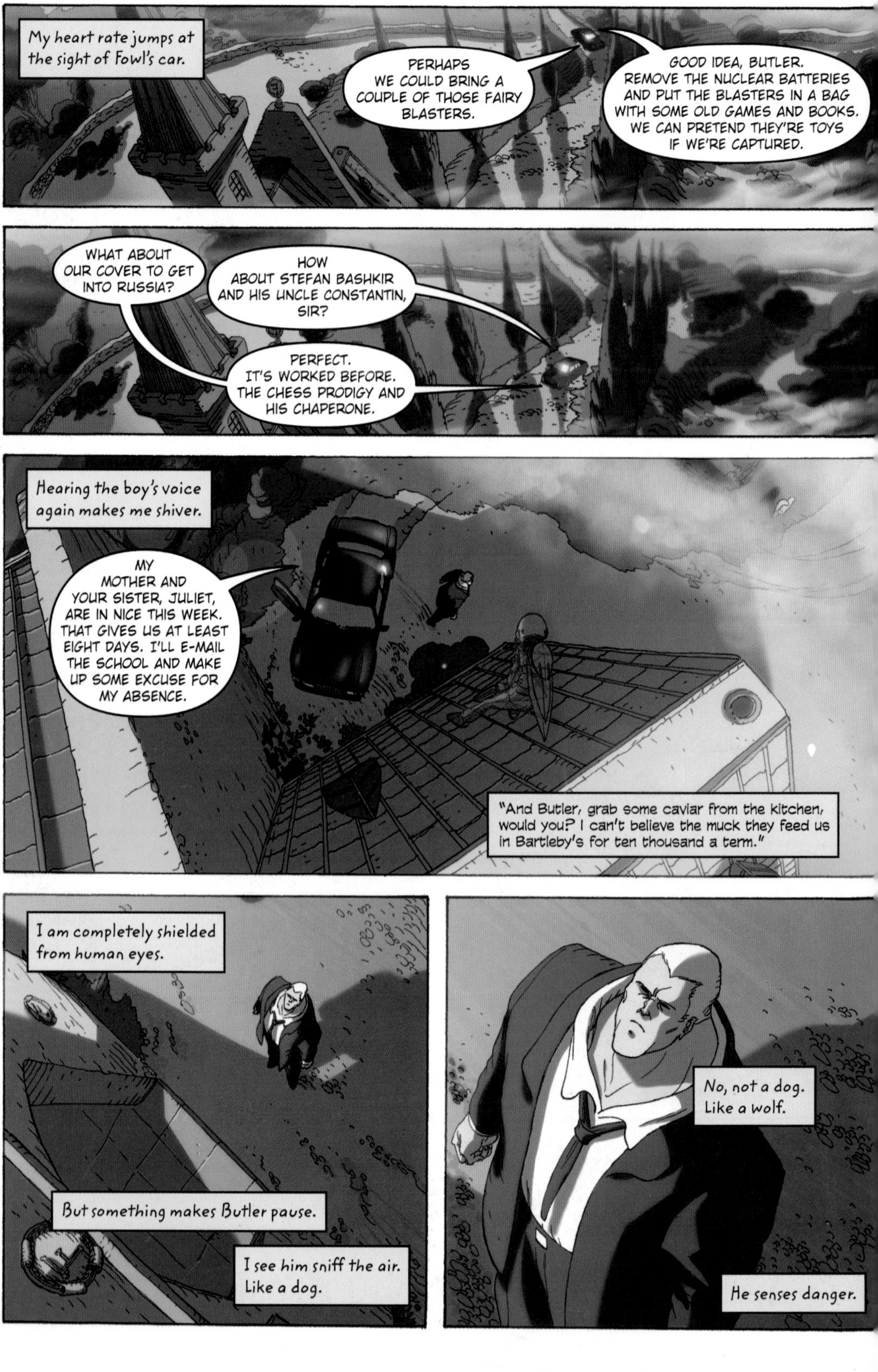
My heart rate jumps at the sight of Fowl's car.
PERHAPS WE COULD BRING A COUPLE OF THOSE FAIRY BLASTERS.
GOOD IDEA, BUTLER. REMOVE THE NUCLEAR BATTERIES AND PUT THE BLASTERS IN A BAG WITH SOME OLD GAMES AND BOOKS. WE CAN PRETEND THEY'RE TOYS IF WE'RE CAPTURED.
WHAT ABOUT OUR COVER TO GET INTO RUSSIA?
HOW ABOUT STEFAN BASHKIR AND HIS UNCLE CONSTANTIN, SIR?
PERFECT. IT'S WORKED BEFORE. THE CHESS PRODIGY AND HIS CHAPERONE.
Hearing the boy's voice again makes me shiver.
MY MOTHER AND YOUR SISTER, JULIET, ARE IN NICE THIS WEEK. THAT GIVES US AT LEAST EIGHT DAYS. I'LL E-MAIL THE SCHOOL AND MAKE UP SOME EXCUSE FOR MY ABSENCE.
"And Butler, grab some caviar from the kitchen, would you? I can't believe the muck they feed us in Bartleby's for ten thousand a term."
I am completely shielded from human eyes.
But something makes Butler pause.
I see him sniff the air. Like a dog.
No, not a dog. Like a wolf.
He senses danger.

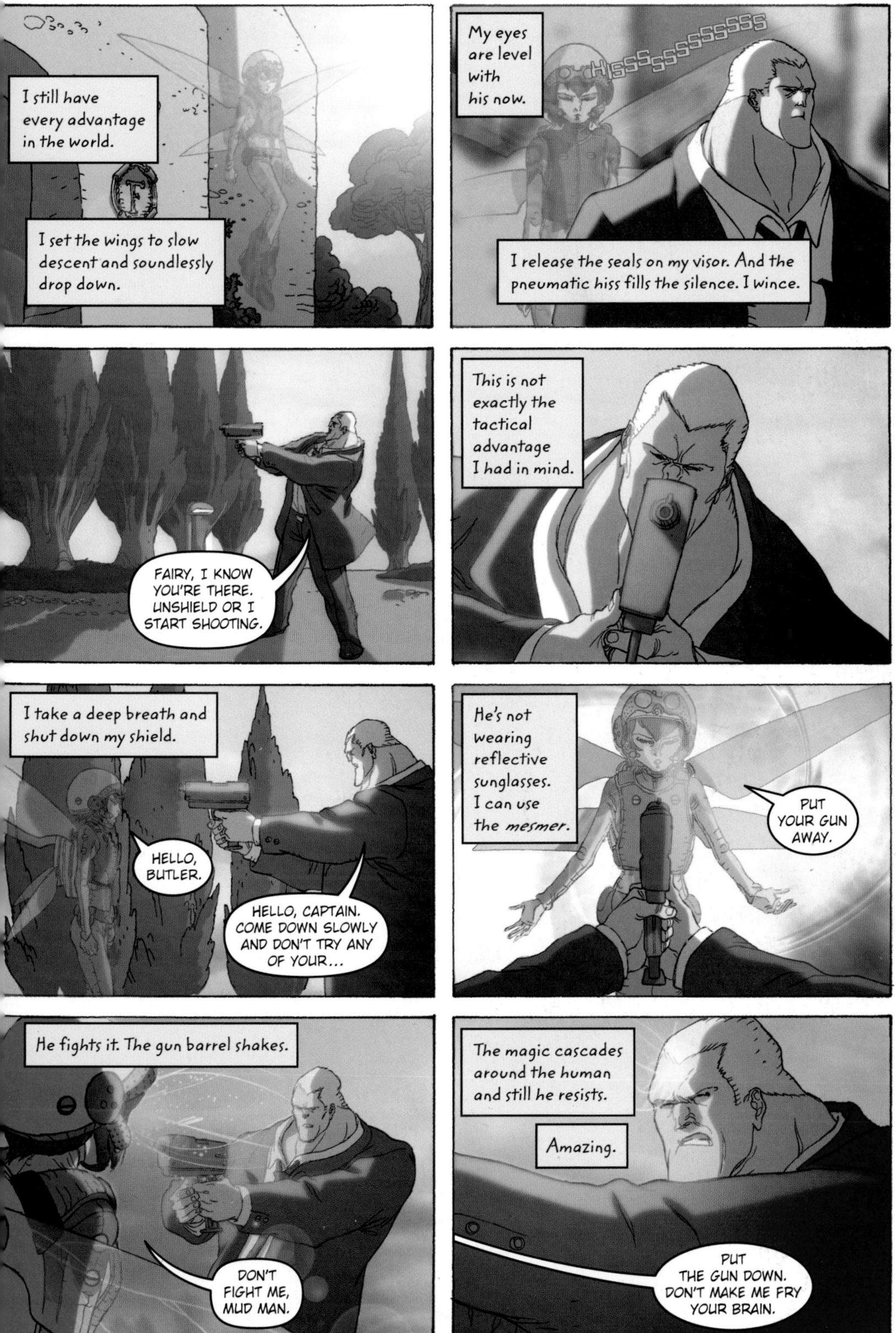
I still have every advantage in the world.
I set the wings to slow descent and soundlessly drop down.
My eyes are level with his now.
HISSSSSSSSSSSSSS
I release the seals on my visor. And the pneumatic hiss fills the silence. I wince.
FAIRY, I KNOW YOU'RE THERE. UNSHIELD OR I START SHOOTING.
This is not exactly the tactical advantage I had in mind.
I take a deep breath and shut down my shield.
HELLO, BUTLER.
HELLO, CAPTAIN. COME DOWN SLOWLY AND DON'T TRY ANY OF YOUR…
He's not wearing reflective sunglasses. I can use the *mesmer*.
PUT YOUR GUN AWAY.
He fights it. The gun barrel shakes.
DON'T FIGHT ME, MUD MAN.
The magic cascades around the human and still he resists.
Amazing.
PUT THE GUN DOWN. DON'T MAKE ME FRY YOUR BRAIN.

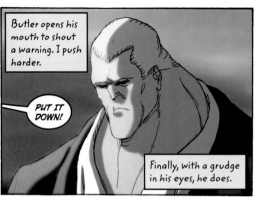

Butler opens his mouth to shout a warning. I push harder.

PUT IT DOWN!

Finally, with a grudge in his eyes, he does.

GOOD. NOW GO BACK TO THE CAR AND OPEN THE DOOR AS THOUGH NOTHING'S WRONG.

I put up my shield again. I'm going to enjoy this.

I press the SEND button. The e-mail should do the trick.

"Dear Principal Guiney, Because of your counselor's tactless interrogation of my little Arty, I have taken him out of school for a course of therapy sessions with real professionals in Switzerland.

"Do not attempt to contact me as that would only serve to irritate me further and, when irritated, I generally call my attorneys. Sincerely, Angeline Fowl"

It would be nice to see Principal Guiney's expression when he reads the e-mail.

I slip inside the car completely silently.

The boy has no idea I am there.

CAPTAIN SHORT, I PRESUME. WHY DON'T YOU STOP VIBRATING AND SETTLE INTO THE VISIBLE SPECTRUM?

That's really very annoying.

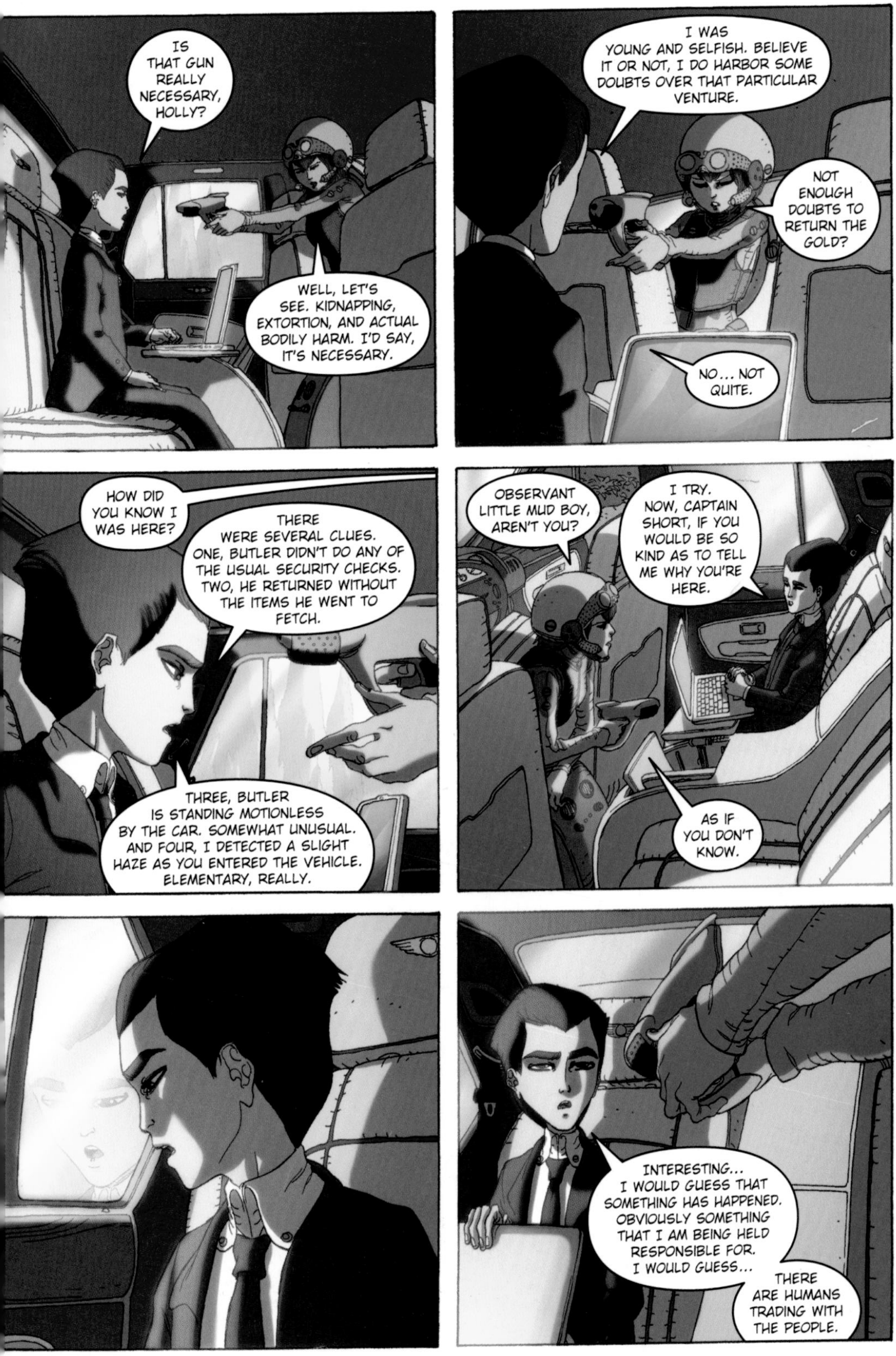
IS THAT GUN REALLY NECESSARY, HOLLY?
WELL, LET'S SEE. KIDNAPPING, EXTORTION, AND ACTUAL BODILY HARM. I'D SAY, IT'S NECESSARY.
I WAS YOUNG AND SELFISH. BELIEVE IT OR NOT, I DO HARBOR SOME DOUBTS OVER THAT PARTICULAR VENTURE.
NOT ENOUGH DOUBTS TO RETURN THE GOLD?
NO... NOT QUITE.
HOW DID YOU KNOW I WAS HERE?
THERE WERE SEVERAL CLUES. ONE, BUTLER DIDN'T DO ANY OF THE USUAL SECURITY CHECKS. TWO, HE RETURNED WITHOUT THE ITEMS HE WENT TO FETCH.
THREE, BUTLER IS STANDING MOTIONLESS BY THE CAR. SOMEWHAT UNUSUAL. AND FOUR, I DETECTED A SLIGHT HAZE AS YOU ENTERED THE VEHICLE. ELEMENTARY, REALLY.
OBSERVANT LITTLE MUD BOY, AREN'T YOU?
I TRY. NOW, CAPTAIN SHORT, IF YOU WOULD BE SO KIND AS TO TELL ME WHY YOU'RE HERE.
AS IF YOU DON'T KNOW.
INTERESTING... I WOULD GUESS THAT SOMETHING HAS HAPPENED. OBVIOUSLY SOMETHING THAT I AM BEING HELD RESPONSIBLE FOR. I WOULD GUESS...
THERE ARE HUMANS TRADING WITH THE PEOPLE.

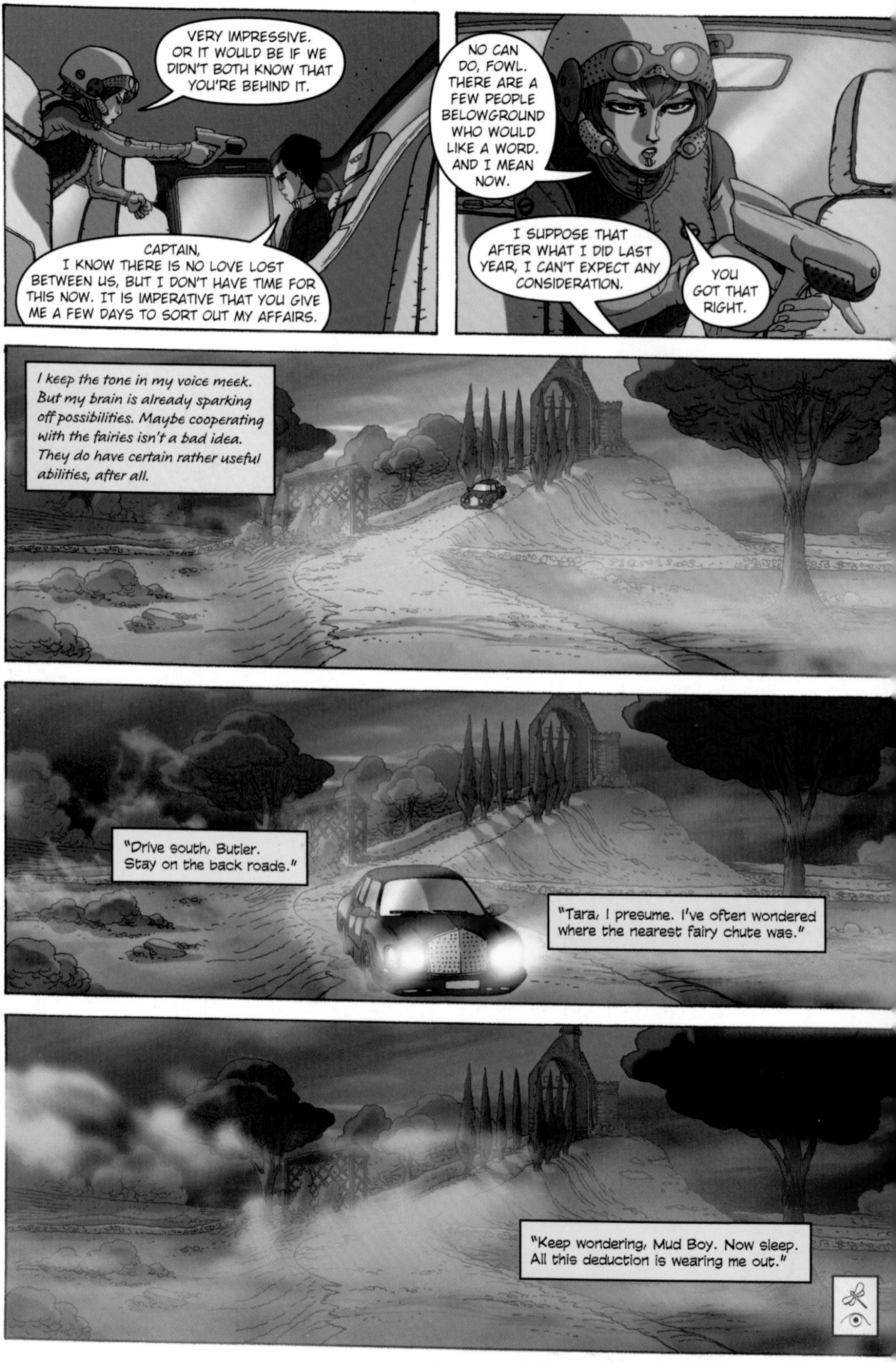
VERY IMPRESSIVE. OR IT WOULD BE IF WE DIDN'T BOTH KNOW THAT YOU'RE BEHIND IT.
CAPTAIN, I KNOW THERE IS NO LOVE LOST BETWEEN US, BUT I DON'T HAVE TIME FOR THIS NOW. IT IS IMPERATIVE THAT YOU GIVE ME A FEW DAYS TO SORT OUT MY AFFAIRS.
NO CAN DO, FOWL. THERE ARE A FEW PEOPLE BELOWGROUND WHO WOULD LIKE A WORD. AND I MEAN NOW.
I SUPPOSE THAT AFTER WHAT I DID LAST YEAR, I CAN'T EXPECT ANY CONSIDERATION.
YOU GOT THAT RIGHT.
I keep the tone in my voice meek. But my brain is already sparking off possibilities. Maybe cooperating with the fairies isn't a bad idea. They do have certain rather useful abilities, after all.
"Drive south, Butler. Stay on the back roads."
"Tara, I presume. I've often wondered where the nearest fairy chute was."
"Keep wondering, Mud Boy. Now sleep. All this deduction is wearing me out."

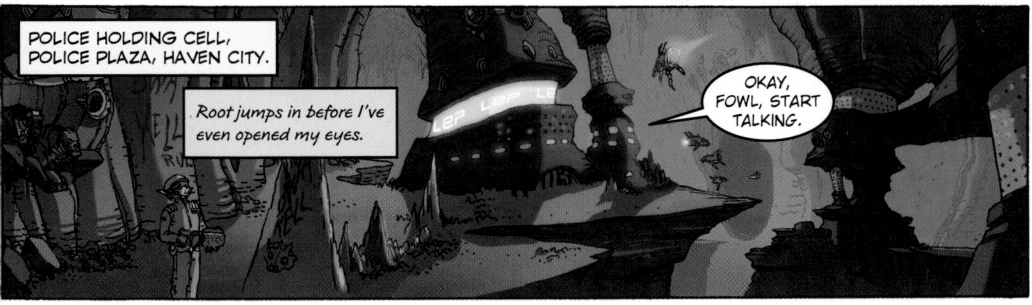
POLICE HOLDING CELL, POLICE PLAZA, HAVEN CITY.
Root jumps in before I've even opened my eyes.
OKAY, FOWL, START TALKING.

CHAPTER 4: FOWL IS FAIR

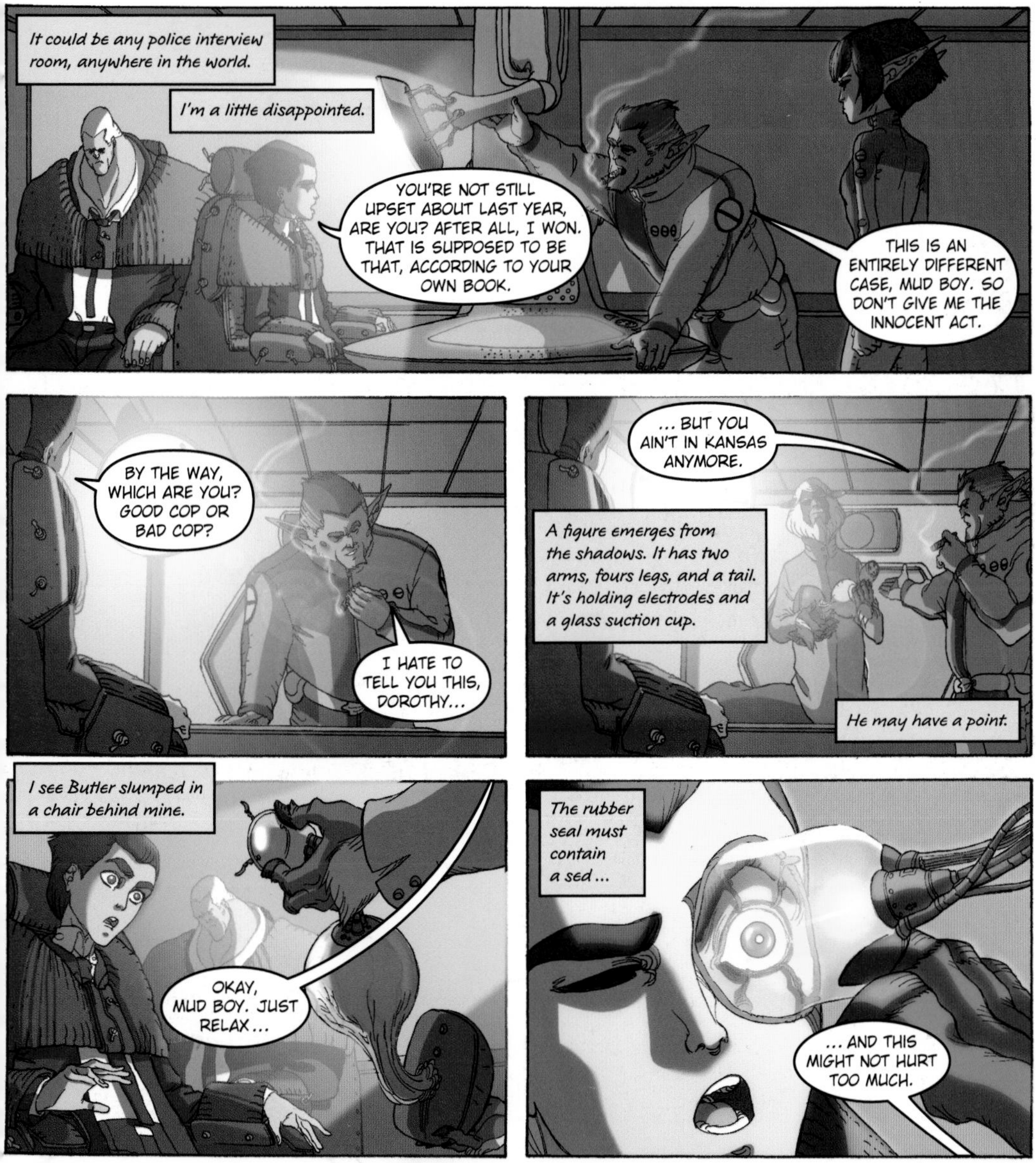
It could be any police interview room, anywhere in the world.
I'm a little disappointed.
YOU'RE NOT STILL UPSET ABOUT LAST YEAR, ARE YOU? AFTER ALL, I WON. THAT IS SUPPOSED TO BE THAT, ACCORDING TO YOUR OWN BOOK.
THIS IS AN ENTIRELY DIFFERENT CASE, MUD BOY. SO DON'T GIVE ME THE INNOCENT ACT.
BY THE WAY, WHICH ARE YOU? GOOD COP OR BAD COP?
I HATE TO TELL YOU THIS, DOROTHY...
... BUT YOU AIN'T IN KANSAS ANYMORE.
A figure emerges from the shadows. It has two arms, fours legs, and a tail. It's holding electrodes and a glass suction cup.
He may have a point.
I see Butler slumped in a chair behind mine.
OKAY, MUD BOY. JUST RELAX...
The rubber seal must contain a sed...
... AND THIS MIGHT NOT HURT TOO MUCH.

THE SEDATIVE IS IN THE RUBBER SEALS. THEY NEVER SEE IT COMING. TELL ME I'M NOT THE CLEVEREST INDIVIDUAL IN THE UNIVERSE.
OH, I DON'T KNOW. THAT PIXIE, OPAL KOBOI, IS ONE PRETTY SHARP SCIENTIST. GOOD AT BUSINESS TOO.
The commander winks at me. Foaly takes the bait, like always.
KOBOI? KOBOI? IF YOU ASK ME, WE'RE ALL USING FAR TOO MUCH KOBOI TECHNOLOGY THESE DAYS. IT'S NOT GOOD TO LET ONE COMPANY HAVE SO MUCH POLICE BUSINESS.
I'M SERIOUS, JULIUS. I KNOW OPAL KOBOI FROM MY DAYS AT UNIVERSITY. SHE'S NOT STABLE.
KOBOI JUST UPGRADED EVERY GUN AND VEHICLE IN THE ENTIRE FORCE. YOU'RE JUST UPSET BECAUSE SHE'S BETTER THAN YOU. RICHER, TOO.
YEAH, WELL, MAYBE I'LL GO PRIVATE WITH THIS RETIMAGER.
WHICH DOES WHAT EXACTLY?
EVERY SINGLE THING A HUMAN EYE LOOKS AT LEAVES AN IMPRINT ON THE RETINA. LIKE A TINY ETCHING. WE CAN SEARCH FOR MATCHES. IF HE'S LYING, WE'LL KNOW.
"For every matching point, we get a hit. About two hundred hits is normal. Anything above that and he's seen a goblin before."
HIT RATE: 186
RESULT—NEGATIVE
HIT RATE: 164
RESULT—NEGATIVE
HIT RATE: 158
RESULT—NEGATIVE
"Could they have mind-wiped him?"
NO, THAT'S THE BEAUTY OF THIS BABY. IT OPERATES ON ACTUAL PHYSICAL EVIDENCE. YOU'D HAVE TO SCRUB THE RETINAS.
SORRY, COMMANDER, BUT MASTER FOWL HERE IS INNOCENT. HE'S NEVER EVEN SEEN A GOBLIN, MUCH LESS TRADED WITH THE B'WA KELL.

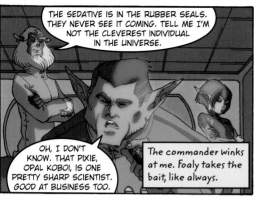

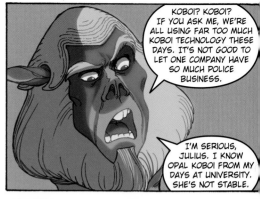

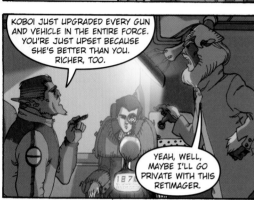

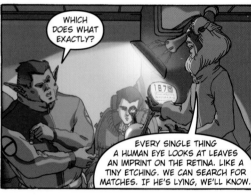

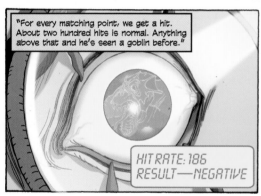

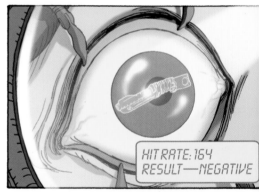

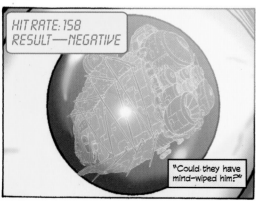

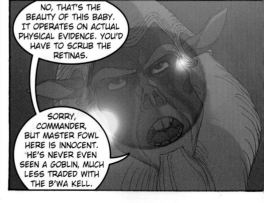

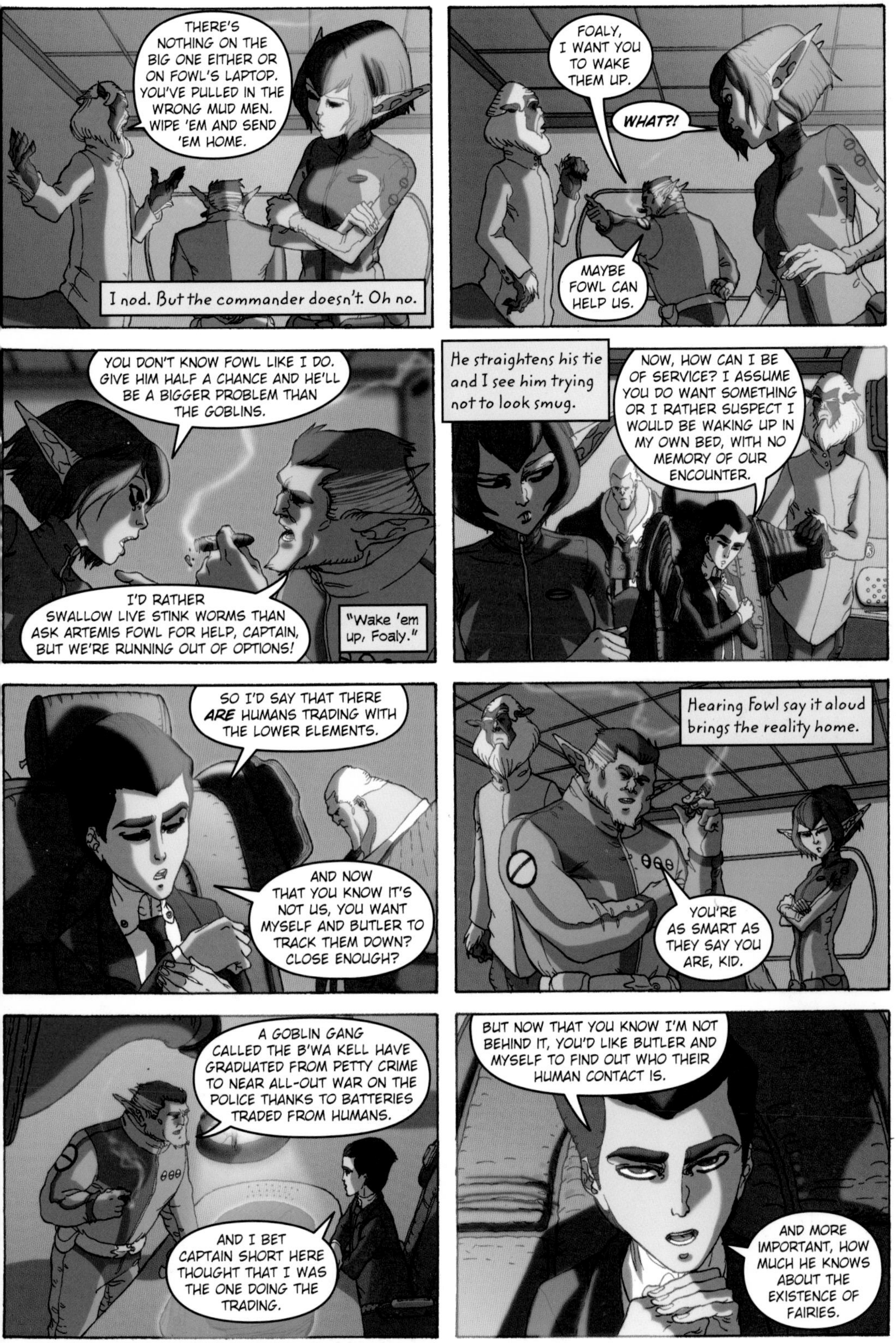
THERE'S NOTHING ON THE BIG ONE EITHER OR ON FOWL'S LAPTOP. YOU'VE PULLED IN THE WRONG MUD MEN. WIPE 'EM AND SEND 'EM HOME.
I nod. But the commander doesn't. Oh no.
FOALY, I WANT YOU TO WAKE THEM UP.
WHAT?!
MAYBE FOWL CAN HELP US.
YOU DON'T KNOW FOWL LIKE I DO. GIVE HIM HALF A CHANCE AND HE'LL BE A BIGGER PROBLEM THAN THE GOBLINS.
I'D RATHER SWALLOW LIVE STINK WORMS THAN ASK ARTEMIS FOWL FOR HELP, CAPTAIN, BUT WE'RE RUNNING OUT OF OPTIONS!
"Wake 'em up, Foaly."
He straightens his tie and I see him trying not to look smug.
NOW, HOW CAN I BE OF SERVICE? I ASSUME YOU DO WANT SOMETHING OR I RATHER SUSPECT I WOULD BE WAKING UP IN MY OWN BED, WITH NO MEMORY OF OUR ENCOUNTER.
SO I'D SAY THAT THERE ARE HUMANS TRADING WITH THE LOWER ELEMENTS.
AND NOW THAT YOU KNOW IT'S NOT US, YOU WANT MYSELF AND BUTLER TO TRACK THEM DOWN? CLOSE ENOUGH?
Hearing Fowl say it aloud brings the reality home.
YOU'RE AS SMART AS THEY SAY YOU ARE, KID.
A GOBLIN GANG CALLED THE B'WA KELL HAVE GRADUATED FROM PETTY CRIME TO NEAR ALL-OUT WAR ON THE POLICE THANKS TO BATTERIES TRADED FROM HUMANS.
AND I BET CAPTAIN SHORT HERE THOUGHT THAT I WAS THE ONE DOING THE TRADING.
BUT NOW THAT YOU KNOW I'M NOT BEHIND IT, YOU'D LIKE BUTLER AND MYSELF TO FIND OUT WHO THEIR HUMAN CONTACT IS.
AND MORE IMPORTANT, HOW MUCH HE KNOWS ABOUT THE EXISTENCE OF FAIRIES.

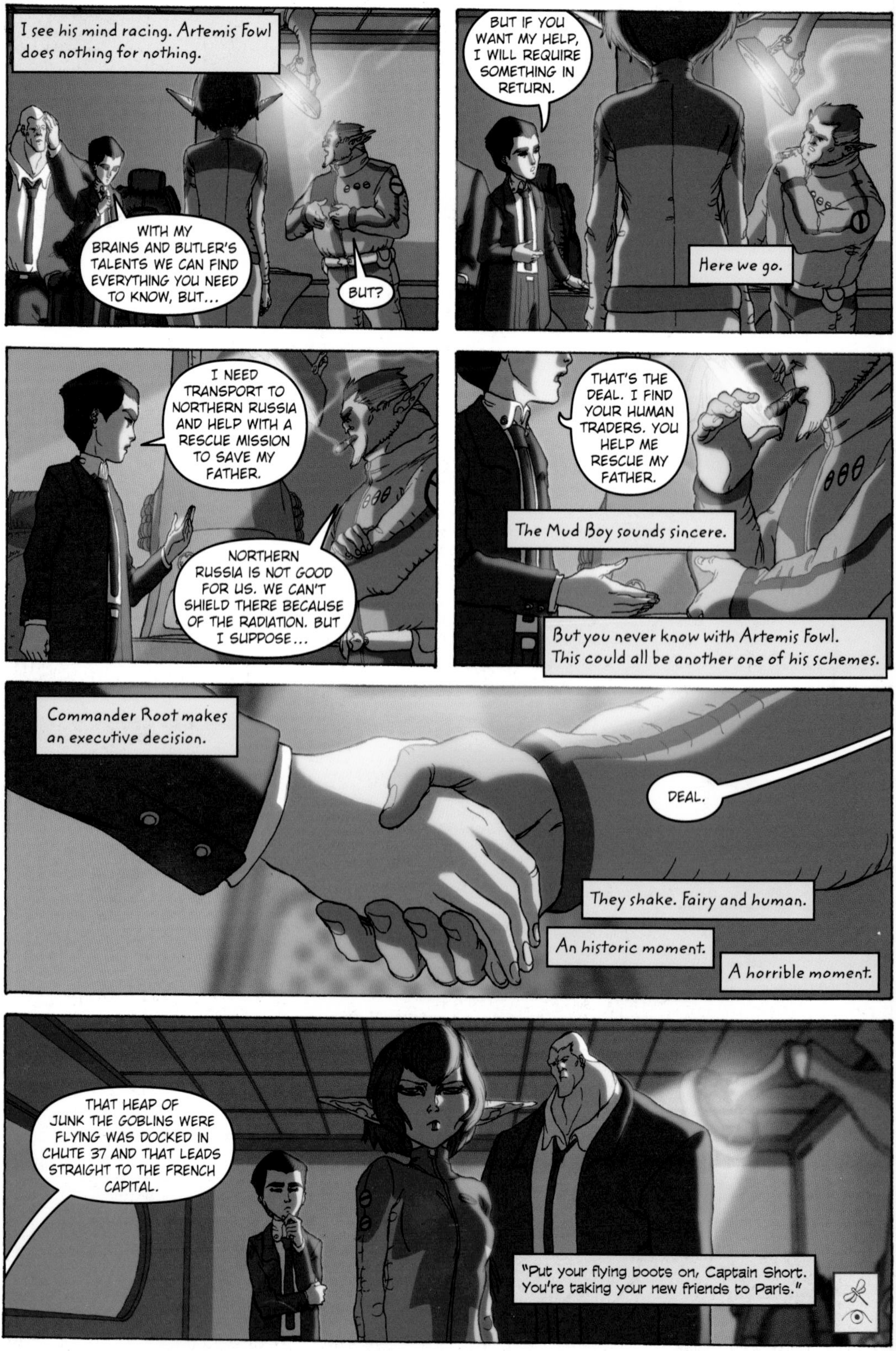
I see his mind racing. Artemis Fowl does nothing for nothing.
WITH MY BRAINS AND BUTLER'S TALENTS WE CAN FIND EVERYTHING YOU NEED TO KNOW, BUT...
BUT?
BUT IF YOU WANT MY HELP, I WILL REQUIRE SOMETHING IN RETURN.
Here we go.
I NEED TRANSPORT TO NORTHERN RUSSIA AND HELP WITH A RESCUE MISSION TO SAVE MY FATHER.
NORTHERN RUSSIA IS NOT GOOD FOR US. WE CAN'T SHIELD THERE BECAUSE OF THE RADIATION. BUT I SUPPOSE...
THAT'S THE DEAL. I FIND YOUR HUMAN TRADERS. YOU HELP ME RESCUE MY FATHER.
The Mud Boy sounds sincere.
But you never know with Artemis Fowl. This could all be another one of his schemes.
Commander Root makes an executive decision.
DEAL.
They shake. Fairy and human.
An historic moment.
A horrible moment.
THAT HEAP OF JUNK THE GOBLINS WERE FLYING WAS DOCKED IN CHUTE 37 AND THAT LEADS STRAIGHT TO THE FRENCH CAPITAL.
"Put your flying boots on, Captain Short. You're taking your new friends to Paris."

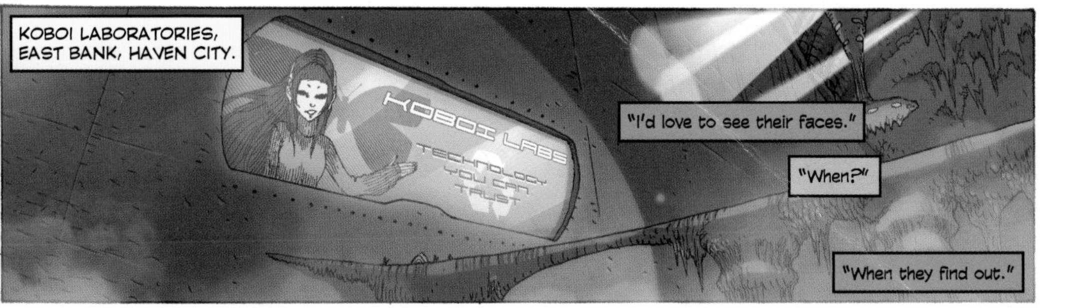
KOBOI LABORATORIES, EAST BANK, HAVEN CITY.
KOBOI LABS
TECHNOLOGY YOU CAN TRUST
"I'd love to see their faces."
"When?"
"When they find out."

CHAPTER 5: DADDY'S GIRL

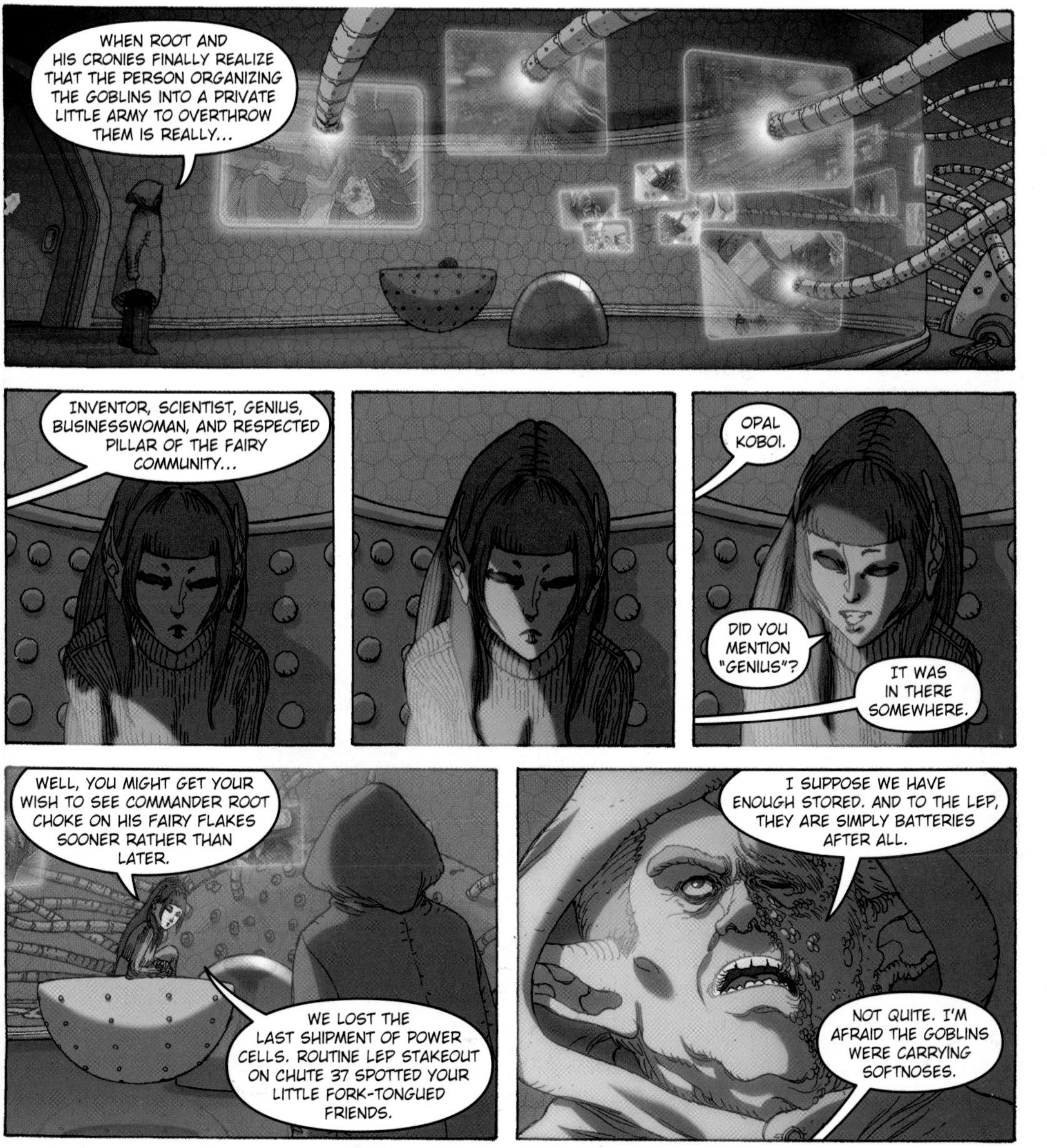
WHEN ROOT AND HIS CRONIES FINALLY REALIZE THAT THE PERSON ORGANIZING THE GOBLINS INTO A PRIVATE LITTLE ARMY TO OVERTHROW THEM IS REALLY...
INVENTOR, SCIENTIST, GENIUS, BUSINESSWOMAN, AND RESPECTED PILLAR OF THE FAIRY COMMUNITY...
OPAL KOBOI.
DID YOU MENTION "GENIUS"?
IT WAS IN THERE SOMEWHERE.
WELL, YOU MIGHT GET YOUR WISH TO SEE COMMANDER ROOT CHOKE ON HIS FAIRY FLAKES SOONER RATHER THAN LATER.
WE LOST THE LAST SHIPMENT OF POWER CELLS. ROUTINE LEP STAKEOUT ON CHUTE 37 SPOTTED YOUR LITTLE FORK-TONGUED FRIENDS.
I SUPPOSE WE HAVE ENOUGH STORED. AND TO THE LEP, THEY ARE SIMPLY BATTERIES AFTER ALL.
NOT QUITE. I'M AFRAID THE GOBLINS WERE CARRYING SOFTNOSES.

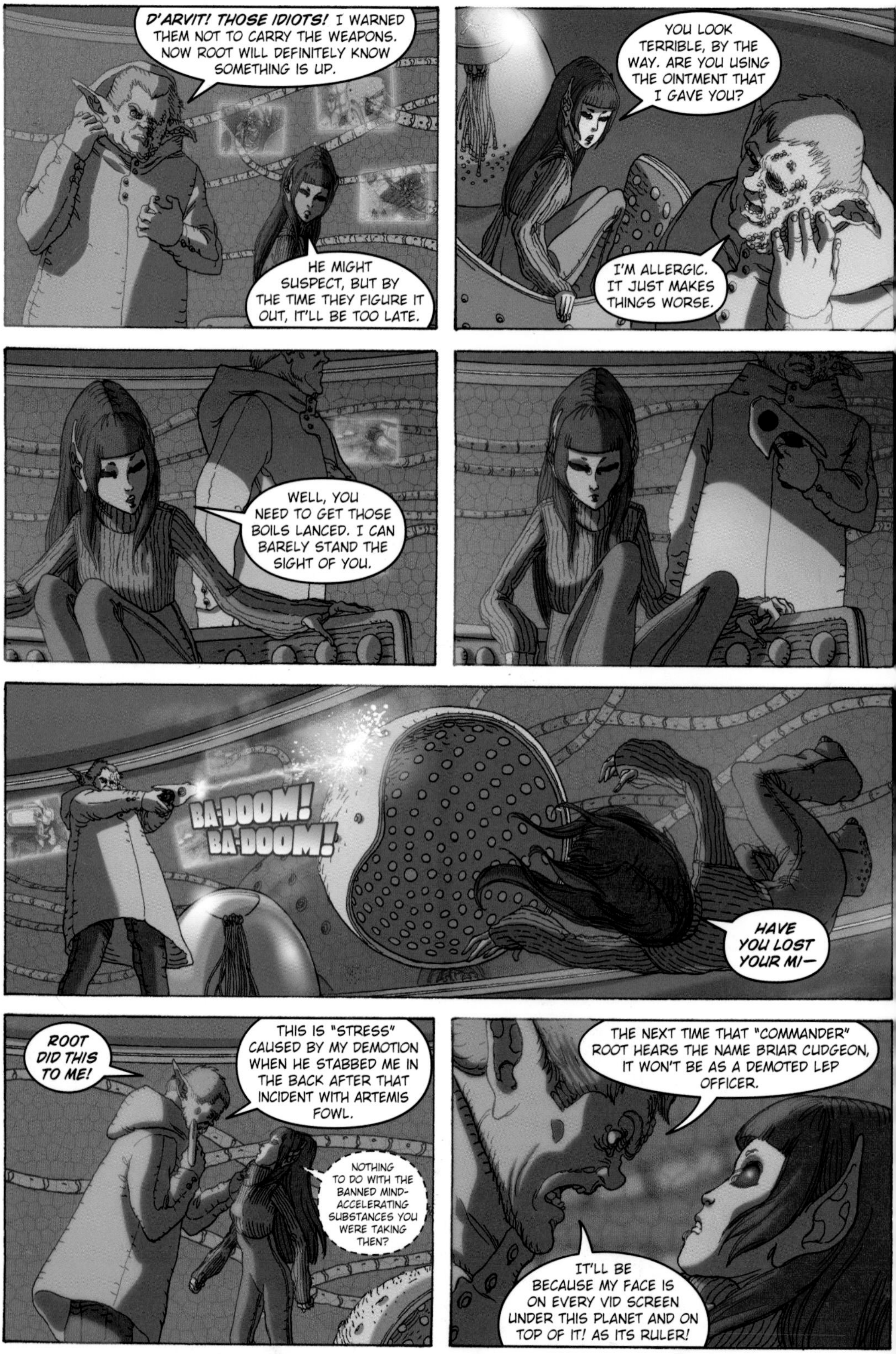
D'ARVIT! THOSE IDIOTS! I WARNED THEM NOT TO CARRY THE WEAPONS. NOW ROOT WILL DEFINITELY KNOW SOMETHING IS UP.
HE MIGHT SUSPECT, BUT BY THE TIME THEY FIGURE IT OUT, IT'LL BE TOO LATE.
YOU LOOK TERRIBLE, BY THE WAY. ARE YOU USING THE OINTMENT THAT I GAVE YOU?
I'M ALLERGIC. IT JUST MAKES THINGS WORSE.
WELL, YOU NEED TO GET THOSE BOILS LANCED. I CAN BARELY STAND THE SIGHT OF YOU.
BA-DOOM! BA-DOOM!
HAVE YOU LOST YOUR MI—
ROOT DID THIS TO ME!
THIS IS "STRESS" CAUSED BY MY DEMOTION WHEN HE STABBED ME IN THE BACK AFTER THAT INCIDENT WITH ARTEMIS FOWL.
NOTHING TO DO WITH THE BANNED MIND-ACCELERATING SUBSTANCES YOU WERE TAKING THEN?
THE NEXT TIME THAT "COMMANDER" ROOT HEARS THE NAME BRIAR CUDGEON, IT WON'T BE AS A DEMOTED LEP OFFICER.
IT'LL BE BECAUSE MY FACE IS ON EVERY VID SCREEN UNDER THIS PLANET AND ON TOP OF IT! AS ITS RULER!

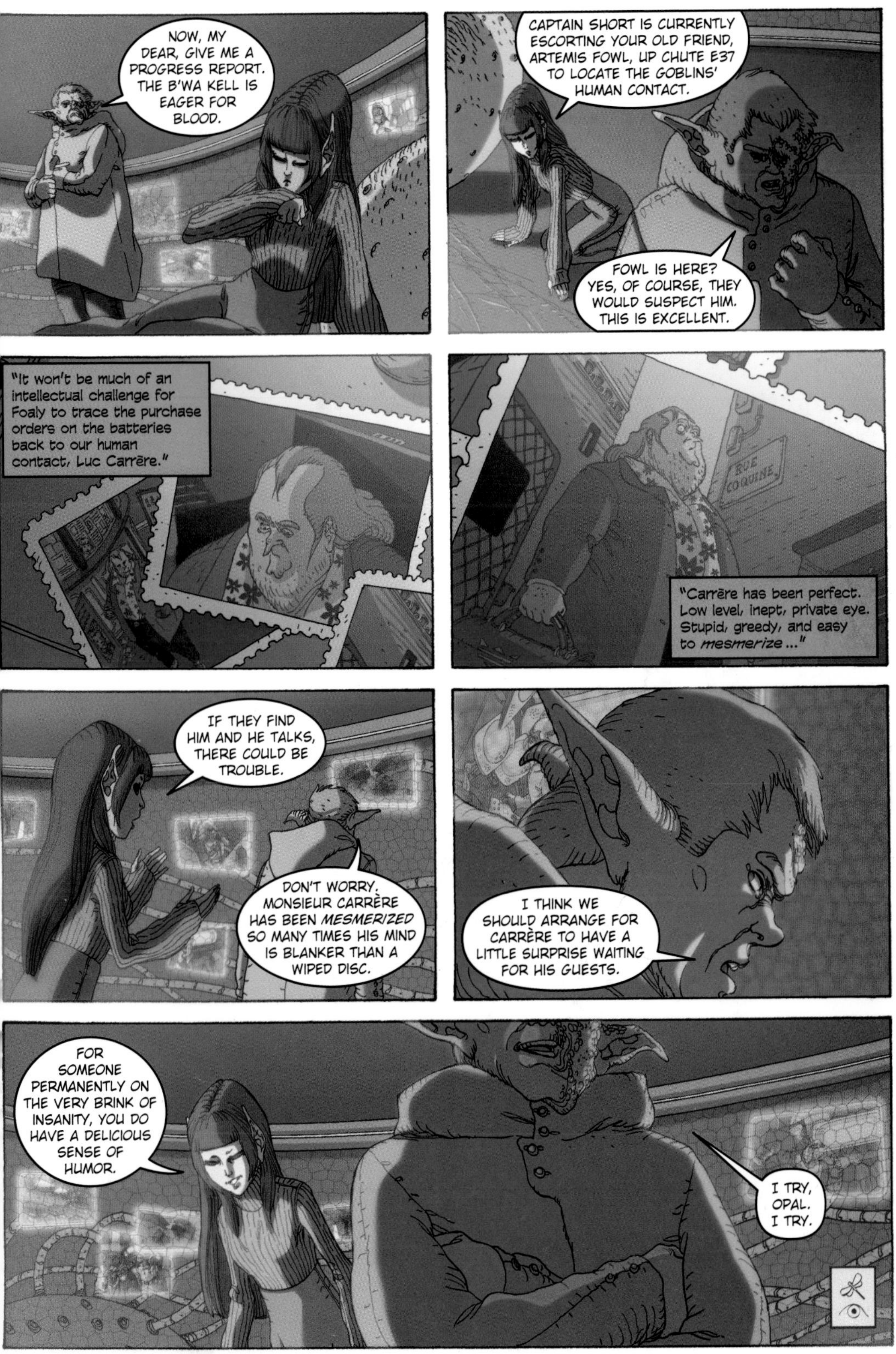

NOW, MY DEAR, GIVE ME A PROGRESS REPORT. THE B'WA KELL IS EAGER FOR BLOOD.
CAPTAIN SHORT IS CURRENTLY ESCORTING YOUR OLD FRIEND, ARTEMIS FOWL, UP CHUTE E37 TO LOCATE THE GOBLINS' HUMAN CONTACT.
FOWL IS HERE? YES, OF COURSE, THEY WOULD SUSPECT HIM. THIS IS EXCELLENT.
"It won't be much of an intellectual challenge for Foaly to trace the purchase orders on the batteries back to our human contact, Luc Carrère."
RUE COQUINE
"Carrère has been perfect. Low level, inept, private eye. Stupid, greedy, and easy to *mesmerize* ..."
IF THEY FIND HIM AND HE TALKS, THERE COULD BE TROUBLE.
DON'T WORRY. MONSIEUR CARRÈRE HAS BEEN *MESMERIZED* SO MANY TIMES HIS MIND IS BLANKER THAN A WIPED DISC.
I THINK WE SHOULD ARRANGE FOR CARRÈRE TO HAVE A LITTLE SURPRISE WAITING FOR HIS GUESTS.
FOR SOMEONE PERMANENTLY ON THE VERY BRINK OF INSANITY, YOU DO HAVE A DELICIOUS SENSE OF HUMOR.
I TRY, OPAL. I TRY.

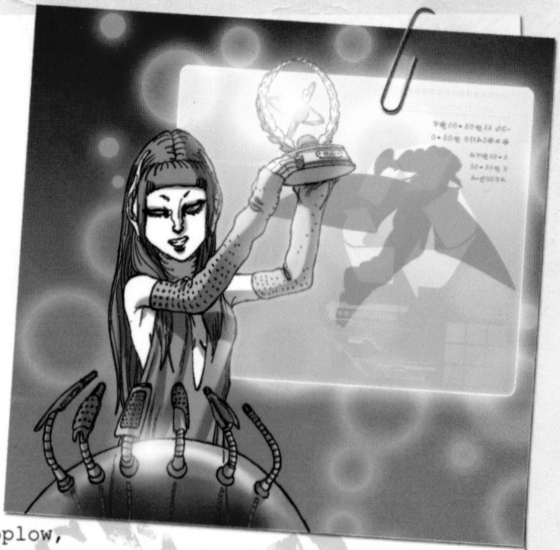

CASE FILE:
210764

CASE OFFICER:
Wing Commander Vinyáya

CASE TYPE:
Missing Person

CASE HISTORY:
Student journalist, Zanel Tapplow, disappeared while researching an unauthorized biography of Koboi Laboratories mogul, Opal Koboi. His room in student halls was found stripped of all his personal effects. A printed note said that he was going to seek work in Atlantis. Investigations revealed no travel permit was ever issued in his name. Two pages of his notes were later recovered from an alley near the goblin correctional facility, Howler's Peak.

CASE UNSOLVED

FUTURE RESEARCH

Is Opal funding secret research into illegal cloning technology?

If so, where is the greenhouse lab?

Are Opal's parents still alive in Cumulus House?

Why is she so interested in the Mud Man environmentalist, Giovanni Zito?

What is "The Core" project?

What's this thing with lemurs???

Opal Koboi—born to family of old-money pixies on Principality Hill. Father was Ferall Koboi, the business tycoon. As a child was said to be beautiful, but extremely precocious and headstrong. Scored over 300 on standard IQ test. Ditched her History of Art degree in favor of a master's in the male-oriented Brotherhood of Engineers. Bitter rivalry with the centaur, Foaly, after he beat her to win their year's science medal at university. Destroyed her own father's company and bought control of it when shares hit rock bottom. Launched Koboi Laboratories. Within five years, had more defense and LEP contracts than any rival. Concerns about Opal's influence over LEP weapons policy raised at Council level and dismissed.

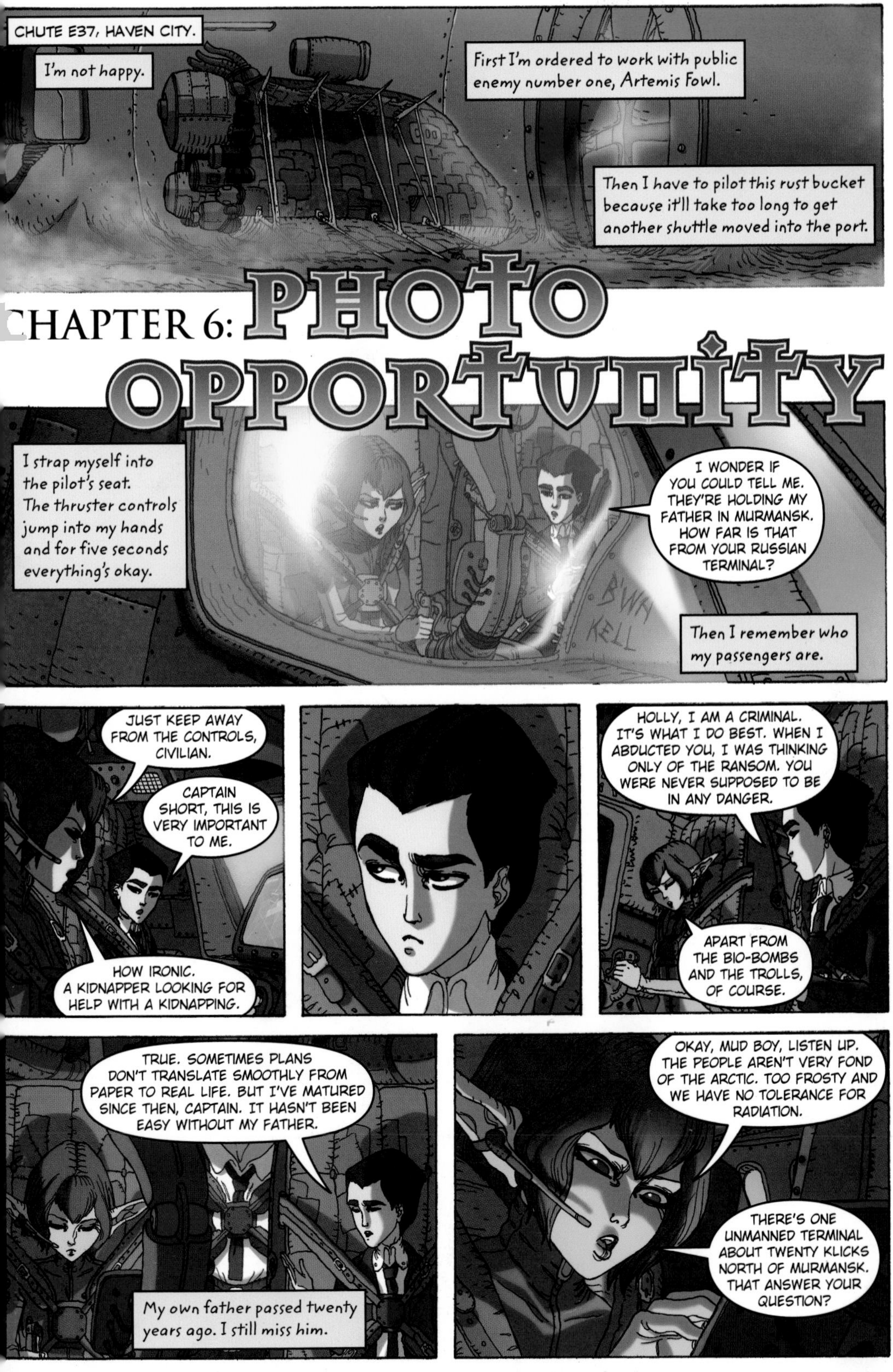
CHUTE E37, HAVEN CITY.
I'm not happy.
First I'm ordered to work with public enemy number one, Artemis Fowl.
Then I have to pilot this rust bucket because it'll take too long to get another shuttle moved into the port.
CHAPTER 6: PHOTO OPPORTUNITY
I strap myself into the pilot's seat. The thruster controls jump into my hands and for five seconds everything's okay.
I WONDER IF YOU COULD TELL ME. THEY'RE HOLDING MY FATHER IN MURMANSK. HOW FAR IS THAT FROM YOUR RUSSIAN TERMINAL?
B'WA KELL
Then I remember who my passengers are.
JUST KEEP AWAY FROM THE CONTROLS, CIVILIAN.
CAPTAIN SHORT, THIS IS VERY IMPORTANT TO ME.
HOW IRONIC. A KIDNAPPER LOOKING FOR HELP WITH A KIDNAPPING.
HOLLY, I AM A CRIMINAL. IT'S WHAT I DO BEST. WHEN I ABDUCTED YOU, I WAS THINKING ONLY OF THE RANSOM. YOU WERE NEVER SUPPOSED TO BE IN ANY DANGER.
APART FROM THE BIO-BOMBS AND THE TROLLS, OF COURSE.
TRUE. SOMETIMES PLANS DON'T TRANSLATE SMOOTHLY FROM PAPER TO REAL LIFE. BUT I'VE MATURED SINCE THEN, CAPTAIN. IT HASN'T BEEN EASY WITHOUT MY FATHER.
My own father passed twenty years ago. I still miss him.
OKAY, MUD BOY, LISTEN UP. THE PEOPLE AREN'T VERY FOND OF THE ARCTIC. TOO FROSTY AND WE HAVE NO TOLERANCE FOR RADIATION.
THERE'S ONE UNMANNED TERMINAL ABOUT TWENTY KLICKS NORTH OF MURMANSK. THAT ANSWER YOUR QUESTION?

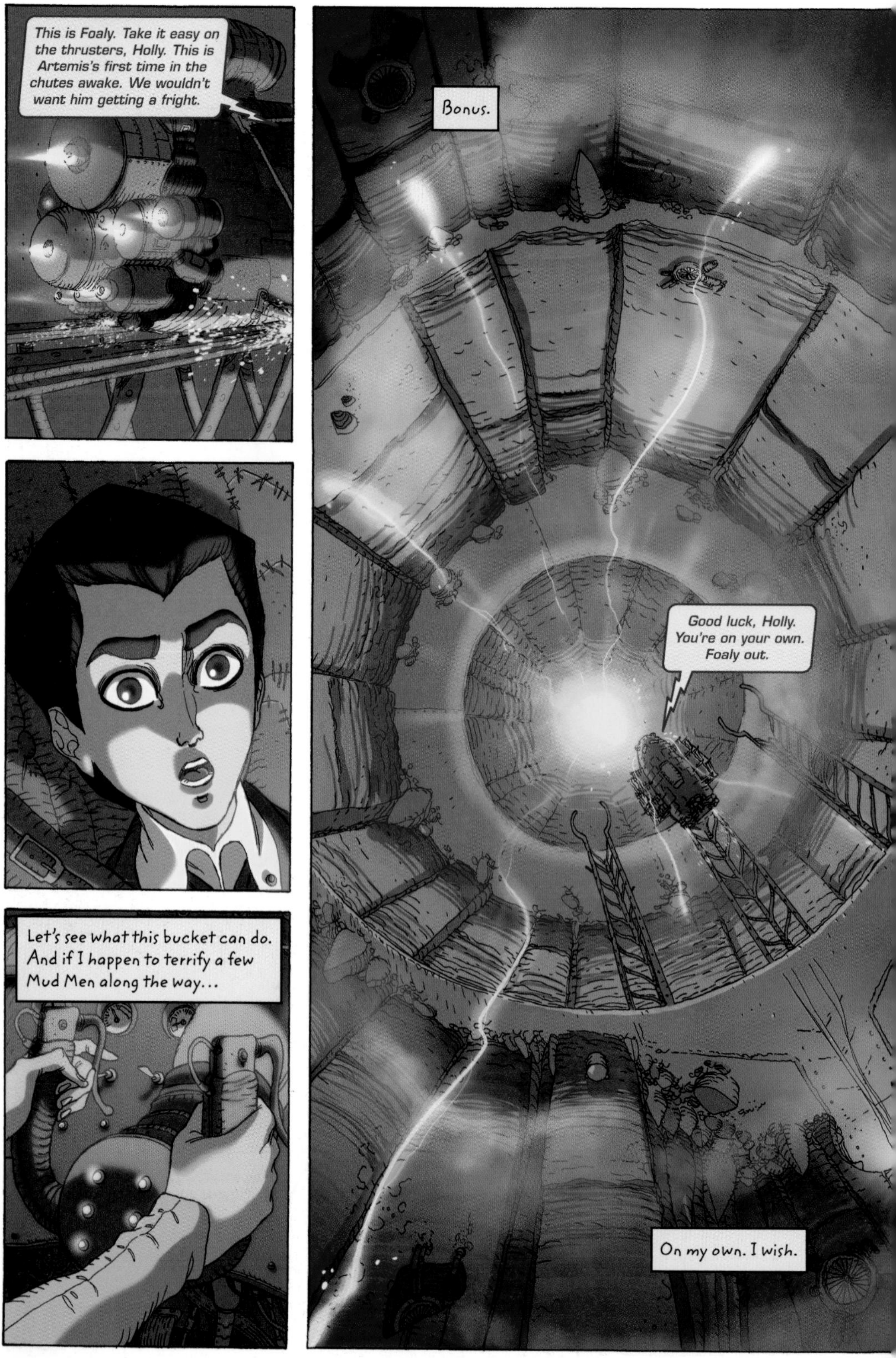
This is Foaly. Take it easy on the thrusters, Holly. This is Artemis's first time in the chutes awake. We wouldn't want him getting a fright.
Let's see what this bucket can do. And if I happen to terrify a few Mud Men along the way...
Bonus.
Good luck, Holly. You're on your own. Foaly out.
On my own. I wish.

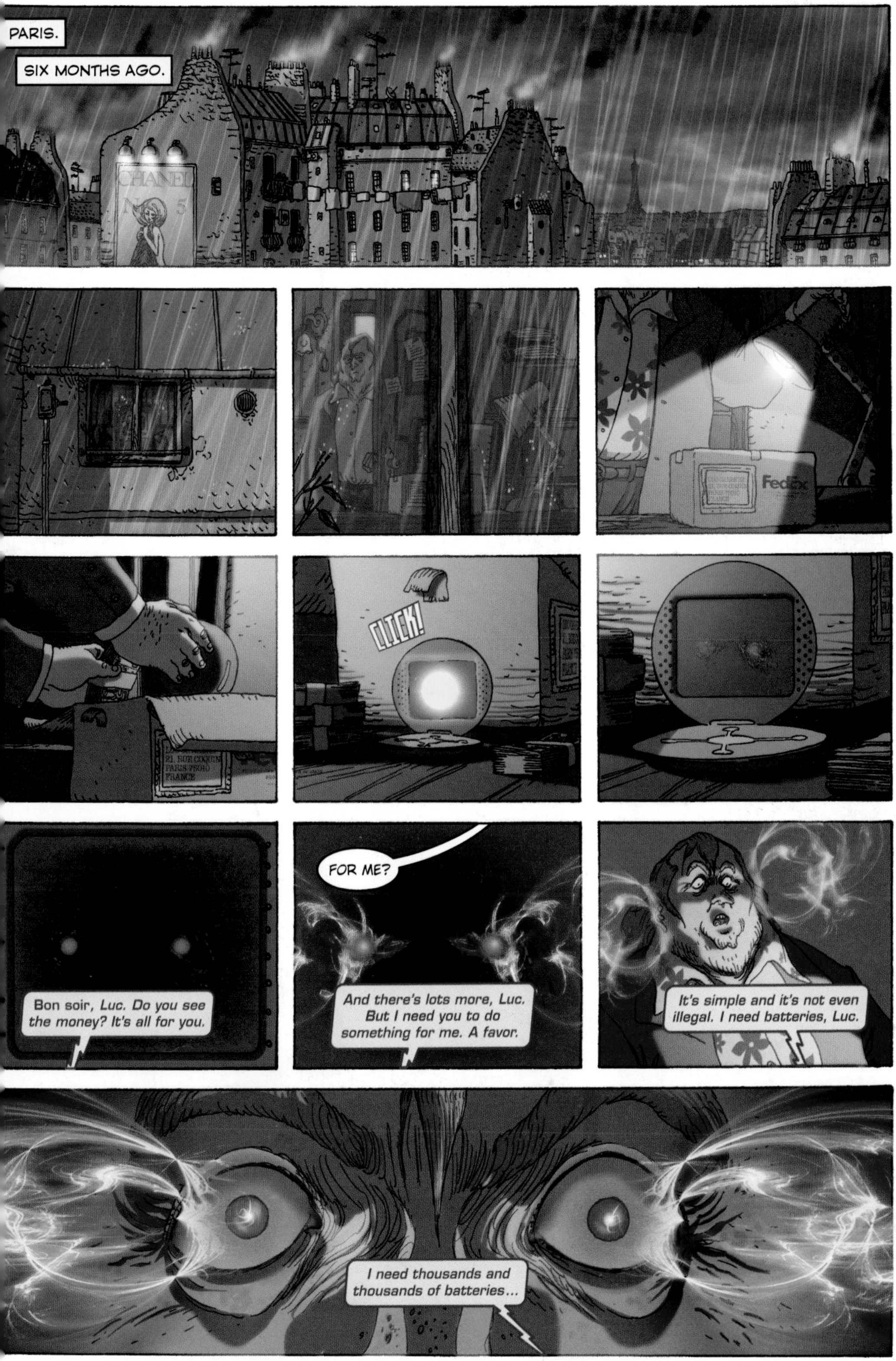
PARIS.
SIX MONTHS AGO.
CHANEL
N 5
FedEx
21, RUE COQUIN
PARIS 75010
FRANCE
CLICK!
Bon soir, Luc. Do you see the money? It's all for you.
FOR ME?
And there's lots more, Luc. But I need you to do something for me. A favor.
It's simple and it's not even illegal. I need batteries, Luc.
I need thousands and thousands of batteries...

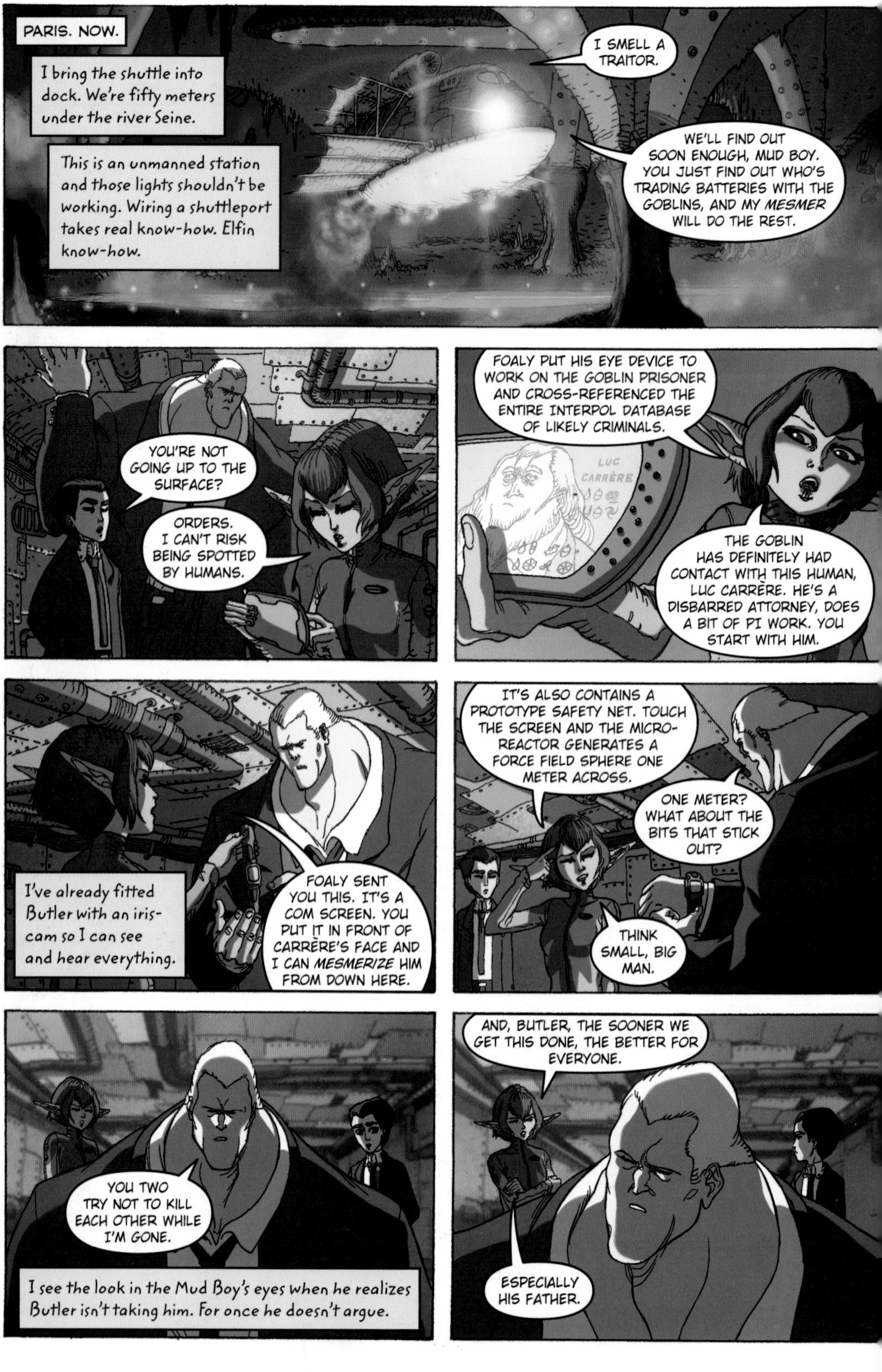
PARIS. NOW.
I bring the shuttle into dock. We're fifty meters under the river Seine.
This is an unmanned station and those lights shouldn't be working. Wiring a shuttleport takes real know-how. Elfin know-how.
I SMELL A TRAITOR.
WE'LL FIND OUT SOON ENOUGH, MUD BOY. YOU JUST FIND OUT WHO'S TRADING BATTERIES WITH THE GOBLINS, AND MY MESMER WILL DO THE REST.
YOU'RE NOT GOING UP TO THE SURFACE?
ORDERS. I CAN'T RISK BEING SPOTTED BY HUMANS.
FOALY PUT HIS EYE DEVICE TO WORK ON THE GOBLIN PRISONER AND CROSS-REFERENCED THE ENTIRE INTERPOL DATABASE OF LIKELY CRIMINALS.
LUC CARRÈRE
THE GOBLIN HAS DEFINITELY HAD CONTACT WITH THIS HUMAN, LUC CARRÈRE. HE'S A DISBARRED ATTORNEY, DOES A BIT OF PI WORK. YOU START WITH HIM.
I've already fitted Butler with an iris-cam so I can see and hear everything.
FOALY SENT YOU THIS. IT'S A COM SCREEN. YOU PUT IT IN FRONT OF CARRÈRE'S FACE AND I CAN MESMERIZE HIM FROM DOWN HERE.
IT'S ALSO CONTAINS A PROTOTYPE SAFETY NET. TOUCH THE SCREEN AND THE MICRO-REACTOR GENERATES A FORCE FIELD SPHERE ONE METER ACROSS.
ONE METER? WHAT ABOUT THE BITS THAT STICK OUT?
THINK SMALL, BIG MAN.
YOU TWO TRY NOT TO KILL EACH OTHER WHILE I'M GONE.
I see the look in the Mud Boy's eyes when he realizes Butler isn't taking him. For once he doesn't argue.
AND, BUTLER, THE SOONER WE GET THIS DONE, THE BETTER FOR EVERYONE.
ESPECIALLY HIS FATHER.

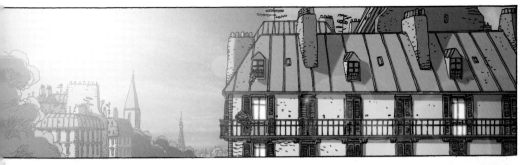

Bonjour, *Luc.* Ça va?

I have a special assignment for you today. You like your new apartment, don't you? Well, do this right and you will never have to worry about money again.

CLICK!

BIEN.

WHAT IS IT?

It's a special camera, Luc, that's all. If you pull the thing that looks like a trigger, then it takes a picture.

Some friends of mine are coming to visit you and I want you to take their picture. It's just a game we play.

HOW WILL I KNOW YOUR FRIENDS?

They will ask you questions about the batteries. Then you take their picture.

Don't worry, Luc. I would never ask you to do anything wrong, now, would I? Trust me and you'll be rich forever...

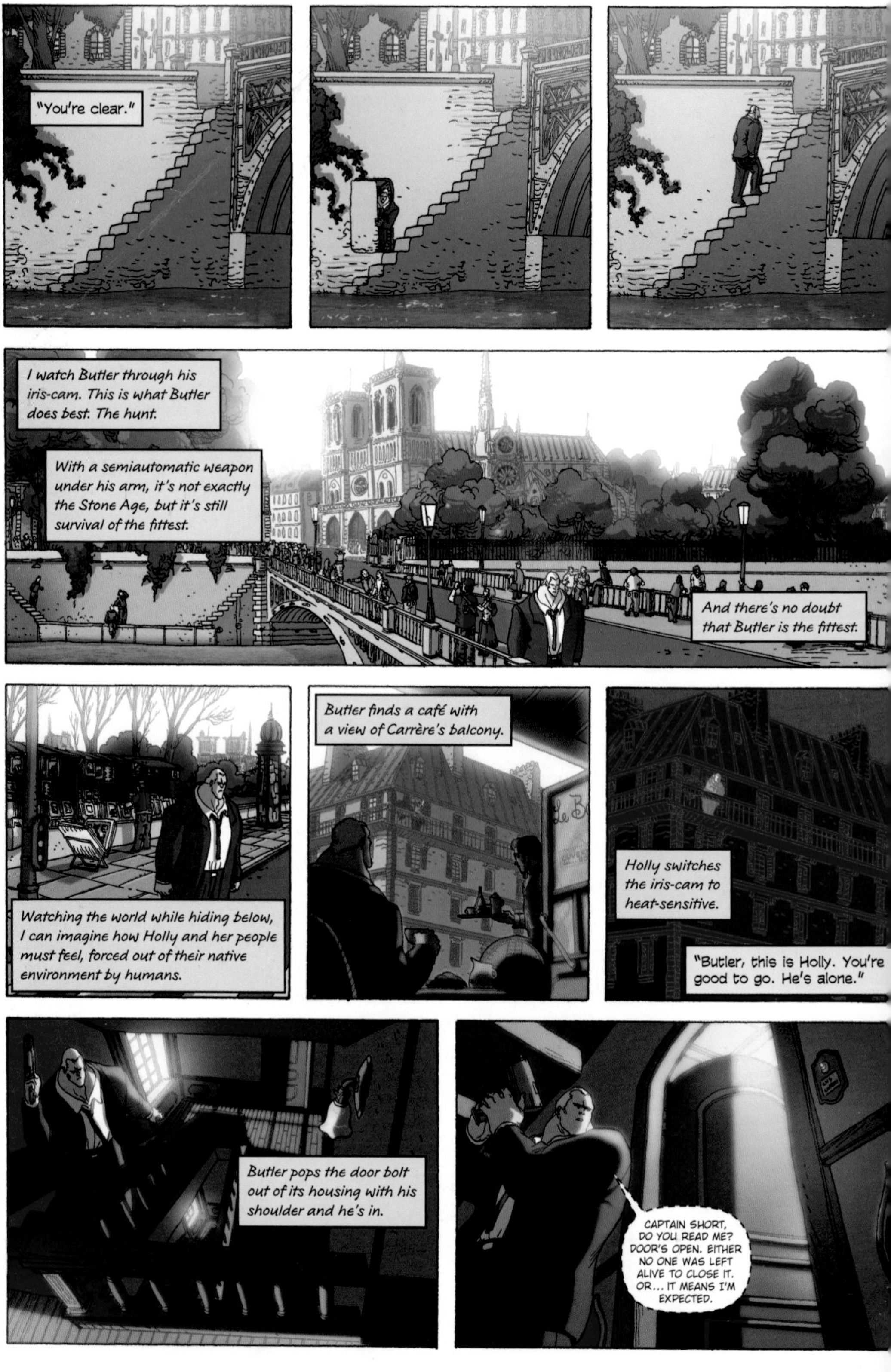
"You're clear."
I watch Butler through his iris-cam. This is what Butler does best. The hunt.
With a semiautomatic weapon under his arm, it's not exactly the Stone Age, but it's still survival of the fittest.
And there's no doubt that Butler is the fittest.
Watching the world while hiding below, I can imagine how Holly and her people must feel, forced out of their native environment by humans.
Butler finds a café with a view of Carrère's balcony.
Holly switches the iris-cam to heat-sensitive.
"Butler, this is Holly. You're good to go. He's alone."
Butler pops the door bolt out of its housing with his shoulder and he's in.
CAPTAIN SHORT, DO YOU READ ME? DOOR'S OPEN. EITHER NO ONE WAS LEFT ALIVE TO CLOSE IT. OR... IT MEANS I'M EXPECTED.

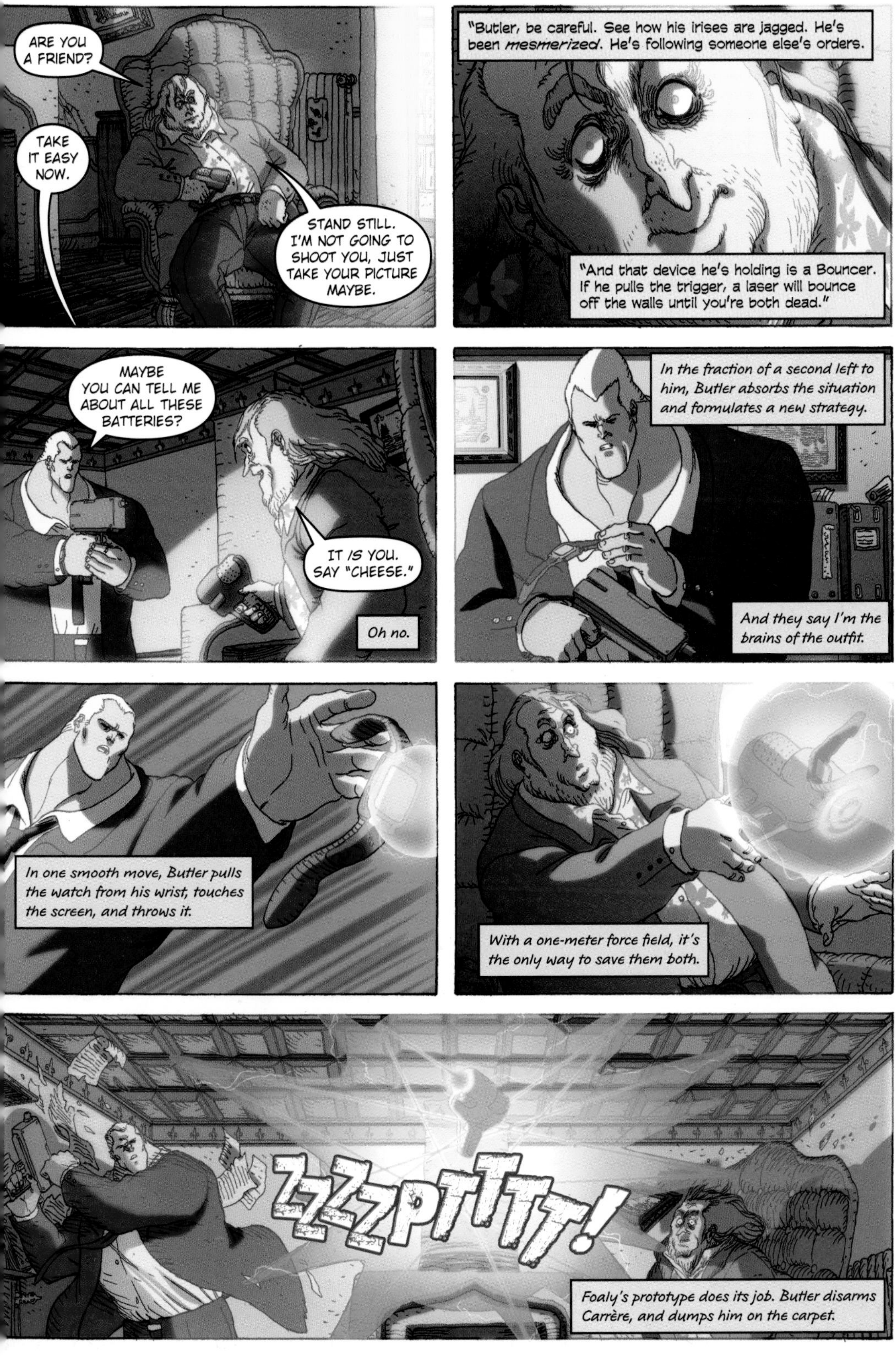
ARE YOU A FRIEND?
TAKE IT EASY NOW.
STAND STILL. I'M NOT GOING TO SHOOT YOU, JUST TAKE YOUR PICTURE MAYBE.
"Butler, be careful. See how his irises are jagged. He's been *mesmerized*. He's following someone else's orders.
"And that device he's holding is a Bouncer. If he pulls the trigger, a laser will bounce off the walls until you're both dead."
MAYBE YOU CAN TELL ME ABOUT ALL THESE BATTERIES?
IT *IS* YOU. SAY "CHEESE."
Oh no.
In the fraction of a second left to him, Butler absorbs the situation and formulates a new strategy.
And they say I'm the brains of the outfit.
In one smooth move, Butler pulls the watch from his wrist, touches the screen, and throws it.
With a one-meter force field, it's the only way to save them both.
ZZZZPTTTTT!
Foaly's prototype does its job. Butler disarms Carrère, and dumps him on the carpet.

The explosion seems to bring Carrère out of his trance.

THERE'S BEEN AN ACCIDENT, BUT YOU'RE FINE. I'M GOING TO CHECK YOUR VITALS.

Butler presses his hand against Carrère's heart.

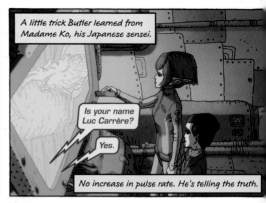

A little trick Butler learned from Madame Ko, his Japanese sensei.

Is your name Luc Carrère?

Yes.

No increase in pulse rate. He's telling the truth.

ARE YOU A PRIVATE EYE?

I PREFER THE TITLE "INVESTIGATOR."

Also true.

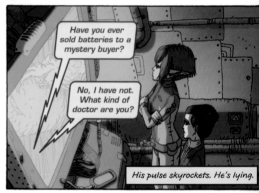

Have you ever sold batteries to a mystery buyer?

No, I have not. What kind of doctor are you?

His pulse skyrockets. He's lying.

Now the big one.

HAVE YOU EVER HAD DEALINGS WITH GOBLINS?

ARE YOU CRAZY? GOBLINS? WHAT ARE YOU TALKING ABOUT?

He's telling the truth. He's never had any direct dealings with the goblins.

THANK FROND.

Holly breathes a sigh of relief. He doesn't know Holly's people exist.

I tell Butler to get out of there. The police will be on their way after that explosion.

How Monsieur explains why his apartment is full of what I suspect are counterfeit euros is his concern.

We have work to do.

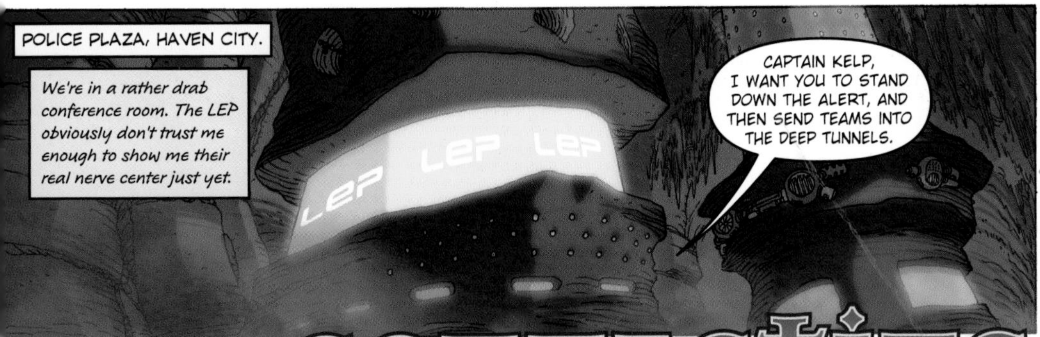
POLICE PLAZA, HAVEN CITY.
We're in a rather drab conference room. The LEP obviously don't trust me enough to show me their real nerve center just yet.
LEP LEP LEP
CAPTAIN KELP, I WANT YOU TO STAND DOWN THE ALERT, AND THEN SEND TEAMS INTO THE DEEP TUNNELS.

CHAPTER 7: CONNECTING THE DOTS

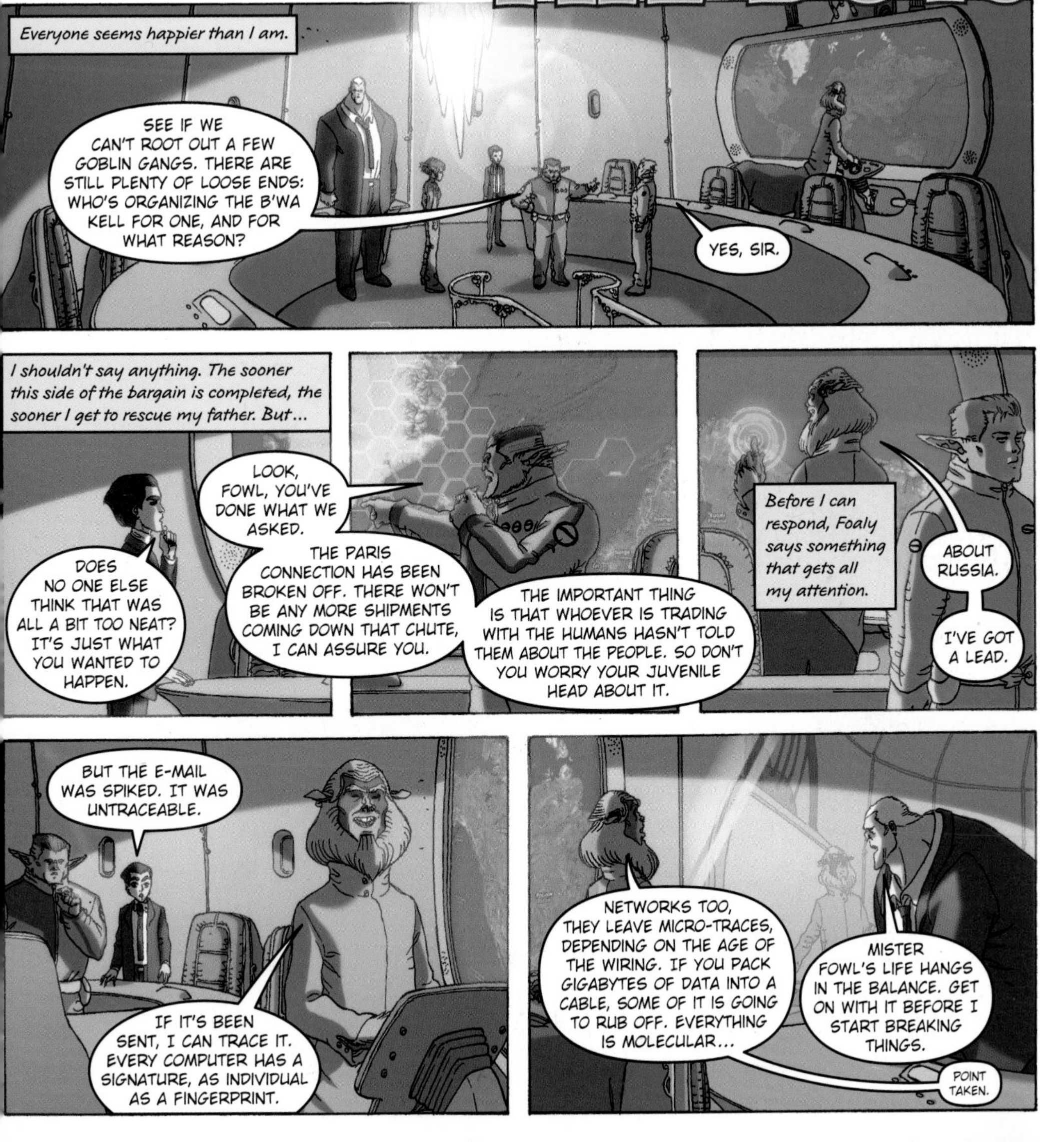
Everyone seems happier than I am.
SEE IF WE CAN'T ROOT OUT A FEW GOBLIN GANGS. THERE ARE STILL PLENTY OF LOOSE ENDS: WHO'S ORGANIZING THE B'WA KELL FOR ONE, AND FOR WHAT REASON?
YES, SIR.
I shouldn't say anything. The sooner this side of the bargain is completed, the sooner I get to rescue my father. But...
DOES NO ONE ELSE THINK THAT WAS ALL A BIT TOO NEAT? IT'S JUST WHAT YOU WANTED TO HAPPEN.
LOOK, FOWL, YOU'VE DONE WHAT WE ASKED.
THE PARIS CONNECTION HAS BEEN BROKEN OFF. THERE WON'T BE ANY MORE SHIPMENTS COMING DOWN THAT CHUTE, I CAN ASSURE YOU.
THE IMPORTANT THING IS THAT WHOEVER IS TRADING WITH THE HUMANS HASN'T TOLD THEM ABOUT THE PEOPLE. SO DON'T YOU WORRY YOUR JUVENILE HEAD ABOUT IT.
Before I can respond, Foaly says something that gets all my attention.
ABOUT RUSSIA.
I'VE GOT A LEAD.
BUT THE E-MAIL WAS SPIKED. IT WAS UNTRACEABLE.
IF IT'S BEEN SENT, I CAN TRACE IT. EVERY COMPUTER HAS A SIGNATURE, AS INDIVIDUAL AS A FINGERPRINT.
NETWORKS TOO, THEY LEAVE MICRO-TRACES, DEPENDING ON THE AGE OF THE WIRING. IF YOU PACK GIGABYTES OF DATA INTO A CABLE, SOME OF IT IS GOING TO RUB OFF. EVERYTHING IS MOLECULAR...
MISTER FOWL'S LIFE HANGS IN THE BALANCE. GET ON WITH IT BEFORE I START BREAKING THINGS.
POINT TAKEN.

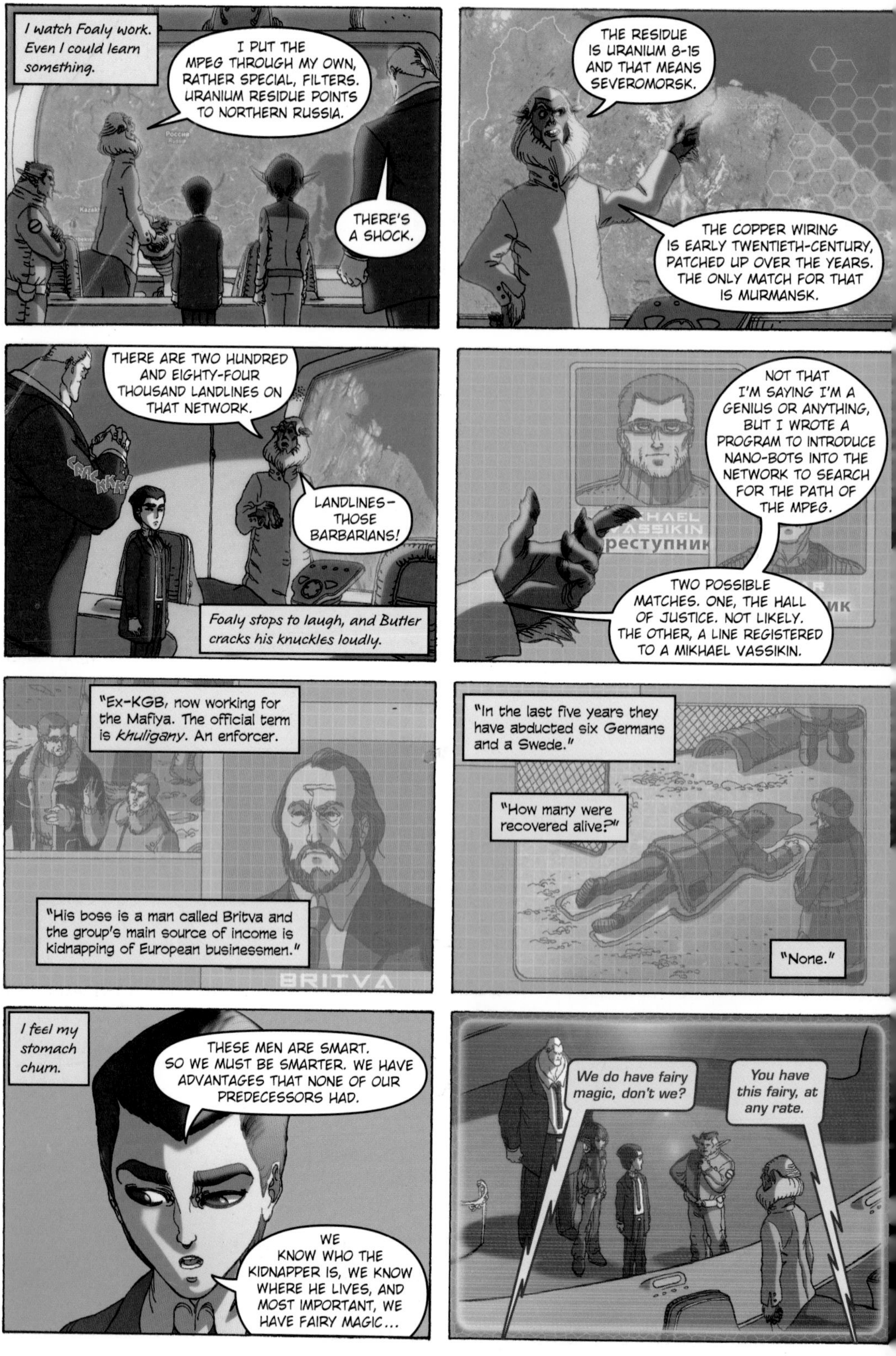
I watch Foaly work. Even I could learn something.
I PUT THE MPEG THROUGH MY OWN, RATHER SPECIAL, FILTERS. URANIUM RESIDUE POINTS TO NORTHERN RUSSIA.
THERE'S A SHOCK.
THE RESIDUE IS URANIUM 8-15 AND THAT MEANS SEVEROMORSK.
THE COPPER WIRING IS EARLY TWENTIETH-CENTURY, PATCHED UP OVER THE YEARS. THE ONLY MATCH FOR THAT IS MURMANSK.
THERE ARE TWO HUNDRED AND EIGHTY-FOUR THOUSAND LANDLINES ON THAT NETWORK.
LANDLINES– THOSE BARBARIANS!
Foaly stops to laugh, and Butler cracks his knuckles loudly.
NOT THAT I'M SAYING I'M A GENIUS OR ANYTHING, BUT I WROTE A PROGRAM TO INTRODUCE NANO-BOTS INTO THE NETWORK TO SEARCH FOR THE PATH OF THE MPEG.
TWO POSSIBLE MATCHES. ONE, THE HALL OF JUSTICE. NOT LIKELY. THE OTHER, A LINE REGISTERED TO A MIKHAEL VASSIKIN.
"Ex-KGB, now working for the Mafiya. The official term is *khuligany*. An enforcer.
"His boss is a man called Britva and the group's main source of income is kidnapping of European businessmen."
BRITVA
"In the last five years they have abducted six Germans and a Swede."
"How many were recovered alive?"
"None."
I feel my stomach churn.
THESE MEN ARE SMART. SO WE MUST BE SMARTER. WE HAVE ADVANTAGES THAT NONE OF OUR PREDECESSORS HAD.
WE KNOW WHO THE KIDNAPPER IS, WE KNOW WHERE HE LIVES, AND MOST IMPORTANT, WE HAVE FAIRY MAGIC...
We do have fairy magic, don't we?
You have this fairy, at any rate.

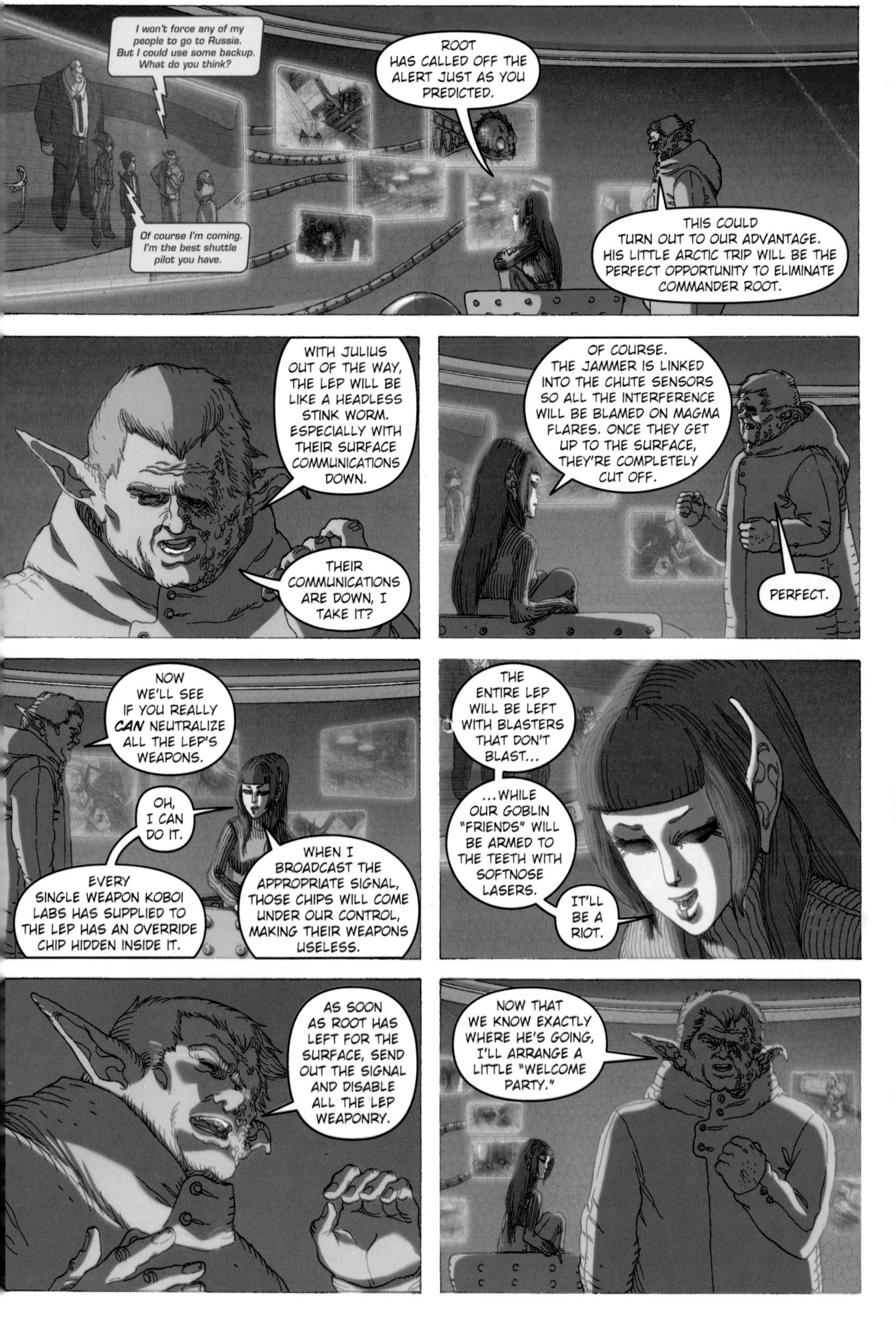
I won't force any of my people to go to Russia. But I could use some backup. What do you think?
Of course I'm coming. I'm the best shuttle pilot you have.
ROOT HAS CALLED OFF THE ALERT JUST AS YOU PREDICTED.
THIS COULD TURN OUT TO OUR ADVANTAGE. HIS LITTLE ARCTIC TRIP WILL BE THE PERFECT OPPORTUNITY TO ELIMINATE COMMANDER ROOT.
WITH JULIUS OUT OF THE WAY, THE LEP WILL BE LIKE A HEADLESS STINK WORM. ESPECIALLY WITH THEIR SURFACE COMMUNICATIONS DOWN.
THEIR COMMUNICATIONS ARE DOWN, I TAKE IT?
OF COURSE. THE JAMMER IS LINKED INTO THE CHUTE SENSORS SO ALL THE INTERFERENCE WILL BE BLAMED ON MAGMA FLARES. ONCE THEY GET UP TO THE SURFACE, THEY'RE COMPLETELY CUT OFF.
PERFECT.
NOW WE'LL SEE IF YOU REALLY CAN NEUTRALIZE ALL THE LEP'S WEAPONS.
OH, I CAN DO IT.
EVERY SINGLE WEAPON KOBOI LABS HAS SUPPLIED TO THE LEP HAS AN OVERRIDE CHIP HIDDEN INSIDE IT.
WHEN I BROADCAST THE APPROPRIATE SIGNAL, THOSE CHIPS WILL COME UNDER OUR CONTROL, MAKING THEIR WEAPONS USELESS.
THE ENTIRE LEP WILL BE LEFT WITH BLASTERS THAT DON'T BLAST...
...WHILE OUR GOBLIN "FRIENDS" WILL BE ARMED TO THE TEETH WITH SOFTNOSE LASERS.
IT'LL BE A RIOT.
AS SOON AS ROOT HAS LEFT FOR THE SURFACE, SEND OUT THE SIGNAL AND DISABLE ALL THE LEP WEAPONRY.
NOW THAT WE KNOW EXACTLY WHERE HE'S GOING, I'LL ARRANGE A LITTLE "WELCOME PARTY."

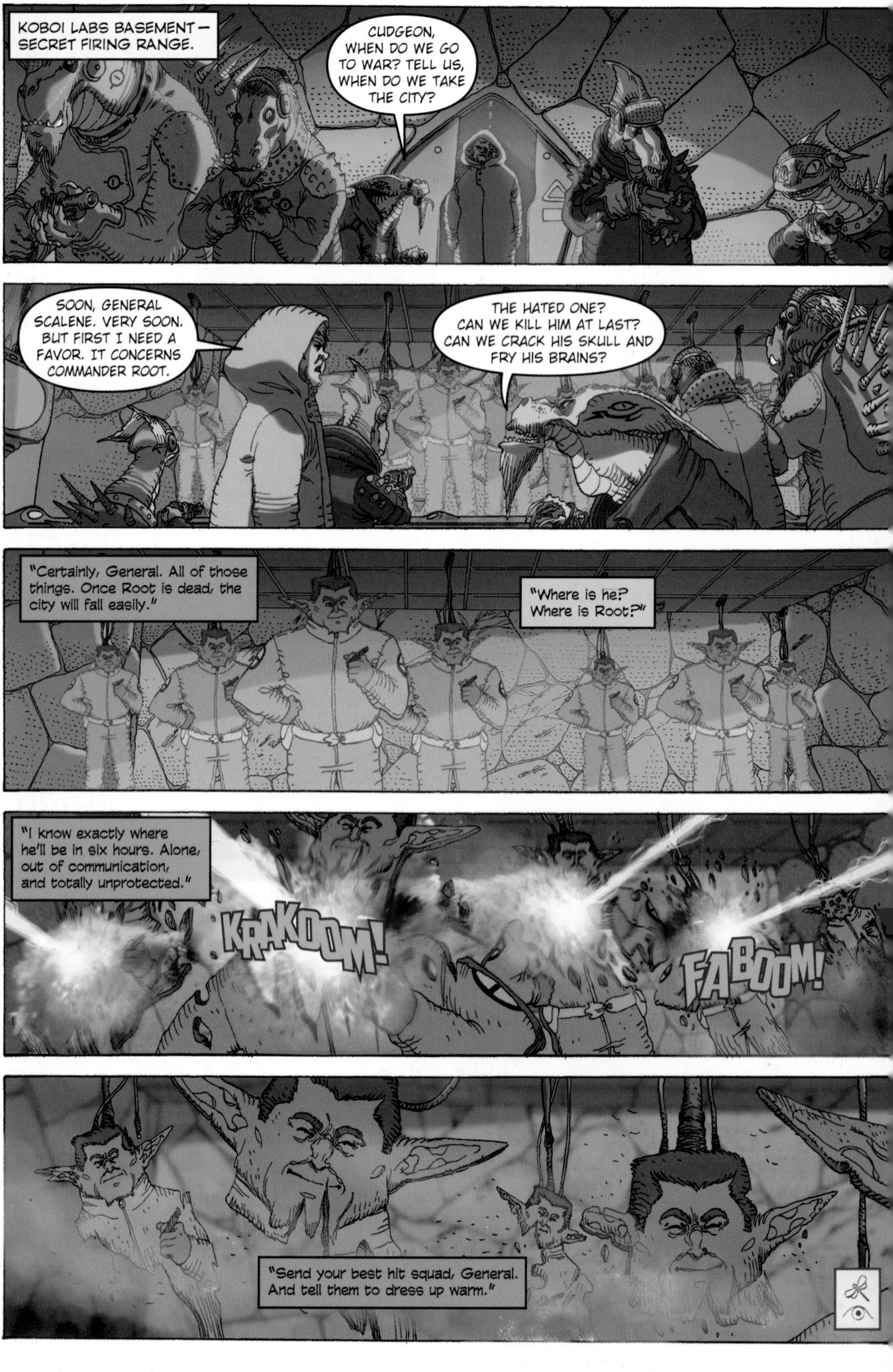
KOBOI LABS BASEMENT—SECRET FIRING RANGE.
CUDGEON, WHEN DO WE GO TO WAR? TELL US, WHEN DO WE TAKE THE CITY?
SOON, GENERAL SCALENE. VERY SOON. BUT FIRST I NEED A FAVOR. IT CONCERNS COMMANDER ROOT.
THE HATED ONE? CAN WE KILL HIM AT LAST? CAN WE CRACK HIS SKULL AND FRY HIS BRAINS?
"Certainly, General. All of those things. Once Root is dead, the city will fall easily."
"Where is he? Where is Root?"
"I know exactly where he'll be in six hours. Alone, out of communication, and totally unprotected."
KRAKOOM!
FABOOM!
"Send your best hit squad, General. And tell them to dress up warm."

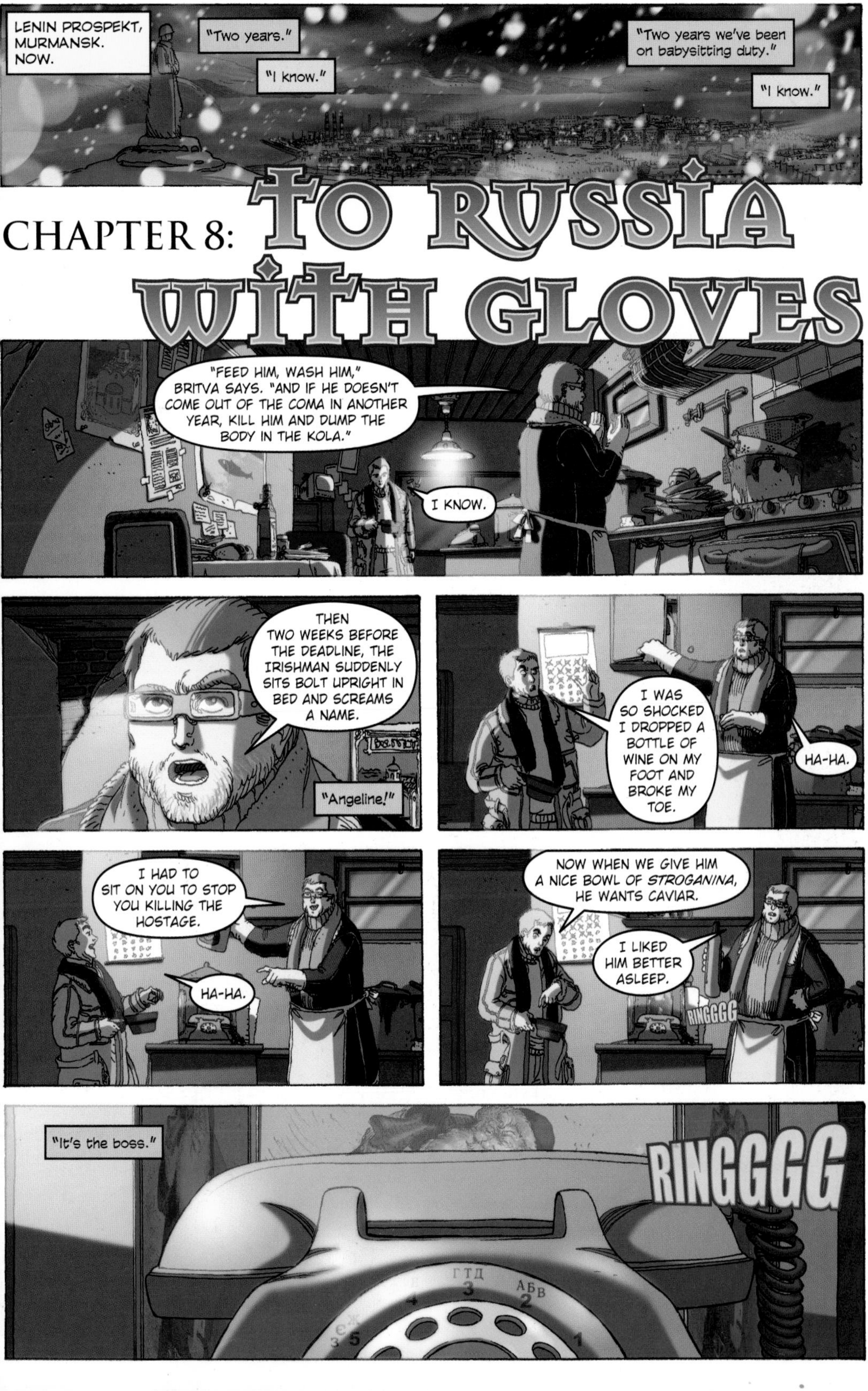
LENIN PROSPEKT, MURMANSK. NOW.
"Two years."
"I know."
"Two years we've been on babysitting duty."
"I know."
CHAPTER 8: TO RUSSIA WITH GLOVES
"FEED HIM, WASH HIM," BRITVA SAYS. "AND IF HE DOESN'T COME OUT OF THE COMA IN ANOTHER YEAR, KILL HIM AND DUMP THE BODY IN THE KOLA."
I KNOW.
THEN TWO WEEKS BEFORE THE DEADLINE, THE IRISHMAN SUDDENLY SITS BOLT UPRIGHT IN BED AND SCREAMS A NAME.
"Angeline!"
I WAS SO SHOCKED I DROPPED A BOTTLE OF WINE ON MY FOOT AND BROKE MY TOE.
HA-HA.
I HAD TO SIT ON YOU TO STOP YOU KILLING THE HOSTAGE.
HA-HA.
NOW WHEN WE GIVE HIM A NICE BOWL OF *STROGANINA*, HE WANTS CAVIAR.
I LIKED HIM BETTER ASLEEP.
RINGGGG
"It's the boss."
RINGGGG

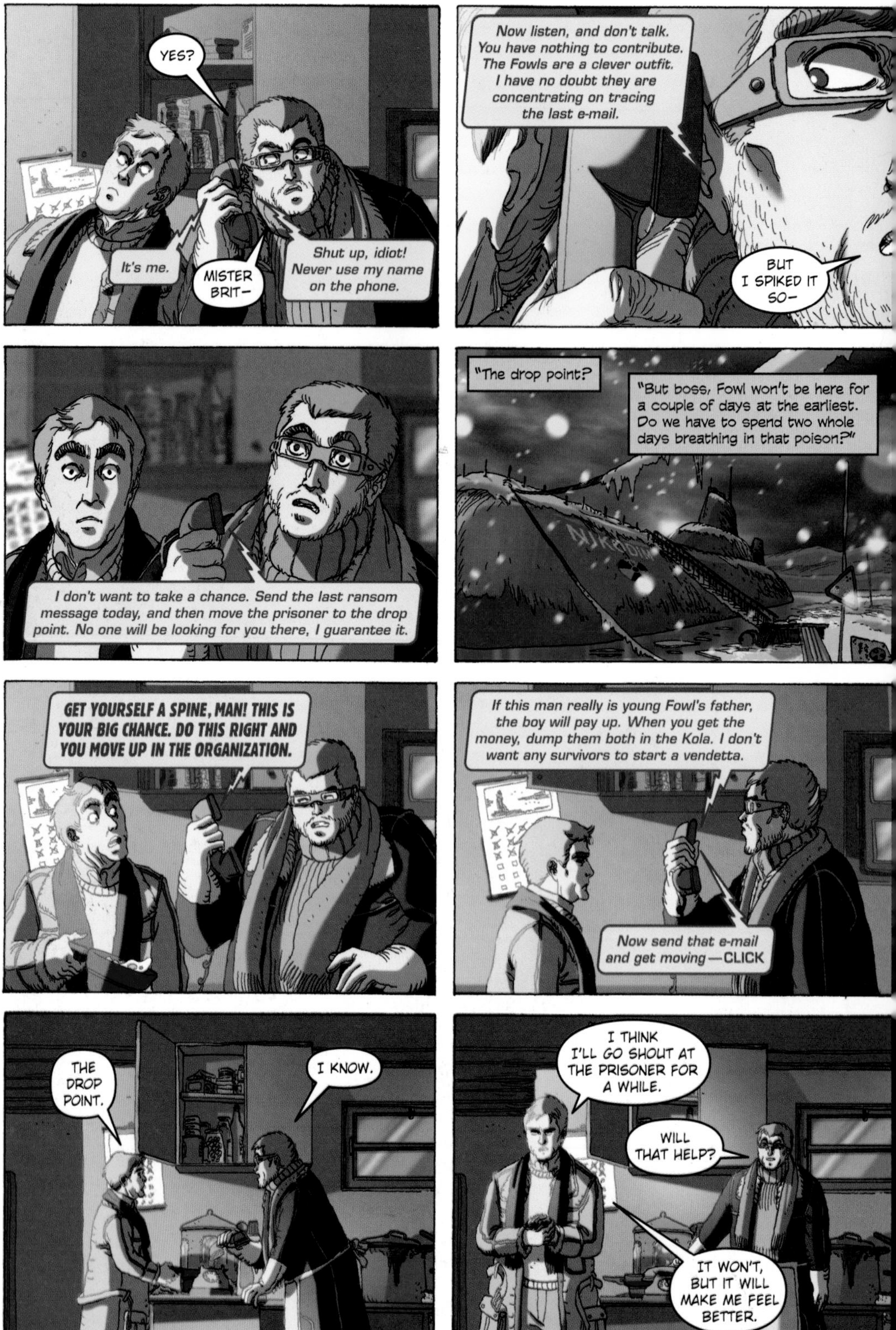
YES?
It's me.
MISTER BRIT—
Shut up, idiot! Never use my name on the phone.
Now listen, and don't talk. You have nothing to contribute. The Fowls are a clever outfit. I have no doubt they are concentrating on tracing the last e-mail.
BUT I SPIKED IT SO—
I don't want to take a chance. Send the last ransom message today, and then move the prisoner to the drop point. No one will be looking for you there, I guarantee it.
"The drop point?
"But boss, Fowl won't be here for a couple of days at the earliest. Do we have to spend two whole days breathing in that poison?"
GET YOURSELF A SPINE, MAN! THIS IS YOUR BIG CHANCE. DO THIS RIGHT AND YOU MOVE UP IN THE ORGANIZATION.
If this man really is young Fowl's father, the boy will pay up. When you get the money, dump them both in the Kola. I don't want any survivors to start a vendetta.
Now send that e-mail and get moving—CLICK
THE DROP POINT.
I KNOW.
I THINK I'LL GO SHOUT AT THE PRISONER FOR A WHILE.
WILL THAT HELP?
IT WON'T, BUT IT WILL MAKE ME FEEL BETTER.

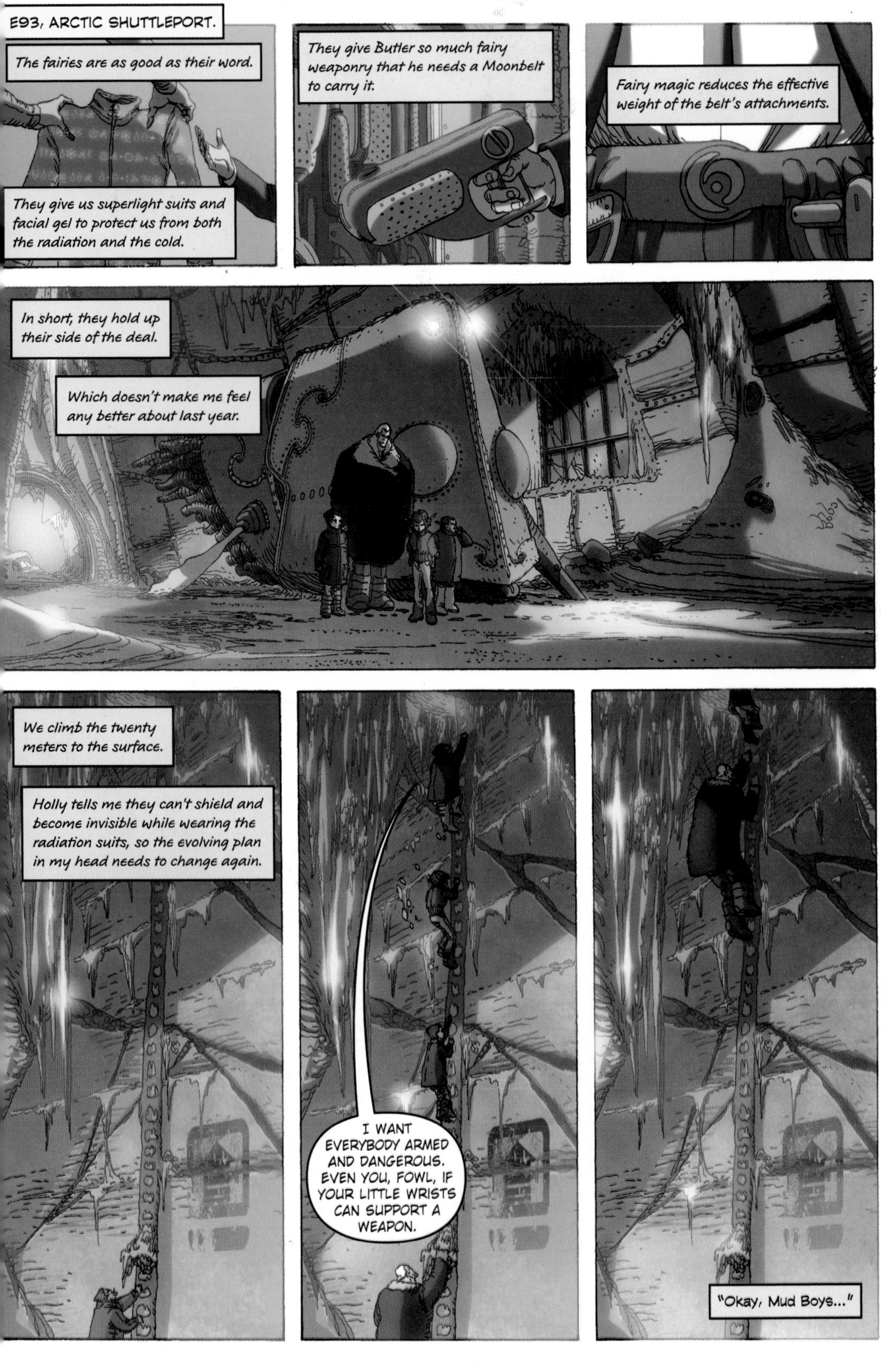
E93, ARCTIC SHUTTLEPORT.
The fairies are as good as their word.
They give us superlight suits and facial gel to protect us from both the radiation and the cold.
They give Butler so much fairy weaponry that he needs a Moonbelt to carry it.
Fairy magic reduces the effective weight of the belt's attachments.
In short, they hold up their side of the deal.
Which doesn't make me feel any better about last year.
We climb the twenty meters to the surface.
Holly tells me they can't shield and become invisible while wearing the radiation suits, so the evolving plan in my head needs to change again.
I WANT EVERYBODY ARMED AND DANGEROUS. EVEN YOU, FOWL, IF YOUR LITTLE WRISTS CAN SUPPORT A WEAPON.
"Okay, Mud Boys..."

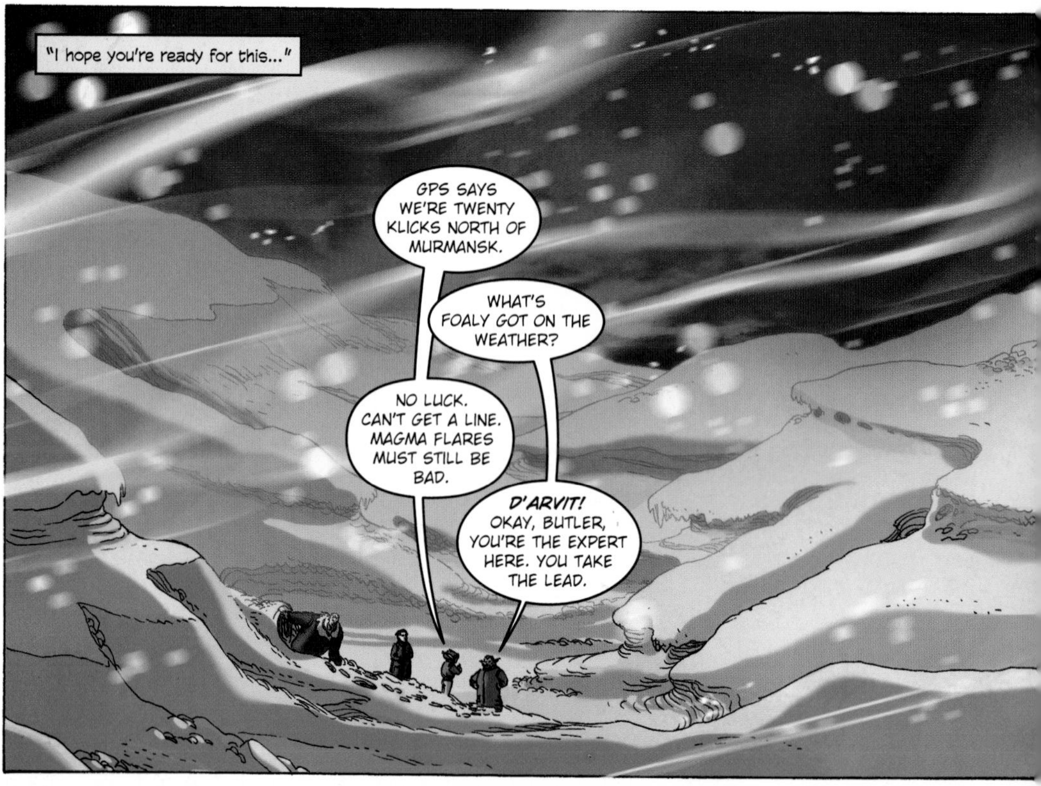
"I hope you're ready for this..."
GPS SAYS WE'RE TWENTY KLICKS NORTH OF MURMANSK.
WHAT'S FOALY GOT ON THE WEATHER?
NO LUCK. CAN'T GET A LINE. MAGMA FLARES MUST STILL BE BAD.
D'ARVIT! OKAY, BUTLER, YOU'RE THE EXPERT HERE. YOU TAKE THE LEAD.

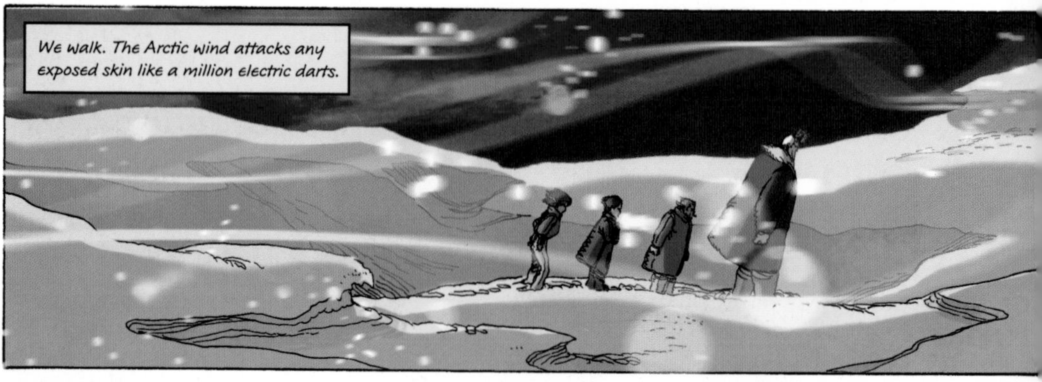
We walk. The Arctic wind attacks any exposed skin like a million electric darts.

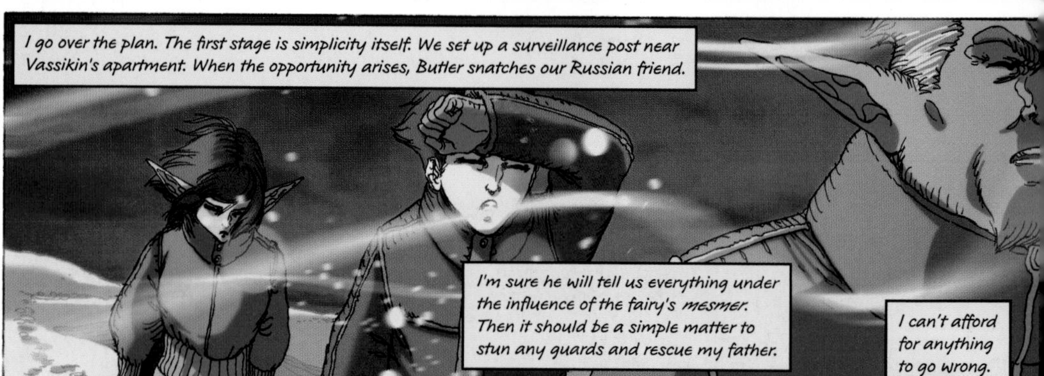
I go over the plan. The first stage is simplicity itself. We set up a surveillance post near Vassikin's apartment. When the opportunity arises, Butler snatches our Russian friend.
I'm sure he will tell us everything under the influence of the fairy's *mesmer*. Then it should be a simple matter to stun any guards and rescue my father.
I can't afford for anything to go wrong.

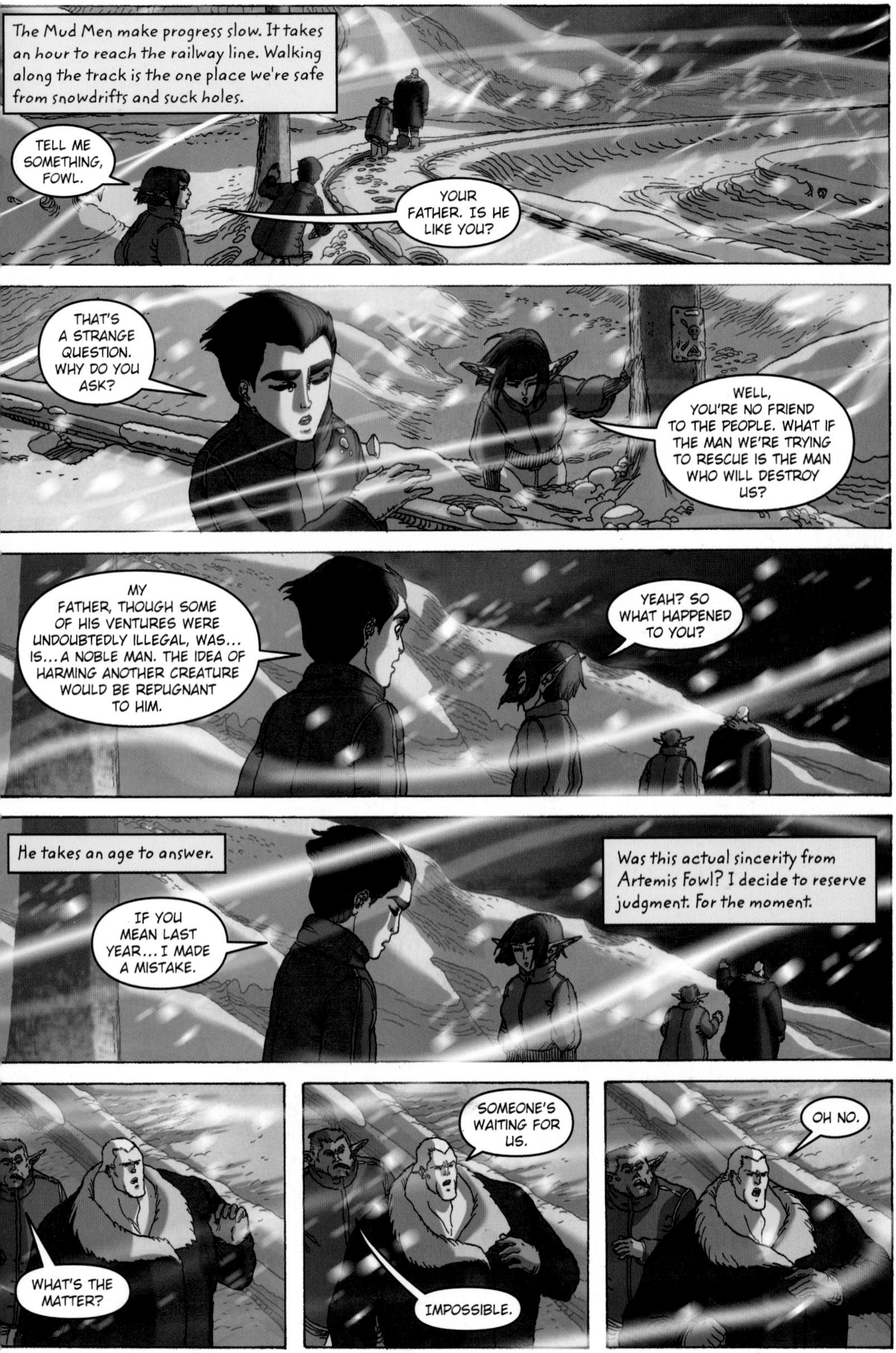
The Mud Men make progress slow. It takes an hour to reach the railway line. Walking along the track is the one place we're safe from snowdrifts and suck holes.
TELL ME SOMETHING, FOWL.
YOUR FATHER. IS HE LIKE YOU?
THAT'S A STRANGE QUESTION. WHY DO YOU ASK?
WELL, YOU'RE NO FRIEND TO THE PEOPLE. WHAT IF THE MAN WE'RE TRYING TO RESCUE IS THE MAN WHO WILL DESTROY US?
MY FATHER, THOUGH SOME OF HIS VENTURES WERE UNDOUBTEDLY ILLEGAL, WAS... IS... A NOBLE MAN. THE IDEA OF HARMING ANOTHER CREATURE WOULD BE REPUGNANT TO HIM.
YEAH? SO WHAT HAPPENED TO YOU?
He takes an age to answer.
IF YOU MEAN LAST YEAR... I MADE A MISTAKE.
Was this actual sincerity from Artemis Fowl? I decide to reserve judgment. For the moment.
WHAT'S THE MATTER?
SOMEONE'S WAITING FOR US.
IMPOSSIBLE.
OH NO.

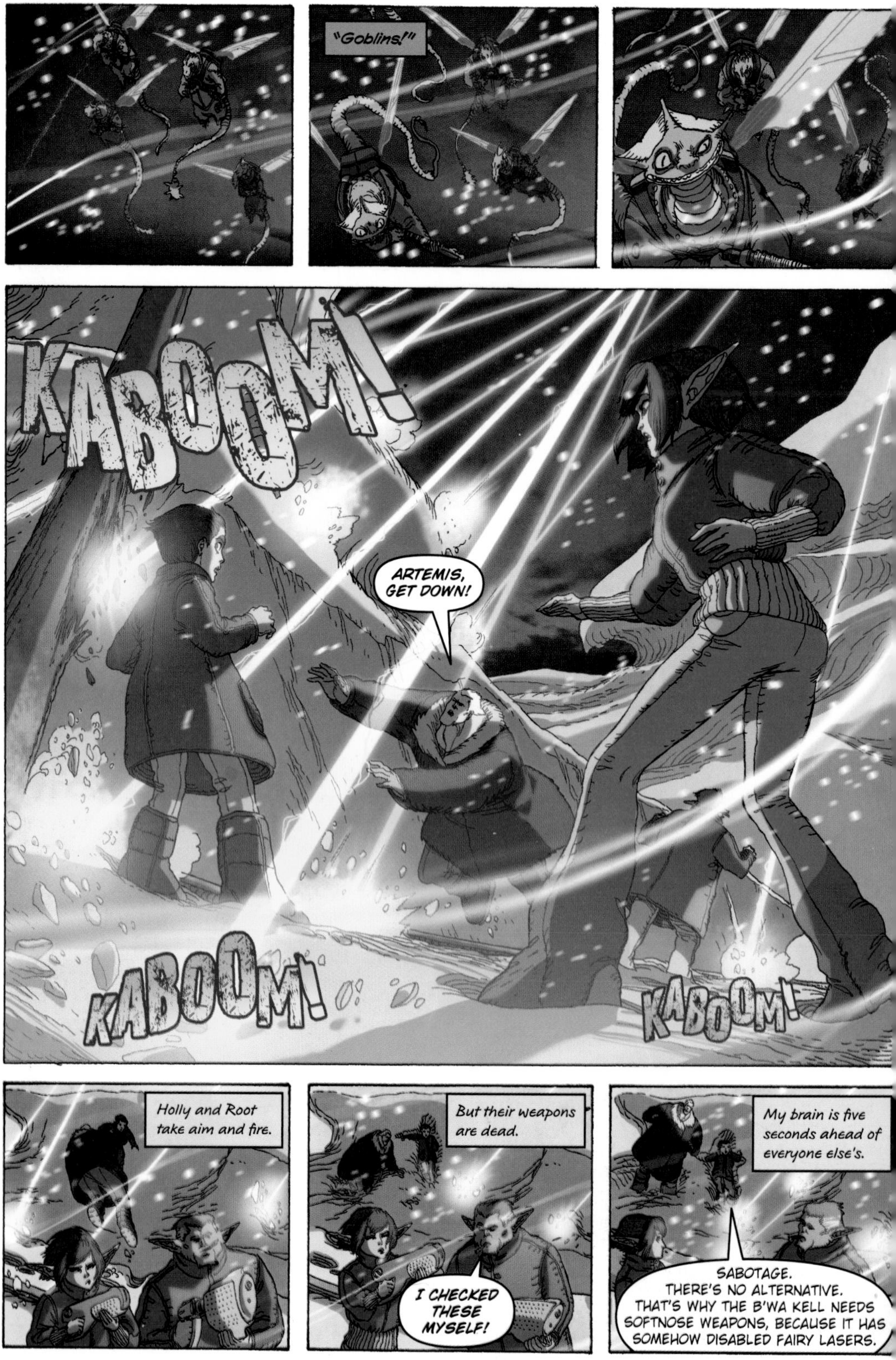
"Goblins!"
KABOOM!
ARTEMIS, GET DOWN!
KABOOM!
KABOOM!
Holly and Root take aim and fire.
But their weapons are dead.
I CHECKED THESE MYSELF!
My brain is five seconds ahead of everyone else's.
SABOTAGE. THERE'S NO ALTERNATIVE. THAT'S WHY THE B'WA KELL NEEDS SOFTNOSE WEAPONS, BECAUSE IT HAS SOMEHOW DISABLED FAIRY LASERS.

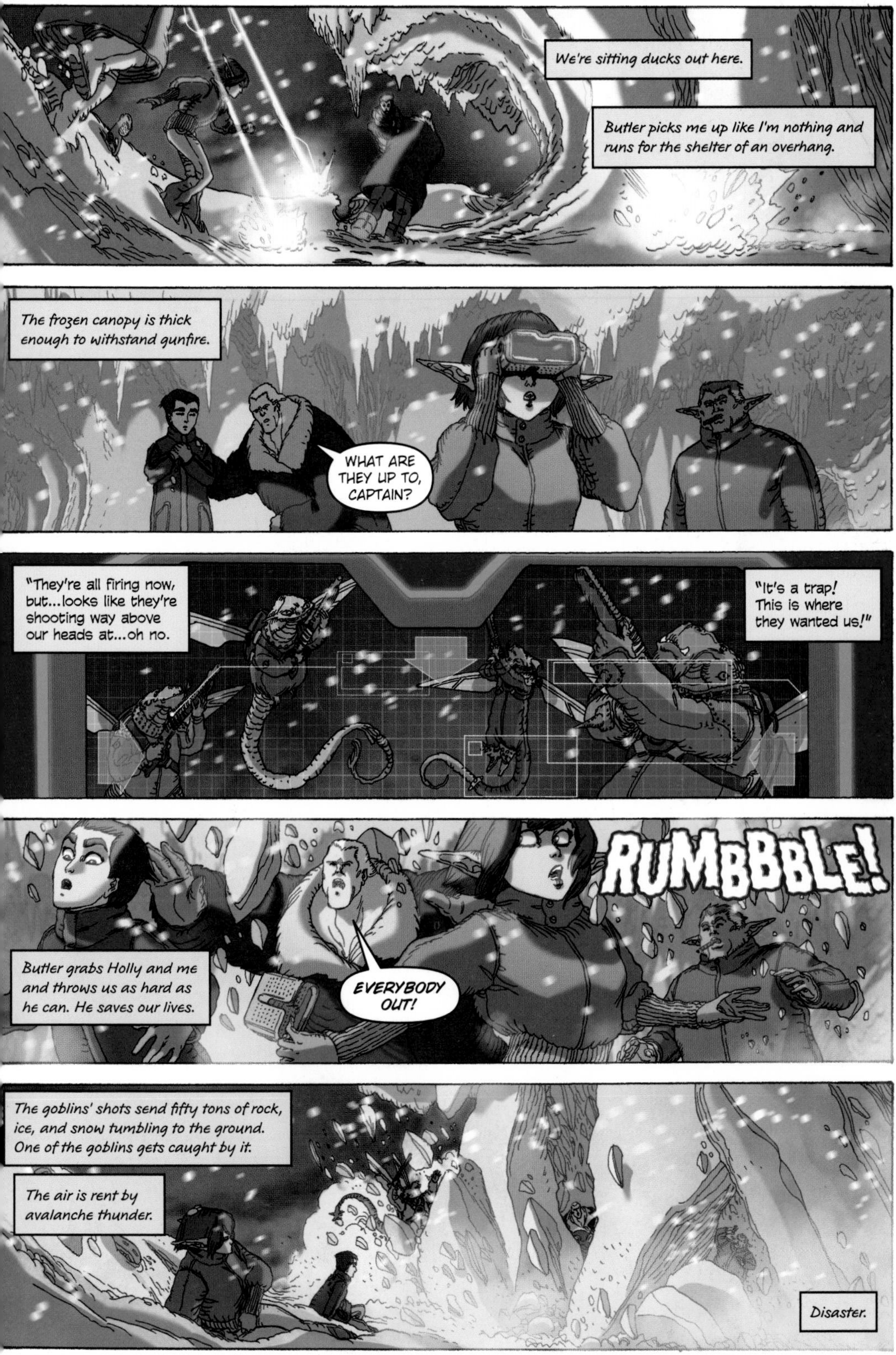
We're sitting ducks out here.
Butler picks me up like I'm nothing and runs for the shelter of an overhang.
The frozen canopy is thick enough to withstand gunfire.
WHAT ARE THEY UP TO, CAPTAIN?
"They're all firing now, but...looks like they're shooting way above our heads at...oh no.
"It's a trap! This is where they wanted us!"
RUMBBBLE!
Butler grabs Holly and me and throws us as hard as he can. He saves our lives.
EVERYBODY OUT!
The goblins' shots send fifty tons of rock, ice, and snow tumbling to the ground. One of the goblins gets caught by it.
The air is rent by avalanche thunder.
Disaster.

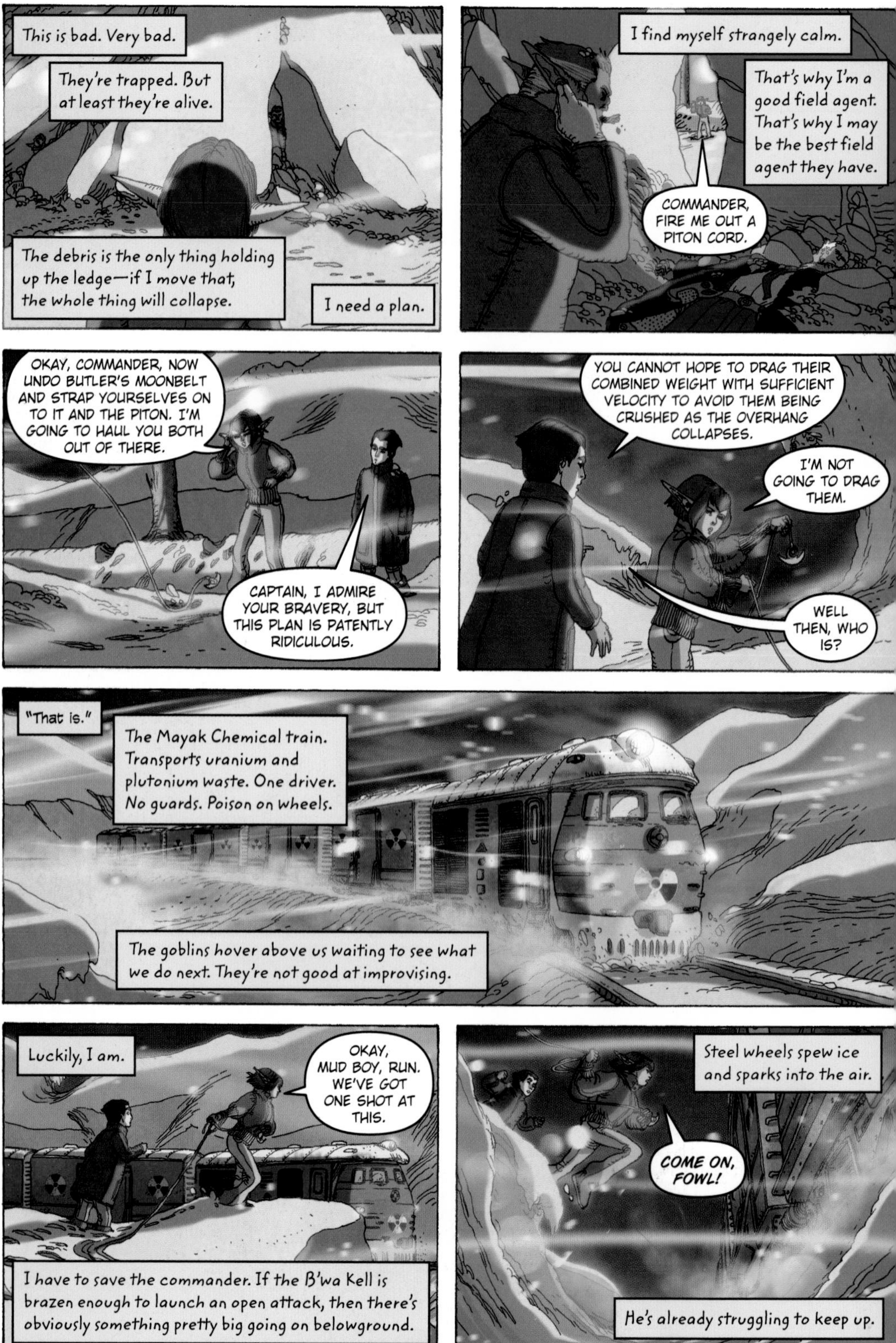

This is bad. Very bad.
They're trapped. But at least they're alive.
The debris is the only thing holding up the ledge—if I move that, the whole thing will collapse.
I need a plan.
I find myself strangely calm.
That's why I'm a good field agent. That's why I may be the best field agent they have.
COMMANDER, FIRE ME OUT A PITON CORD.
OKAY, COMMANDER, NOW UNDO BUTLER'S MOONBELT AND STRAP YOURSELVES ON TO IT AND THE PITON. I'M GOING TO HAUL YOU BOTH OUT OF THERE.
CAPTAIN, I ADMIRE YOUR BRAVERY, BUT THIS PLAN IS PATENTLY RIDICULOUS.
YOU CANNOT HOPE TO DRAG THEIR COMBINED WEIGHT WITH SUFFICIENT VELOCITY TO AVOID THEM BEING CRUSHED AS THE OVERHANG COLLAPSES.
I'M NOT GOING TO DRAG THEM.
WELL THEN, WHO IS?
"That is."
The Mayak Chemical train. Transports uranium and plutonium waste. One driver. No guards. Poison on wheels.
The goblins hover above us waiting to see what we do next. They're not good at improvising.
Luckily, I am.
OKAY, MUD BOY, RUN. WE'VE GOT ONE SHOT AT THIS.
I have to save the commander. If the B'wa Kell is brazen enough to launch an open attack, then there's obviously something pretty big going on belowground.
Steel wheels spew ice and sparks into the air.
COME ON, FOWL!
He's already struggling to keep up.

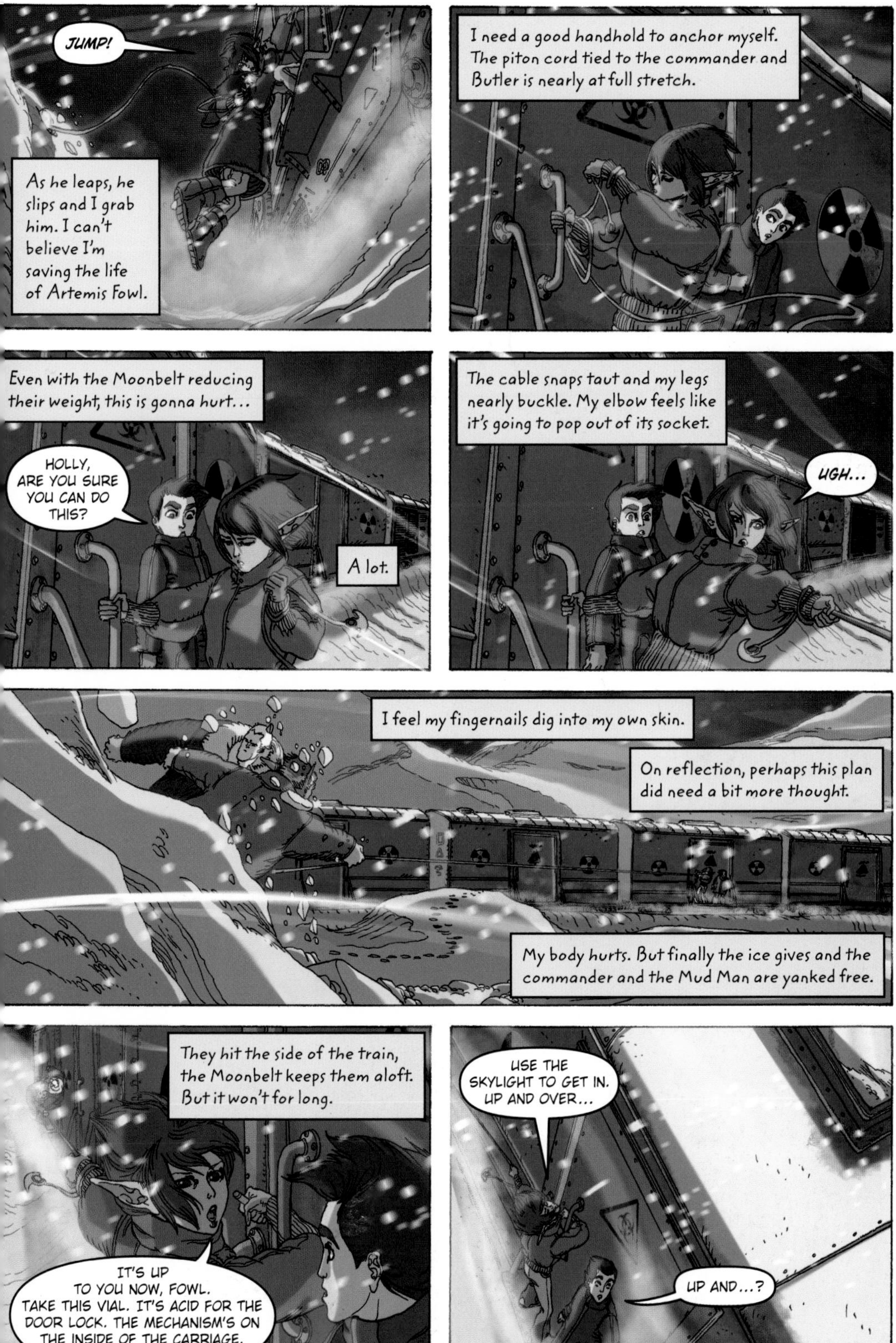
JUMP!
As he leaps, he slips and I grab him. I can't believe I'm saving the life of Artemis Fowl.
I need a good handhold to anchor myself. The piton cord tied to the commander and Butler is nearly at full stretch.
Even with the Moonbelt reducing their weight, this is gonna hurt...
HOLLY, ARE YOU SURE YOU CAN DO THIS?
A lot.
The cable snaps taut and my legs nearly buckle. My elbow feels like it's going to pop out of its socket.
UGH...
I feel my fingernails dig into my own skin.
On reflection, perhaps this plan did need a bit more thought.
My body hurts. But finally the ice gives and the commander and the Mud Man are yanked free.
They hit the side of the train, the Moonbelt keeps them aloft. But it won't for long.
IT'S UP TO YOU NOW, FOWL. TAKE THIS VIAL. IT'S ACID FOR THE DOOR LOCK. THE MECHANISM'S ON THE INSIDE OF THE CARRIAGE.
USE THE SKYLIGHT TO GET IN. UP AND OVER...
UP AND...?

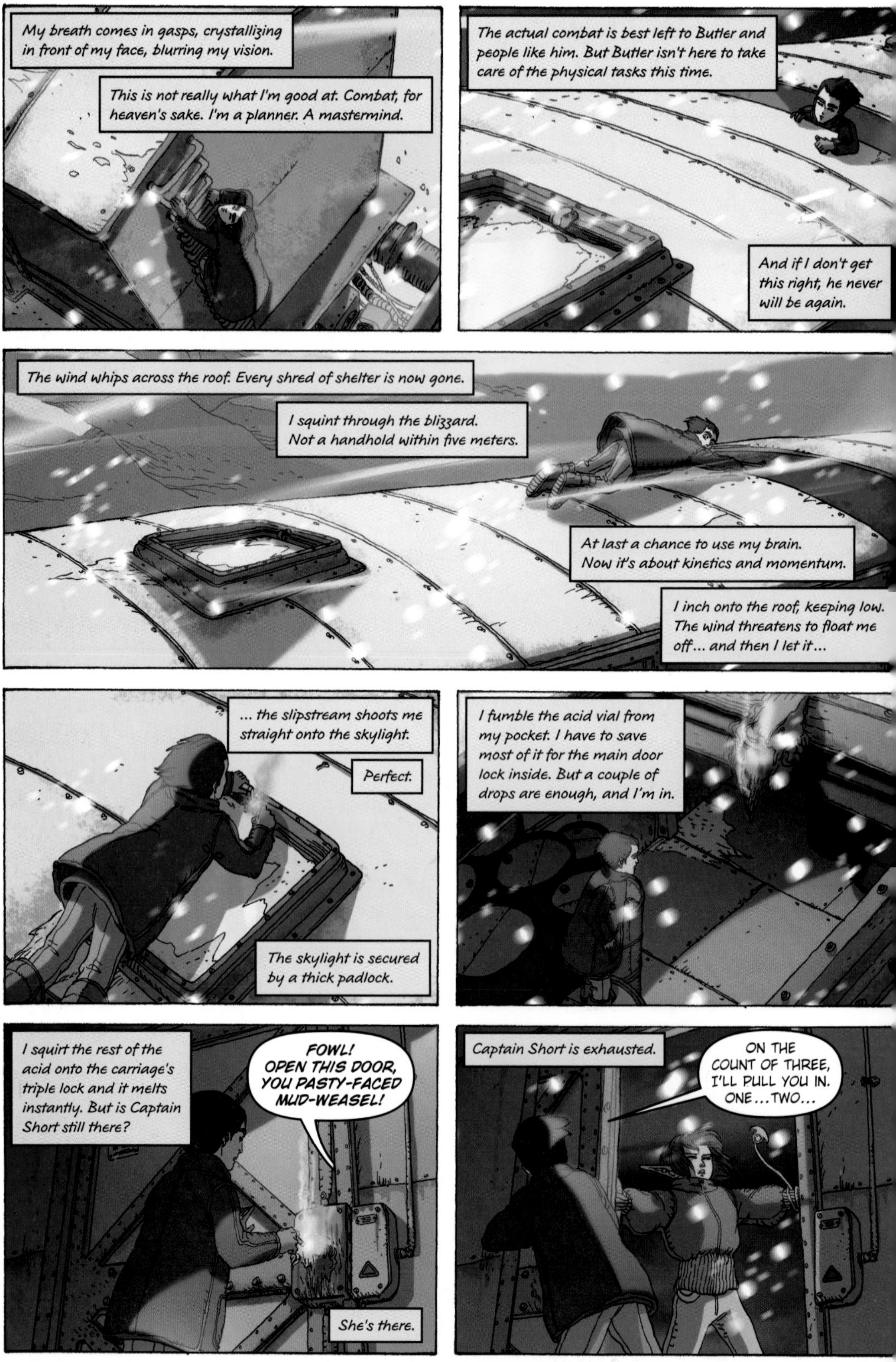

My breath comes in gasps, crystallizing in front of my face, blurring my vision.
This is not really what I'm good at. Combat, for heaven's sake. I'm a planner. A mastermind.
The actual combat is best left to Butler and people like him. But Butler isn't here to take care of the physical tasks this time.
And if I don't get this right, he never will be again.
The wind whips across the roof. Every shred of shelter is now gone.
I squint through the blizzard. Not a handhold within five meters.
At last a chance to use my brain. Now it's about kinetics and momentum.
I inch onto the roof, keeping low. The wind threatens to float me off... and then I let it...
... the slipstream shoots me straight onto the skylight.
Perfect.
The skylight is secured by a thick padlock.
I fumble the acid vial from my pocket. I have to save most of it for the main door lock inside. But a couple of drops are enough, and I'm in.
I squirt the rest of the acid onto the carriage's triple lock and it melts instantly. But is Captain Short still there?
FOWL! OPEN THIS DOOR, YOU PASTY-FACED MUD-WEASEL!
She's there.
Captain Short is exhausted.
ON THE COUNT OF THREE, I'LL PULL YOU IN. ONE...TWO...

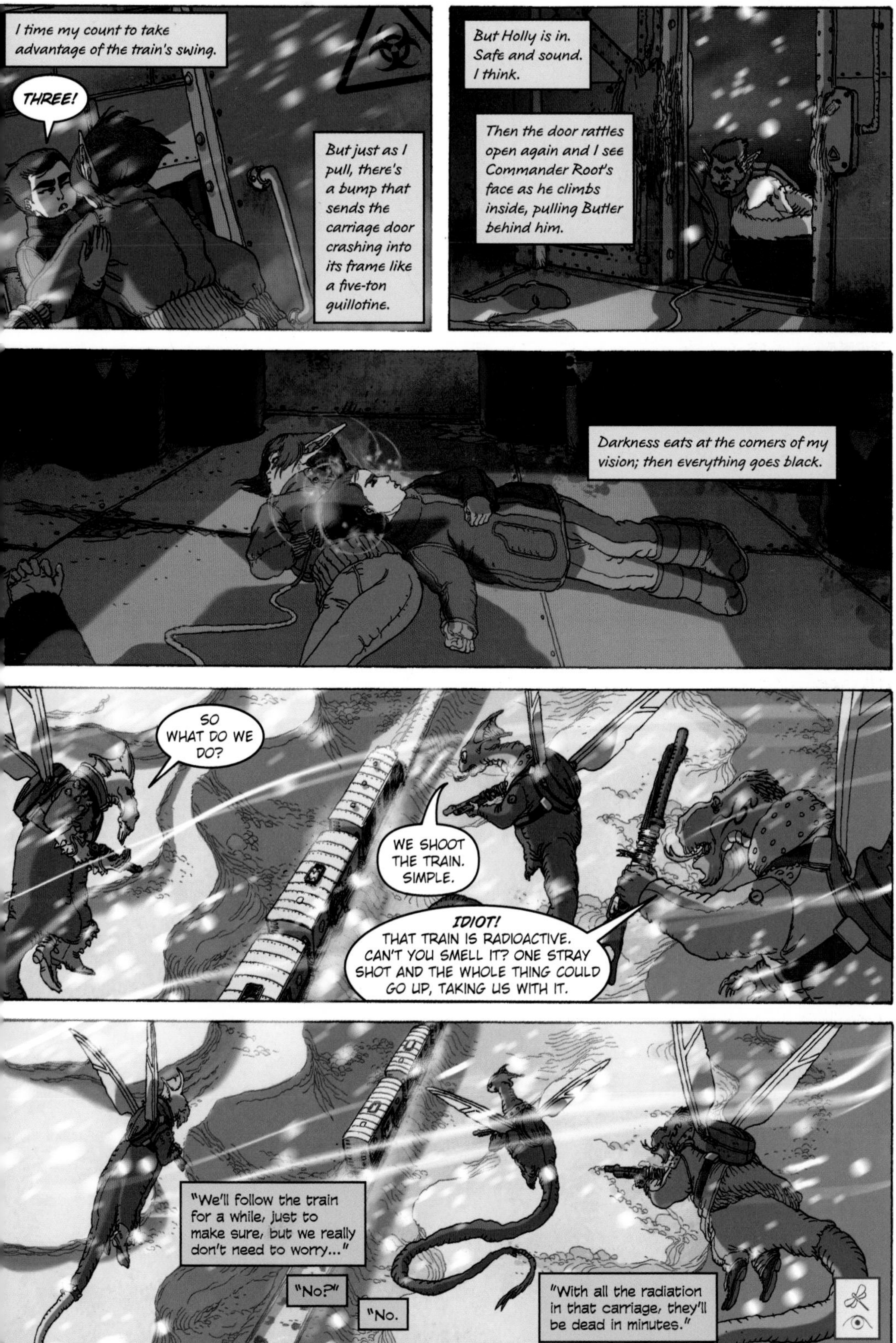
I time my count to take advantage of the train's swing.
THREE!
But just as I pull, there's a bump that sends the carriage door crashing into its frame like a five-ton guillotine.
But Holly is in. Safe and sound. I think.
Then the door rattles open again and I see Commander Root's face as he climbs inside, pulling Butler behind him.
Darkness eats at the corners of my vision; then everything goes black.
SO WHAT DO WE DO?
WE SHOOT THE TRAIN. SIMPLE.
IDIOT! THAT TRAIN IS RADIOACTIVE. CAN'T YOU SMELL IT? ONE STRAY SHOT AND THE WHOLE THING COULD GO UP, TAKING US WITH IT.
"We'll follow the train for a while, just to make sure, but we really don't need to worry..."
"No?"
"No.
"With all the radiation in that carriage, they'll be dead in minutes."

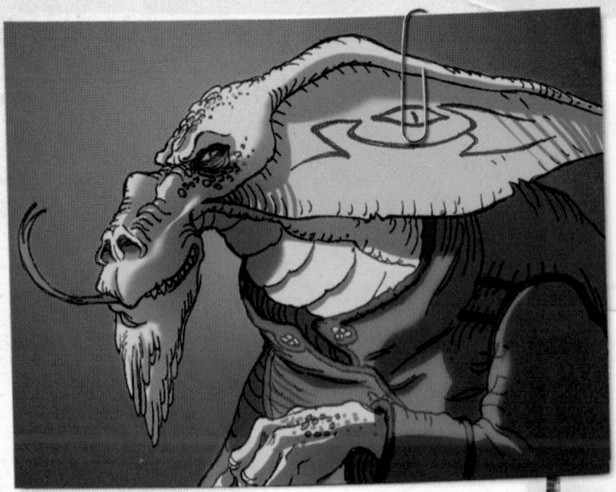

DOCUMENTS RECOVERED FROM THE UPSTAIRS OF THE SECOND SKIN NIGHTCLUB, A NOTORIOUS B'WA KELL GOBLIN HANGOUT.

GENERAL SCALENE'S "TO DO" LIST:

1. Arson attack for Opal
2. Lick own eyeballs
3. Fleece a tourist
4. Shed skin
5. Backstabbing
6. Backbiting
7. General vindictiveness
8. Bit of smuggling
9. Kill Commander Root

HANDSOME, INTELLIGENT, SOON-TO-BE-RICH, OLDER GOBLIN SEEKS YOUNG FEMALE COMPANION FOR FIREBALLS AND WALKS IN THE DARK. MUST HAVE OWN TEETH. I AM CURRENTLY INVOLVED IN A PLOT TO OVERTHROW THE COUNCIL OF HAVEN CITY AND SO MUST REMAIN ANONYMOUS. APPLY GENERAL SCALENE, BOX 2441, HAVEN CITY.

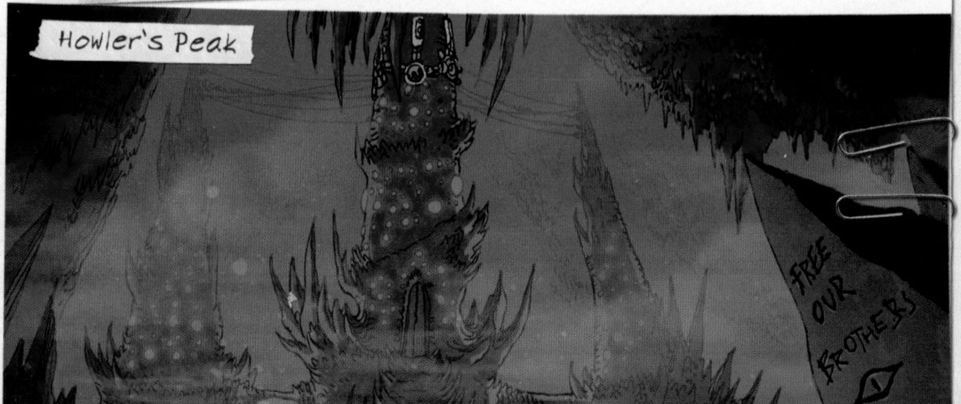
Howler's Peak
FREE OUR BROTHERS

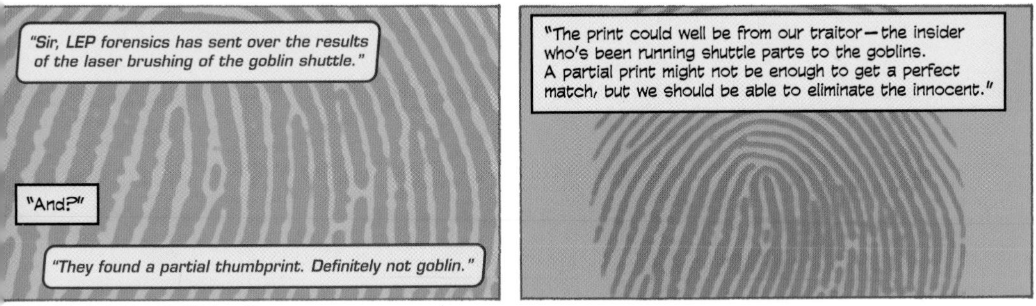
"Sir, LEP forensics has sent over the results of the laser brushing of the goblin shuttle."
"And?"
"They found a partial thumbprint. Definitely not goblin."
"The print could well be from our traitor—the insider who's been running shuttle parts to the goblins.
A partial print might not be enough to get a perfect match, but we should be able to eliminate the innocent."

CHAPTER 9:
NO SAFE HAVEN

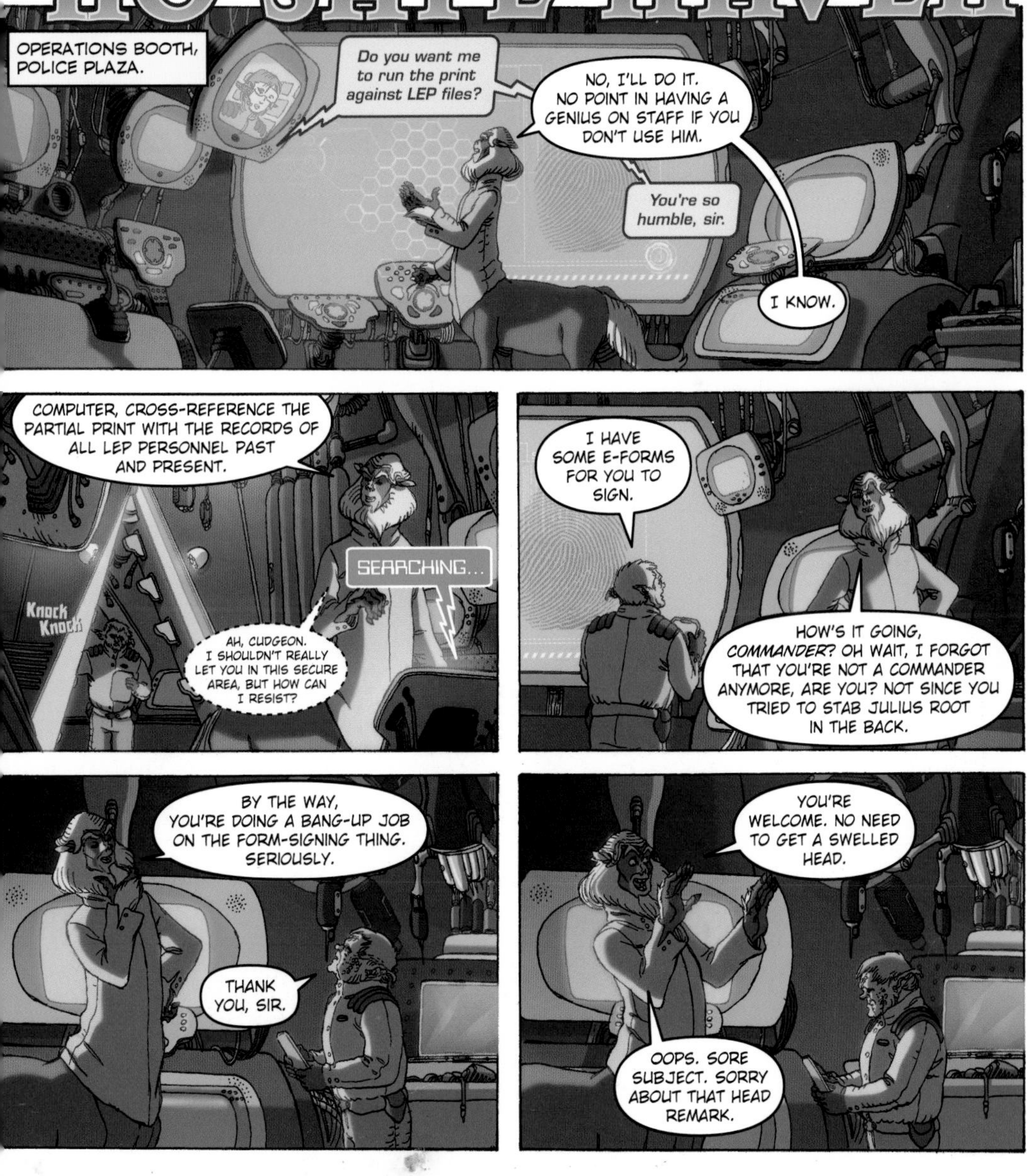
OPERATIONS BOOTH, POLICE PLAZA.
Do you want me to run the print against LEP files?
NO, I'LL DO IT. NO POINT IN HAVING A GENIUS ON STAFF IF YOU DON'T USE HIM.
You're so humble, sir.
I KNOW.
COMPUTER, CROSS-REFERENCE THE PARTIAL PRINT WITH THE RECORDS OF ALL LEP PERSONNEL PAST AND PRESENT.
SEARCHING...
Knock Knock
AH, CUDGEON. I SHOULDN'T REALLY LET YOU IN THIS SECURE AREA, BUT HOW CAN I RESIST?
I HAVE SOME E-FORMS FOR YOU TO SIGN.
HOW'S IT GOING, COMMANDER? OH WAIT, I FORGOT THAT YOU'RE NOT A COMMANDER ANYMORE, ARE YOU? NOT SINCE YOU TRIED TO STAB JULIUS ROOT IN THE BACK.
BY THE WAY, YOU'RE DOING A BANG-UP JOB ON THE FORM-SIGNING THING. SERIOUSLY.
THANK YOU, SIR.
YOU'RE WELCOME. NO NEED TO GET A SWELLED HEAD.
OOPS. SORE SUBJECT. SORRY ABOUT THAT HEAD REMARK.

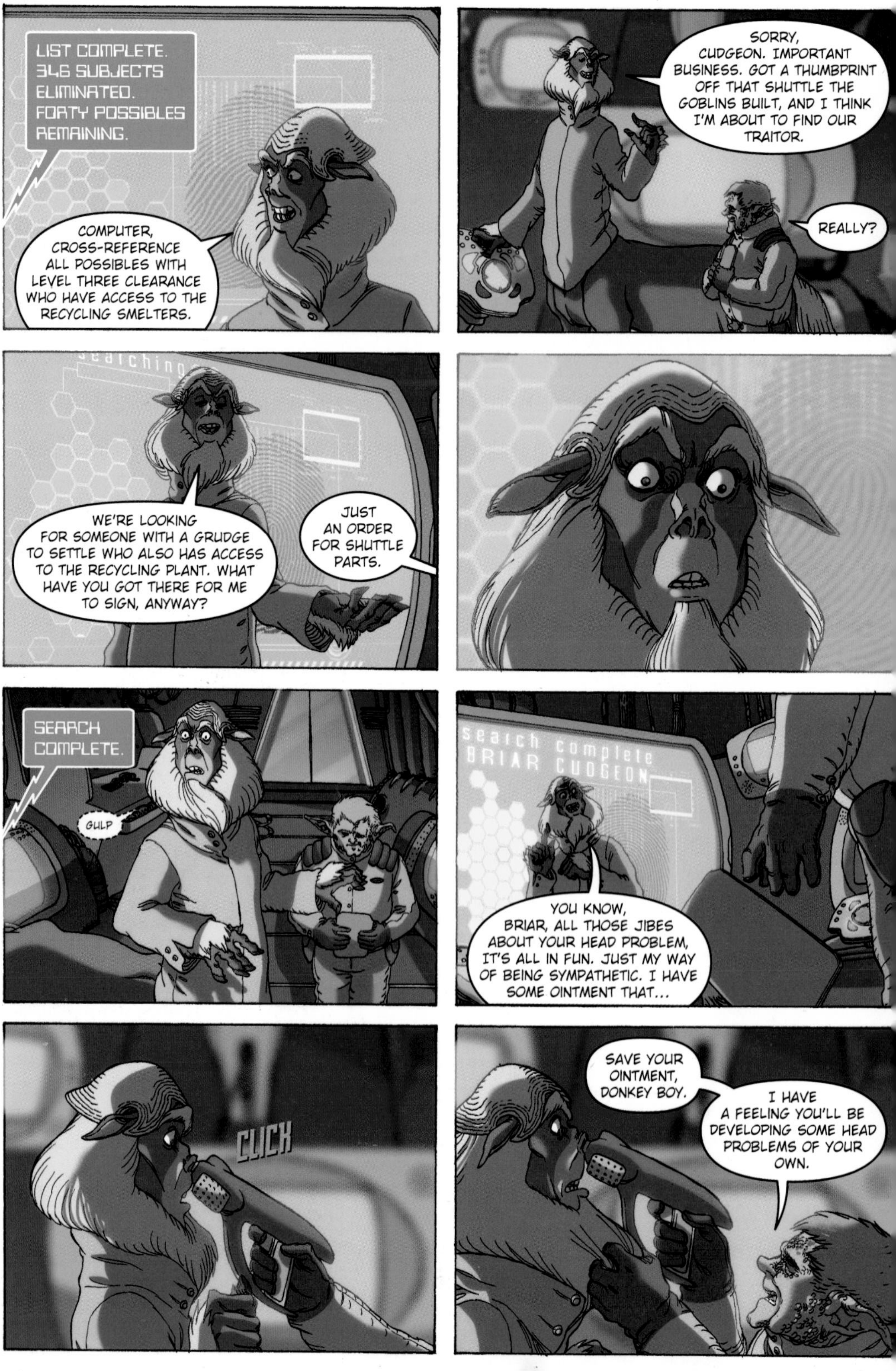
LIST COMPLETE. 346 SUBJECTS ELIMINATED. FORTY POSSIBLES REMAINING.
COMPUTER, CROSS-REFERENCE ALL POSSIBLES WITH LEVEL THREE CLEARANCE WHO HAVE ACCESS TO THE RECYCLING SMELTERS.
SORRY, CUDGEON. IMPORTANT BUSINESS. GOT A THUMBPRINT OFF THAT SHUTTLE THE GOBLINS BUILT, AND I THINK I'M ABOUT TO FIND OUR TRAITOR.
REALLY?
WE'RE LOOKING FOR SOMEONE WITH A GRUDGE TO SETTLE WHO ALSO HAS ACCESS TO THE RECYCLING PLANT. WHAT HAVE YOU GOT THERE FOR ME TO SIGN, ANYWAY?
JUST AN ORDER FOR SHUTTLE PARTS.
SEARCH COMPLETE.
GULP
search complete
BRIAR CUDGEON
YOU KNOW, BRIAR, ALL THOSE JIBES ABOUT YOUR HEAD PROBLEM, IT'S ALL IN FUN. JUST MY WAY OF BEING SYMPATHETIC. I HAVE SOME OINTMENT THAT...
CLICK
SAVE YOUR OINTMENT, DONKEY BOY.
I HAVE A FEELING YOU'LL BE DEVELOPING SOME HEAD PROBLEMS OF YOUR OWN.

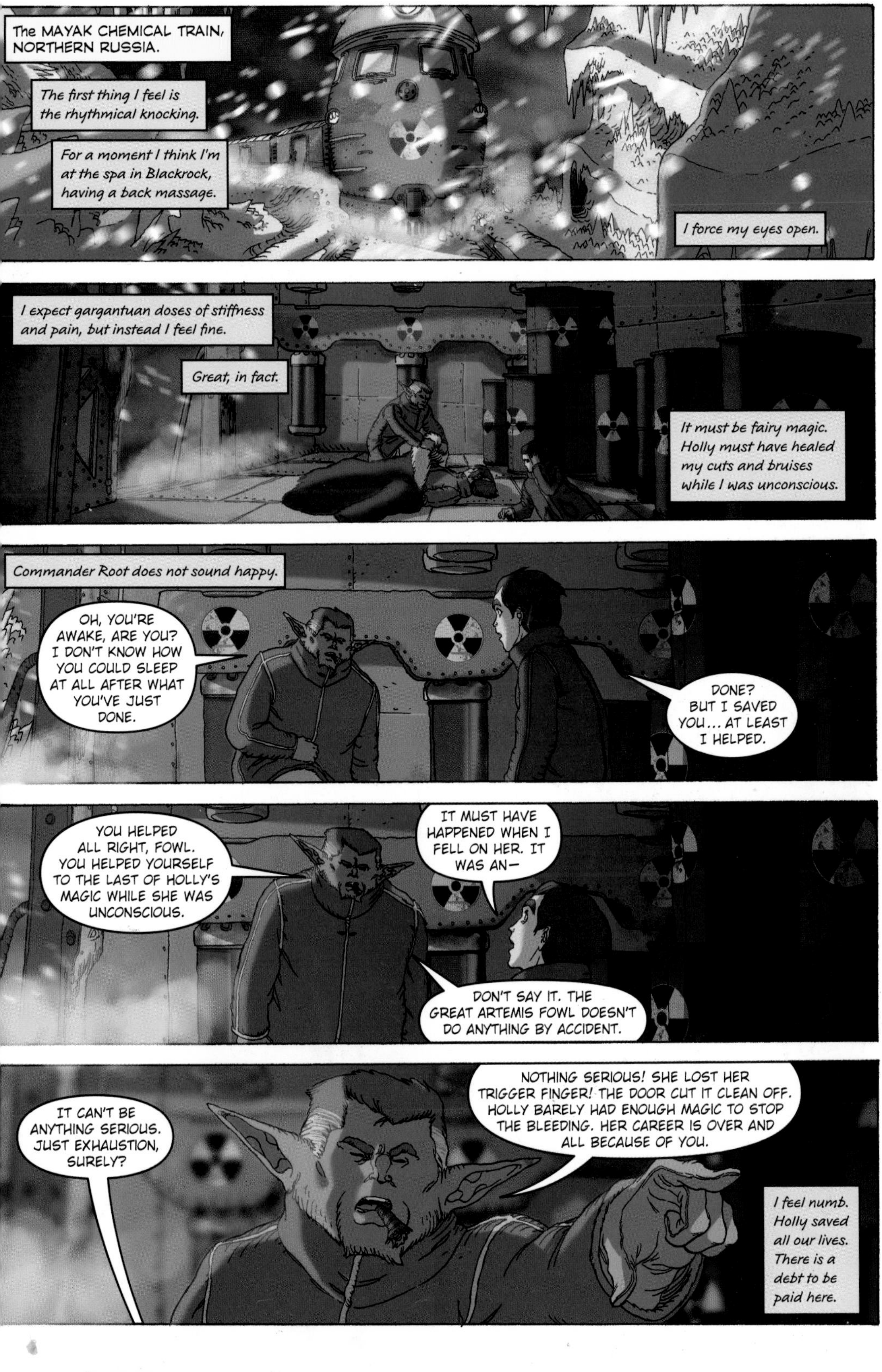
The MAYAK CHEMICAL TRAIN, NORTHERN RUSSIA.
The first thing I feel is the rhythmical knocking.
For a moment I think I'm at the spa in Blackrock, having a back massage.
I force my eyes open.
I expect gargantuan doses of stiffness and pain, but instead I feel fine.
Great, in fact.
It must be fairy magic. Holly must have healed my cuts and bruises while I was unconscious.
Commander Root does not sound happy.
OH, YOU'RE AWAKE, ARE YOU? I DON'T KNOW HOW YOU COULD SLEEP AT ALL AFTER WHAT YOU'VE JUST DONE.
DONE? BUT I SAVED YOU... AT LEAST I HELPED.
YOU HELPED ALL RIGHT, FOWL. YOU HELPED YOURSELF TO THE LAST OF HOLLY'S MAGIC WHILE SHE WAS UNCONSCIOUS.
IT MUST HAVE HAPPENED WHEN I FELL ON HER. IT WAS AN—
DON'T SAY IT. THE GREAT ARTEMIS FOWL DOESN'T DO ANYTHING BY ACCIDENT.
IT CAN'T BE ANYTHING SERIOUS. JUST EXHAUSTION, SURELY?
NOTHING SERIOUS! SHE LOST HER TRIGGER FINGER! THE DOOR CUT IT CLEAN OFF. HOLLY BARELY HAD ENOUGH MAGIC TO STOP THE BLEEDING. HER CAREER IS OVER AND ALL BECAUSE OF YOU.
I feel numb. Holly saved all our lives. There is a debt to be paid here.

THERE'S STILL TIME. WE CAN SAVE THE FINGER. WHAT ABOUT THE RITUAL?

HOW CAN WE COMPLETE THE RITUAL HERE?

In order to replenish their magical powers, the People had to periodically complete the Ritual, which means planting a seed from an ancient oak tree straight into the earth.

I scramble across the floor and start searching Holly.

IN HEAVEN'S NAME, MUD BOY, WHAT ARE YOU DOING?

LAST YEAR IN FOWL MANOR, HOLLY ESCAPED BECAUSE SHE HAD AN ACORN...

I REMEMBER FOALY AND HOLLY PUT TOGETHER SOME PROPOSAL FOR A SEALED ACORN UNIT, BUT THE COUNCIL REJECTED IT. SAID IT WAS "HERESY."

... AN OFFICER LIKE HOLLY WOULDN'T FORGET SOMETHING LIKE THAT.

Yes. There are two tiny items on the gold chain around her neck. One is her copy of the Book, the fairy bible. The other is a small Plexiglas sphere filled with earth.

NOW ALL WE NEED TO DO IS BURY IT AND FAST.

Commander Root tells me that's against regulations, but he doesn't sound too upset.

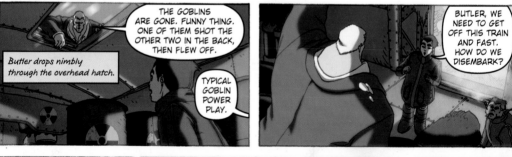

Butler drops nimbly through the overhead hatch.

THE GOBLINS ARE GONE. FUNNY THING. ONE OF THEM SHOT THE OTHER TWO IN THE BACK, THEN FLEW OFF.

TYPICAL GOBLIN POWER PLAY.

BUTLER, WE NEED TO GET OFF THIS TRAIN AND FAST. HOW DO WE DISEMBARK?

Butler grins.

"Artemis, I'm afraid 'disembark' is a pretty gentle term for what I have in mind."

OPERATIONS BOOTH, POLICE PLAZA.

WHY?

WHY? YOU HAVE THE GALL TO ASK ME WHY?

"I was the Council's golden boy! In fifty years I would have been chairman! And then along comes the Artemis Fowl Affair.

"In one short day, all my hopes are dashed. I end up deformed and demoted! And all because of you, Foaly. You and Root!"

SOON JULIUS WILL BE DEAD AND DISHONORED, AND YOU WILL BE BLAMED FOR ALL THE GOBLIN ATTACKS.

"We'll see about that, baboon face."

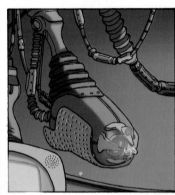

NO PLASMA DEFENSES. NO VOICE-ACTIVATED LASER.

YOU REALLY ARE SLIPPING, FOALY.

EVERYTHING YOU USED TO CONTROL FROM YOUR PRECIOUS OPS ROOM IS NOW WIRED INTO THIS LITTLE BEAUTY.

YOU MEAN...?

ZAPP!

THAT'S RIGHT. NOTHING WORKS UNLESS I PRESS THE BUTTON.

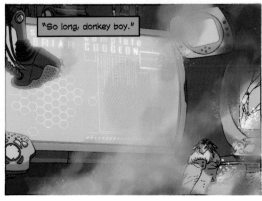

"So long, donkey boy."

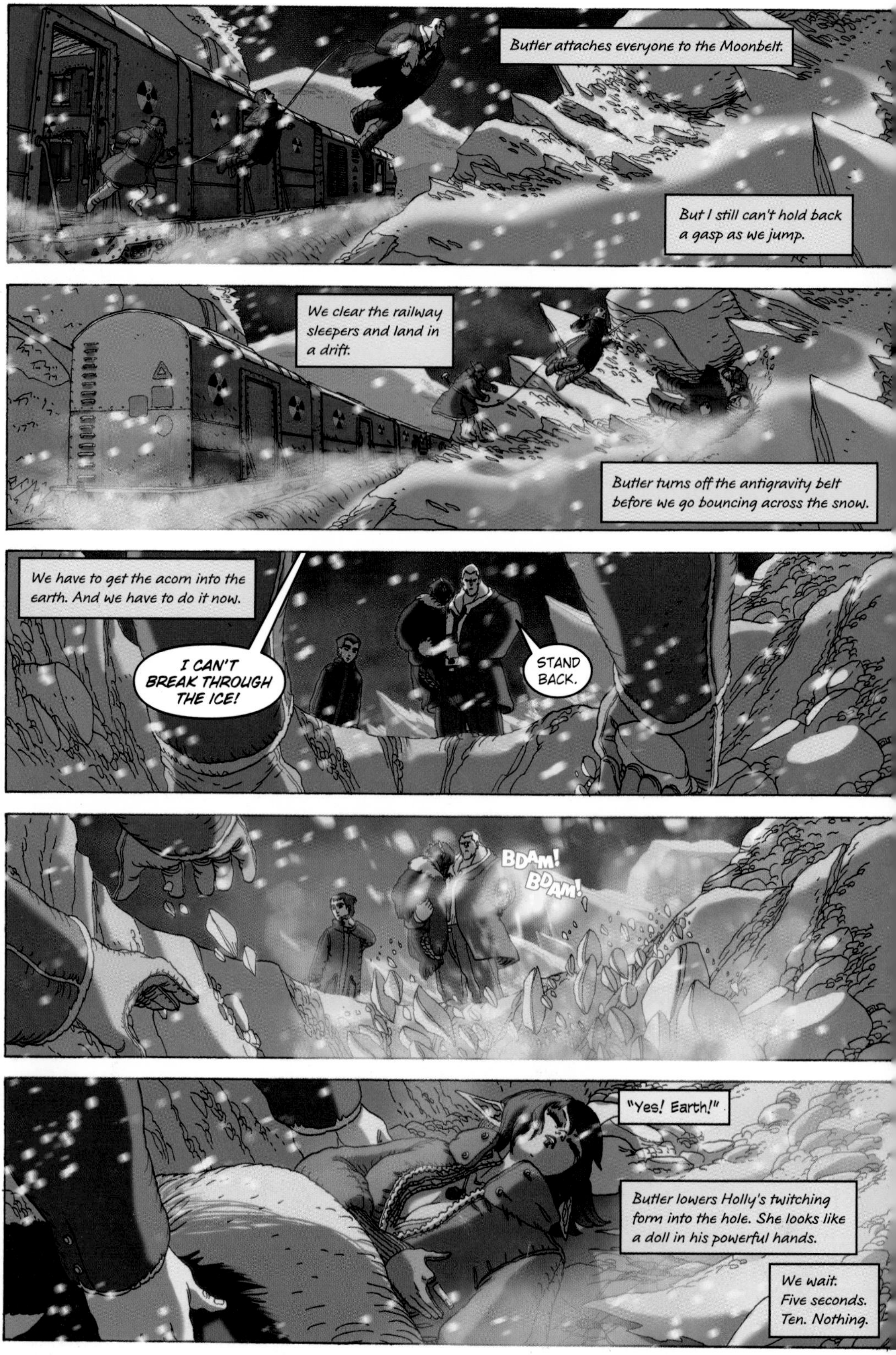

Butler attaches everyone to the Moonbelt.
But I still can't hold back a gasp as we jump.
We clear the railway sleepers and land in a drift.
Butler turns off the antigravity belt before we go bouncing across the snow.
We have to get the acorn into the earth. And we have to do it now.
I CAN'T BREAK THROUGH THE ICE!
STAND BACK.
BDAM!
BDAM!
"Yes! Earth!"
Butler lowers Holly's twitching form into the hole. She looks like a doll in his powerful hands.
We wait. Five seconds. Ten. Nothing.

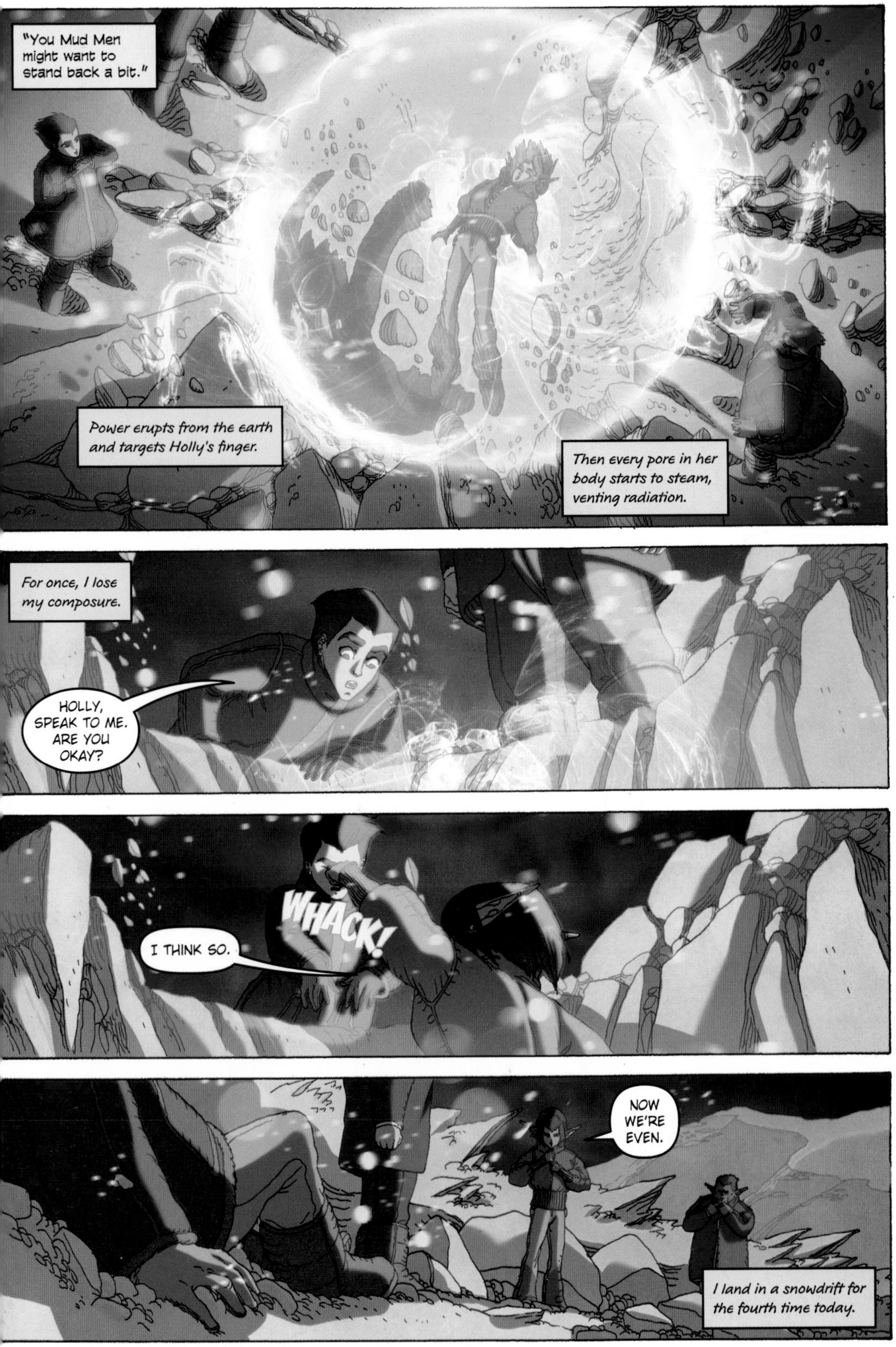
"You Mud Men might want to stand back a bit."
Power erupts from the earth and targets Holly's finger.
Then every pore in her body starts to steam, venting radiation.
For once, I lose my composure.
HOLLY, SPEAK TO ME. ARE YOU OKAY?
WHACK!
I THINK SO.
NOW WE'RE EVEN.
I land in a snowdrift for the fourth time today.

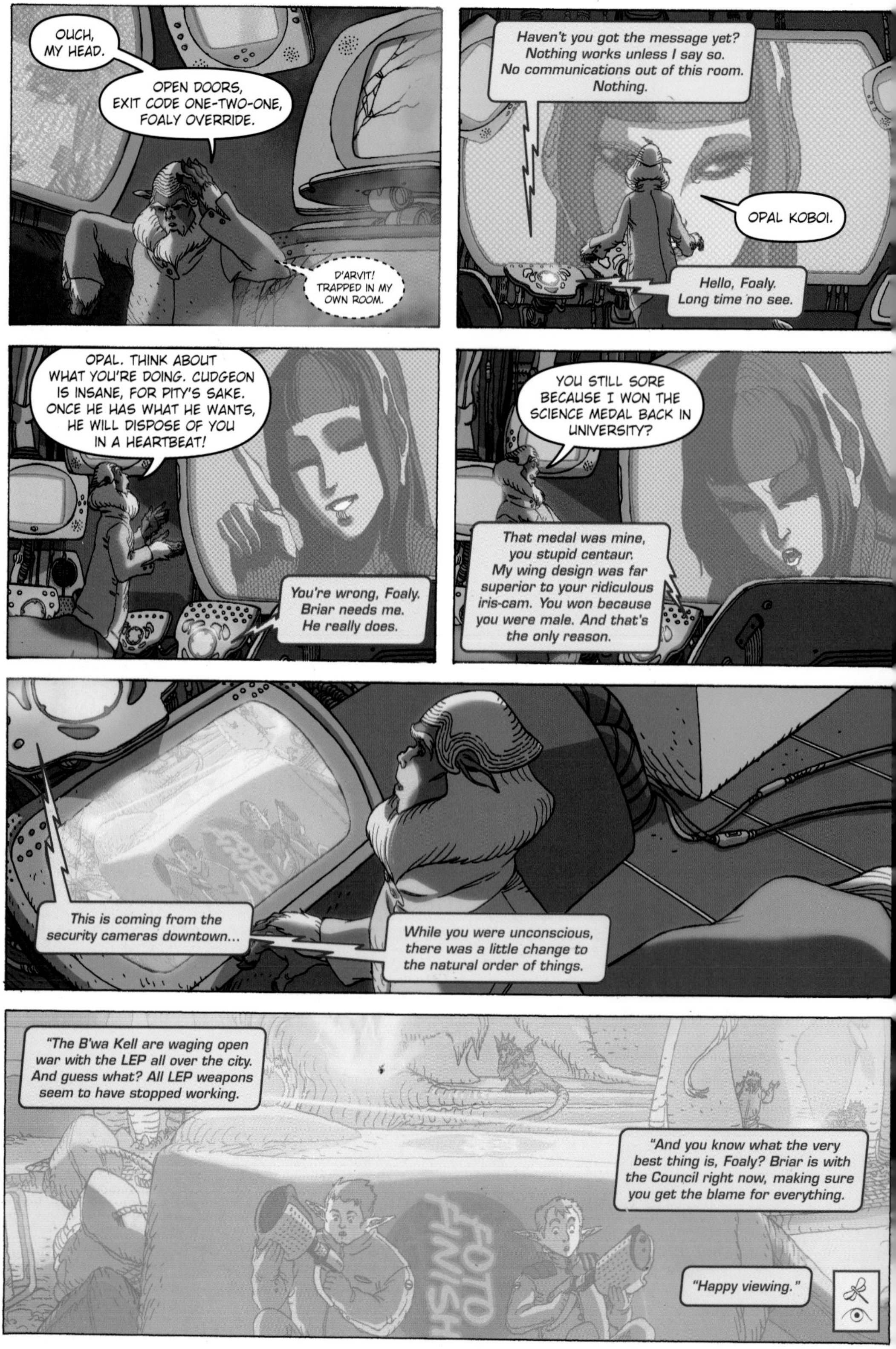
OUCH, MY HEAD.
OPEN DOORS, EXIT CODE ONE-TWO-ONE, FOALY OVERRIDE.
D'ARVIT! TRAPPED IN MY OWN ROOM.
Haven't you got the message yet? Nothing works unless I say so. No communications out of this room. Nothing.
OPAL KOBOI.
Hello, Foaly. Long time no see.
OPAL. THINK ABOUT WHAT YOU'RE DOING. CUDGEON IS INSANE, FOR PITY'S SAKE. ONCE HE HAS WHAT HE WANTS, HE WILL DISPOSE OF YOU IN A HEARTBEAT!
You're wrong, Foaly. Briar needs me. He really does.
YOU STILL SORE BECAUSE I WON THE SCIENCE MEDAL BACK IN UNIVERSITY?
That medal was mine, you stupid centaur. My wing design was far superior to your ridiculous iris-cam. You won because you were male. And that's the only reason.
This is coming from the security cameras downtown...
While you were unconscious, there was a little change to the natural order of things.
"The B'wa Kell are waging open war with the LEP all over the city. And guess what? All LEP weapons seem to have stopped working.
"And you know what the very best thing is, Foaly? Briar is with the Council right now, making sure you get the blame for everything.
"Happy viewing."
FOTO FINISH

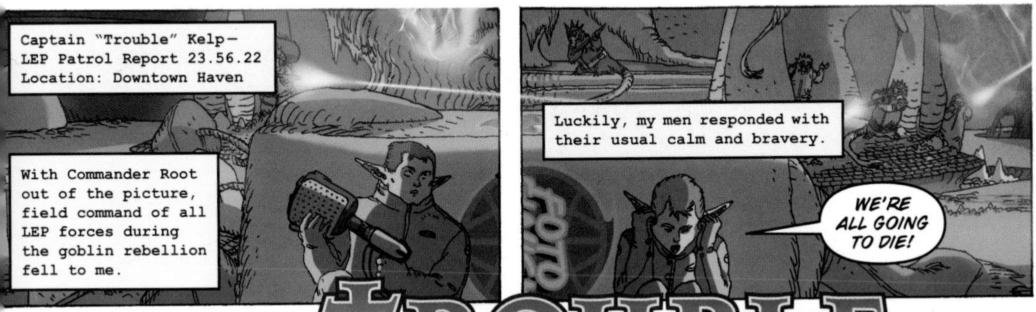
Captain "Trouble" Kelp—
LEP Patrol Report 23.56.22
Location: Downtown Haven
With Commander Root out of the picture, field command of all LEP forces during the goblin rebellion fell to me.
Luckily, my men responded with their usual calm and bravery.
WE'RE ALL GOING TO DIE!

CHAPTER 10: TROUBLE AND STRIFE

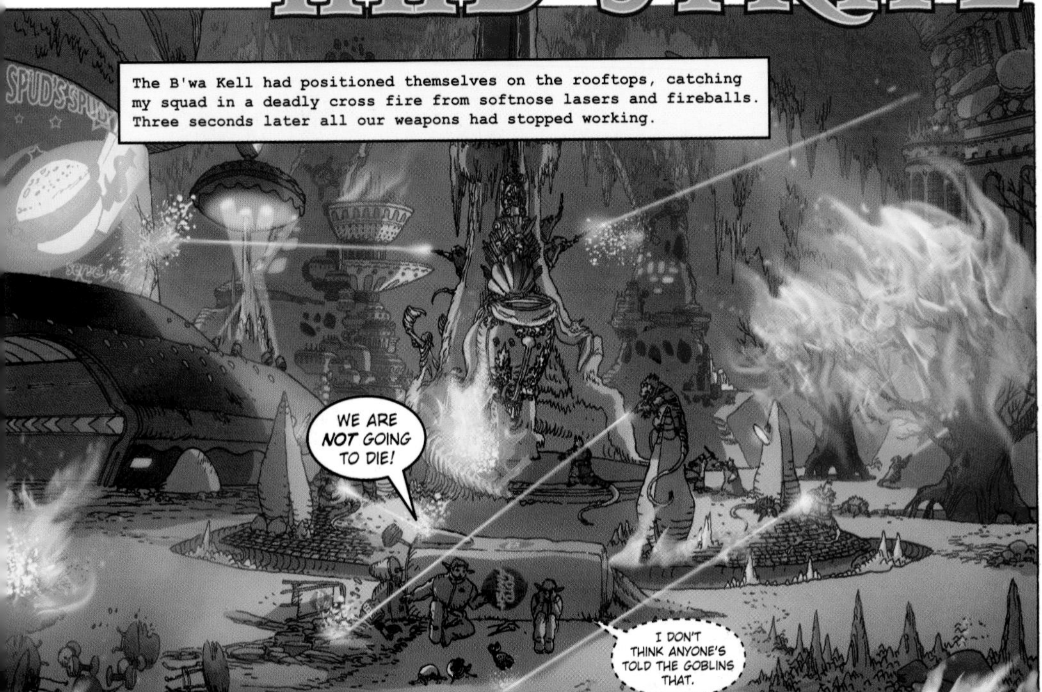
The B'wa Kell had positioned themselves on the rooftops, catching my squad in a deadly cross fire from softnose lasers and fireballs. Three seconds later all our weapons had stopped working.
WE ARE NOT GOING TO DIE!
I DON'T THINK ANYONE'S TOLD THE GOBLINS THAT.

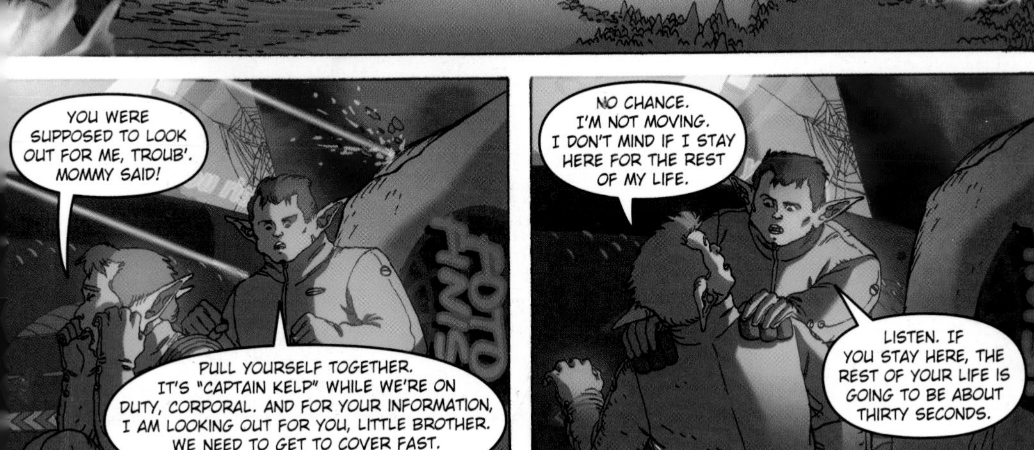
YOU WERE SUPPOSED TO LOOK OUT FOR ME, TROUB'. MOMMY SAID!
PULL YOURSELF TOGETHER. IT'S "CAPTAIN KELP" WHILE WE'RE ON DUTY, CORPORAL. AND FOR YOUR INFORMATION, I AM LOOKING OUT FOR YOU, LITTLE BROTHER. WE NEED TO GET TO COVER FAST.
NO CHANCE. I'M NOT MOVING. I DON'T MIND IF I STAY HERE FOR THE REST OF MY LIFE.
LISTEN. IF YOU STAY HERE, THE REST OF YOUR LIFE IS GOING TO BE ABOUT THIRTY SECONDS.

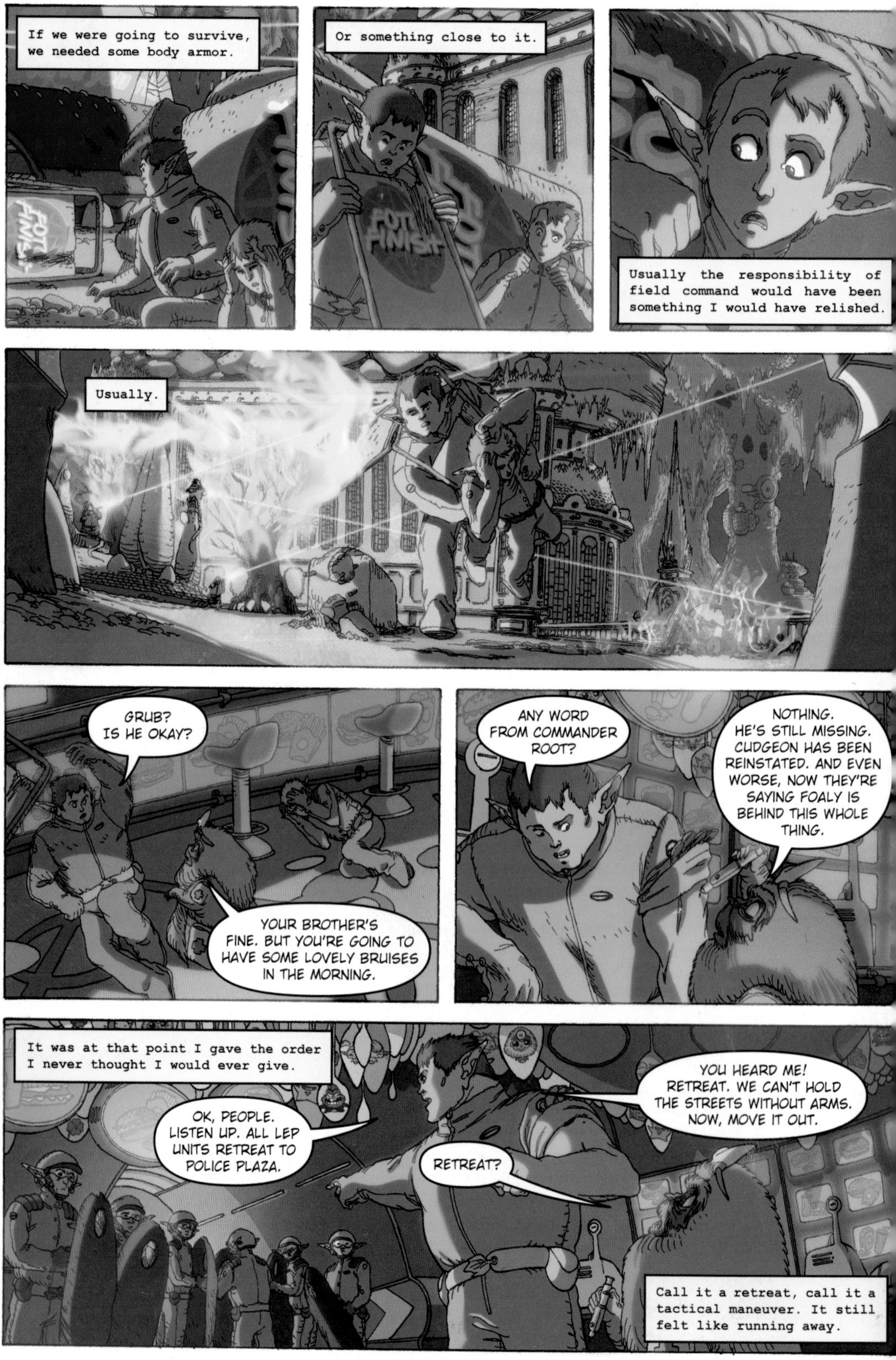

If we were going to survive, we needed some body armor.
FOT FINISH
Or something close to it.
FOT FINISH
Usually the responsibility of field command would have been something I would have relished.
Usually.
GRUB? IS HE OKAY?
YOUR BROTHER'S FINE. BUT YOU'RE GOING TO HAVE SOME LOVELY BRUISES IN THE MORNING.
ANY WORD FROM COMMANDER ROOT?
NOTHING. HE'S STILL MISSING. CUDGEON HAS BEEN REINSTATED. AND EVEN WORSE, NOW THEY'RE SAYING FOALY IS BEHIND THIS WHOLE THING.
It was at that point I gave the order I never thought I would ever give.
OK, PEOPLE. LISTEN UP. ALL LEP UNITS RETREAT TO POLICE PLAZA.
RETREAT?
YOU HEARD ME! RETREAT. WE CAN'T HOLD THE STREETS WITHOUT ARMS. NOW, MOVE IT OUT.
Call it a retreat, call it a tactical maneuver. It still felt like running away.

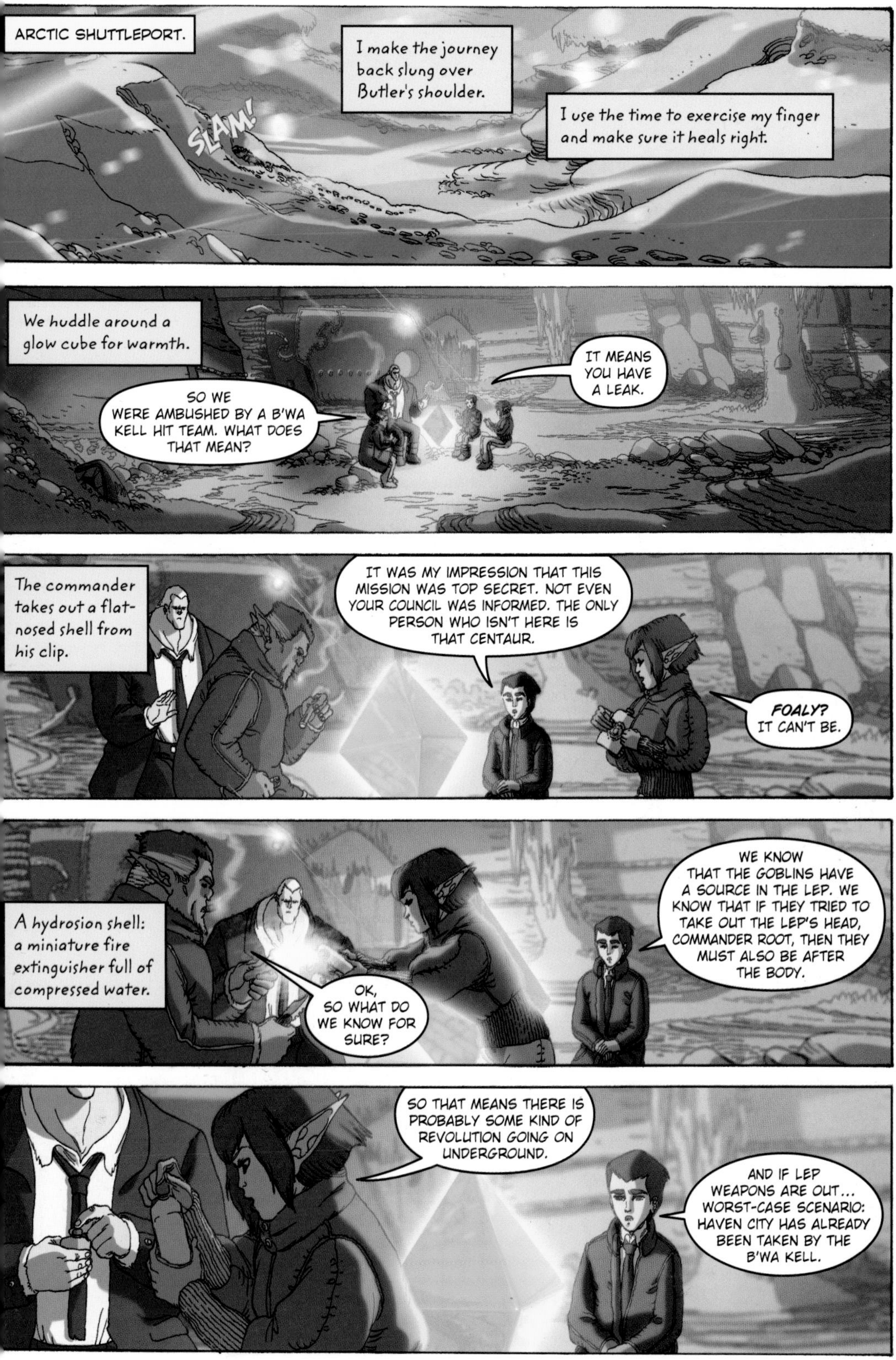
ARCTIC SHUTTLEPORT.
I make the journey back slung over Butler's shoulder.
SLAM!
I use the time to exercise my finger and make sure it heals right.
We huddle around a glow cube for warmth.
SO WE WERE AMBUSHED BY A B'WA KELL HIT TEAM. WHAT DOES THAT MEAN?
IT MEANS YOU HAVE A LEAK.
The commander takes out a flat-nosed shell from his clip.
IT WAS MY IMPRESSION THAT THIS MISSION WAS TOP SECRET. NOT EVEN YOUR COUNCIL WAS INFORMED. THE ONLY PERSON WHO ISN'T HERE IS THAT CENTAUR.
FOALY? IT CAN'T BE.
A hydrosion shell: a miniature fire extinguisher full of compressed water.
OK, SO WHAT DO WE KNOW FOR SURE?
WE KNOW THAT THE GOBLINS HAVE A SOURCE IN THE LEP. WE KNOW THAT IF THEY TRIED TO TAKE OUT THE LEP'S HEAD, COMMANDER ROOT, THEN THEY MUST ALSO BE AFTER THE BODY.
SO THAT MEANS THERE IS PROBABLY SOME KIND OF REVOLUTION GOING ON UNDERGROUND.
AND IF LEP WEAPONS ARE OUT... WORST-CASE SCENARIO: HAVEN CITY HAS ALREADY BEEN TAKEN BY THE B'WA KELL.

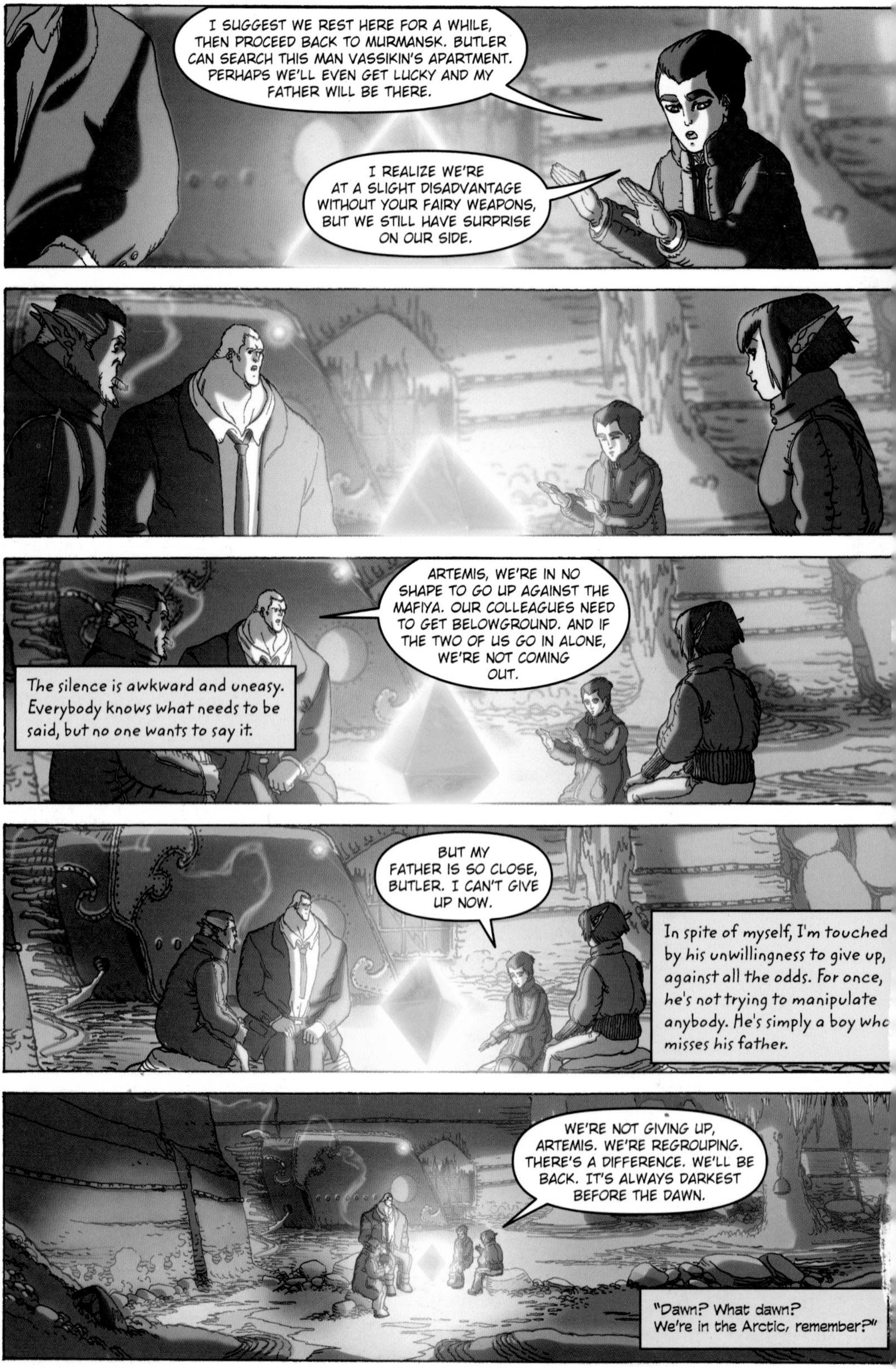
I SUGGEST WE REST HERE FOR A WHILE, THEN PROCEED BACK TO MURMANSK. BUTLER CAN SEARCH THIS MAN VASSIKIN'S APARTMENT. PERHAPS WE'LL EVEN GET LUCKY AND MY FATHER WILL BE THERE.
I REALIZE WE'RE AT A SLIGHT DISADVANTAGE WITHOUT YOUR FAIRY WEAPONS, BUT WE STILL HAVE SURPRISE ON OUR SIDE.
The silence is awkward and uneasy. Everybody knows what needs to be said, but no one wants to say it.
ARTEMIS, WE'RE IN NO SHAPE TO GO UP AGAINST THE MAFIYA. OUR COLLEAGUES NEED TO GET BELOWGROUND. AND IF THE TWO OF US GO IN ALONE, WE'RE NOT COMING OUT.
BUT MY FATHER IS SO CLOSE, BUTLER. I CAN'T GIVE UP NOW.
In spite of myself, I'm touched by his unwillingness to give up, against all the odds. For once, he's not trying to manipulate anybody. He's simply a boy who misses his father.
WE'RE NOT GIVING UP, ARTEMIS. WE'RE REGROUPING. THERE'S A DIFFERENCE. WE'LL BE BACK. IT'S ALWAYS DARKEST BEFORE THE DAWN.
"Dawn? What dawn? We're in the Arctic, remember?"

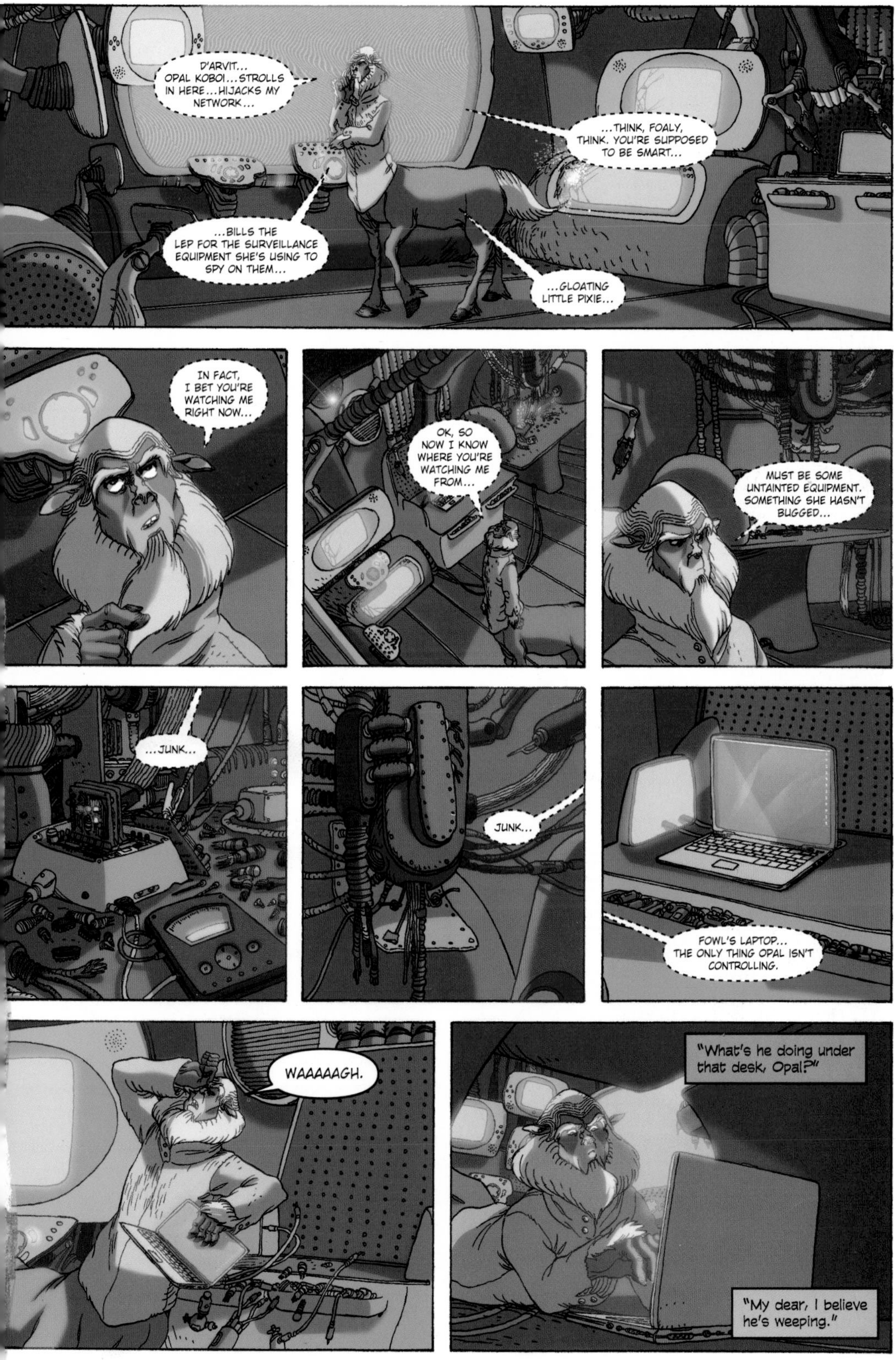
D'ARVIT... OPAL KOBOI...STROLLS IN HERE...HIJACKS MY NETWORK...
...BILLS THE LEP FOR THE SURVEILLANCE EQUIPMENT SHE'S USING TO SPY ON THEM...
...THINK, FOALY, THINK. YOU'RE SUPPOSED TO BE SMART...
...GLOATING LITTLE PIXIE...
IN FACT, I BET YOU'RE WATCHING ME RIGHT NOW...
OK, SO NOW I KNOW WHERE YOU'RE WATCHING ME FROM...
MUST BE SOME UNTAINTED EQUIPMENT. SOMETHING SHE HASN'T BUGGED...
...JUNK...
JUNK...
FOWL'S LAPTOP... THE ONLY THING OPAL ISN'T CONTROLLING.
WAAAAAGH.
"What's he doing under that desk, Opal?"
"My dear, I believe he's weeping."

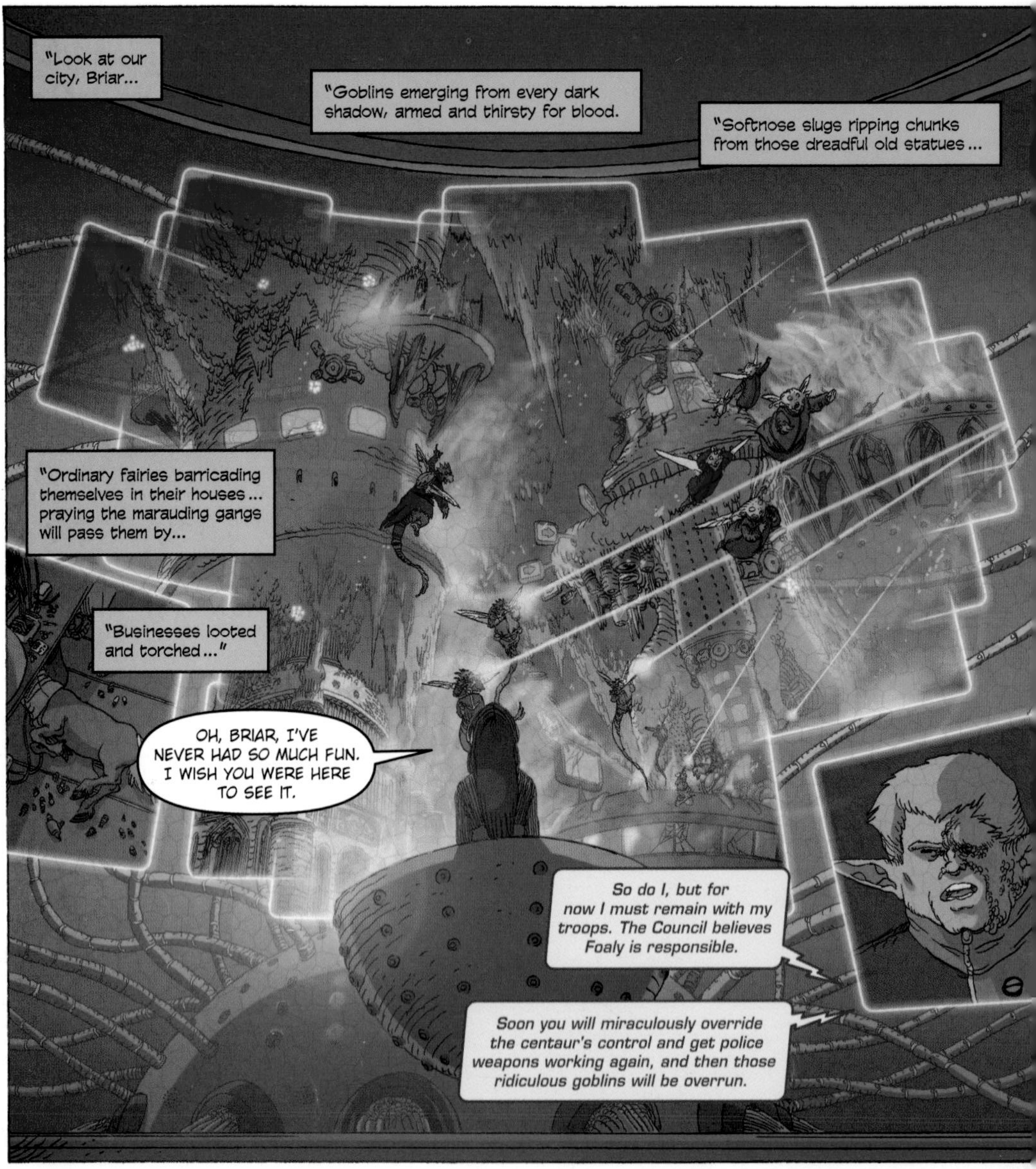
"Look at our city, Briar...
"Goblins emerging from every dark shadow, armed and thirsty for blood.
"Softnose slugs ripping chunks from those dreadful old statues...
"Ordinary fairies barricading themselves in their houses... praying the marauding gangs will pass them by...
"Businesses looted and torched..."
OH, BRIAR, I'VE NEVER HAD SO MUCH FUN. I WISH YOU WERE HERE TO SEE IT.
So do I, but for now I must remain with my troops. The Council believes Foaly is responsible.
Soon you will miraculously override the centaur's control and get police weapons working again, and then those ridiculous goblins will be overrun.

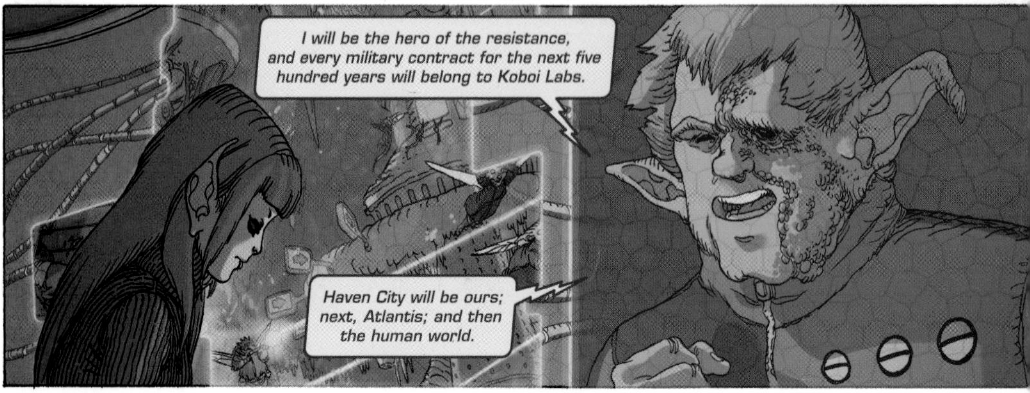
I will be the hero of the resistance, and every military contract for the next five hundred years will belong to Koboi Labs.
Haven City will be ours; next, Atlantis; and then the human world.

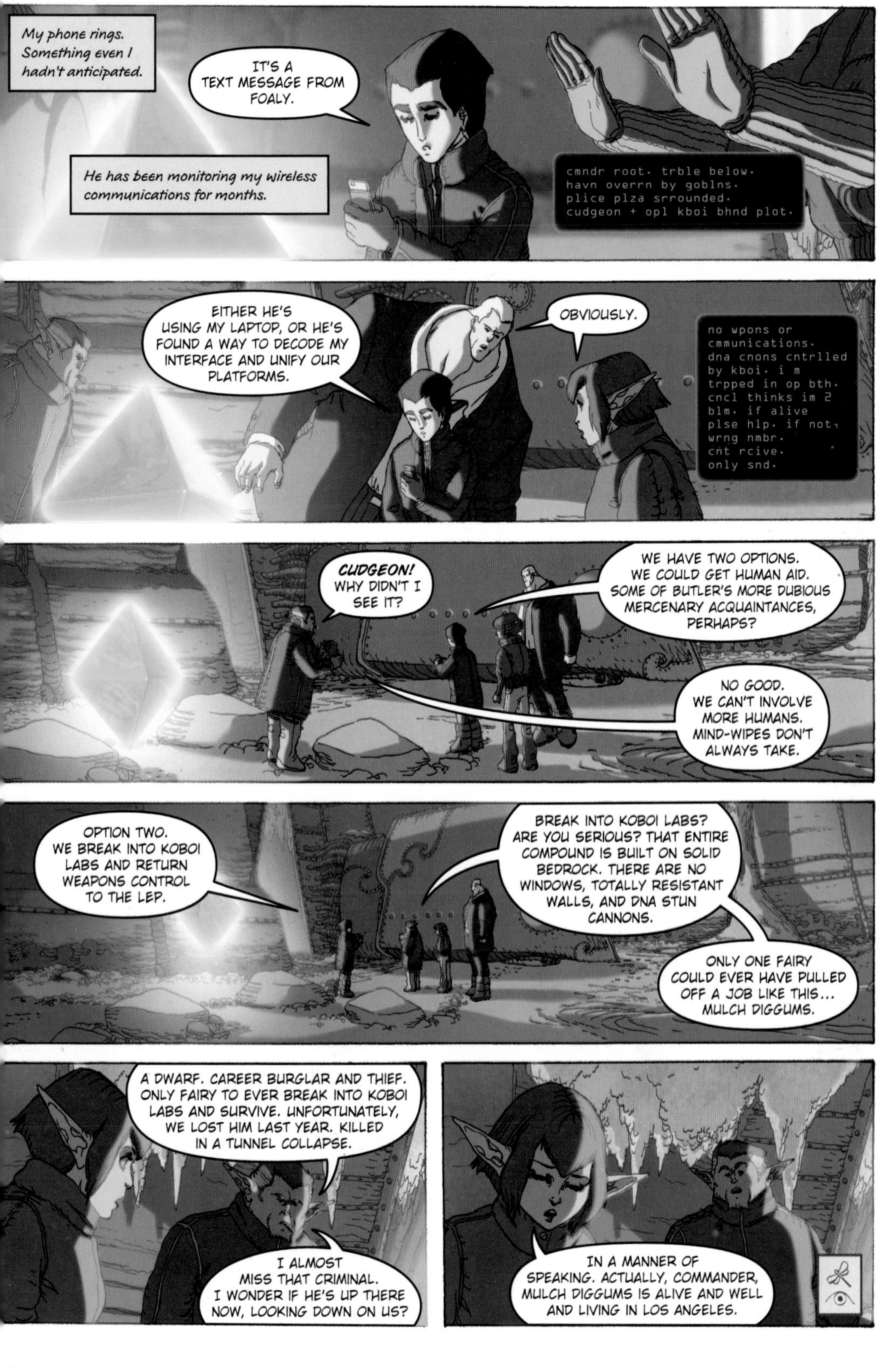

My phone rings. Something even I hadn't anticipated.
IT'S A TEXT MESSAGE FROM FOALY.
He has been monitoring my wireless communications for months.
cmndr root. trble below. havn overrn by goblns. plice plza srrounded. cudgeon + opl kboi bhnd plot.
EITHER HE'S USING MY LAPTOP, OR HE'S FOUND A WAY TO DECODE MY INTERFACE AND UNIFY OUR PLATFORMS.
OBVIOUSLY.
no wpons or cmmunications. dna cnons cntrlled by kboi. i m trpped in op bth. cncl thinks im 2 blm. if alive plse hlp. if not, wrng nmbr. cnt rcive. only snd.
CUDGEON! WHY DIDN'T I SEE IT?
WE HAVE TWO OPTIONS. WE COULD GET HUMAN AID. SOME OF BUTLER'S MORE DUBIOUS MERCENARY ACQUAINTANCES, PERHAPS?
NO GOOD. WE CAN'T INVOLVE MORE HUMANS. MIND-WIPES DON'T ALWAYS TAKE.
OPTION TWO. WE BREAK INTO KOBOI LABS AND RETURN WEAPONS CONTROL TO THE LEP.
BREAK INTO KOBOI LABS? ARE YOU SERIOUS? THAT ENTIRE COMPOUND IS BUILT ON SOLID BEDROCK. THERE ARE NO WINDOWS, TOTALLY RESISTANT WALLS, AND DNA STUN CANNONS.
ONLY ONE FAIRY COULD EVER HAVE PULLED OFF A JOB LIKE THIS... MULCH DIGGUMS.
A DWARF. CAREER BURGLAR AND THIEF. ONLY FAIRY TO EVER BREAK INTO KOBOI LABS AND SURVIVE. UNFORTUNATELY, WE LOST HIM LAST YEAR. KILLED IN A TUNNEL COLLAPSE.
I ALMOST MISS THAT CRIMINAL. I WONDER IF HE'S UP THERE NOW, LOOKING DOWN ON US?
IN A MANNER OF SPEAKING. ACTUALLY, COMMANDER, MULCH DIGGUMS IS ALIVE AND WELL AND LIVING IN LOS ANGELES.

MULCH DIGGUMS

DOCUMENT RECOVERED FROM THE PENTHOUSE SUITE OF THE CROWLEY HOTEL IN LOS ANGELES FOLLOWING THE SUDDEN DISAPPEARANCE OF ITS OCCUPANT, MR. LANCE DIGGER.

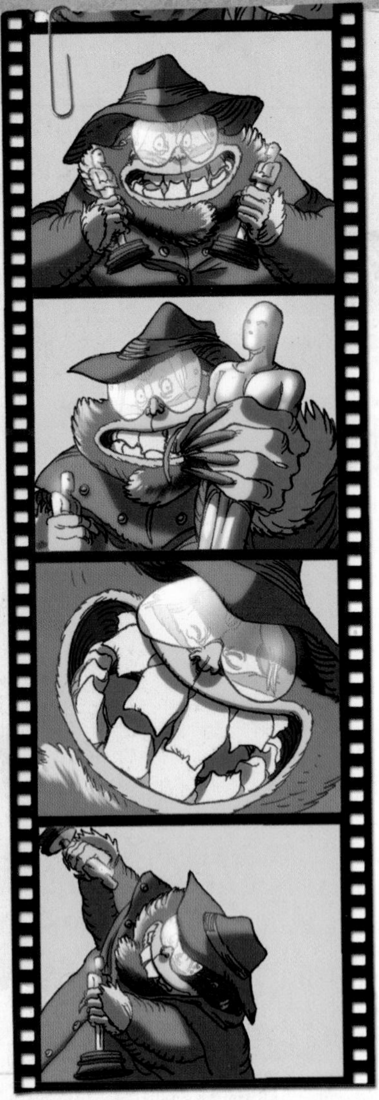

THE DWARF WHO WALKED TALL
A FILM TREATMENT
BY
MULCH DIGGUMS

ESTIMATED BUDGET: approx $350 million.

NOTE: Not only is this screenplay entirely autobiographical, but it is also based on my own life story.

SYNOPSIS:
The hero of our film is Mulch Diggums to be played by new Hollywood heartthrob, Mulch Diggums. Mulch is a handsome, debonair, sophisticated, master thief who suffers from a bit of windiness down below. Mulch lives by a simple moral code: he robs the rich to give to those less fortunate, i.e. himself. Returning home from a harmless and entirely innocent midnight jaunt suddenly in possession of the crown jewels of England, Mulch finds himself

OSCAR LIST

~~FILM~~
~~DIRECTOR~~
~~ACT~~OR
ACTRESS
~~SCREENPLAY~~
~~ADAPTED SCREENPLAY~~
~~BEST FOREIGN LANGUAGE F~~
~~MUSICAL SCORE~~
~~SPECIAL EFFECTS~~

SHOPPING LIST:
To catch a Thief (DVD)
catch me if you can (DVD)
Gone with the wind (DVD)
Beef jerky (Lots)
Nice friendly cat
(In case still peckish)

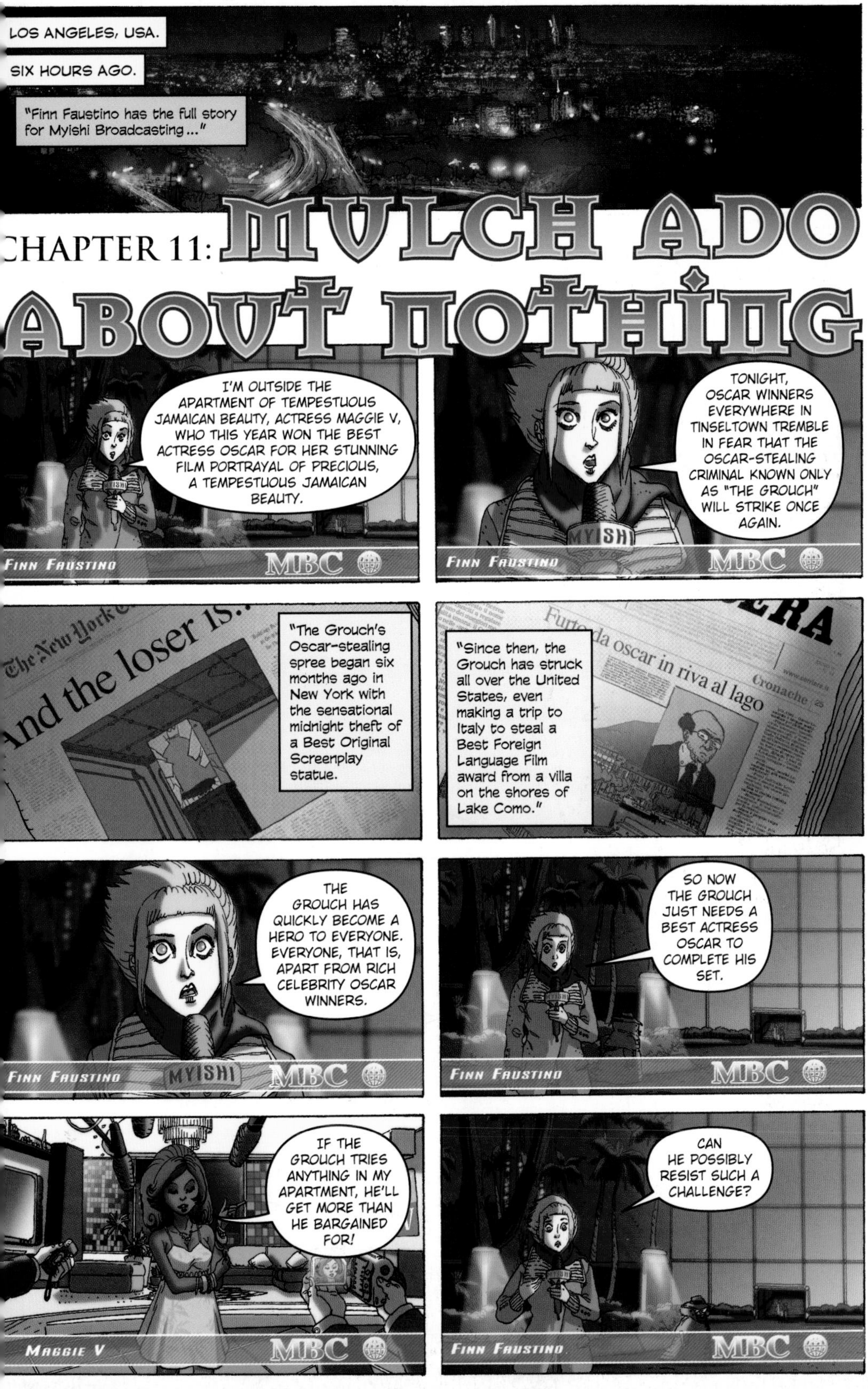

LOS ANGELES, USA.
SIX HOURS AGO.
"Finn Faustino has the full story for Myishi Broadcasting..."
CHAPTER 11: MULCH ADO ABOUT NOTHING
I'M OUTSIDE THE APARTMENT OF TEMPESTUOUS JAMAICAN BEAUTY, ACTRESS MAGGIE V, WHO THIS YEAR WON THE BEST ACTRESS OSCAR FOR HER STUNNING FILM PORTRAYAL OF PRECIOUS, A TEMPESTUOUS JAMAICAN BEAUTY.
FINN FAUSTINO
MBC
TONIGHT, OSCAR WINNERS EVERYWHERE IN TINSELTOWN TREMBLE IN FEAR THAT THE OSCAR-STEALING CRIMINAL KNOWN ONLY AS "THE GROUCH" WILL STRIKE ONCE AGAIN.
MYISHI
FINN FAUSTINO
MBC
And the loser is...
"The Grouch's Oscar-stealing spree began six months ago in New York with the sensational midnight theft of a Best Original Screenplay statue.
"Since then, the Grouch has struck all over the United States, even making a trip to Italy to steal a Best Foreign Language Film award from a villa on the shores of Lake Como."
Furto da oscar in riva al lago
Cronache
THE GROUCH HAS QUICKLY BECOME A HERO TO EVERYONE. EVERYONE, THAT IS, APART FROM RICH CELEBRITY OSCAR WINNERS.
FINN FAUSTINO
MYISHI
MBC
SO NOW THE GROUCH JUST NEEDS A BEST ACTRESS OSCAR TO COMPLETE HIS SET.
FINN FAUSTINO
MBC
IF THE GROUCH TRIES ANYTHING IN MY APARTMENT, HE'LL GET MORE THAN HE BARGAINED FOR!
MAGGIE V
MBC
CAN HE POSSIBLY RESIST SUCH A CHALLENGE?
FINN FAUSTINO
MBC

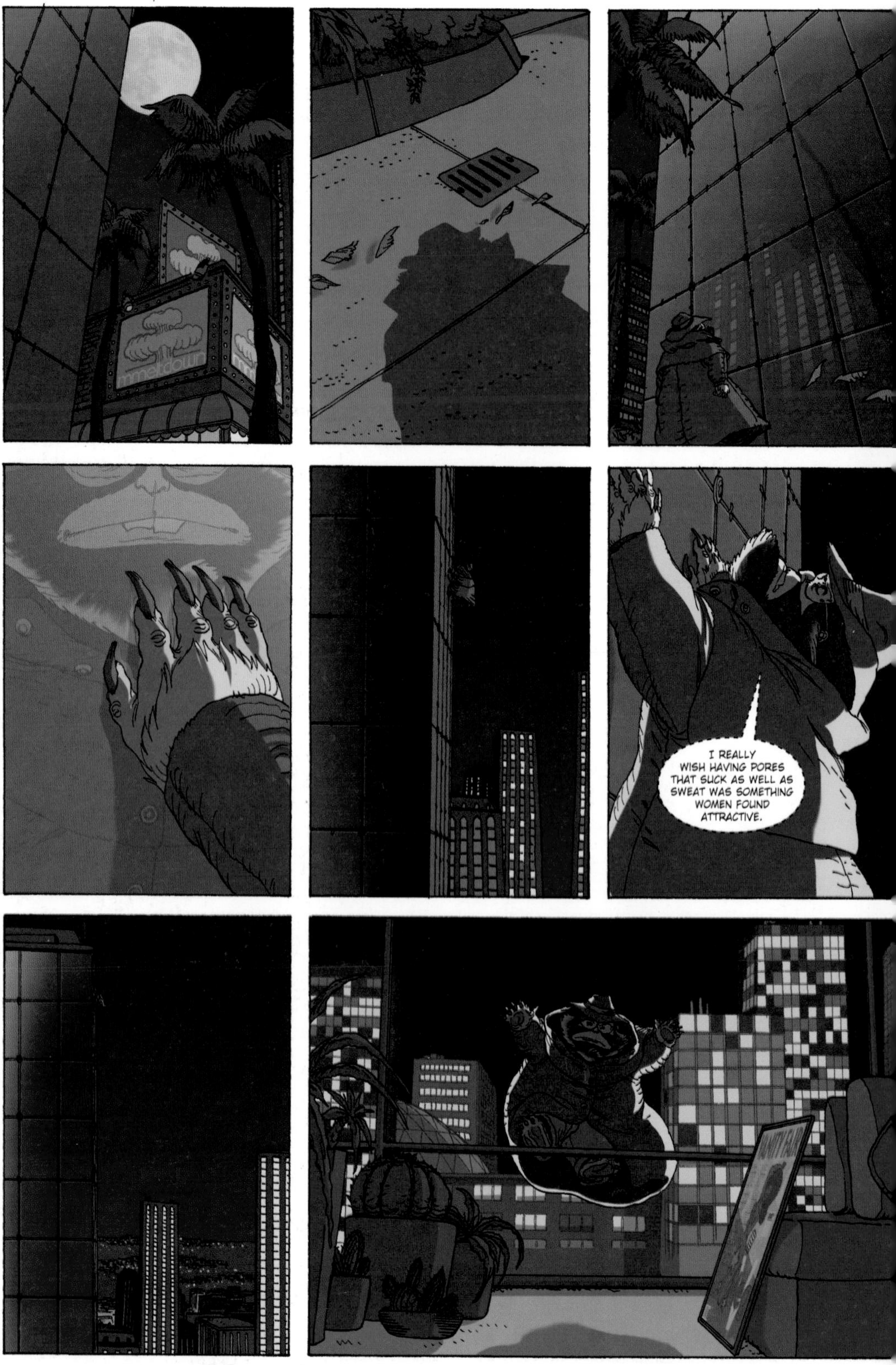
I REALLY WISH HAVING PORES THAT SUCK AS WELL AS SWEAT WAS SOMETHING WOMEN FOUND ATTRACTIVE.

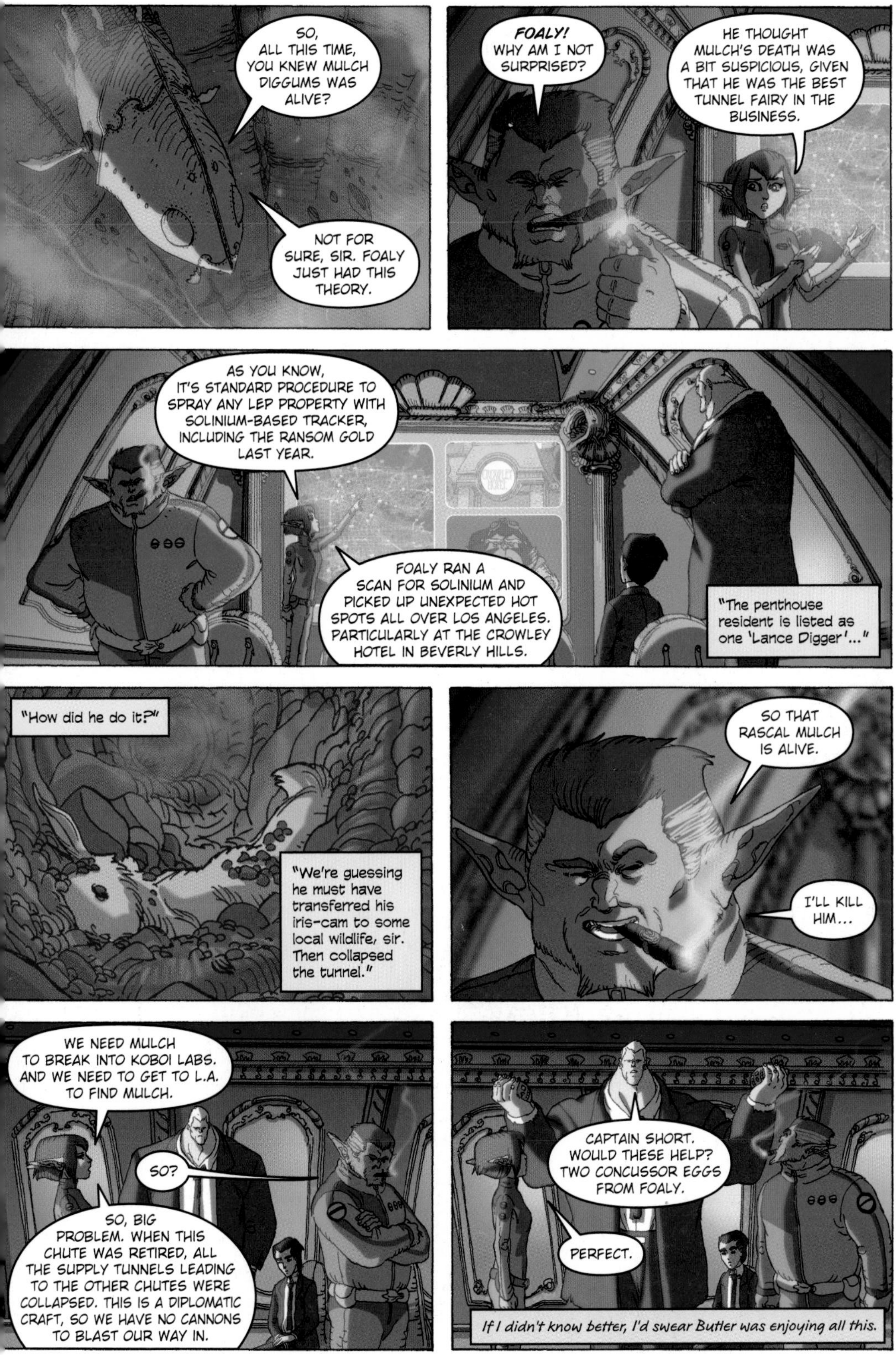
SO, ALL THIS TIME, YOU KNEW MULCH DIGGUMS WAS ALIVE?
NOT FOR SURE, SIR. FOALY JUST HAD THIS THEORY.
FOALY! WHY AM I NOT SURPRISED?
HE THOUGHT MULCH'S DEATH WAS A BIT SUSPICIOUS, GIVEN THAT HE WAS THE BEST TUNNEL FAIRY IN THE BUSINESS.
AS YOU KNOW, IT'S STANDARD PROCEDURE TO SPRAY ANY LEP PROPERTY WITH SOLINIUM-BASED TRACKER, INCLUDING THE RANSOM GOLD LAST YEAR.
FOALY RAN A SCAN FOR SOLINIUM AND PICKED UP UNEXPECTED HOT SPOTS ALL OVER LOS ANGELES. PARTICULARLY AT THE CROWLEY HOTEL IN BEVERLY HILLS.
"The penthouse resident is listed as one 'Lance Digger'..."
"How did he do it?"
"We're guessing he must have transferred his iris-cam to some local wildlife, sir. Then collapsed the tunnel."
SO THAT RASCAL MULCH IS ALIVE.
I'LL KILL HIM...
WE NEED MULCH TO BREAK INTO KOBOI LABS. AND WE NEED TO GET TO L.A. TO FIND MULCH.
SO?
SO, BIG PROBLEM. WHEN THIS CHUTE WAS RETIRED, ALL THE SUPPLY TUNNELS LEADING TO THE OTHER CHUTES WERE COLLAPSED. THIS IS A DIPLOMATIC CRAFT, SO WE HAVE NO CANNONS TO BLAST OUR WAY IN.
CAPTAIN SHORT. WOULD THESE HELP? TWO CONCUSSOR EGGS FROM FOALY.
PERFECT.
If I didn't know better, I'd swear Butler was enjoying all this.

LOS ANGELES, USA. FIVE HOURS, FIFTY MINUTES AGO.

DWARF ROCK POLISH... NO HUMAN GLASS CAN WITHSTAND IT.

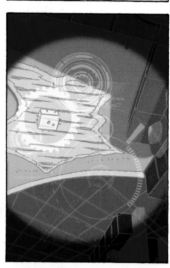

CLICK

WOOOOOOOOOOOO!

UH-OH. MULCH, YOU IDIOT!

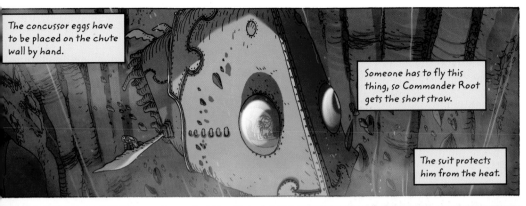

The concussor eggs have to be placed on the chute wall by hand.

Someone has to fly this thing, so Commander Root gets the short straw.

The suit protects him from the heat.

In theory.

MY FINGERS ARE TIGHTENING AROUND MULCH DIGGUMS'S THROAT... MY FINGERS ARE TIGHTENING AROUND MULCH DIGGUMS'S THROAT...

It isn't the five-meter swing on a piton cord that's the problem. It's the lack of handholds on the wall and the bone-crushing drop if you miss.

The commander fires his piton dart to swing back to the shuttle ... and misses.

The commander unhooks the piton dart from his belt and lets it fall.

He reaches for his spare line, and at the same moment we both realize he used it in Russia.

He's trapped.

I KNOW HOW TO SAVE YOU, BUT YOU'RE NOT GOING TO LIKE IT.

"Tell me. That's an order."

I tell him.

He doesn't like it.

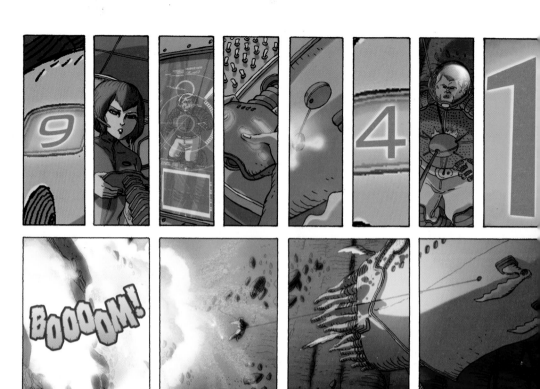

The commander is in the shuttle's sick bay in less than a minute.

WHAT THE HELL WERE YOU THINKING? I COULD HAVE BEEN KILLED.

FIVE MORE SECONDS AND YOU WOULD HAVE BEEN. IT'S THANKS TO HOLLY YOU'RE STILL ALIVE.

HOLLY... PLEASE...

HEAL.

The commander's eyes roll back and the magic shuts him down for recuperation.

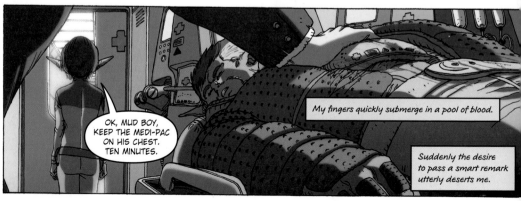

OK, MUD BOY, KEEP THE MEDI-PAC ON HIS CHEST. TEN MINUTES.

My fingers quickly submerge in a pool of blood.

Suddenly the desire to pass a smart remark utterly deserts me.

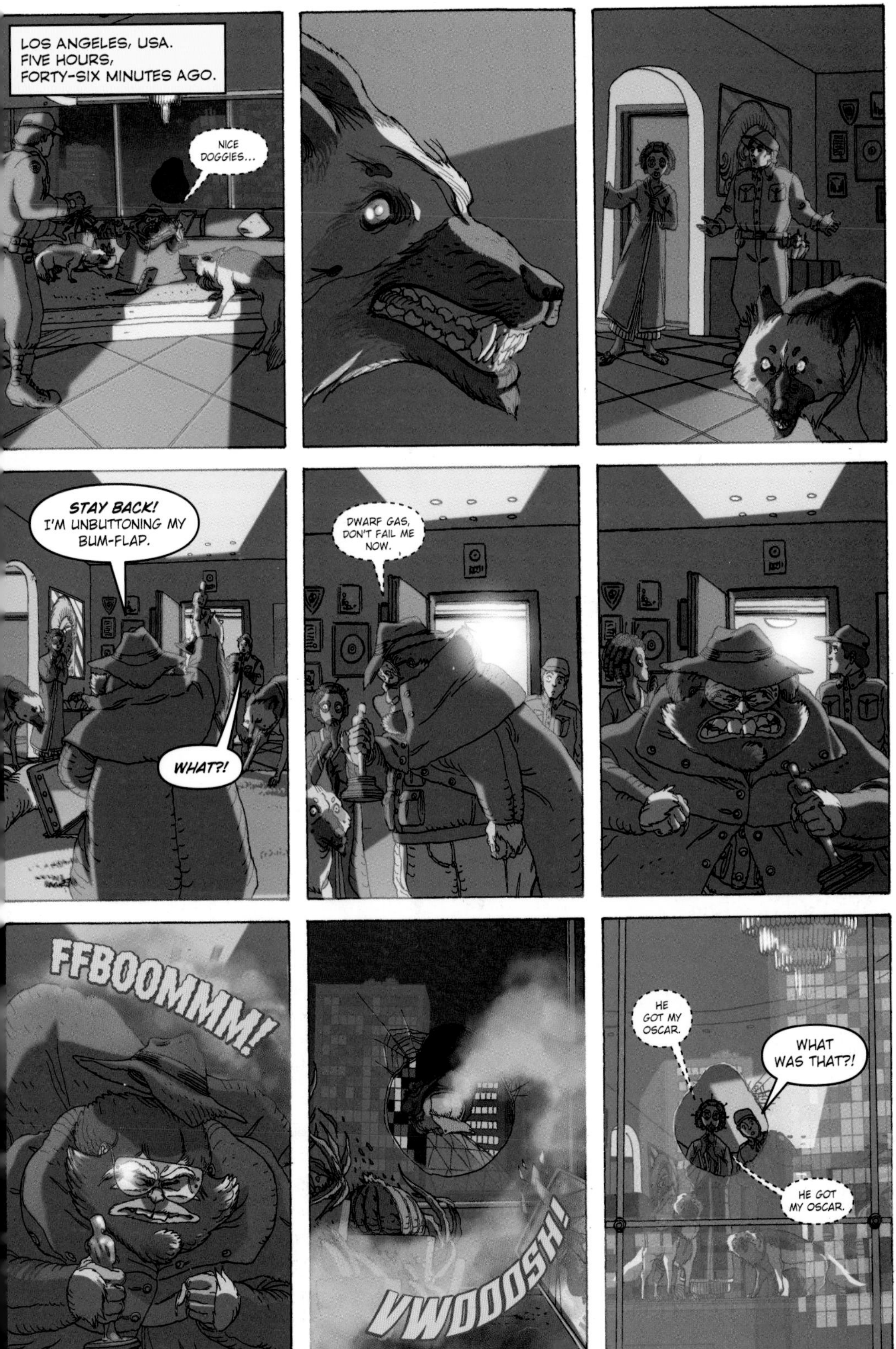
LOS ANGELES, USA.
FIVE HOURS,
FORTY-SIX MINUTES AGO.
NICE DOGGIES...
STAY BACK! I'M UNBUTTONING MY BUM-FLAP.
WHAT?!
DWARF GAS, DON'T FAIL ME NOW.
FFBOOMMMM!
VWOOOSH!
HE GOT MY OSCAR.
WHAT WAS THAT?!
HE GOT MY OSCAR.

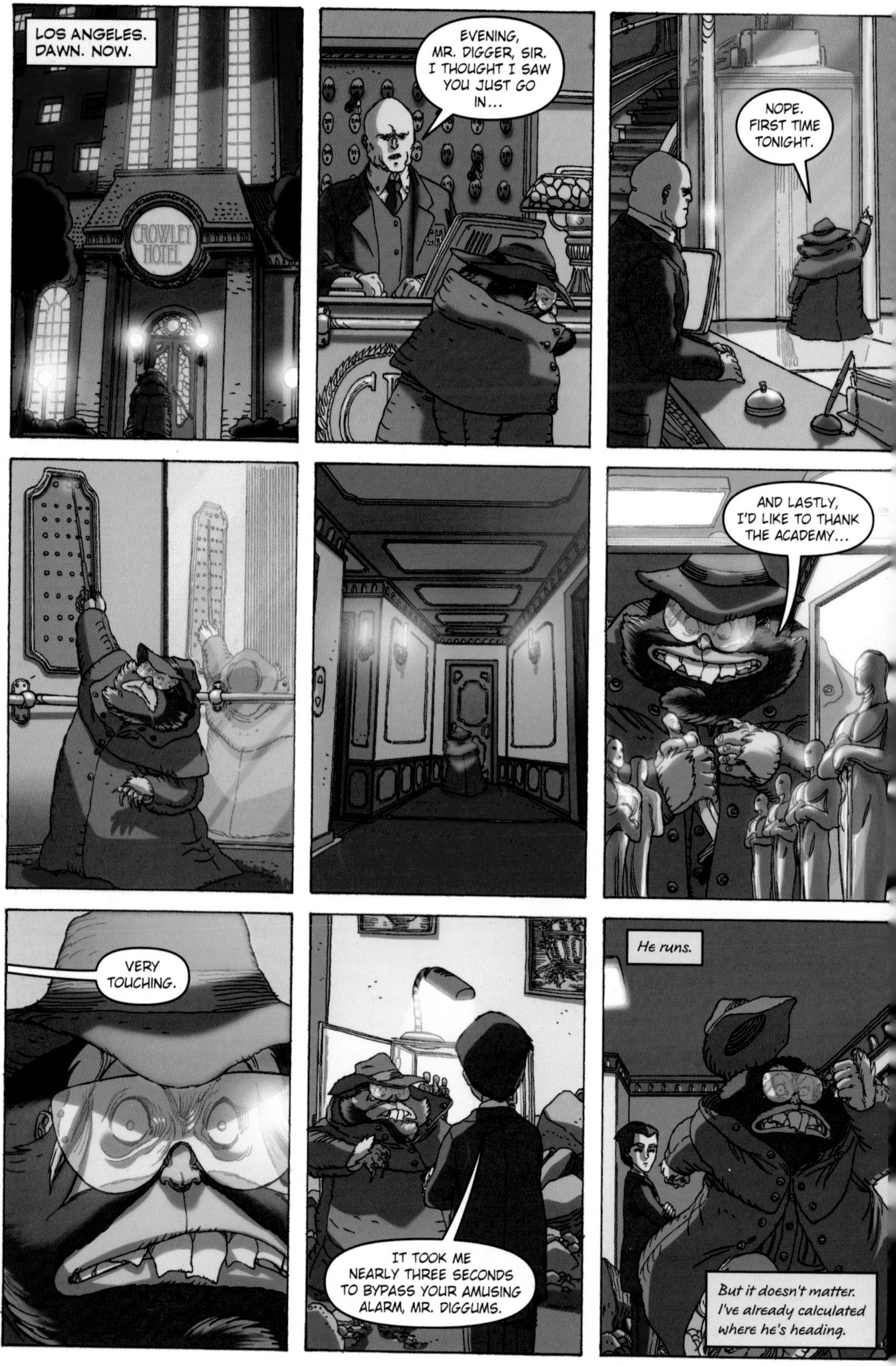
LOS ANGELES. DAWN. NOW.
CROWLEY HOTEL
EVENING, MR. DIGGER, SIR. I THOUGHT I SAW YOU JUST GO IN...
NOPE. FIRST TIME TONIGHT.
AND LASTLY, I'D LIKE TO THANK THE ACADEMY...
VERY TOUCHING.
IT TOOK ME NEARLY THREE SECONDS TO BYPASS YOUR AMUSING ALARM, MR. DIGGUMS.
He runs.
But it doesn't matter. I've already calculated where he's heading.

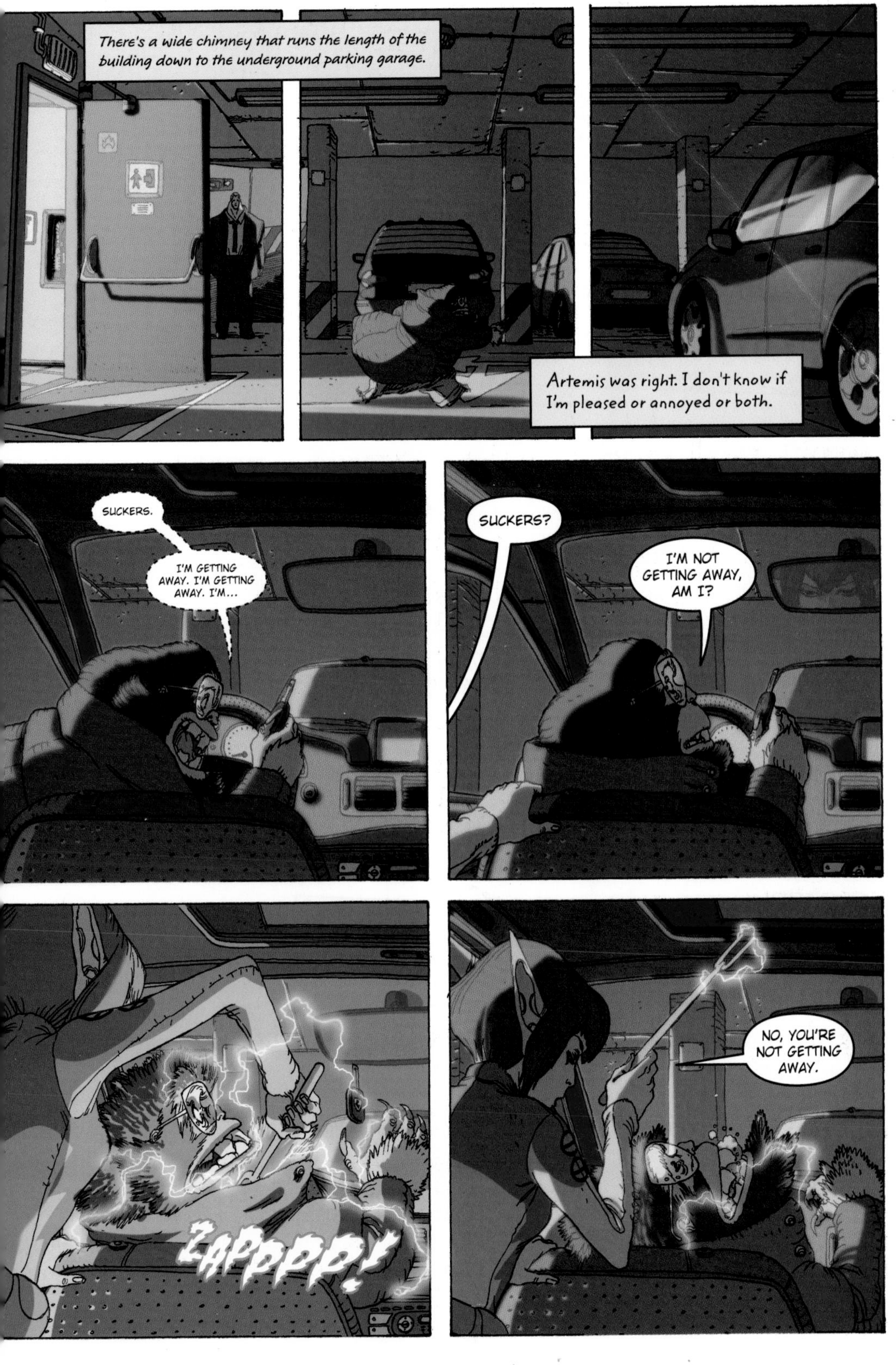
There's a wide chimney that runs the length of the building down to the underground parking garage.
Artemis was right. I don't know if I'm pleased or annoyed or both.
SUCKERS.
I'M GETTING AWAY. I'M GETTING AWAY. I'M...
SUCKERS?
I'M NOT GETTING AWAY, AM I?
ZAPPPP!
NO, YOU'RE NOT GETTING AWAY.

CHUTE E116, HIDDEN SIXTEEN MILES SOUTH OF LOS ANGELES.

"Well, well, if it isn't my favorite reprobate, back from the dead."

HOW COME YOU NEVER PAY ME A SOCIAL VISIT, JULIUS? AFTER ALL, I DID SAVE YOUR CAREER BACK IN IRELAND.

WE HAD A DEAL, CONVICT. YOU BROKE IT BY FAKING YOUR OWN DEATH AND ESCAPING. NOW I'M BRINGING YOU IN.

I AM BESIDE MYSELF WITH FEAR. UMM... YOU KNOW THIS SQUID PATÉ COULD USE A LITTLE BEETLE JUICE.

LISTEN TO ME, CONVICT. I DID NOT COME ALL THIS WAY TO FEED YOUR STOMACH.

JUST OUT OF INTEREST, JULIUS, WHY *HAVE* YOU TRAVELED ALL THIS WAY? THE GREAT COMMANDER ROOT COMMANDEERING AN AMBASSADOR'S SHUTTLE AND WORKING WITH MUD MEN JUST TO APPREHEND LITTLE OLD ME? I DON'T THINK SO.

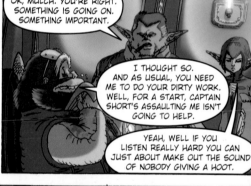

OK, MULCH. YOU'RE RIGHT. SOMETHING IS GOING ON. SOMETHING IMPORTANT.

I THOUGHT SO. AND AS USUAL, YOU NEED ME TO DO YOUR DIRTY WORK. WELL, FOR A START, CAPTAIN SHORT'S ASSAULTING ME ISN'T GOING TO HELP.

YEAH, WELL IF YOU LISTEN REALLY HARD YOU CAN JUST ABOUT MAKE OUT THE SOUND OF NOBODY GIVING A HOOT.

MAY I REMIND YOU THAT WHILE YOU'RE EXCHANGING WITTICISMS, MY FATHER IS FREEZING SOMEWHERE IN THE ARCTIC.

THE ARCTIC? DWARFS HATE ICE. YOU WANT ME TO RESCUE ARTEMIS FOWL'S FATHER FROM THE ARCTIC?

I WISH IT WERE THAT SIMPLE. AND IN A FEW MINUTES SO WILL YOU.

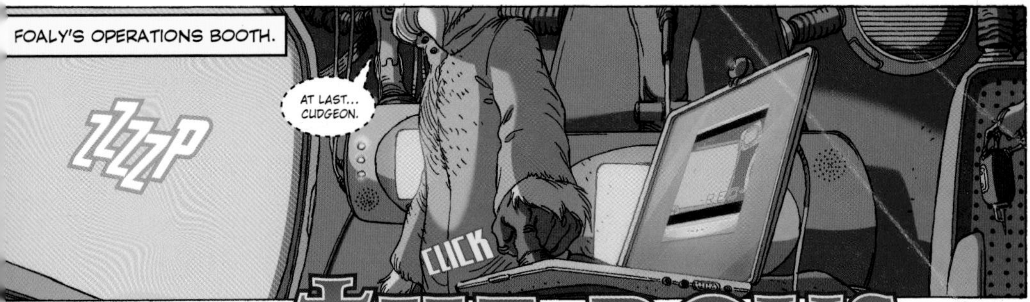
FOALY'S OPERATIONS BOOTH.
ZZZZP
AT LAST... CUDGEON.
CLICK

CHAPTER 12: THE BOYS ARE BACK

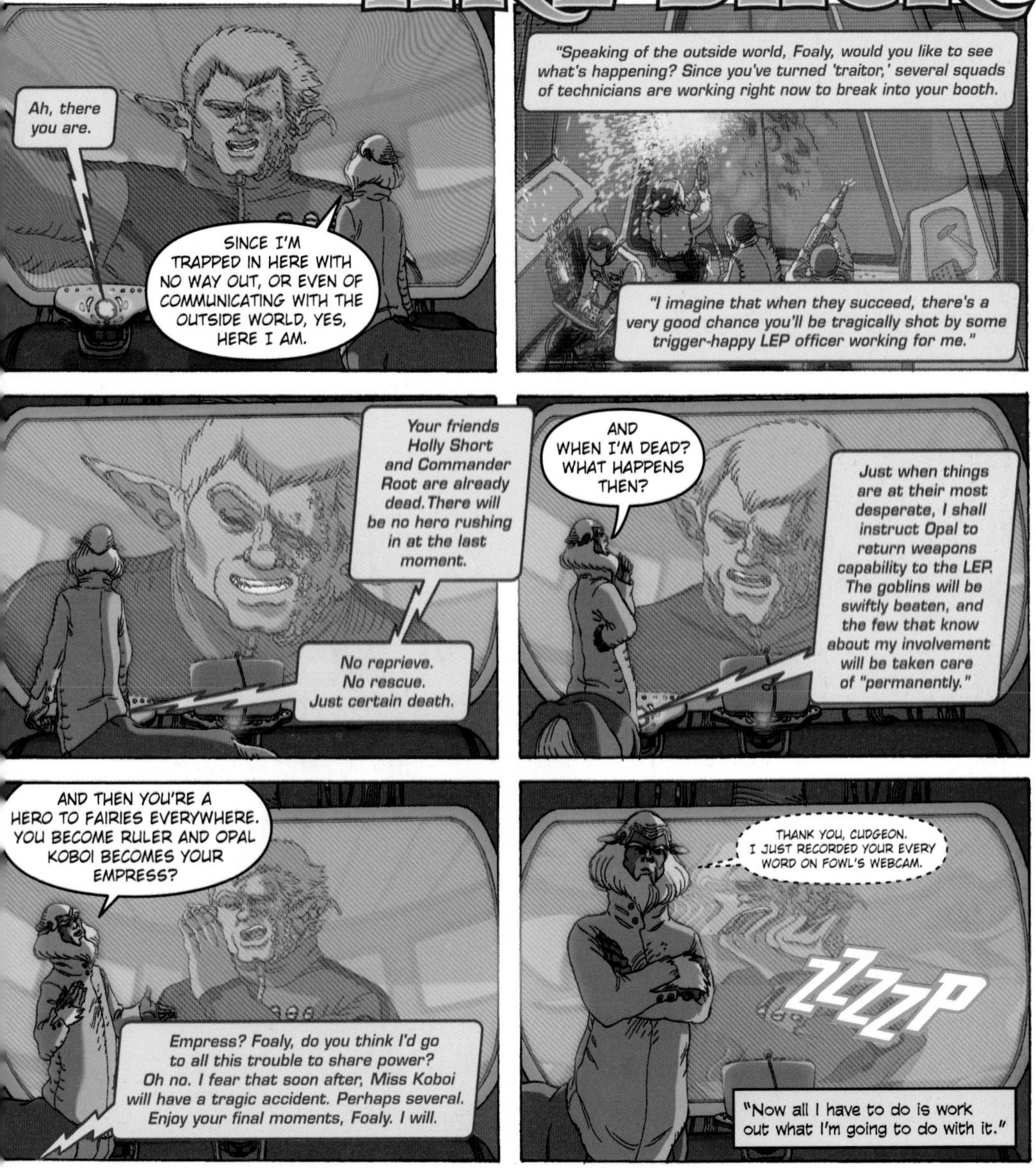
Ah, there you are.
SINCE I'M TRAPPED IN HERE WITH NO WAY OUT, OR EVEN OF COMMUNICATING WITH THE OUTSIDE WORLD, YES, HERE I AM.
"Speaking of the outside world, Foaly, would you like to see what's happening? Since you've turned 'traitor,' several squads of technicians are working right now to break into your booth.
"I imagine that when they succeed, there's a very good chance you'll be tragically shot by some trigger-happy LEP officer working for me."
Your friends Holly Short and Commander Root are already dead. There will be no hero rushing in at the last moment.
No reprieve. No rescue. Just certain death.
AND WHEN I'M DEAD? WHAT HAPPENS THEN?
Just when things are at their most desperate, I shall instruct Opal to return weapons capability to the LEP. The goblins will be swiftly beaten, and the few that know about my involvement will be taken care of "permanently."
AND THEN YOU'RE A HERO TO FAIRIES EVERYWHERE. YOU BECOME RULER AND OPAL KOBOI BECOMES YOUR EMPRESS?
Empress? Foaly, do you think I'd go to all this trouble to share power? Oh no. I fear that soon after, Miss Koboi will have a tragic accident. Perhaps several. Enjoy your final moments, Foaly. I will.
THANK YOU, CUDGEON. I JUST RECORDED YOUR EVERY WORD ON FOWL'S WEBCAM.
ZZZZP
"Now all I have to do is work out what I'm going to do with it."

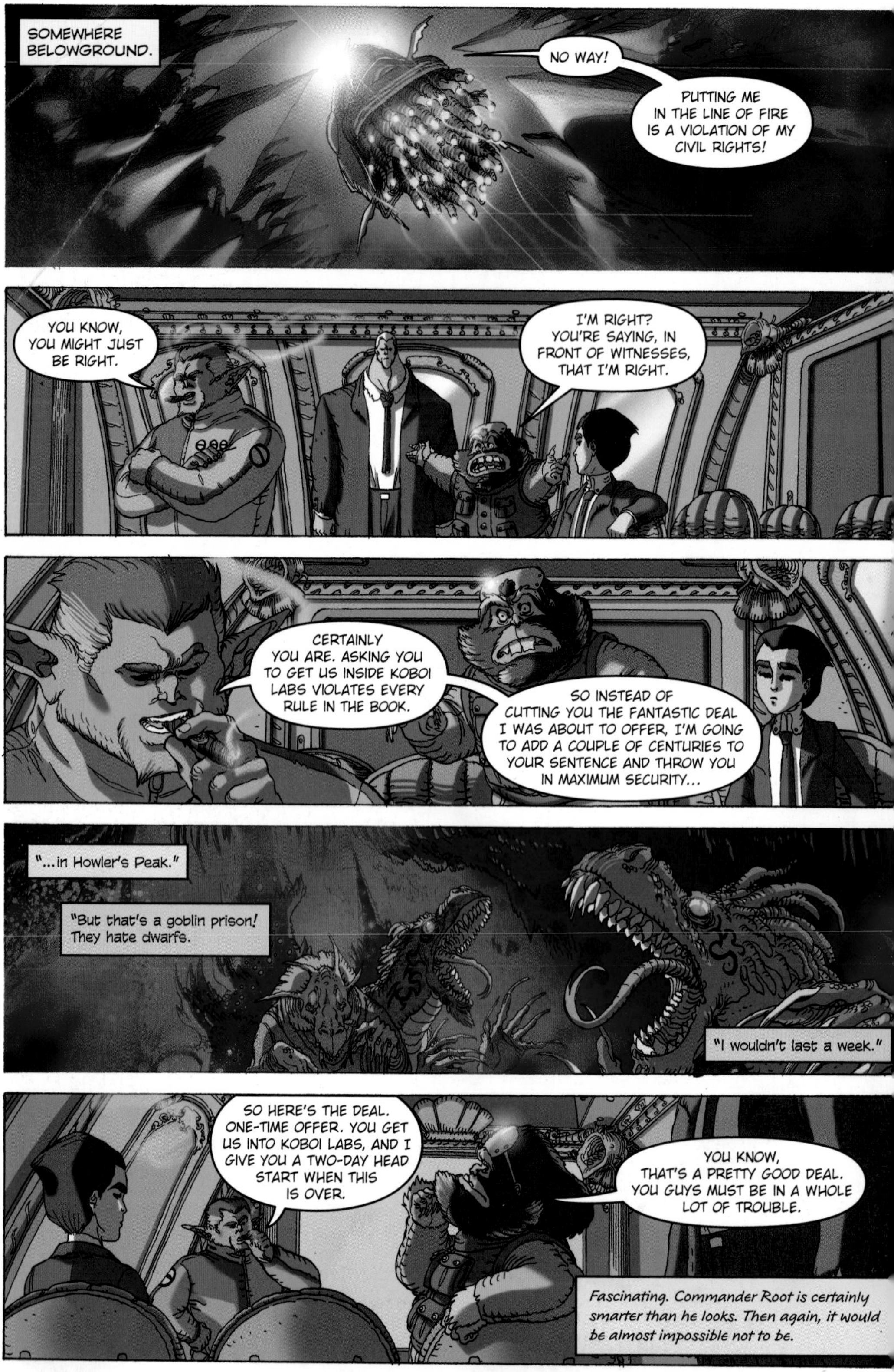
SOMEWHERE BELOWGROUND.
NO WAY!
PUTTING ME IN THE LINE OF FIRE IS A VIOLATION OF MY CIVIL RIGHTS!
YOU KNOW, YOU MIGHT JUST BE RIGHT.
I'M RIGHT? YOU'RE SAYING, IN FRONT OF WITNESSES, THAT I'M RIGHT.
CERTAINLY YOU ARE. ASKING YOU TO GET US INSIDE KOBOI LABS VIOLATES EVERY RULE IN THE BOOK.
SO INSTEAD OF CUTTING YOU THE FANTASTIC DEAL I WAS ABOUT TO OFFER, I'M GOING TO ADD A COUPLE OF CENTURIES TO YOUR SENTENCE AND THROW YOU IN MAXIMUM SECURITY...
"...in Howler's Peak."
"But that's a goblin prison! They hate dwarfs.
"I wouldn't last a week."
SO HERE'S THE DEAL. ONE-TIME OFFER. YOU GET US INTO KOBOI LABS, AND I GIVE YOU A TWO-DAY HEAD START WHEN THIS IS OVER.
YOU KNOW, THAT'S A PRETTY GOOD DEAL. YOU GUYS MUST BE IN A WHOLE LOT OF TROUBLE.
Fascinating. Commander Root is certainly smarter than he looks. Then again, it would be almost impossible not to be.

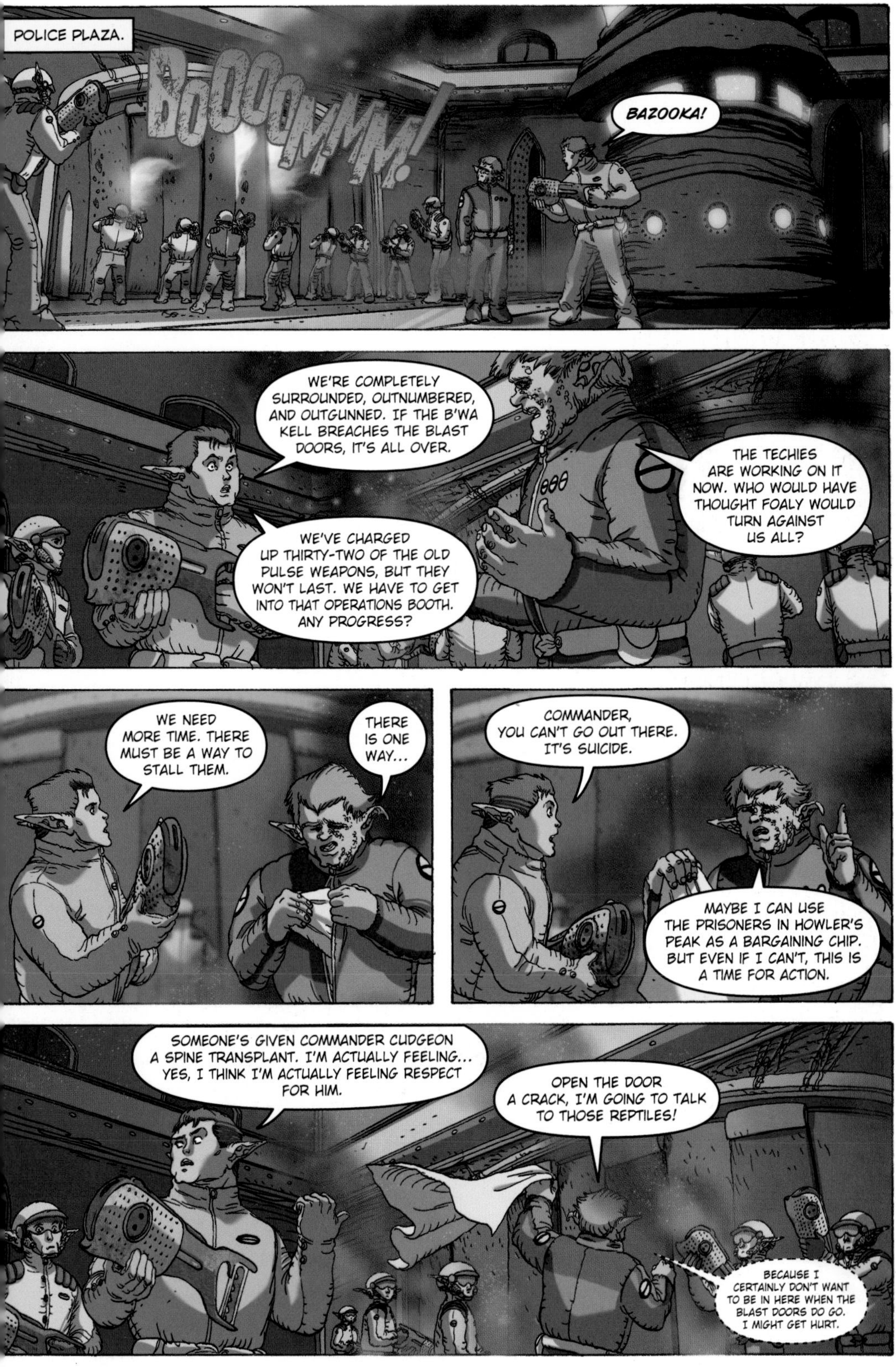
POLICE PLAZA.
BOOOOMMM!
BAZOOKA!
WE'RE COMPLETELY SURROUNDED, OUTNUMBERED, AND OUTGUNNED. IF THE B'WA KELL BREACHES THE BLAST DOORS, IT'S ALL OVER.
WE'VE CHARGED UP THIRTY-TWO OF THE OLD PULSE WEAPONS, BUT THEY WON'T LAST. WE HAVE TO GET INTO THAT OPERATIONS BOOTH. ANY PROGRESS?
THE TECHIES ARE WORKING ON IT NOW. WHO WOULD HAVE THOUGHT FOALY WOULD TURN AGAINST US ALL?
WE NEED MORE TIME. THERE MUST BE A WAY TO STALL THEM.
THERE IS ONE WAY...
COMMANDER, YOU CAN'T GO OUT THERE. IT'S SUICIDE.
MAYBE I CAN USE THE PRISONERS IN HOWLER'S PEAK AS A BARGAINING CHIP. BUT EVEN IF I CAN'T, THIS IS A TIME FOR ACTION.
SOMEONE'S GIVEN COMMANDER CUDGEON A SPINE TRANSPLANT. I'M ACTUALLY FEELING... YES, I THINK I'M ACTUALLY FEELING RESPECT FOR HIM.
OPEN THE DOOR A CRACK, I'M GOING TO TALK TO THOSE REPTILES!
BECAUSE I CERTAINLY DON'T WANT TO BE IN HERE WHEN THE BLAST DOORS DO GO. I MIGHT GET HURT.

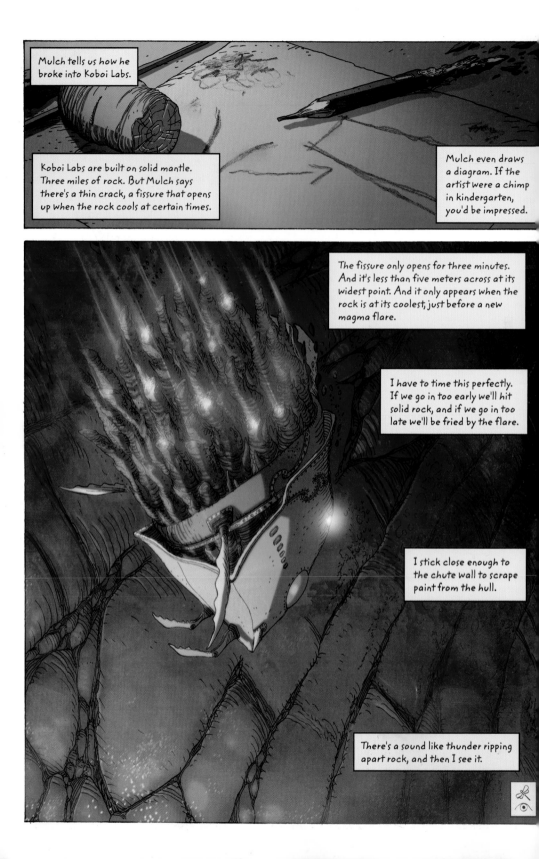

Mulch tells us how he broke into Koboi Labs.

Koboi Labs are built on solid mantle. Three miles of rock. But Mulch says there's a thin crack, a fissure that opens up when the rock cools at certain times.

Mulch even draws a diagram. If the artist were a chimp in kindergarten, you'd be impressed.

The fissure only opens for three minutes. And it's less than five meters across at its widest point. And it only appears when the rock is at its coolest, just before a new magma flare.

I have to time this perfectly. If we go in too early we'll hit solid rock, and if we go in too late we'll be fried by the flare.

I stick close enough to the chute wall to scrape paint from the hull.

There's a sound like thunder ripping apart rock, and then I see it.

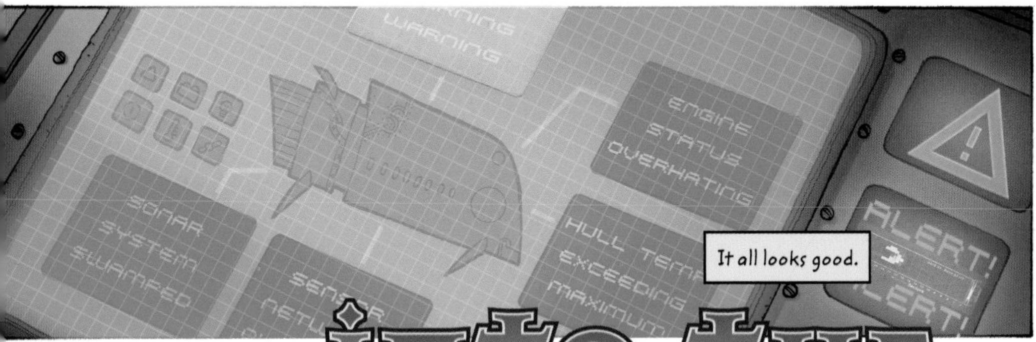
WARNING
ENGINE STATUS OVERHATING
SONAR SYSTEM SWAMPED
HULL TEMP EXCEEDING MAXIMUM
ALERT!
It all looks good.

CHAPTER 13: INTO THE BREACH

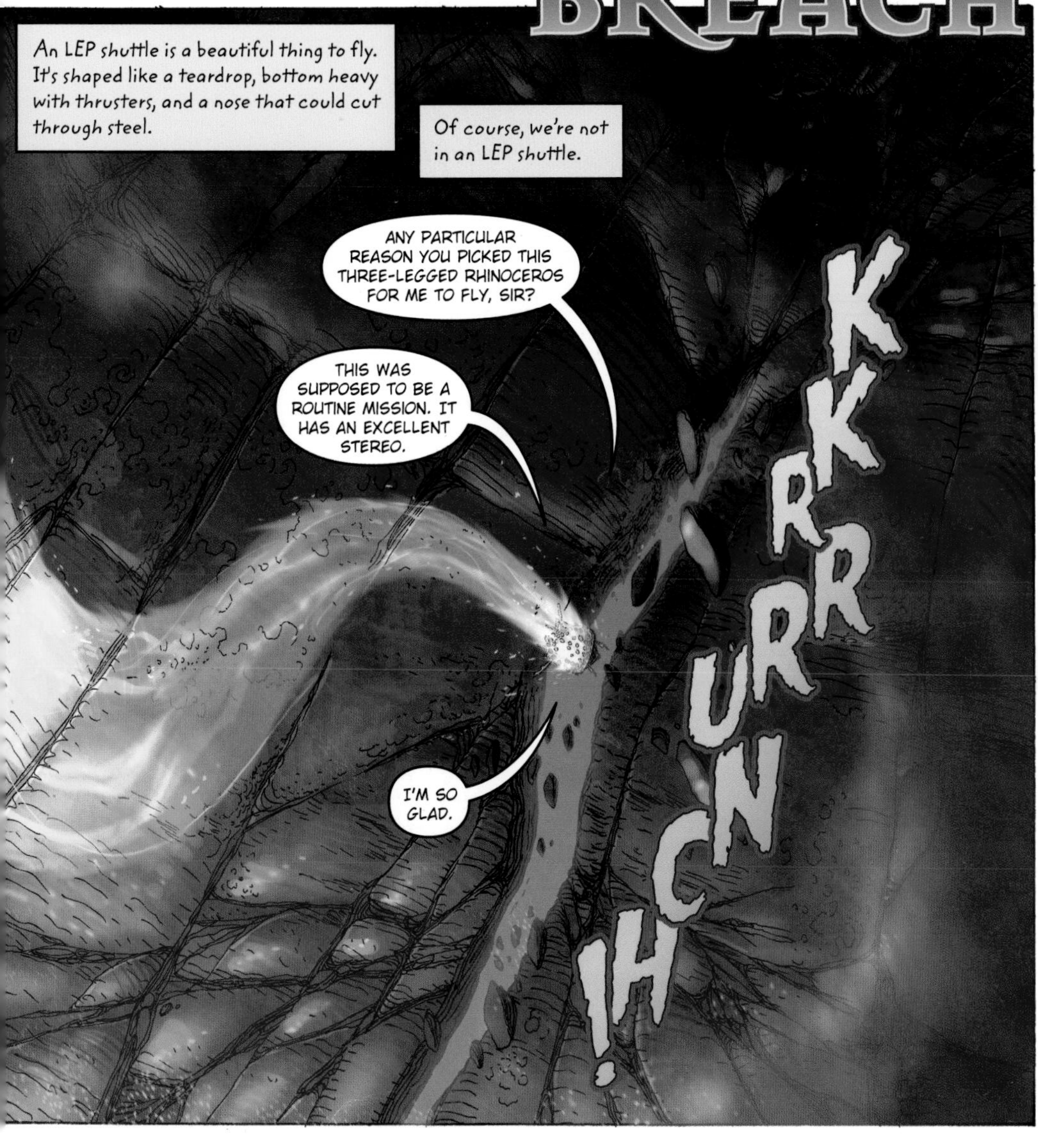
An LEP shuttle is a beautiful thing to fly. It's shaped like a teardrop, bottom heavy with thrusters, and a nose that could cut through steel.
Of course, we're not in an LEP shuttle.
ANY PARTICULAR REASON YOU PICKED THIS THREE-LEGGED RHINOCEROS FOR ME TO FLY, SIR?
THIS WAS SUPPOSED TO BE A ROUTINE MISSION. IT HAS AN EXCELLENT STEREO.
I'M SO GLAD.
KRKRRRUNCH!

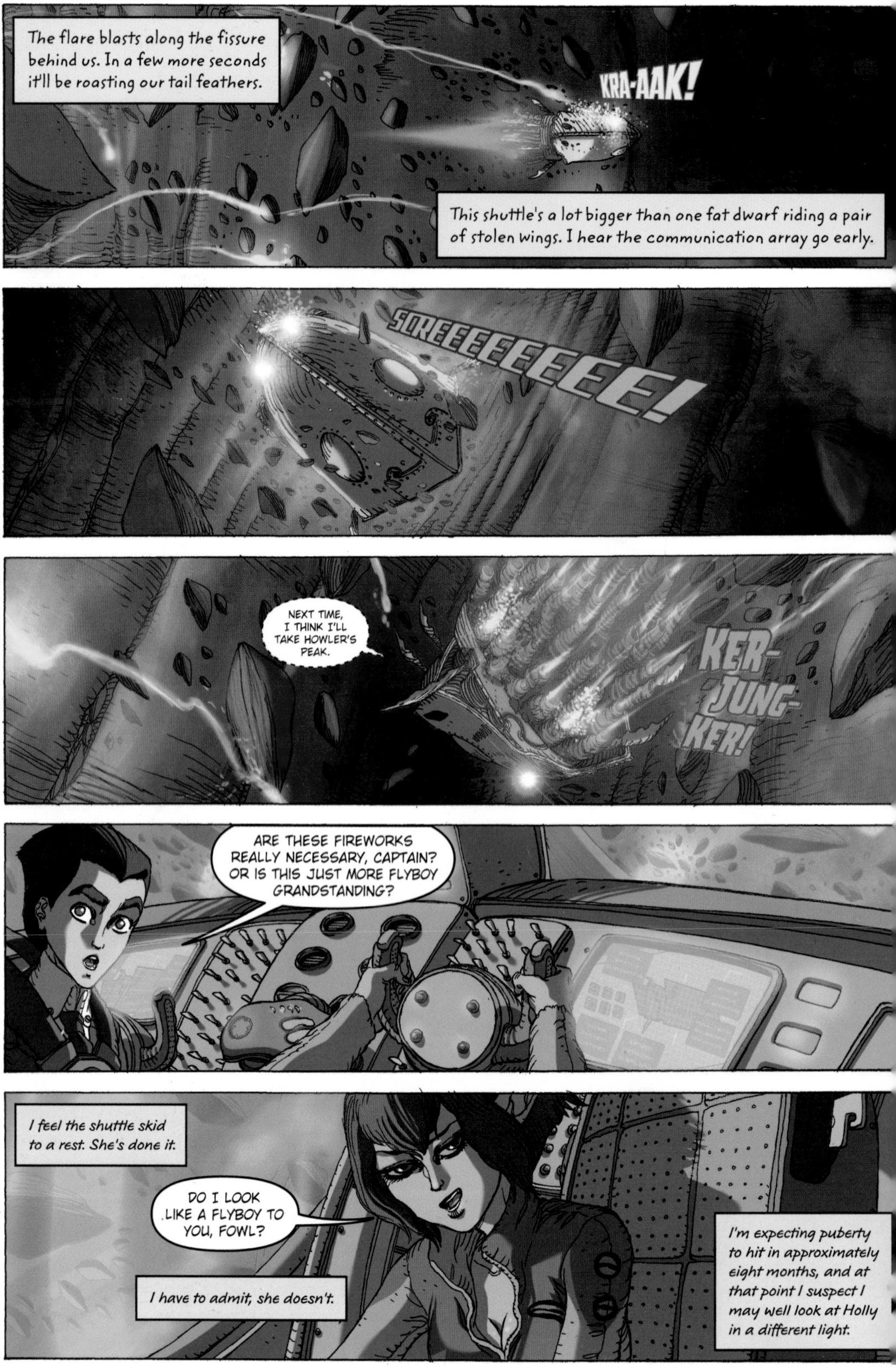
The flare blasts along the fissure behind us. In a few more seconds it'll be roasting our tail feathers.
KRA-AAK!
This shuttle's a lot bigger than one fat dwarf riding a pair of stolen wings. I hear the communication array go early.
SCREEEEEEEEEE!
NEXT TIME, I THINK I'LL TAKE HOWLER'S PEAK.
KER-JUNG-KER!
ARE THESE FIREWORKS REALLY NECESSARY, CAPTAIN? OR IS THIS JUST MORE FLYBOY GRANDSTANDING?
I feel the shuttle skid to a rest. She's done it.
DO I LOOK LIKE A FLYBOY TO YOU, FOWL?
I have to admit, she doesn't.
I'm expecting puberty to hit in approximately eight months, and at that point I suspect I may well look at Holly in a different light.

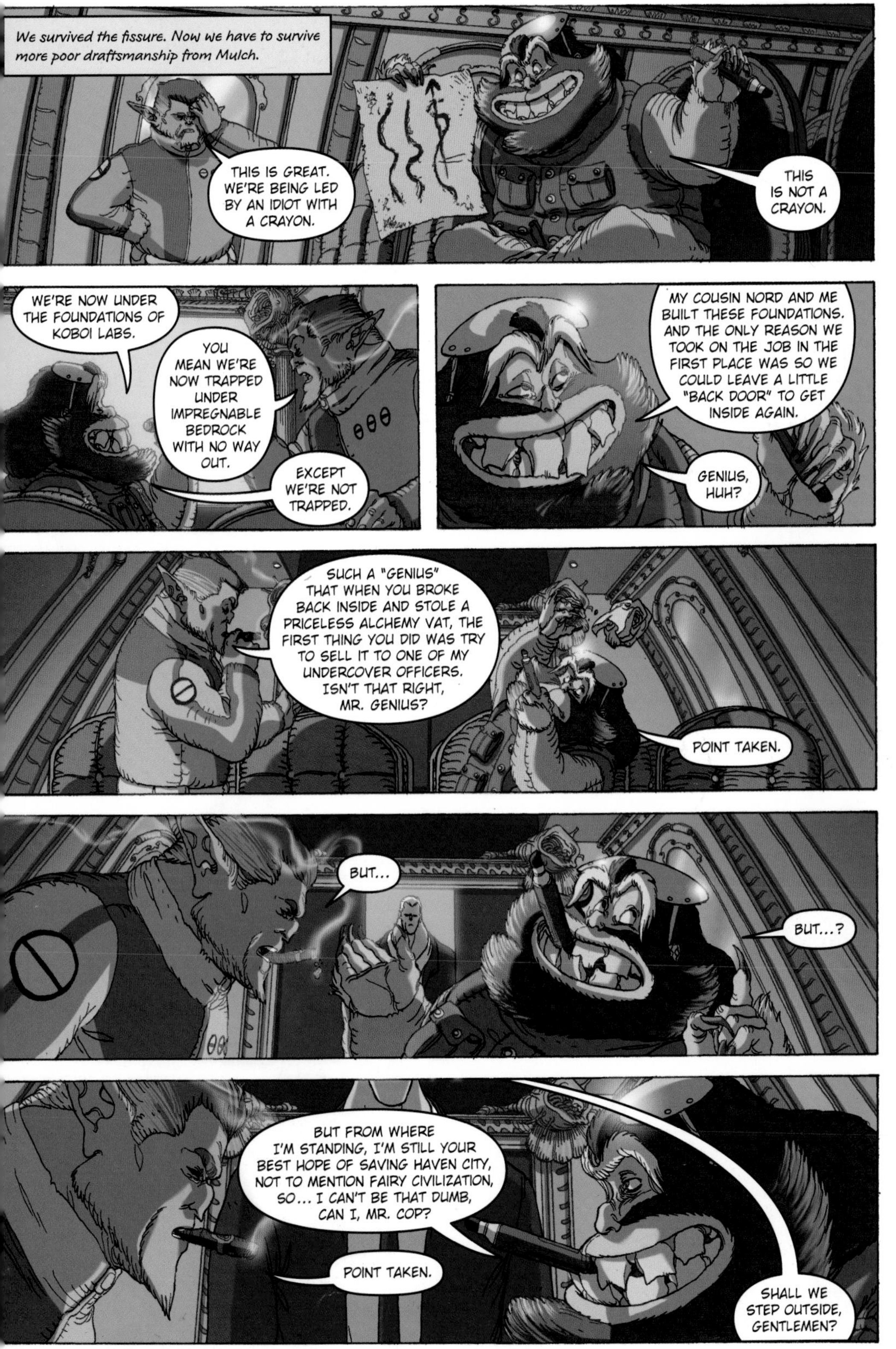
We survived the fissure. Now we have to survive more poor draftsmanship from Mulch.
THIS IS GREAT. WE'RE BEING LED BY AN IDIOT WITH A CRAYON.
THIS IS NOT A CRAYON.
WE'RE NOW UNDER THE FOUNDATIONS OF KOBOI LABS.
YOU MEAN WE'RE NOW TRAPPED UNDER IMPREGNABLE BEDROCK WITH NO WAY OUT.
EXCEPT WE'RE NOT TRAPPED.
MY COUSIN NORD AND ME BUILT THESE FOUNDATIONS. AND THE ONLY REASON WE TOOK ON THE JOB IN THE FIRST PLACE WAS SO WE COULD LEAVE A LITTLE "BACK DOOR" TO GET INSIDE AGAIN.
GENIUS, HUH?
SUCH A "GENIUS" THAT WHEN YOU BROKE BACK INSIDE AND STOLE A PRICELESS ALCHEMY VAT, THE FIRST THING YOU DID WAS TRY TO SELL IT TO ONE OF MY UNDERCOVER OFFICERS. ISN'T THAT RIGHT, MR. GENIUS?
POINT TAKEN.
BUT...
BUT...?
BUT FROM WHERE I'M STANDING, I'M STILL YOUR BEST HOPE OF SAVING HAVEN CITY, NOT TO MENTION FAIRY CIVILIZATION, SO... I CAN'T BE THAT DUMB, CAN I, MR. COP?
POINT TAKEN.
SHALL WE STEP OUTSIDE, GENTLEMEN?

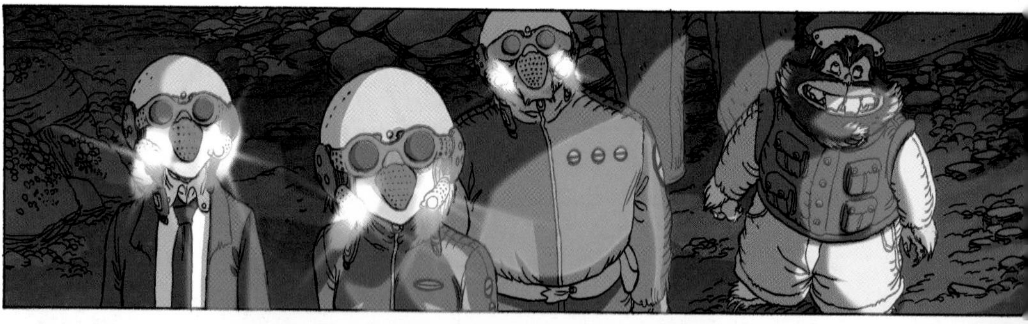

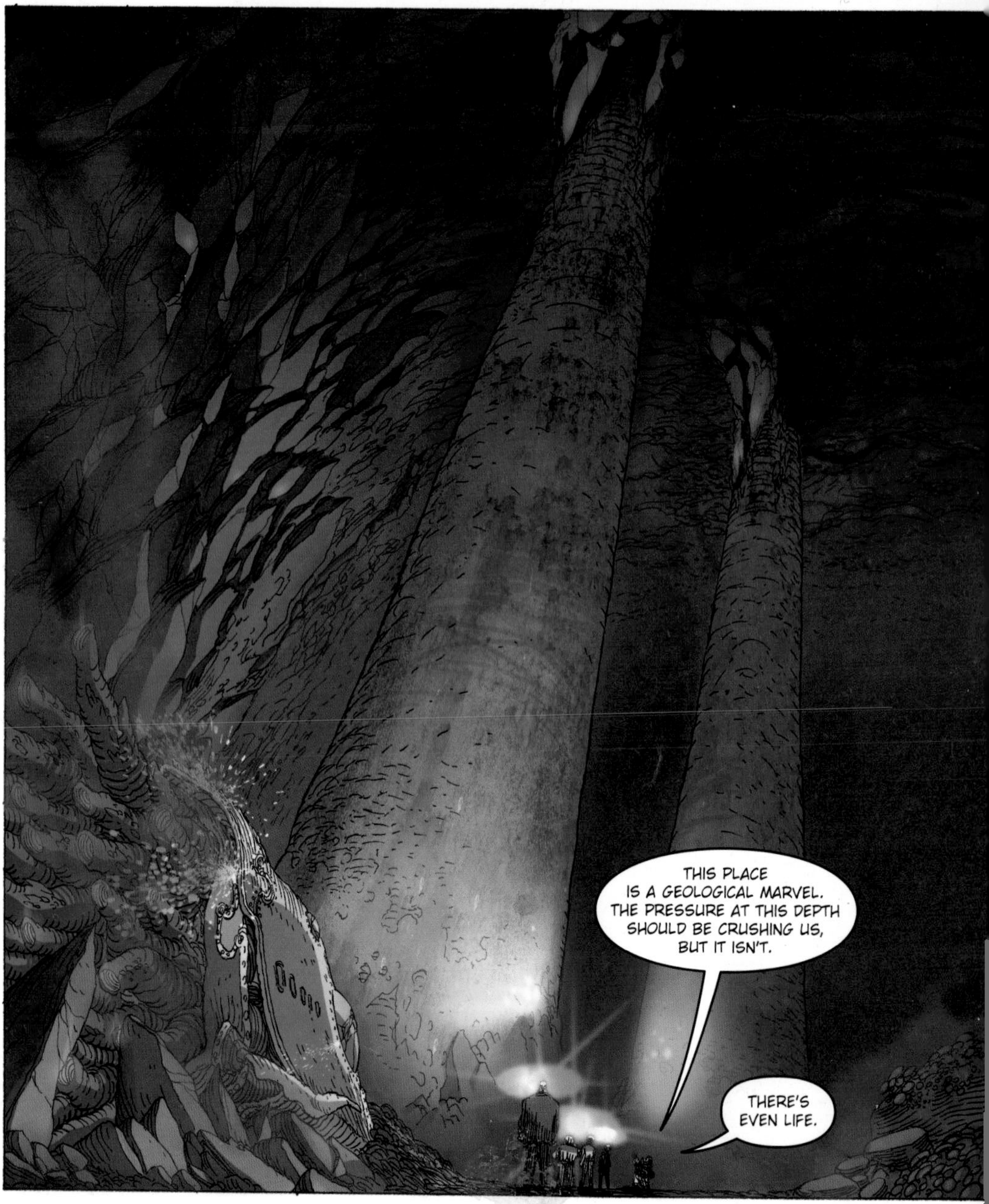
THIS PLACE IS A GEOLOGICAL MARVEL. THE PRESSURE AT THIS DEPTH SHOULD BE CRUSHING US, BUT IT ISN'T.
THERE'S EVEN LIFE.

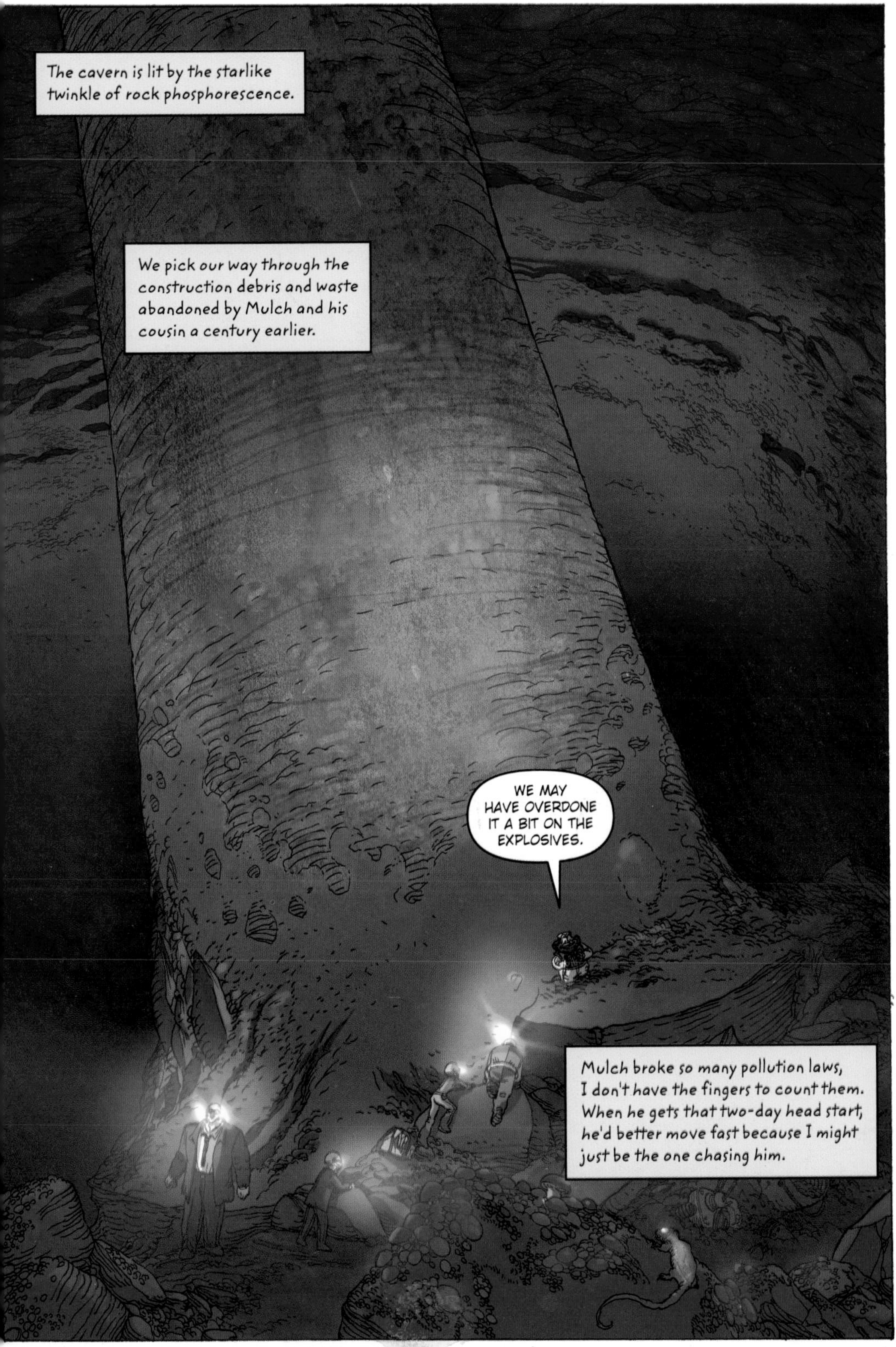
The cavern is lit by the starlike twinkle of rock phosphorescence.
We pick our way through the construction debris and waste abandoned by Mulch and his cousin a century earlier.
WE MAY HAVE OVERDONE IT A BIT ON THE EXPLOSIVES.
Mulch broke so many pollution laws, I don't have the fingers to count them. When he gets that two-day head start, he'd better move fast because I might just be the one chasing him.

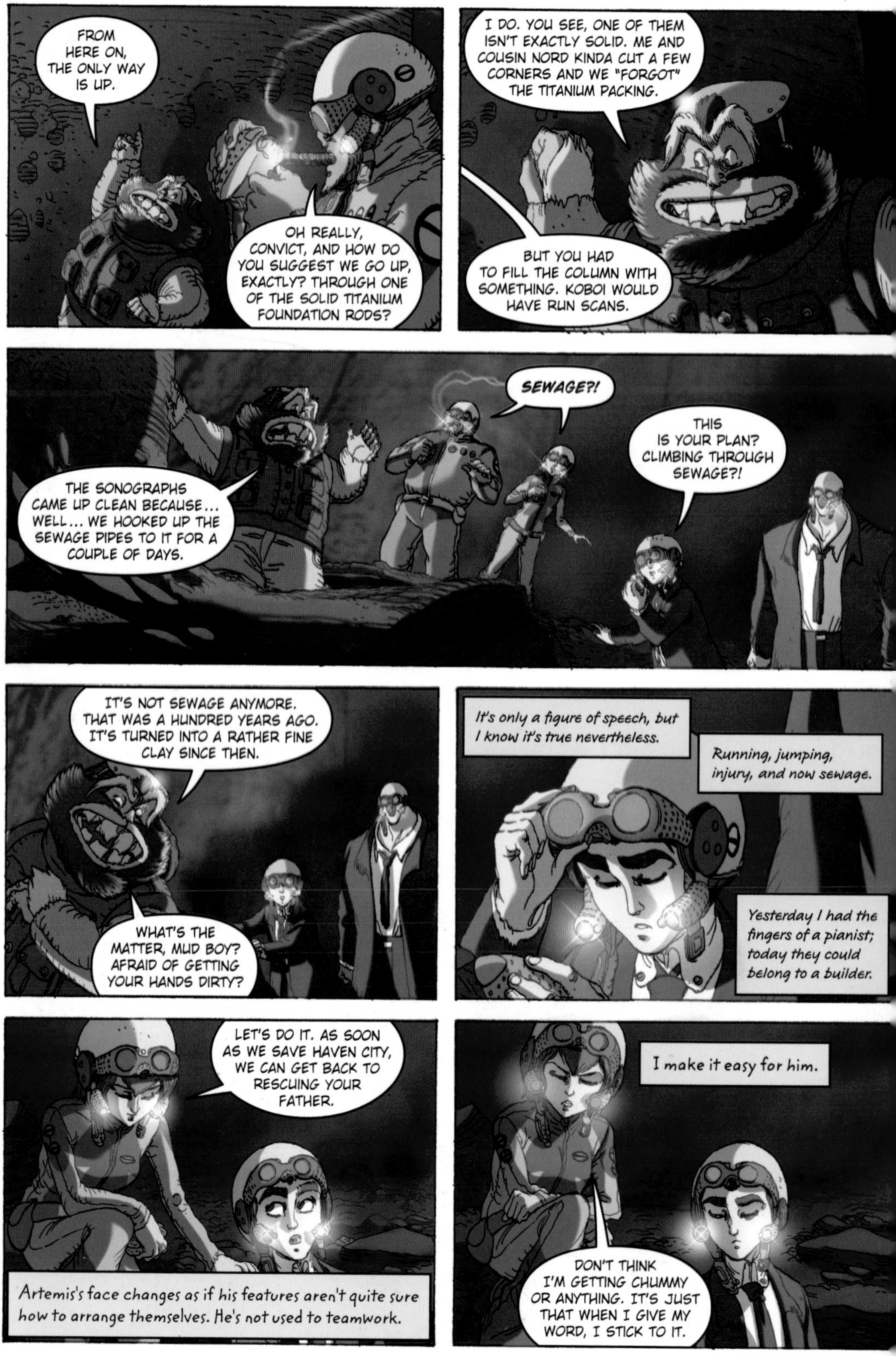
FROM HERE ON, THE ONLY WAY IS UP.
OH REALLY, CONVICT, AND HOW DO YOU SUGGEST WE GO UP, EXACTLY? THROUGH ONE OF THE SOLID TITANIUM FOUNDATION RODS?
I DO. YOU SEE, ONE OF THEM ISN'T EXACTLY SOLID. ME AND COUSIN NORD KINDA CUT A FEW CORNERS AND WE "FORGOT" THE TITANIUM PACKING.
BUT YOU HAD TO FILL THE COLUMN WITH SOMETHING. KOBOI WOULD HAVE RUN SCANS.
THE SONOGRAPHS CAME UP CLEAN BECAUSE... WELL... WE HOOKED UP THE SEWAGE PIPES TO IT FOR A COUPLE OF DAYS.
SEWAGE?!
THIS IS YOUR PLAN? CLIMBING THROUGH SEWAGE?!
IT'S NOT SEWAGE ANYMORE. THAT WAS A HUNDRED YEARS AGO. IT'S TURNED INTO A RATHER FINE CLAY SINCE THEN.
WHAT'S THE MATTER, MUD BOY? AFRAID OF GETTING YOUR HANDS DIRTY?
It's only a figure of speech, but I know it's true nevertheless.
Running, jumping, injury, and now sewage.
Yesterday I had the fingers of a pianist; today they could belong to a builder.
LET'S DO IT. AS SOON AS WE SAVE HAVEN CITY, WE CAN GET BACK TO RESCUING YOUR FATHER.
Artemis's face changes as if his features aren't quite sure how to arrange themselves. He's not used to teamwork.
I make it easy for him.
DON'T THINK I'M GETTING CHUMMY OR ANYTHING. IT'S JUST THAT WHEN I GIVE MY WORD, I STICK TO IT.

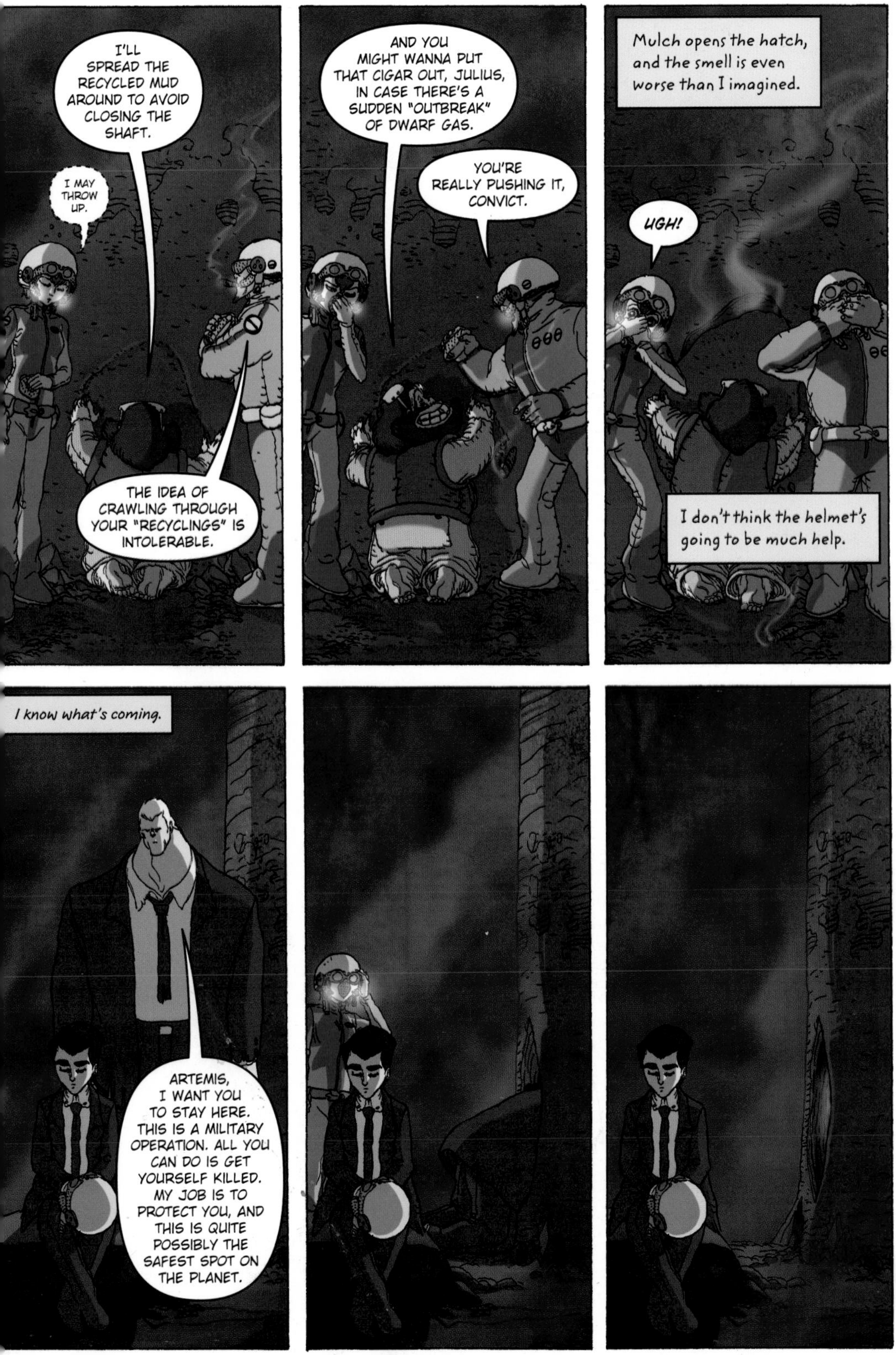
I'LL SPREAD THE RECYCLED MUD AROUND TO AVOID CLOSING THE SHAFT.
I MAY THROW UP.
THE IDEA OF CRAWLING THROUGH YOUR "RECYCLINGS" IS INTOLERABLE.
AND YOU MIGHT WANNA PUT THAT CIGAR OUT, JULIUS, IN CASE THERE'S A SUDDEN "OUTBREAK" OF DWARF GAS.
YOU'RE REALLY PUSHING IT, CONVICT.
Mulch opens the hatch, and the smell is even worse than I imagined.
UGH!
I don't think the helmet's going to be much help.
I know what's coming.
ARTEMIS, I WANT YOU TO STAY HERE. THIS IS A MILITARY OPERATION. ALL YOU CAN DO IS GET YOURSELF KILLED. MY JOB IS TO PROTECT YOU, AND THIS IS QUITE POSSIBLY THE SAFEST SPOT ON THE PLANET.

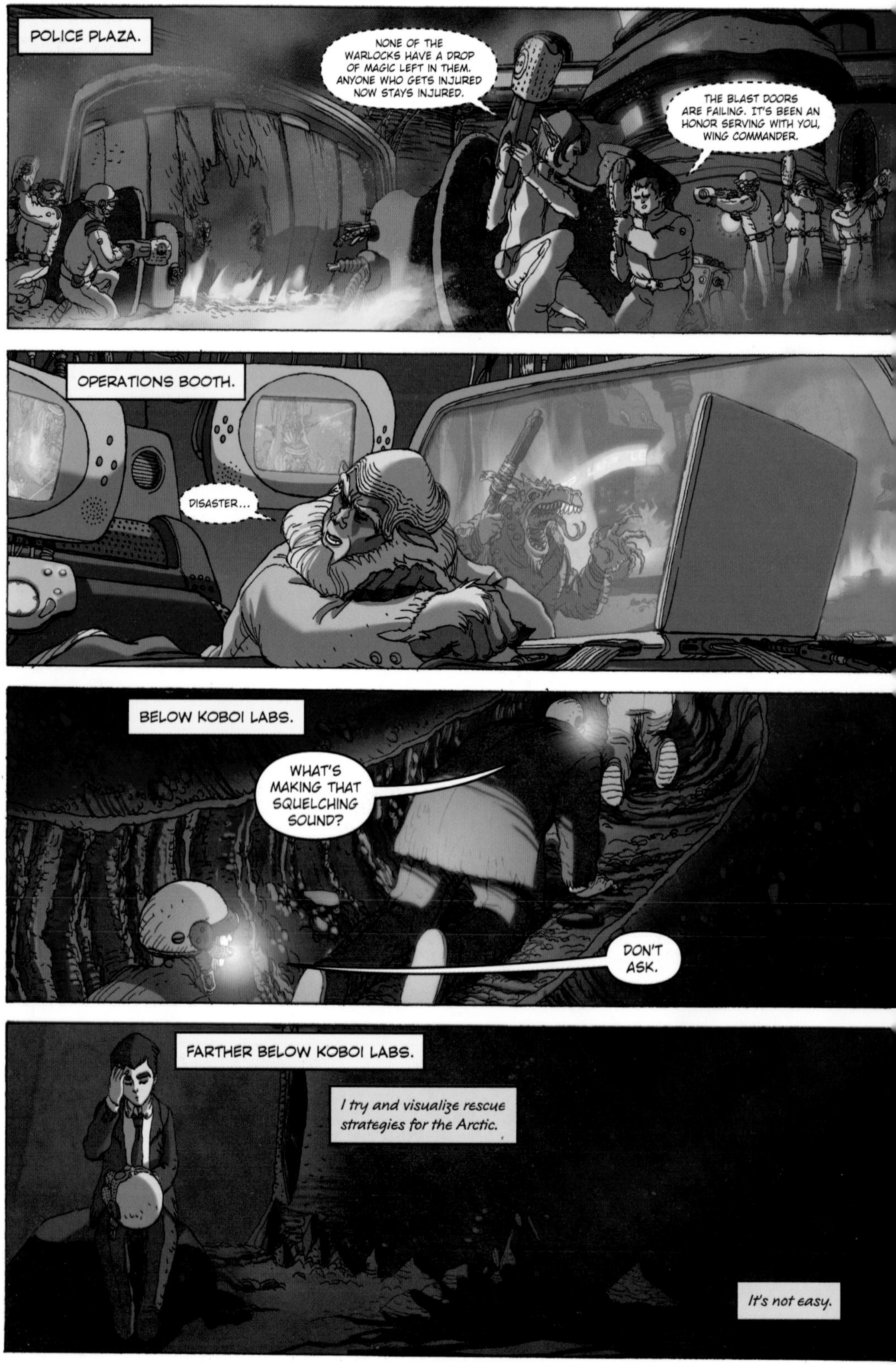
POLICE PLAZA.
NONE OF THE WARLOCKS HAVE A DROP OF MAGIC LEFT IN THEM. ANYONE WHO GETS INJURED NOW STAYS INJURED.
THE BLAST DOORS ARE FAILING. IT'S BEEN AN HONOR SERVING WITH YOU, WING COMMANDER.
OPERATIONS BOOTH.
DISASTER...
BELOW KOBOI LABS.
WHAT'S MAKING THAT SQUELCHING SOUND?
DON'T ASK.
FARTHER BELOW KOBOI LABS.
I try and visualize rescue strategies for the Arctic.
It's not easy.

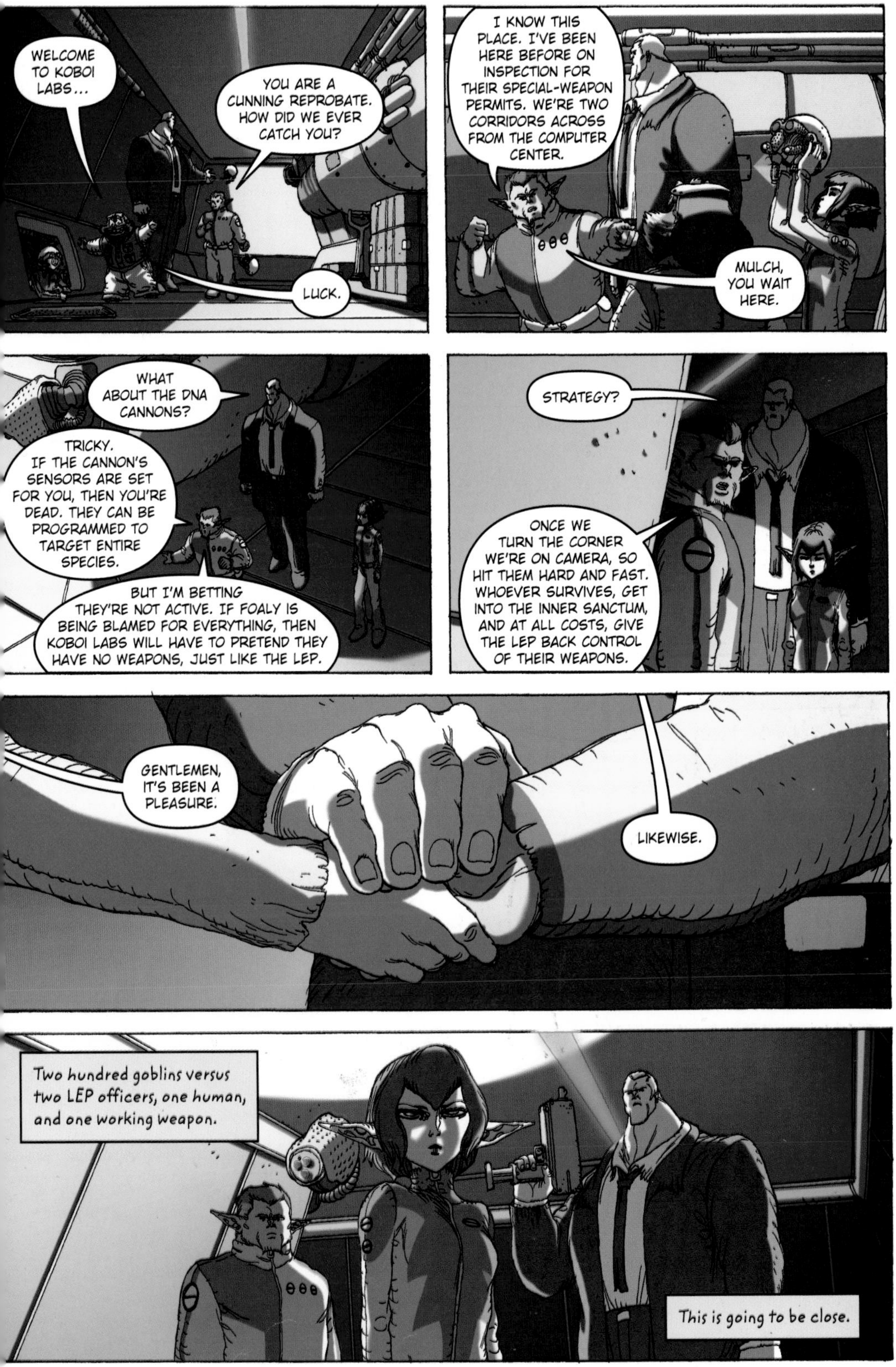
WELCOME TO KOBOI LABS...
YOU ARE A CUNNING REPROBATE. HOW DID WE EVER CATCH YOU?
LUCK.
I KNOW THIS PLACE. I'VE BEEN HERE BEFORE ON INSPECTION FOR THEIR SPECIAL-WEAPON PERMITS. WE'RE TWO CORRIDORS ACROSS FROM THE COMPUTER CENTER.
MULCH, YOU WAIT HERE.
WHAT ABOUT THE DNA CANNONS?
TRICKY. IF THE CANNON'S SENSORS ARE SET FOR YOU, THEN YOU'RE DEAD. THEY CAN BE PROGRAMMED TO TARGET ENTIRE SPECIES.
BUT I'M BETTING THEY'RE NOT ACTIVE. IF FOALY IS BEING BLAMED FOR EVERYTHING, THEN KOBOI LABS WILL HAVE TO PRETEND THEY HAVE NO WEAPONS, JUST LIKE THE LEP.
STRATEGY?
ONCE WE TURN THE CORNER WE'RE ON CAMERA, SO HIT THEM HARD AND FAST. WHOEVER SURVIVES, GET INTO THE INNER SANCTUM, AND AT ALL COSTS, GIVE THE LEP BACK CONTROL OF THEIR WEAPONS.
GENTLEMEN, IT'S BEEN A PLEASURE.
LIKEWISE.
Two hundred goblins versus two LEP officers, one human, and one working weapon.
This is going to be close.

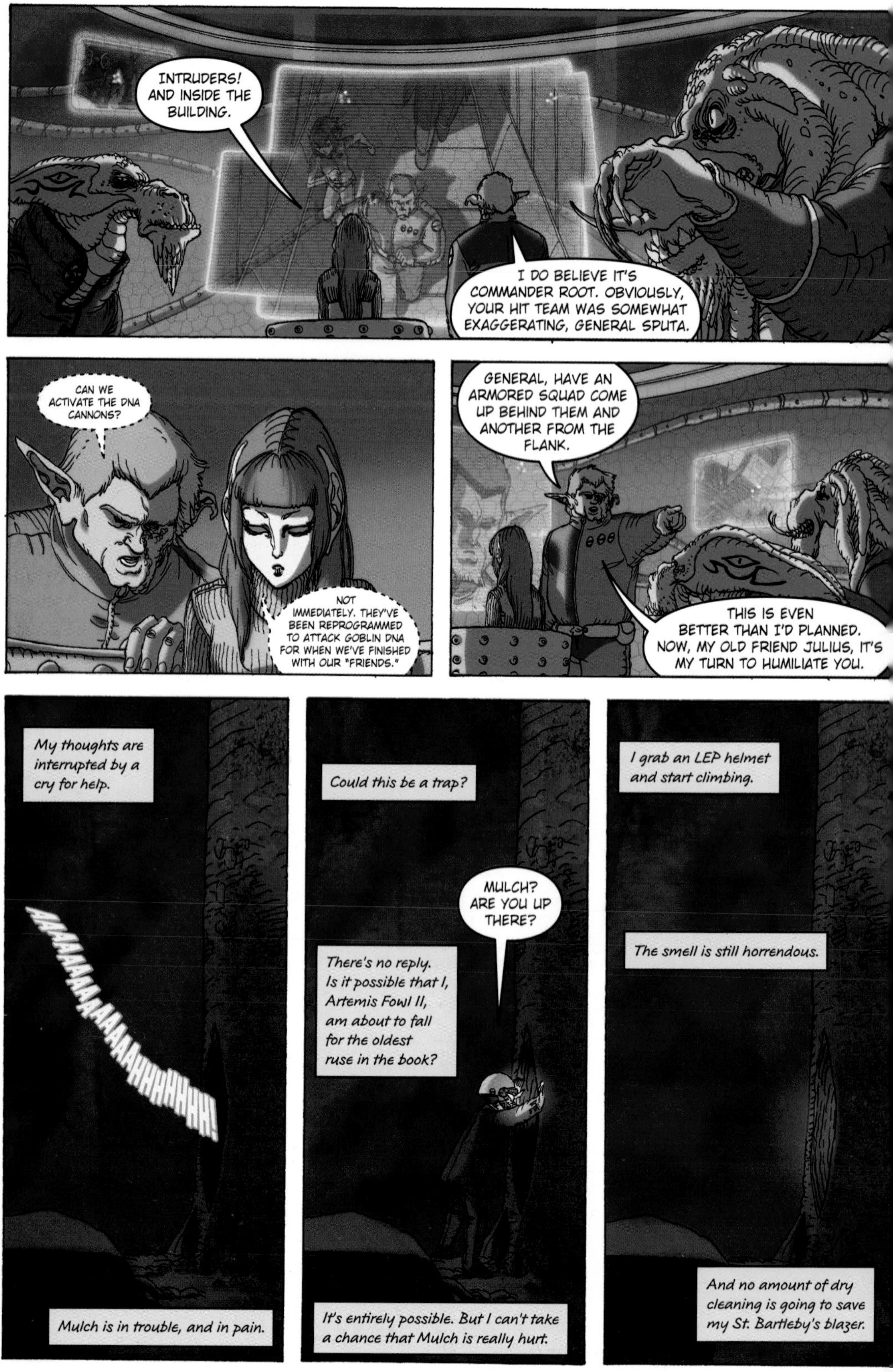
INTRUDERS! AND INSIDE THE BUILDING.
I DO BELIEVE IT'S COMMANDER ROOT. OBVIOUSLY, YOUR HIT TEAM WAS SOMEWHAT EXAGGERATING, GENERAL SPUTA.
CAN WE ACTIVATE THE DNA CANNONS?
NOT IMMEDIATELY. THEY'VE BEEN REPROGRAMMED TO ATTACK GOBLIN DNA FOR WHEN WE'VE FINISHED WITH OUR "FRIENDS."
GENERAL, HAVE AN ARMORED SQUAD COME UP BEHIND THEM AND ANOTHER FROM THE FLANK.
THIS IS EVEN BETTER THAN I'D PLANNED. NOW, MY OLD FRIEND JULIUS, IT'S MY TURN TO HUMILIATE YOU.
My thoughts are interrupted by a cry for help.
AAAAAAAAAAAAAAAAHHHHHHH!
Mulch is in trouble, and in pain.
Could this be a trap?
MULCH? ARE YOU UP THERE?
There's no reply. Is it possible that I, Artemis Fowl II, am about to fall for the oldest ruse in the book?
It's entirely possible. But I can't take a chance that Mulch is really hurt.
I grab an LEP helmet and start climbing.
The smell is still horrendous.
And no amount of dry cleaning is going to save my St. Bartleby's blazer.

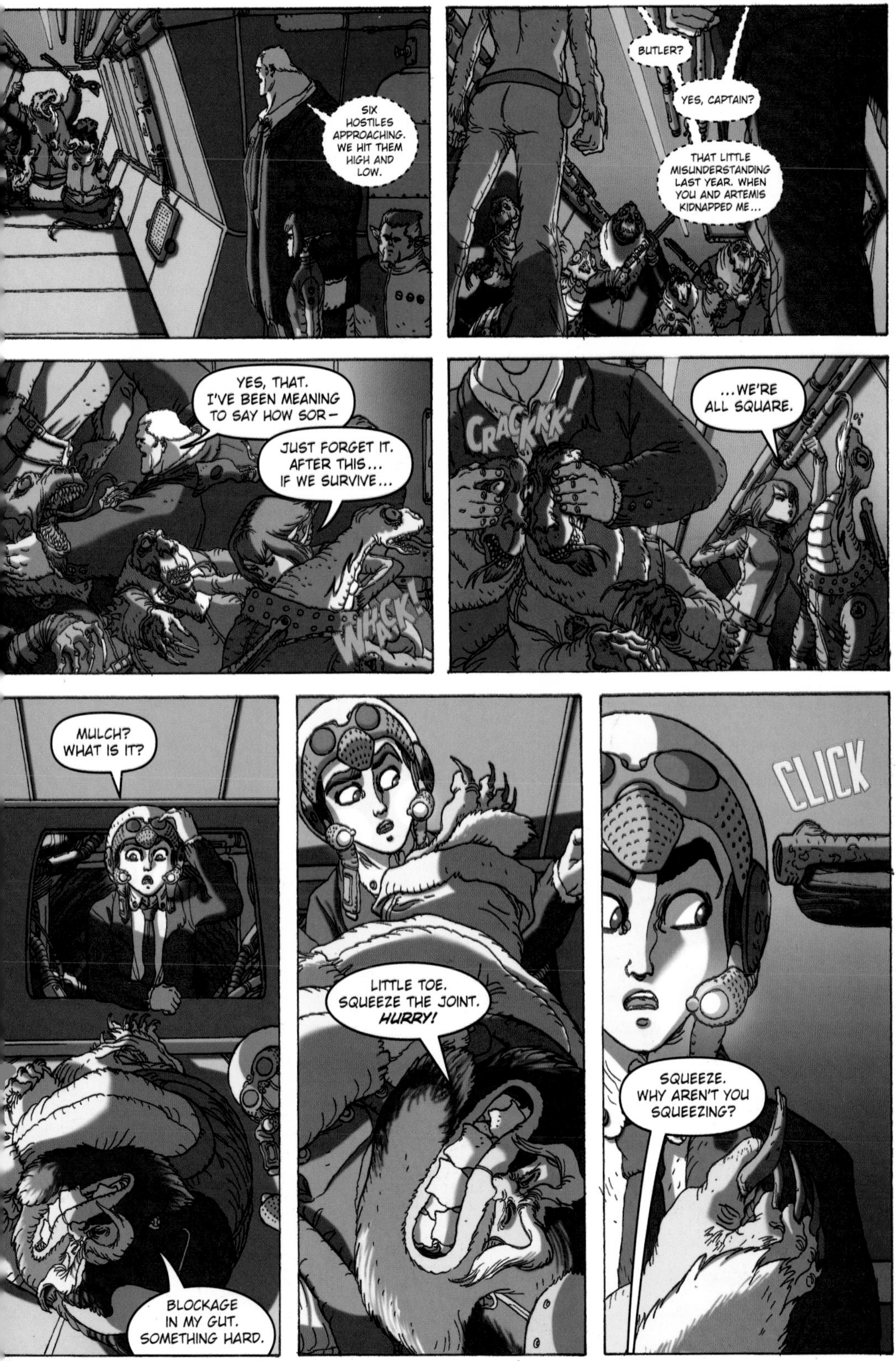
SIX HOSTILES APPROACHING. WE HIT THEM HIGH AND LOW.
BUTLER?
YES, CAPTAIN?
THAT LITTLE MISUNDERSTANDING LAST YEAR. WHEN YOU AND ARTEMIS KIDNAPPED ME...
YES, THAT. I'VE BEEN MEANING TO SAY HOW SOR–
JUST FORGET IT. AFTER THIS... IF WE SURVIVE...
WHACK!
CRACKKK!
...WE'RE ALL SQUARE.
MULCH? WHAT IS IT?
BLOCKAGE IN MY GUT. SOMETHING HARD.
LITTLE TOE. SQUEEZE THE JOINT. HURRY!
CLICK
SQUEEZE. WHY AREN'T YOU SQUEEZING?

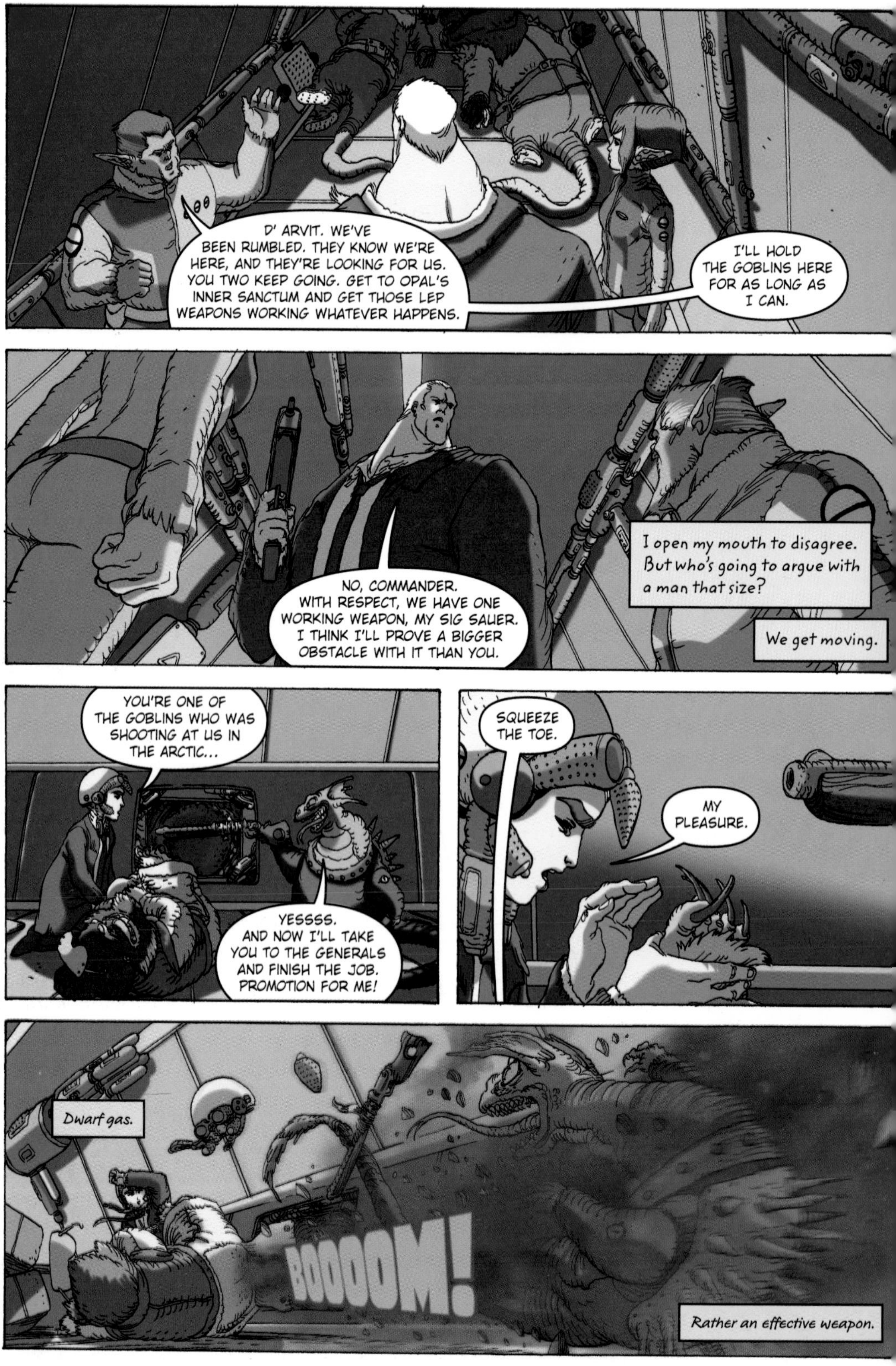
D' ARVIT. WE'VE BEEN RUMBLED. THEY KNOW WE'RE HERE, AND THEY'RE LOOKING FOR US. YOU TWO KEEP GOING. GET TO OPAL'S INNER SANCTUM AND GET THOSE LEP WEAPONS WORKING WHATEVER HAPPENS.
I'LL HOLD THE GOBLINS HERE FOR AS LONG AS I CAN.
NO, COMMANDER. WITH RESPECT, WE HAVE ONE WORKING WEAPON, MY SIG SAUER. I THINK I'LL PROVE A BIGGER OBSTACLE WITH IT THAN YOU.
I open my mouth to disagree. But who's going to argue with a man that size?
We get moving.
YOU'RE ONE OF THE GOBLINS WHO WAS SHOOTING AT US IN THE ARCTIC...
YESSSS. AND NOW I'LL TAKE YOU TO THE GENERALS AND FINISH THE JOB. PROMOTION FOR ME!
SQUEEZE THE TOE.
MY PLEASURE.
Dwarf gas.
BOOOOM!
Rather an effective weapon.

TWELVE MORE SHOTS TILL THEY CLOSE IN.

THANKS, KID. I THOUGHT I WAS A GONER THERE. MUST'VE BEEN A PIECE OF GRANITE OR A DIAMOND STUCK IN MY GUT.

MULCH, YOU KNOW YOUR WAY AROUND THIS PLACE. HOW CAN I GET TO WHAT THEY CALL THE "INNER SANCTUM"?

NOT A SMART MOVE. THIS PLACE IS CRAWLING WITH GOBLINS, AND THEY'RE ALL LOOKING FOR YOU.

I HAVE TO GET IN THERE, MULCH.

"I have to help my... friends."

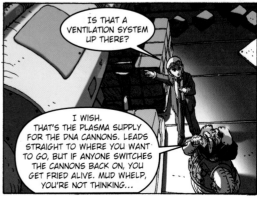

IS THAT A VENTILATION SYSTEM UP THERE?

I WISH. THAT'S THE PLASMA SUPPLY FOR THE DNA CANNONS. LEADS STRAIGHT TO WHERE YOU WANT TO GO, BUT IF ANYONE SWITCHES THE CANNONS BACK ON, YOU GET FRIED ALIVE. MUD WHELP, YOU'RE NOT THINKING...

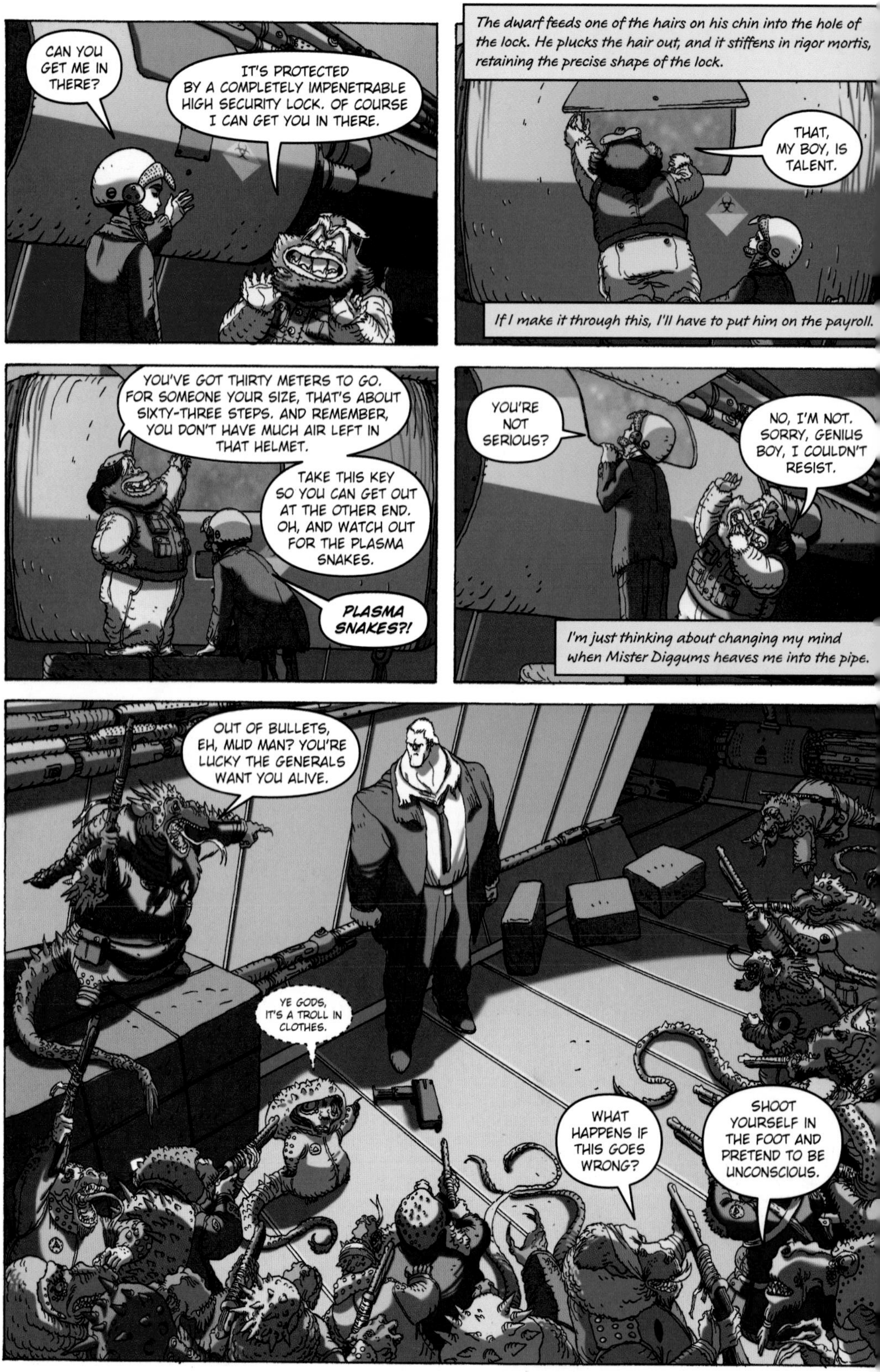
CAN YOU GET ME IN THERE?
IT'S PROTECTED BY A COMPLETELY IMPENETRABLE HIGH SECURITY LOCK. OF COURSE I CAN GET YOU IN THERE.
The dwarf feeds one of the hairs on his chin into the hole of the lock. He plucks the hair out, and it stiffens in rigor mortis, retaining the precise shape of the lock.
THAT, MY BOY, IS TALENT.
If I make it through this, I'll have to put him on the payroll.
YOU'VE GOT THIRTY METERS TO GO. FOR SOMEONE YOUR SIZE, THAT'S ABOUT SIXTY-THREE STEPS. AND REMEMBER, YOU DON'T HAVE MUCH AIR LEFT IN THAT HELMET.
TAKE THIS KEY SO YOU CAN GET OUT AT THE OTHER END. OH, AND WATCH OUT FOR THE PLASMA SNAKES.
PLASMA SNAKES?!
YOU'RE NOT SERIOUS?
NO, I'M NOT. SORRY, GENIUS BOY, I COULDN'T RESIST.
I'm just thinking about changing my mind when Mister Diggums heaves me into the pipe.
OUT OF BULLETS, EH, MUD MAN? YOU'RE LUCKY THE GENERALS WANT YOU ALIVE.
YE GODS, IT'S A TROLL IN CLOTHES.
WHAT HAPPENS IF THIS GOES WRONG?
SHOOT YOURSELF IN THE FOOT AND PRETEND TO BE UNCONSCIOUS.

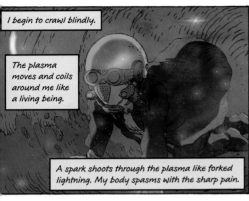

I begin to crawl blindly.

The plasma moves and coils around me like a living being.

A spark shoots through the plasma like forked lightning. My body spasms with the sharp pain.

I'm wading through a turgid sea of orange gel.

For someone with the highest recorded IQ in Europe, this is possibly the most stupid thing I've ever done.

I can taste the recycled air in my helmet getting stale.

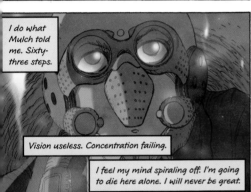

I do what Mulch told me. Sixty-three steps.

Vision useless. Concentration failing.

I feel my mind spiraling off. I'm going to die here alone. I will never be great.

I reach fifty-four. Or is it fifty-six?

The difference is life and death...

And not just for me...

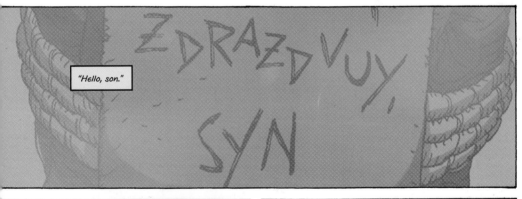

"Hello, son."

I have to get out. I search for the keyhole.

Nothing.

Nothing.

Then ... a passing spark offers illumination.

I pull the key Mulch made out of my pocket and slide it gently into the lock.

The flap drops open.

"That, my boy, is talent!"

There could be anything on the other side. I fall through.

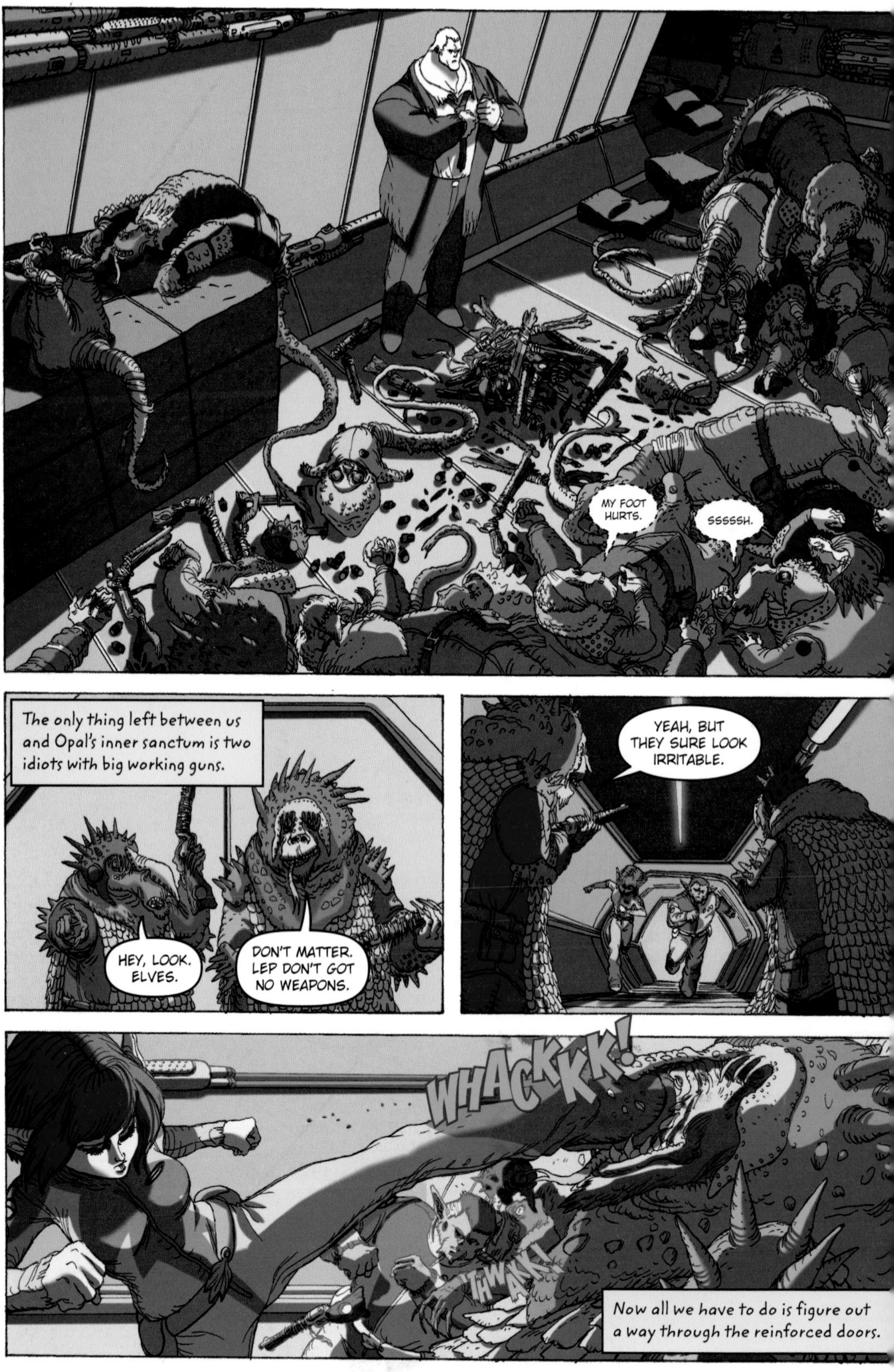
MY FOOT HURTS.
SSSSSH.
The only thing left between us and Opal's inner sanctum is two idiots with big working guns.
HEY, LOOK. ELVES.
DON'T MATTER. LEP DON'T GOT NO WEAPONS.
YEAH, BUT THEY SURE LOOK IRRITABLE.
WHACKKK!
THWAKK!
Now all we have to do is figure out a way through the reinforced doors.

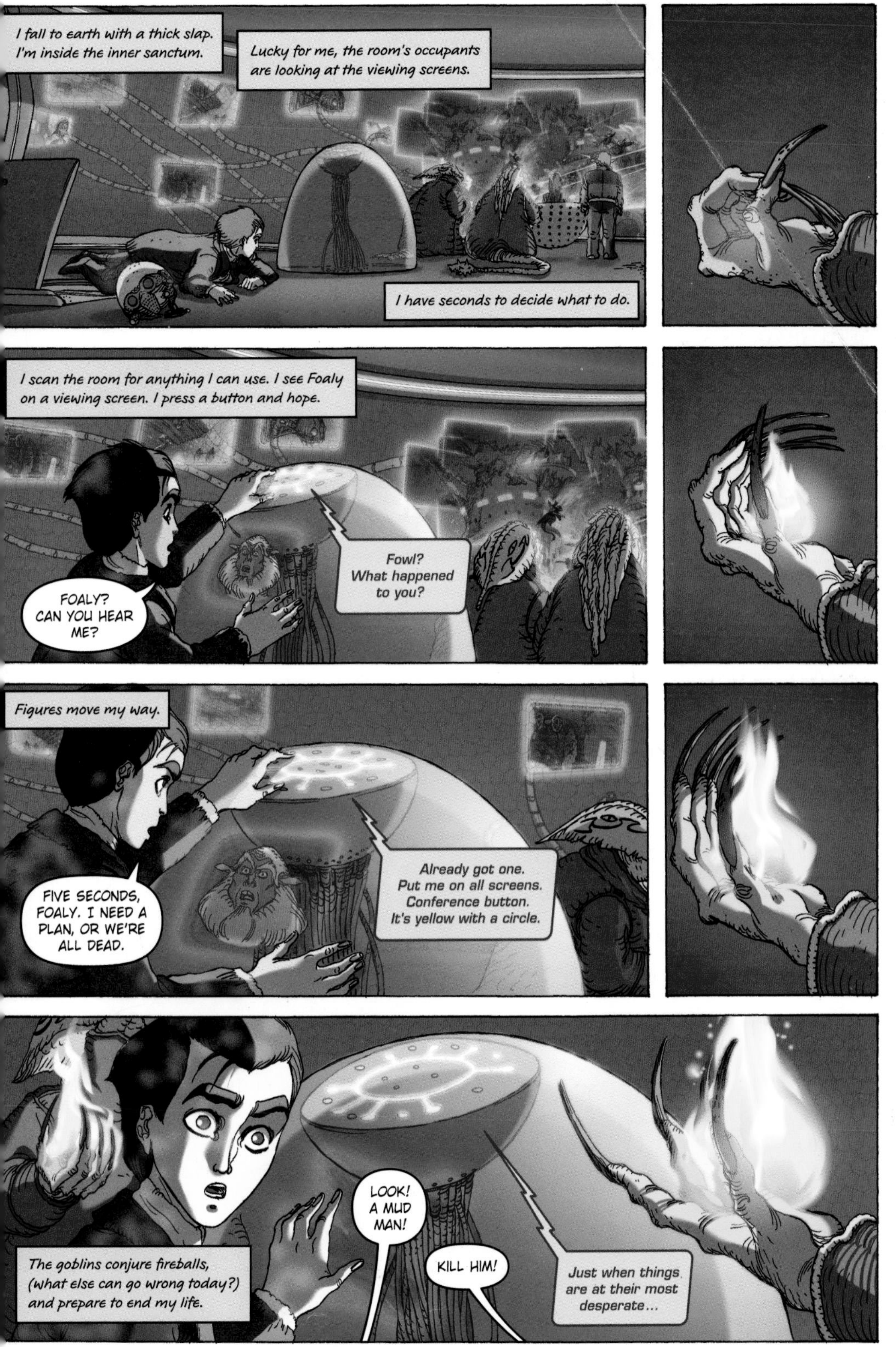
I fall to earth with a thick slap. I'm inside the inner sanctum.
Lucky for me, the room's occupants are looking at the viewing screens.
I have seconds to decide what to do.
I scan the room for anything I can use. I see Foaly on a viewing screen. I press a button and hope.
FOALY? CAN YOU HEAR ME?
Fowl? What happened to you?
Figures move my way.
FIVE SECONDS, FOALY. I NEED A PLAN, OR WE'RE ALL DEAD.
Already got one. Put me on all screens. Conference button. It's yellow with a circle.
LOOK! A MUD MAN!
KILL HIM!
The goblins conjure fireballs, (what else can go wrong today?) and prepare to end my life.
Just when things are at their most desperate...

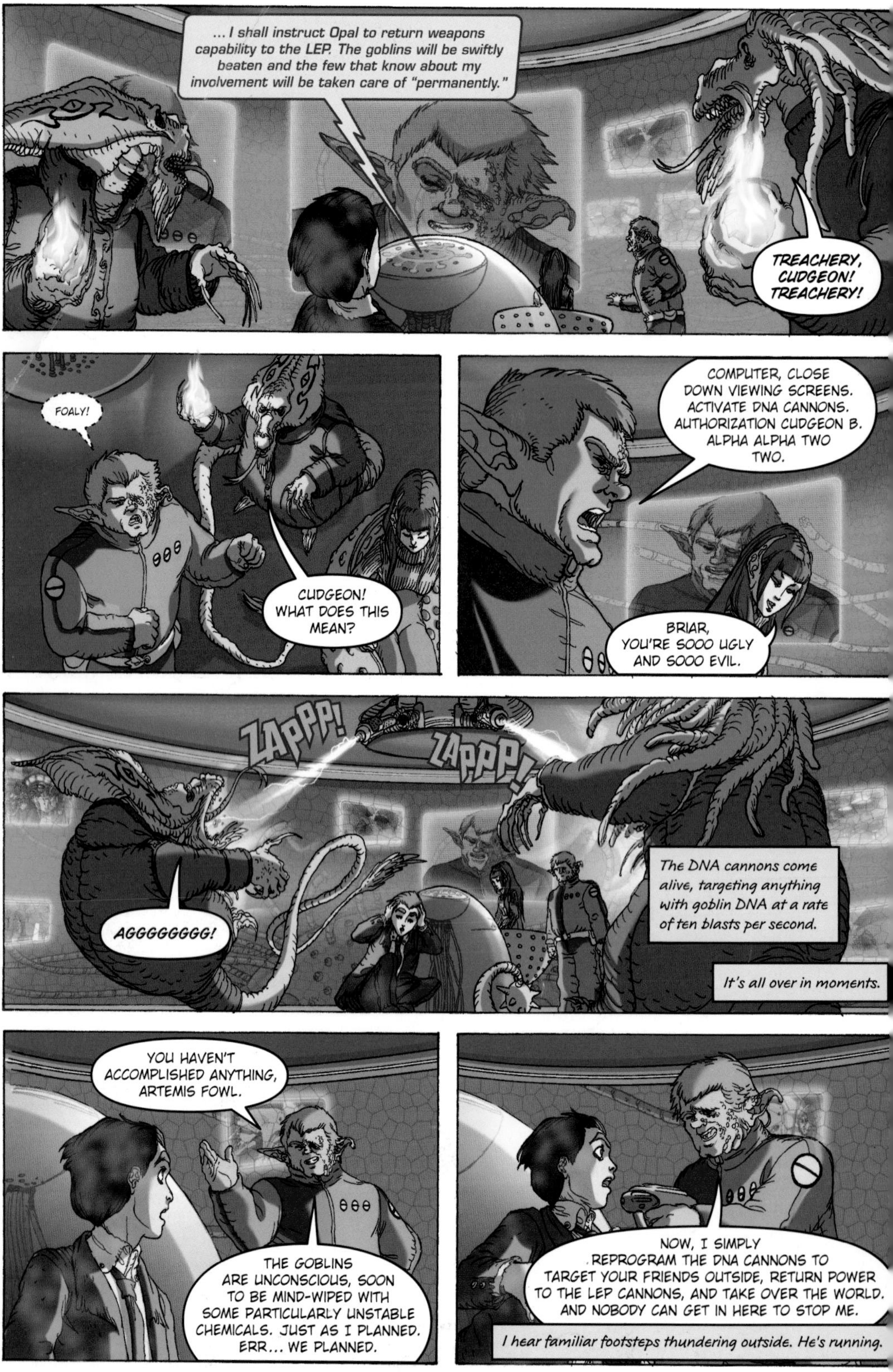

... I shall instruct Opal to return weapons capability to the LEP. The goblins will be swiftly beaten and the few that know about my involvement will be taken care of "permanently."
TREACHERY, CUDGEON! TREACHERY!
FOALY!
CUDGEON! WHAT DOES THIS MEAN?
COMPUTER, CLOSE DOWN VIEWING SCREENS. ACTIVATE DNA CANNONS. AUTHORIZATION CUDGEON B. ALPHA ALPHA TWO TWO.
BRIAR, YOU'RE SOOO UGLY AND SOOO EVIL.
ZAPPP!
ZAPPP!
AGGGGGGGG!
The DNA cannons come alive, targeting anything with goblin DNA at a rate of ten blasts per second.
It's all over in moments.
YOU HAVEN'T ACCOMPLISHED ANYTHING, ARTEMIS FOWL.
THE GOBLINS ARE UNCONSCIOUS, SOON TO BE MIND-WIPED WITH SOME PARTICULARLY UNSTABLE CHEMICALS. JUST AS I PLANNED. ERR... WE PLANNED.
NOW, I SIMPLY REPROGRAM THE DNA CANNONS TO TARGET YOUR FRIENDS OUTSIDE, RETURN POWER TO THE LEP CANNONS, AND TAKE OVER THE WORLD. AND NOBODY CAN GET IN HERE TO STOP ME.
I hear familiar footsteps thundering outside. He's running.

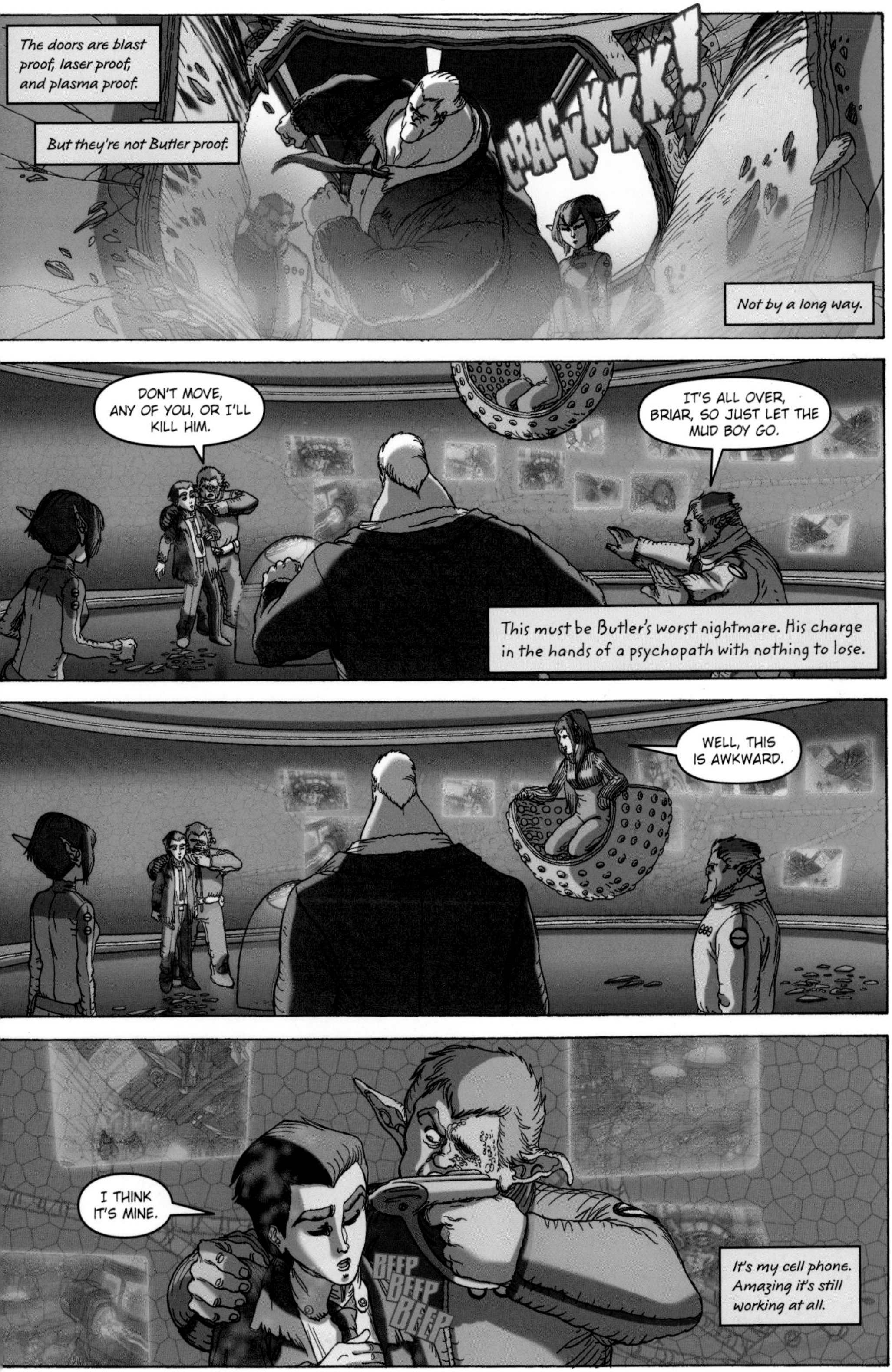
The doors are blast proof, laser proof, and plasma proof.
But they're not Butler proof.
CRACKKKK!
Not by a long way.
DON'T MOVE, ANY OF YOU, OR I'LL KILL HIM.
IT'S ALL OVER, BRIAR, SO JUST LET THE MUD BOY GO.
This must be Butler's worst nightmare. His charge in the hands of a psychopath with nothing to lose.
WELL, THIS IS AWKWARD.
I THINK IT'S MINE.
BEEP BEEP BEEP
It's my cell phone. Amazing it's still working at all.

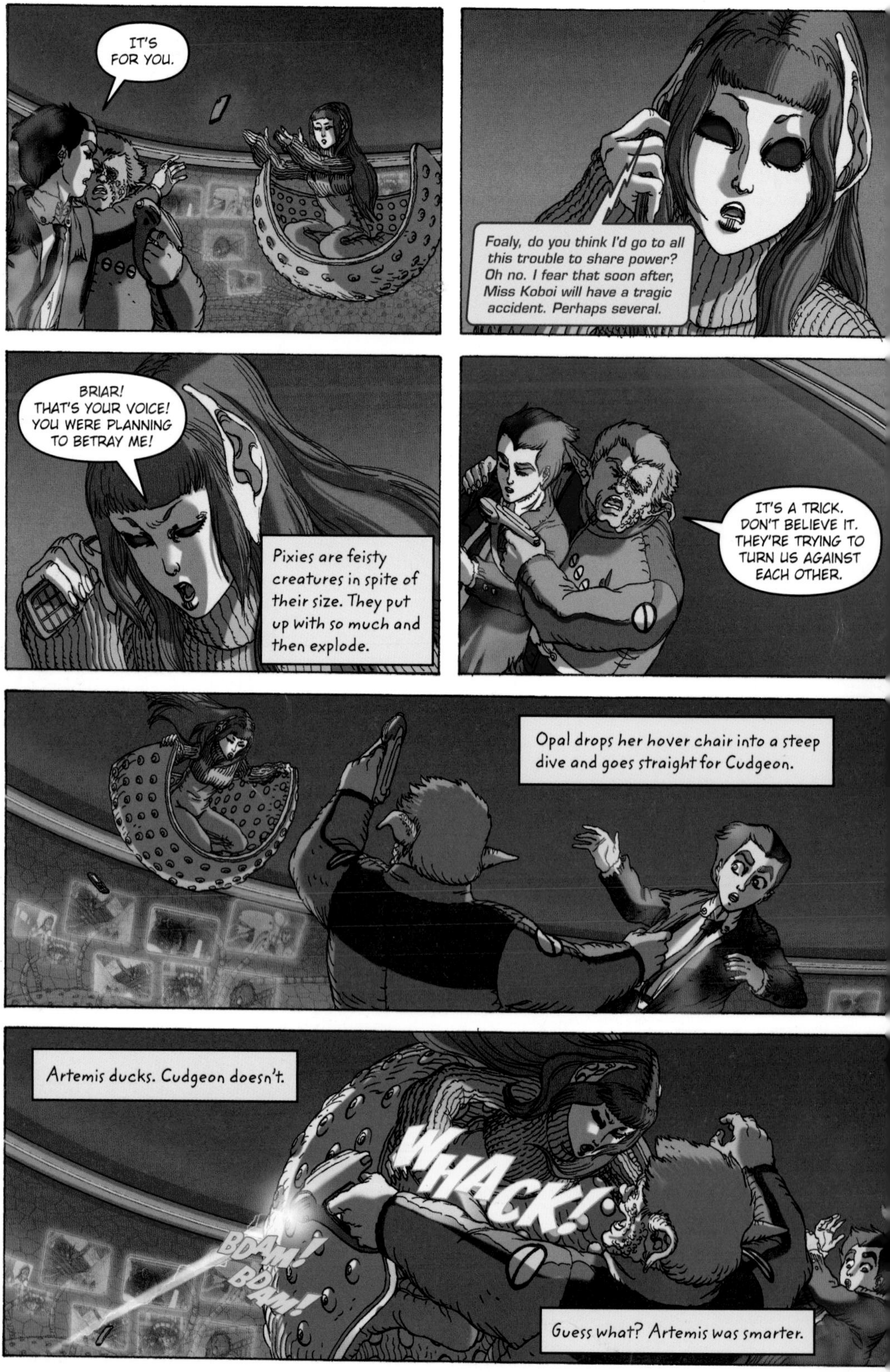
IT'S FOR YOU.
Foaly, do you think I'd go to all this trouble to share power? Oh no. I fear that soon after, Miss Koboi will have a tragic accident. Perhaps several.
BRIAR! THAT'S YOUR VOICE! YOU WERE PLANNING TO BETRAY ME!
Pixies are feisty creatures in spite of their size. They put up with so much and then explode.
IT'S A TRICK. DON'T BELIEVE IT. THEY'RE TRYING TO TURN US AGAINST EACH OTHER.
Opal drops her hover chair into a steep dive and goes straight for Cudgeon.
Artemis ducks. Cudgeon doesn't.
WHACK!
BDAM! BDAM!
Guess what? Artemis was smarter.

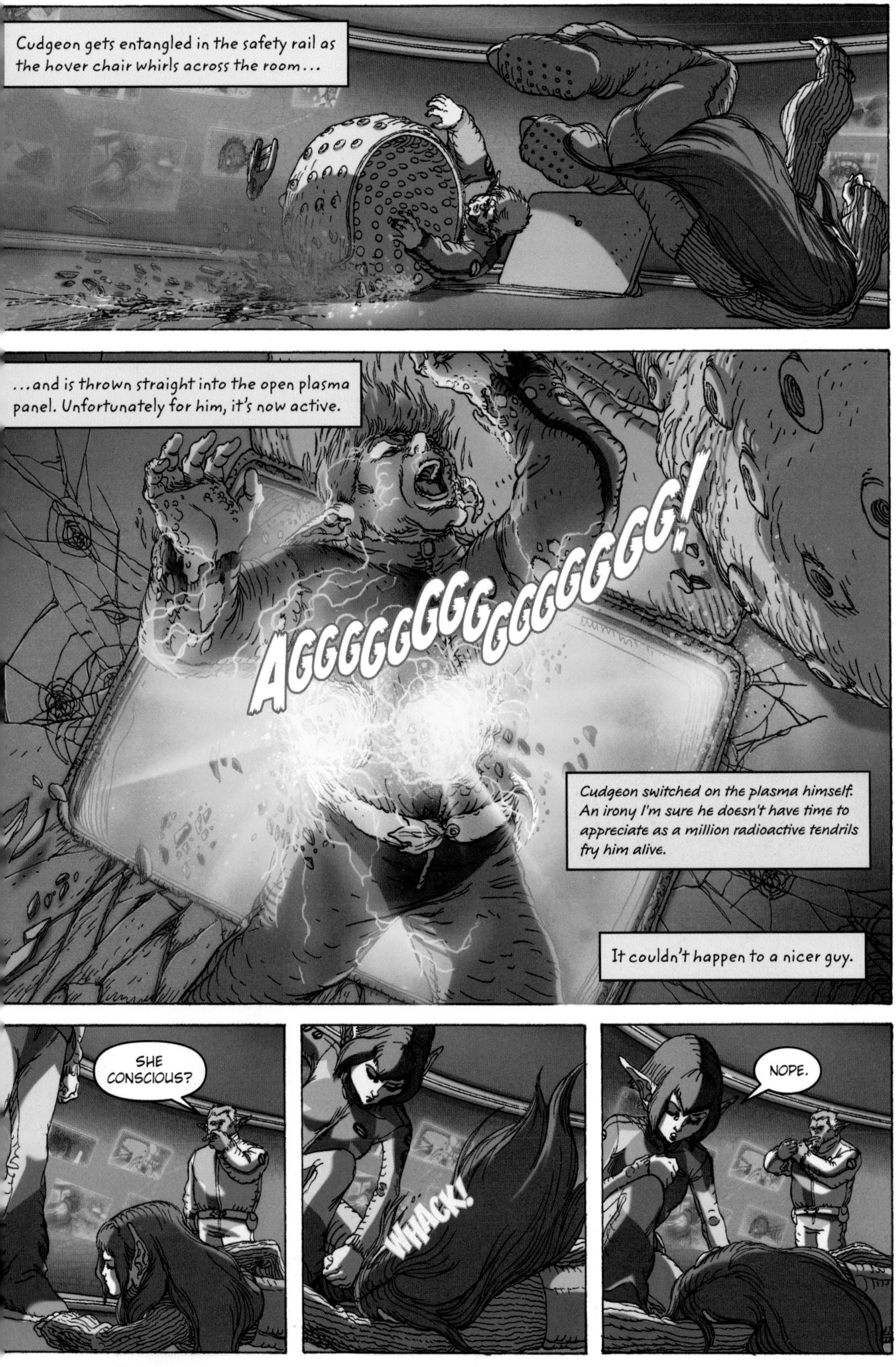
Cudgeon gets entangled in the safety rail as the hover chair whirls across the room . . .
. . . and is thrown straight into the open plasma panel. Unfortunately for him, it's now active.
AGGGGGGGGGGGGGGGG!
Cudgeon switched on the plasma himself. An irony I'm sure he doesn't have time to appreciate as a million radioactive tendrils fry him alive.
It couldn't happen to a nicer guy.
SHE CONSCIOUS?
WHACK!
NOPE.

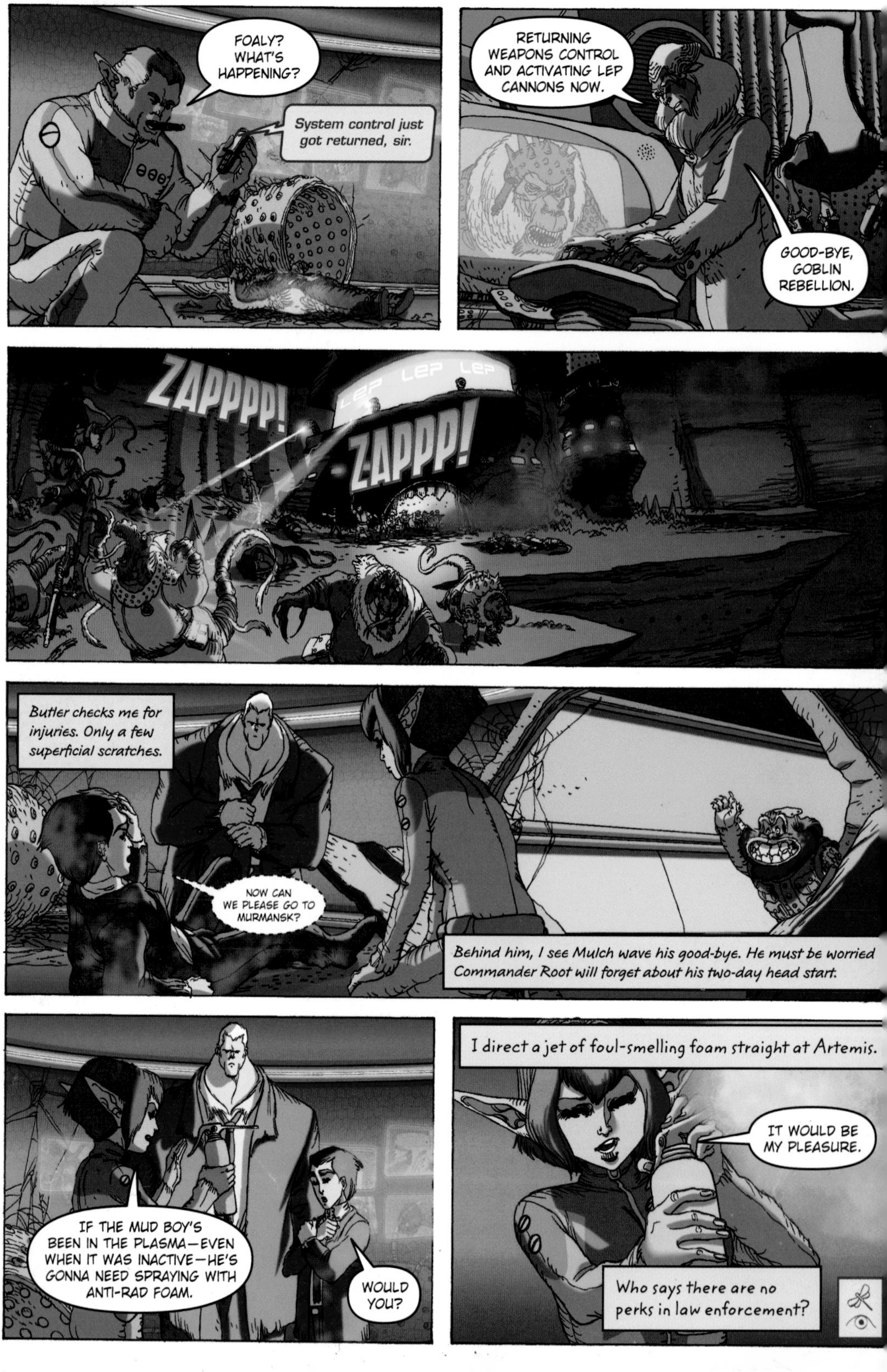
FOALY? WHAT'S HAPPENING?
System control just got returned, sir.
RETURNING WEAPONS CONTROL AND ACTIVATING LEP CANNONS NOW.
GOOD-BYE, GOBLIN REBELLION.
ZAPPPP!
LEP LEP LEP
Z-APPP!
Butter checks me for injuries. Only a few superficial scratches.
NOW CAN WE PLEASE GO TO MURMANSK?
Behind him, I see Mulch wave his good-bye. He must be worried Commander Root will forget about his two-day head start.
IF THE MUD BOY'S BEEN IN THE PLASMA—EVEN WHEN IT WAS INACTIVE—HE'S GONNA NEED SPRAYING WITH ANTI-RAD FOAM.
WOULD YOU?
I direct a jet of foul-smelling foam straight at Artemis.
IT WOULD BE MY PLEASURE.
Who says there are no perks in law enforcement?

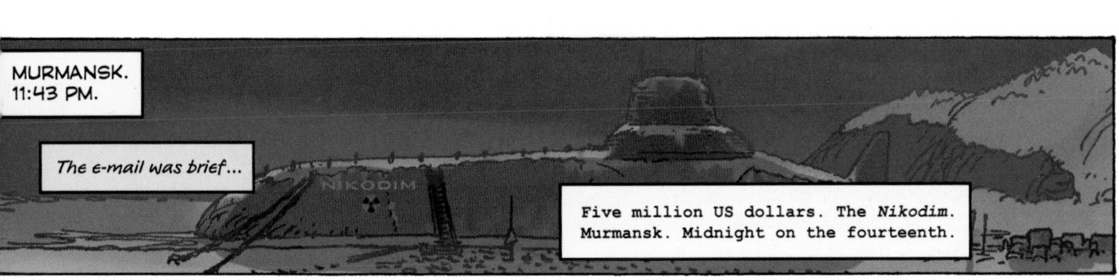
MURMANSK.
11:43 PM.
The e-mail was brief...
NIKODIM
Five million US dollars. The *Nikodim*. Murmansk. Midnight on the fourteenth.

CHAPTER 14: FATHER'S DAY

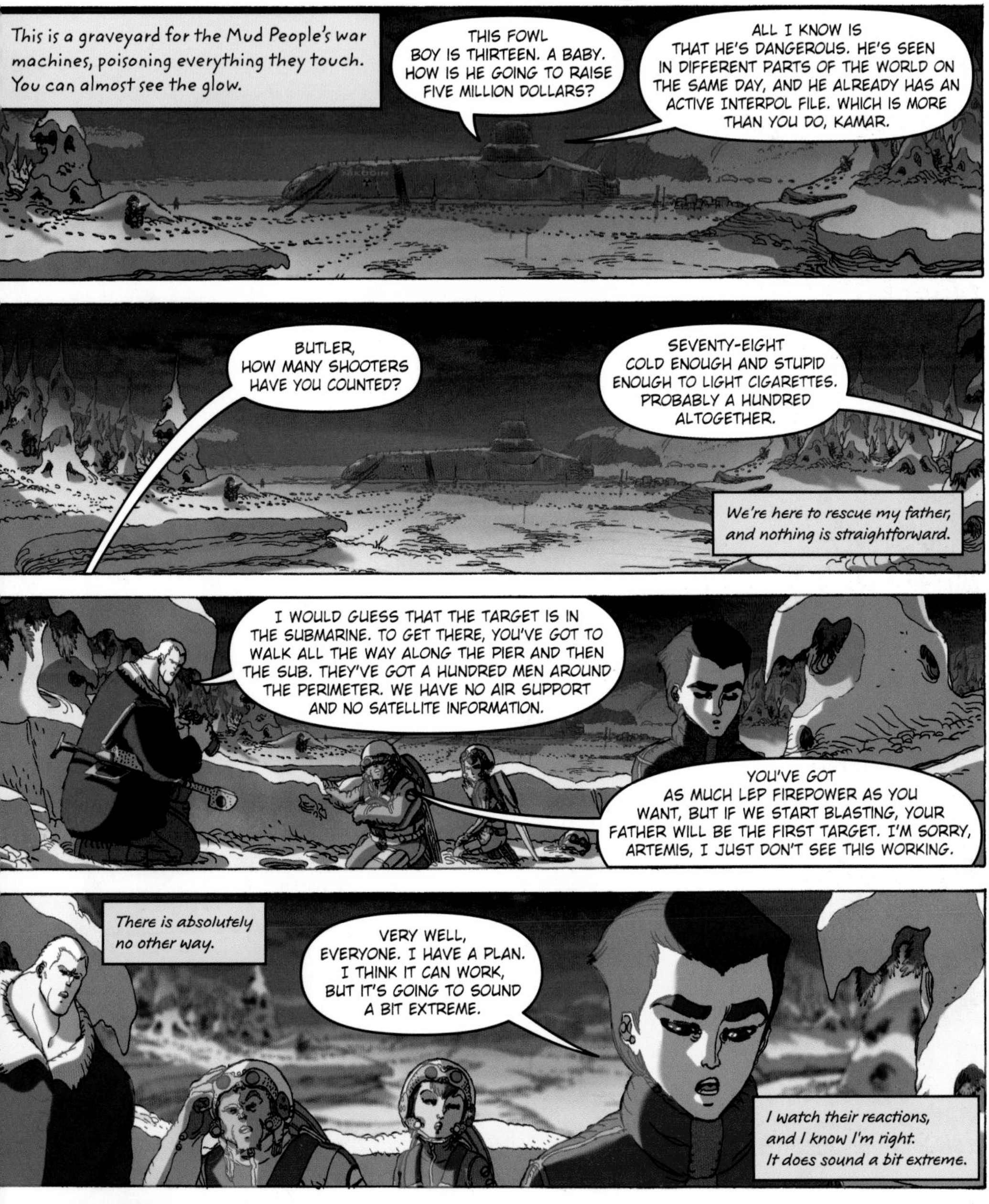
This is a graveyard for the Mud People's war machines, poisoning everything they touch. You can almost see the glow.
THIS FOWL BOY IS THIRTEEN. A BABY. HOW IS HE GOING TO RAISE FIVE MILLION DOLLARS?
ALL I KNOW IS THAT HE'S DANGEROUS. HE'S SEEN IN DIFFERENT PARTS OF THE WORLD ON THE SAME DAY, AND HE ALREADY HAS AN ACTIVE INTERPOL FILE. WHICH IS MORE THAN YOU DO, KAMAR.
BUTLER, HOW MANY SHOOTERS HAVE YOU COUNTED?
SEVENTY-EIGHT COLD ENOUGH AND STUPID ENOUGH TO LIGHT CIGARETTES. PROBABLY A HUNDRED ALTOGETHER.
We're here to rescue my father, and nothing is straightforward.
I WOULD GUESS THAT THE TARGET IS IN THE SUBMARINE. TO GET THERE, YOU'VE GOT TO WALK ALL THE WAY ALONG THE PIER AND THEN THE SUB. THEY'VE GOT A HUNDRED MEN AROUND THE PERIMETER. WE HAVE NO AIR SUPPORT AND NO SATELLITE INFORMATION.
YOU'VE GOT AS MUCH LEP FIREPOWER AS YOU WANT, BUT IF WE START BLASTING, YOUR FATHER WILL BE THE FIRST TARGET. I'M SORRY, ARTEMIS, I JUST DON'T SEE THIS WORKING.
There is absolutely no other way.
VERY WELL, EVERYONE. I HAVE A PLAN. I THINK IT CAN WORK, BUT IT'S GOING TO SOUND A BIT EXTREME.
I watch their reactions, and I know I'm right. It does sound a bit extreme.

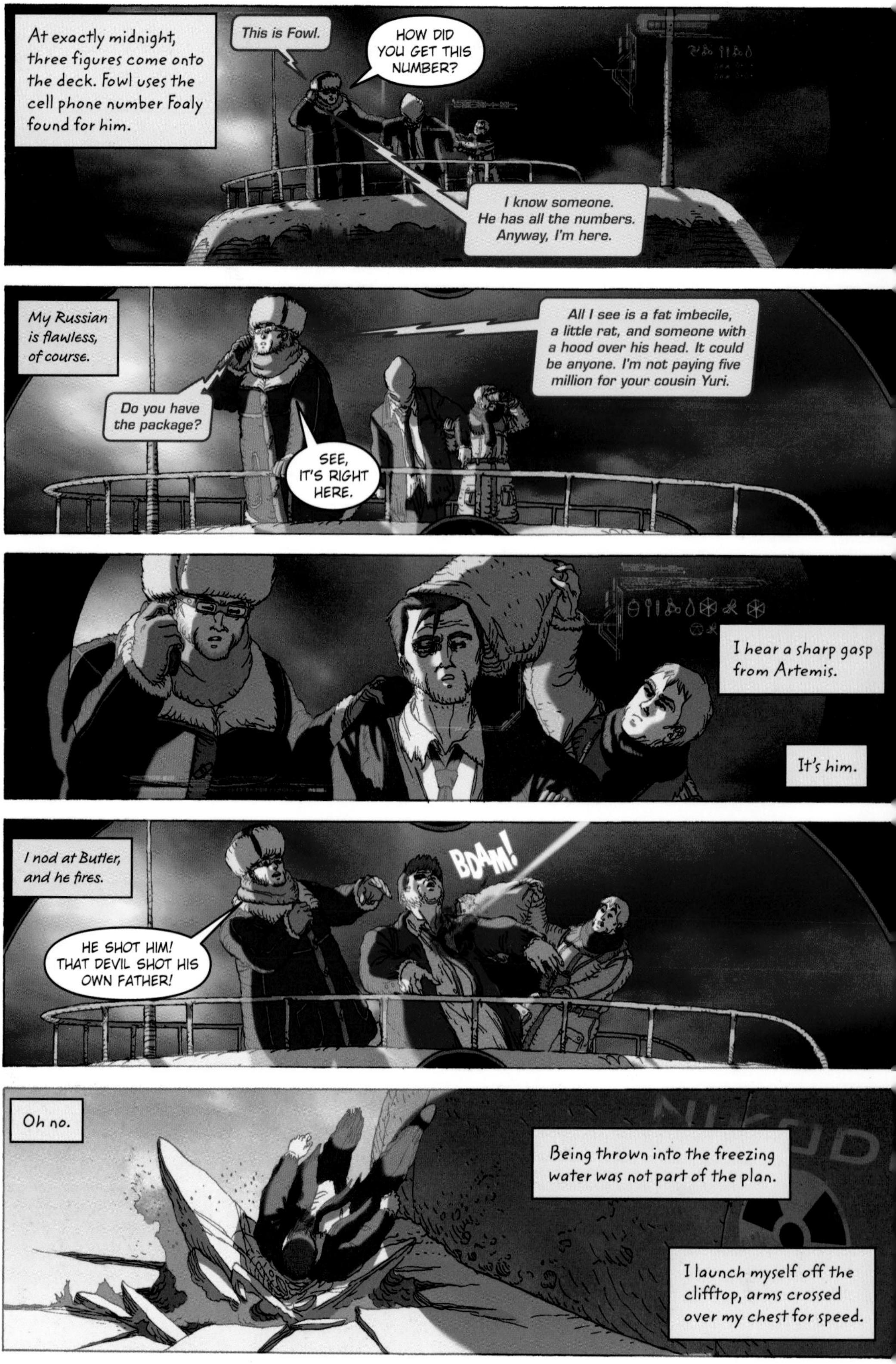
At exactly midnight, three figures come onto the deck. Fowl uses the cell phone number Foaly found for him.
This is Fowl.
HOW DID YOU GET THIS NUMBER?
I know someone. He has all the numbers. Anyway, I'm here.
My Russian is flawless, of course.
All I see is a fat imbecile, a little rat, and someone with a hood over his head. It could be anyone. I'm not paying five million for your cousin Yuri.
Do you have the package?
SEE, IT'S RIGHT HERE.
I hear a sharp gasp from Artemis.
It's him.
I nod at Butler, and he fires.
BDAM!
HE SHOT HIM! THAT DEVIL SHOT HIS OWN FATHER!
Oh no.
Being thrown into the freezing water was not part of the plan.
I launch myself off the clifftop, arms crossed over my chest for speed.

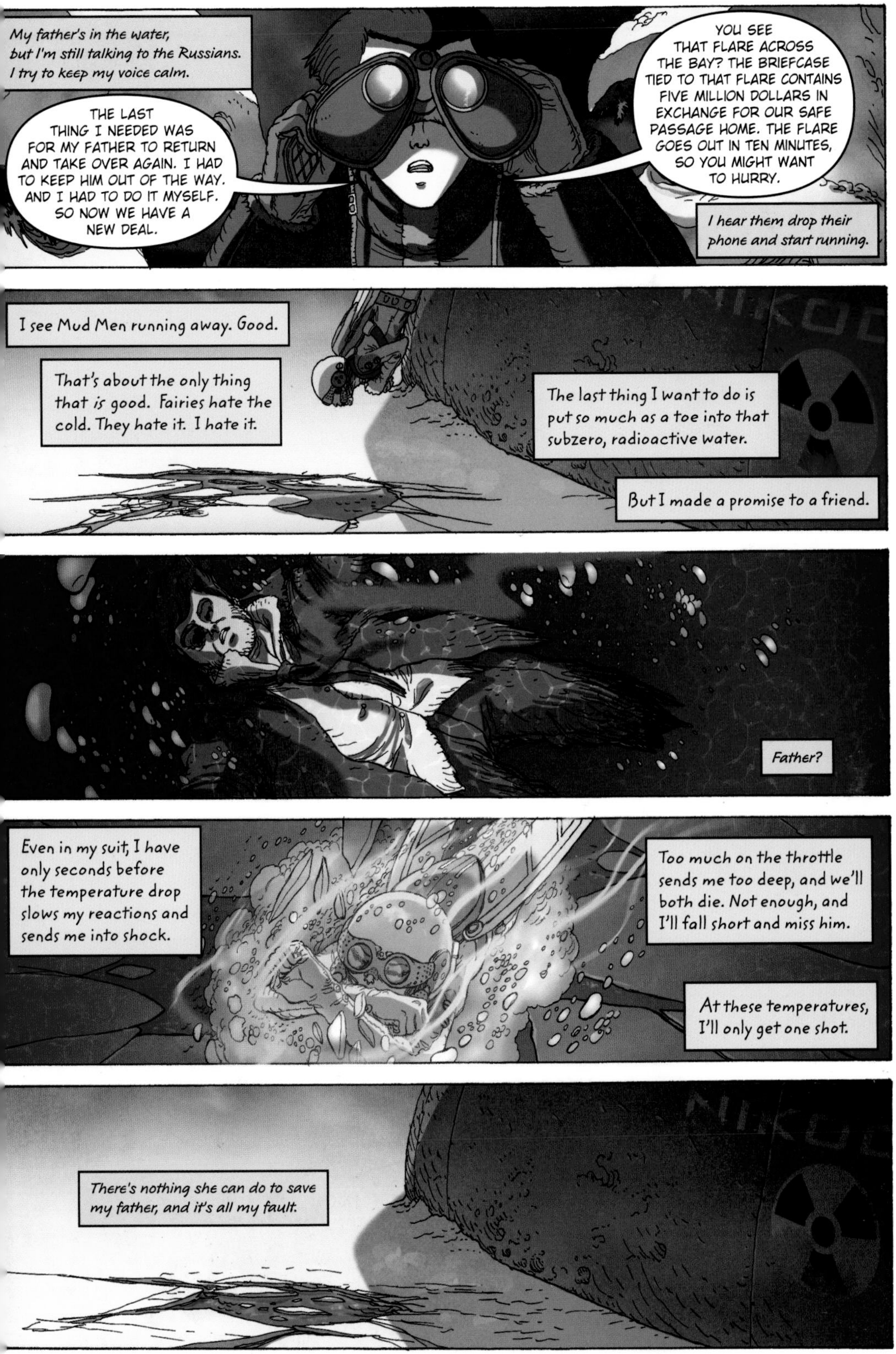
My father's in the water, but I'm still talking to the Russians. I try to keep my voice calm.
THE LAST THING I NEEDED WAS FOR MY FATHER TO RETURN AND TAKE OVER AGAIN. I HAD TO KEEP HIM OUT OF THE WAY. AND I HAD TO DO IT MYSELF. SO NOW WE HAVE A NEW DEAL.
YOU SEE THAT FLARE ACROSS THE BAY? THE BRIEFCASE TIED TO THAT FLARE CONTAINS FIVE MILLION DOLLARS IN EXCHANGE FOR OUR SAFE PASSAGE HOME. THE FLARE GOES OUT IN TEN MINUTES, SO YOU MIGHT WANT TO HURRY.
I hear them drop their phone and start running.
I see Mud Men running away. Good.
That's about the only thing that *is* good. Fairies hate the cold. They hate it. I hate it.
The last thing I want to do is put so much as a toe into that subzero, radioactive water.
But I made a promise to a friend.
Father?
Even in my suit, I have only seconds before the temperature drop slows my reactions and sends me into shock.
Too much on the throttle sends me too deep, and we'll both die. Not enough, and I'll fall short and miss him.
At these temperatures, I'll only get one shot.
There's nothing she can do to save my father, and it's all my fault.

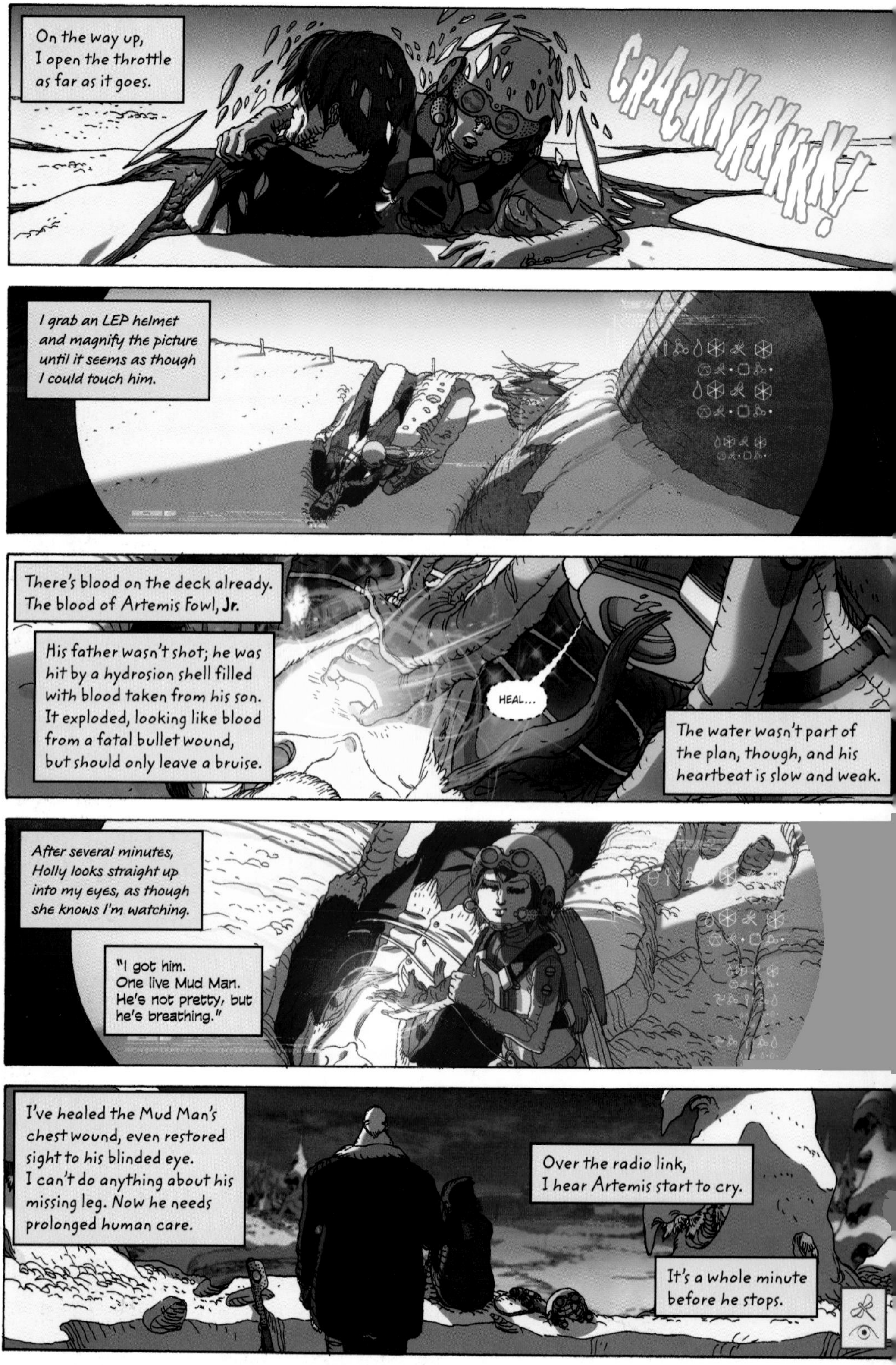
On the way up, I open the throttle as far as it goes.
CRACKKKKKKK!
I grab an LEP helmet and magnify the picture until it seems as though I could touch him.
There's blood on the deck already. The blood of Artemis Fowl, Jr.
His father wasn't shot; he was hit by a hydrosion shell filled with blood taken from his son. It exploded, looking like blood from a fatal bullet wound, but should only leave a bruise.
HEAL...
The water wasn't part of the plan, though, and his heartbeat is slow and weak.
After several minutes, Holly looks straight up into my eyes, as though she knows I'm watching.
"I got him. One live Mud Man. He's not pretty, but he's breathing."
I've healed the Mud Man's chest wound, even restored sight to his blinded eye. I can't do anything about his missing leg. Now he needs prolonged human care.
Over the radio link, I hear Artemis start to cry.
It's a whole minute before he stops.

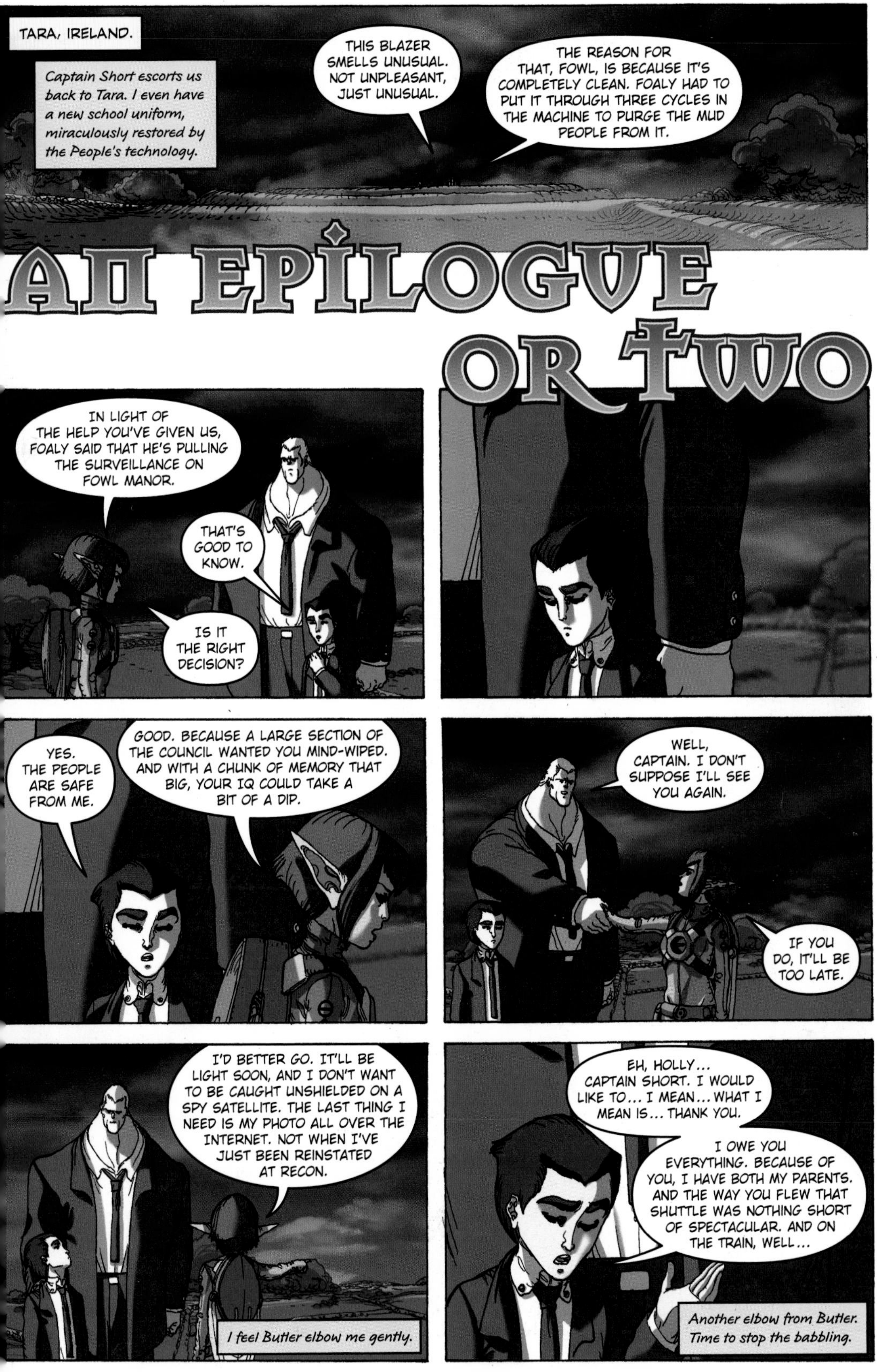
TARA, IRELAND.
Captain Short escorts us back to Tara. I even have a new school uniform, miraculously restored by the People's technology.
THIS BLAZER SMELLS UNUSUAL. NOT UNPLEASANT, JUST UNUSUAL.
THE REASON FOR THAT, FOWL, IS BECAUSE IT'S COMPLETELY CLEAN. FOALY HAD TO PUT IT THROUGH THREE CYCLES IN THE MACHINE TO PURGE THE MUD PEOPLE FROM IT.
AN EPILOGUE OR TWO
IN LIGHT OF THE HELP YOU'VE GIVEN US, FOALY SAID THAT HE'S PULLING THE SURVEILLANCE ON FOWL MANOR.
THAT'S GOOD TO KNOW.
IS IT THE RIGHT DECISION?
YES. THE PEOPLE ARE SAFE FROM ME.
GOOD. BECAUSE A LARGE SECTION OF THE COUNCIL WANTED YOU MIND-WIPED. AND WITH A CHUNK OF MEMORY THAT BIG, YOUR IQ COULD TAKE A BIT OF A DIP.
WELL, CAPTAIN. I DON'T SUPPOSE I'LL SEE YOU AGAIN.
IF YOU DO, IT'LL BE TOO LATE.
I'D BETTER GO. IT'LL BE LIGHT SOON, AND I DON'T WANT TO BE CAUGHT UNSHIELDED ON A SPY SATELLITE. THE LAST THING I NEED IS MY PHOTO ALL OVER THE INTERNET. NOT WHEN I'VE JUST BEEN REINSTATED AT RECON.
I feel Butler elbow me gently.
EH, HOLLY... CAPTAIN SHORT. I WOULD LIKE TO... I MEAN... WHAT I MEAN IS... THANK YOU.
I OWE YOU EVERYTHING. BECAUSE OF YOU, I HAVE BOTH MY PARENTS. AND THE WAY YOU FLEW THAT SHUTTLE WAS NOTHING SHORT OF SPECTACULAR. AND ON THE TRAIN, WELL...
Another elbow from Butler. Time to stop the babbling.

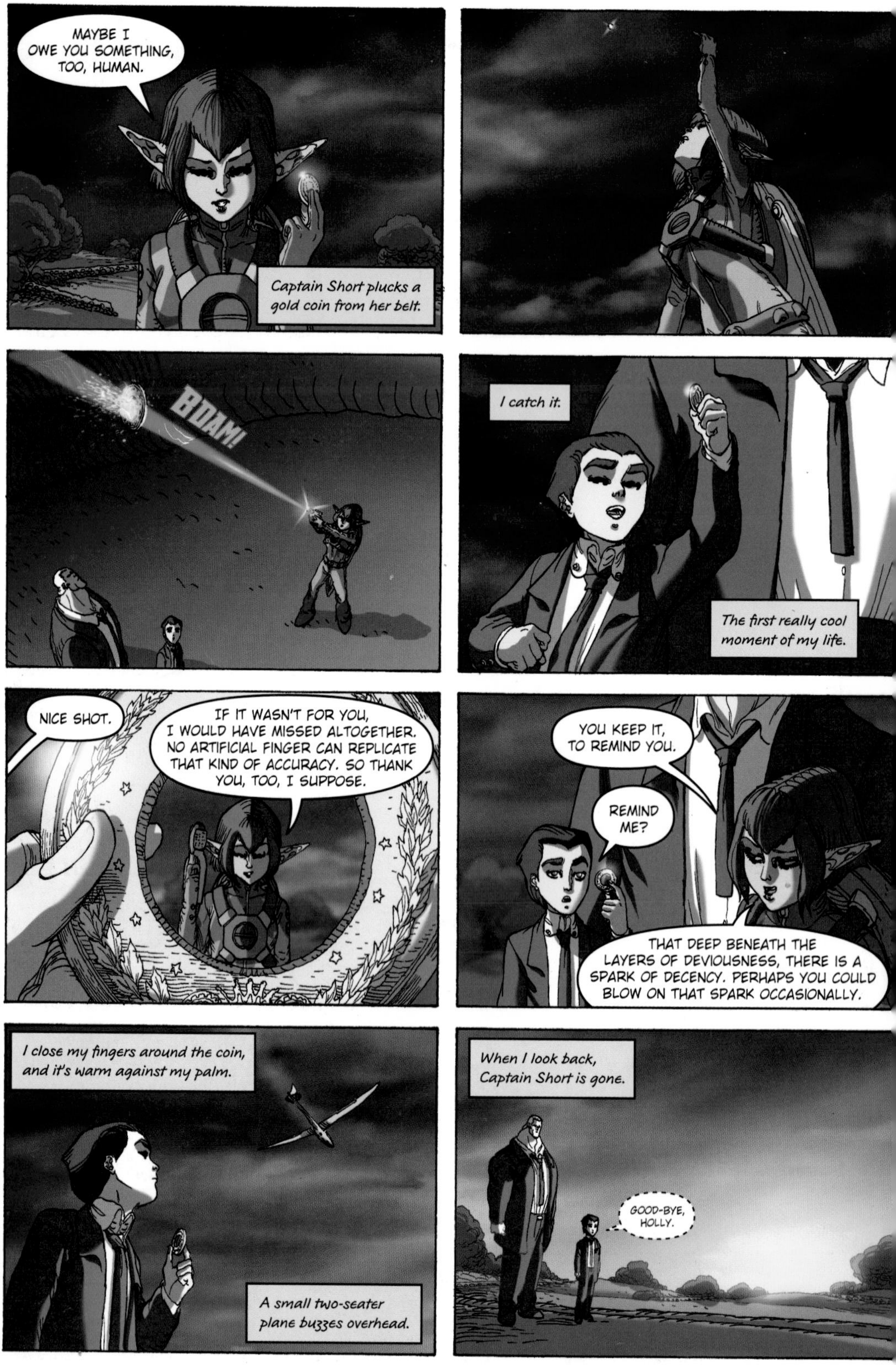
MAYBE I OWE YOU SOMETHING, TOO, HUMAN.
Captain Short plucks a gold coin from her belt.
BDAM!
I catch it.
The first really cool moment of my life.
NICE SHOT.
IF IT WASN'T FOR YOU, I WOULD HAVE MISSED ALTOGETHER. NO ARTIFICIAL FINGER CAN REPLICATE THAT KIND OF ACCURACY. SO THANK YOU, TOO, I SUPPOSE.
YOU KEEP IT, TO REMIND YOU.
REMIND ME?
THAT DEEP BENEATH THE LAYERS OF DEVIOUSNESS, THERE IS A SPARK OF DECENCY. PERHAPS YOU COULD BLOW ON THAT SPARK OCCASIONALLY.
I close my fingers around the coin, and it's warm against my palm.
A small two-seater plane buzzes overhead.
When I look back, Captain Short is gone.
GOOD-BYE, HOLLY.

After she healed him, Holly flew my father southwest to Helsinki, depositing him at the doors of the University Hospital.

They will be able to identify him from the suitably weathered passport Foaly ran up.

I head back to St. Bart's School. I should be there when the news comes through.

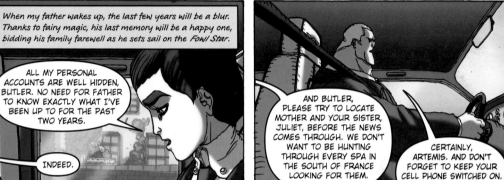

When my father wakes up, the last few years will be a blur. Thanks to fairy magic, his last memory will be a happy one, bidding his family farewell as he sets sail on the *Fowl Star*.

ALL MY PERSONAL ACCOUNTS ARE WELL HIDDEN, BUTLER. NO NEED FOR FATHER TO KNOW EXACTLY WHAT I'VE BEEN UP TO FOR THE PAST TWO YEARS.

INDEED.

AND BUTLER, PLEASE TRY TO LOCATE MOTHER AND YOUR SISTER, JULIET, BEFORE THE NEWS COMES THROUGH. WE DON'T WANT TO BE HUNTING THROUGH EVERY SPA IN THE SOUTH OF FRANCE LOOKING FOR THEM.

CERTAINLY, ARTEMIS. AND DON'T FORGET TO KEEP YOUR CELL PHONE SWITCHED ON.

Suddenly, I shudder.

There's one thing I need to ask...

BUTLER... IN THE ARCTIC, WHEN I ORDERED YOU TO...

YES. YOU DID THE RIGHT THING. IT WAS THE ONLY WAY.

From this moment on, life will be different. With two parents in Fowl Manor, my schemes will have to be much more carefully planned.

I owe it to the People to leave them alone for a good while, but Mulch Diggums... that's a different matter. So many secure facilities, so little time.

Butler drives away, and I watch as the Bentley disappears down the avenue.

Back to St. Bart's, then.

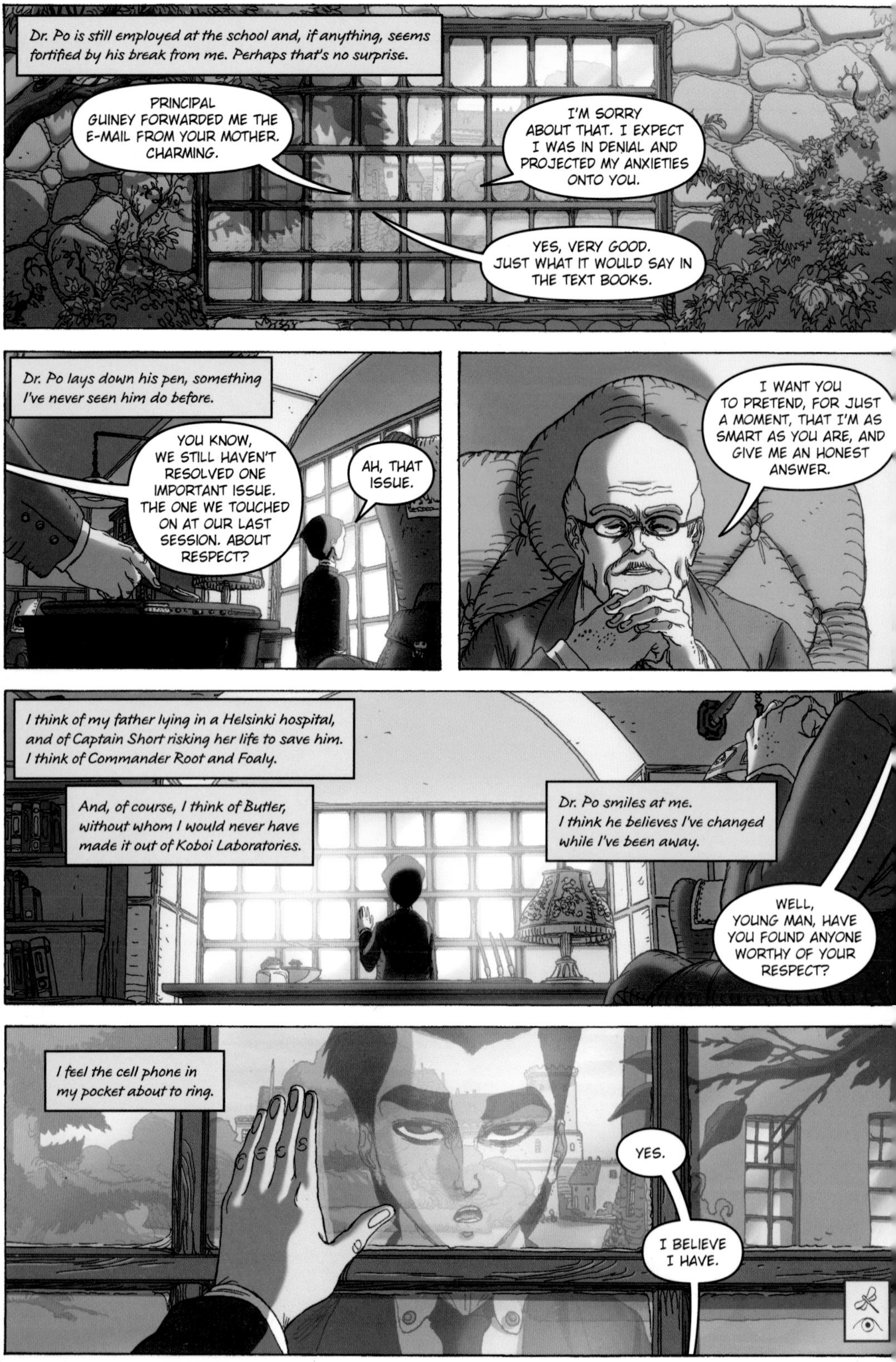
Dr. Po is still employed at the school and, if anything, seems fortified by his break from me. Perhaps that's no surprise.
PRINCIPAL GUINEY FORWARDED ME THE E-MAIL FROM YOUR MOTHER. CHARMING.
I'M SORRY ABOUT THAT. I EXPECT I WAS IN DENIAL AND PROJECTED MY ANXIETIES ONTO YOU.
YES, VERY GOOD. JUST WHAT IT WOULD SAY IN THE TEXT BOOKS.
Dr. Po lays down his pen, something I've never seen him do before.
YOU KNOW, WE STILL HAVEN'T RESOLVED ONE IMPORTANT ISSUE. THE ONE WE TOUCHED ON AT OUR LAST SESSION. ABOUT RESPECT?
AH, THAT ISSUE.
I WANT YOU TO PRETEND, FOR JUST A MOMENT, THAT I'M AS SMART AS YOU ARE, AND GIVE ME AN HONEST ANSWER.
I think of my father lying in a Helsinki hospital, and of Captain Short risking her life to save him. I think of Commander Root and Foaly.
And, of course, I think of Butler, without whom I would never have made it out of Koboi Laboratories.
Dr. Po smiles at me. I think he believes I've changed while I've been away.
WELL, YOUNG MAN, HAVE YOU FOUND ANYONE WORTHY OF YOUR RESPECT?
I feel the cell phone in my pocket about to ring.
YES.
I BELIEVE I HAVE.